***The ex best thing*.**

Fletcher Andrews never believed in promises. Or monogamy. Or love. When you're tall and gorgeous, New York City is one big all-you-can-eat buffet of hot young actors, models, and baristas. Even when living happily with Roger, his sweet, sexy violinist boyfriend, Fletch can't resist an occasional taste. Too bad you don't know what you've got until it's thrown you out for cheating with half the cast of *Disney on Ice*.

Two years and a chance meeting later, Fletch desperately wants Roger back. Roger's new boyfriend, Jeff, will do anything to stop that from happening. But Fletch has a plan to make amends. And with a little help from friends, colleagues—even Roger's Scottish terrier, Haggis—they might find that the love you don't believe in can sweep you right off your feet . . .

Where Do I Start?

Chase Taylor Hackett

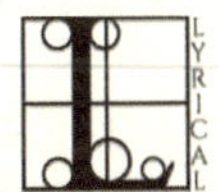

LYRICAL PRESS
Kensington Publishing Corp.
www.kensingtonbooks.com

To the extent that the image or images on the cover of this book depict a person or persons, such person or persons are merely models, and are not intended to portray any character or characters featured in the book.

LYRICAL PRESS BOOKS are published by

Kensington Publishing Corp.
119 West 40th Street
New York, NY 10018

This book is a work of fiction. Names, characters, places, and incidents either are products of the author's imagination or are used fictionally. Any resemblence to actual events or locales or persons living or dead is entirely coincidental.

All Kensington titles, imprints, and distributed lines are available at special quantity discounts for bulk purchases for sales promotion, premiums, fund-raising, educational, or institutional use.

Special book excerpts or customized printings can also be created to fit specific needs. For details, write or phone the office of the Kensington Sales Manager: Kensington Publishing Corp., 119 West 40th Street, New York, NY 10018. Attn. Sales Department. Phone: 1-800-221-2647.

First Electronic Edition: October 2017
eISBN-13: 978-1-5161-0444-4
eISBN-10: 1-5161-0444-7

First Print Edition: October 2017
ISBN-13: 978-1-5161-04445-1
ISBN-10: 1-5161-0445-5

Printed in the United States of America

For Travis because…well…everything.

Just everything.

Chapter 1
A Night at the Opera

FLETCH

"Man-oh-man," I said. "Not too shabby."

I was looking at my reflection in the glass that separated the front seat from the back. I was in a limo, I was wearing a four-thousand-dollar custom tux, and holy moly, I looked frigging fabulous.

I suppose that's as good a place to start as any.

That night, in *that* limo. Even if it *is* sort of smack-dab in the middle of the story. But as Roger later explained to me, sometimes when you don't know where to begin, maybe it doesn't matter, just as long as you do. Begin, I mean. He said he'd learned that from his dog. I'm not really sure what he meant by that, but I can tell you this: Roger has a seriously cool dog.

So I don't know if this is the best place to start, but this is where I'm starting.

I was in a limo, all dressed up like I'd never been dressed up before, and checking out my reflection.

"You're gorgeous-just-gorgeous," yapped Darwin in his odd combination of a southern drawl and a machine-gun delivery. "No need to keep checking because I'll just tell you." He also liked to speak in triplicate. "Gorgeous-gorgeous-gorgeous."

Darwin was my date, and the reason for the limo. And the tux. And the tickets. And everything else.

I was pretty much psyched out of my mind, and it was really hard to sit still. This had to be—hands down—*the* best day of my life.

Okay, we were going to the opera, which might not exactly thrill you, and I'm not the world's biggest opera fan myself—in fact, I know almost nothing about it. I'm not like a total musical idiot. I'd been exposed to some classical music—just not opera.

But this was the opening night of the season of the Metropolitan Opera. In case you didn't know it—and *I* didn't before this—the opening night is like a mini-Oscar night here: tuxedos, designer dresses, celebrities, a red carpet across the plaza, photographers.

You're thinking, all of that for the opera? I know, crazy, right? Welcome to New York.

"I was just admiring the lovely clothes you bought me," I said, answering Darwin's question. "Thank you again."

"You're-welcome-you're-welcome-you're-welcome. Again. You look magnificent-just-magnificent."

"Thanks."

When Darwin asked me if I wanted to go to the opera, I wasn't all that stoked about it, but when he told me what it was going to be like, I jumped at it. Then he told me I would need a tux, and of course, I didn't *have* a tux, so we went shopping, and the next thing you know, he didn't *rent* me a tux, which was what I'd expected. He didn't *buy* me a tux. He'd had this whole suit *made* for me: cream-colored jacket, black pants with a satin stripe down the side, fancy shirt with a wing collar. The whole enchilada—*con queso*. My shirt studs were sterling silver and onyx, if you can believe it.

And right now, I was trying really hard to keep my leg from bouncing. I was too big for my body.

"No need to be quite so tense, Toots. All you have to do is look fetching—something you're so very good at."

Yep, that's what he called me. Toots. Embarrassing as it was. Toots, like Tootsie, as in Tootsie Pop. Something to do with an old TV commercial—don't ask. All I can tell you is I winced every time he said it. But—you know—you don't bite the hand…so Toots it was.

Other than that, I was pretty proud about Darwin. Darwin Stewart Harrison, famous Broadway costume designer.

"How many Tony Awards do you have, Darwin?"

"Not-so-many-not-so-many-not-so-many. Six. But who's counting."

Famous Broadway costume designer with six Tony Awards. For those of you from out of town, those are like the Academy Awards for theatre.

I don't want to tell you how we met.

Darwin also had more money than God, and a huge apartment overlooking the East River. And *he* had asked *me* to go to the opera with him, which was kinda cool, don't you think?

I've been with lots of guys—something which I'm sure is going to come up later—but Darwin was easily the oldest. He was in his forties somewhere, I guessed. Okay, I "hoped" would maybe be more accurate. He wasn't exactly a fit forty-probably-fifty either. He was funny, though. He could be really funny.

And the paunchiest. But he was also extraordinarily generous. Really, practically every week he had some pricey gift for me.

I checked my reflection again.

Man-oh-man, who *wouldn't* go out with me?

The car moved forward a bit.

Darwin had classical music on in the car, and I realized—

"Hey—I know this," I said.

"I'm so glad. What?"

"This piece of music. It's a string quartet—Schubert." Like I said, I'm not a total idiot. How I knew what I knew about Schubert is something else I'm sure you're going to hear more about later. "It's called 'Death and the Maiden.'"

"If-you-say-so-if-you-say-so. I'm sure I don't know."

The opening notes were really distinctive.

Daaaaaaaaaaaaaaaaaaaaaaah
Dadada dum.

I'd even made up stupid words for it, like

Dweeeeeeeeeeeeeeeb!
Where are my shoes?

It went on from there and just got sillier. Yeah, it was dumb but pretty funny at the time. Dweeb was my nickname for the guy I knew who played string quartets. Point is I knew this chunk of a string quartet from before, and thinking about back then distracted me from how scared I was now.

"The title's from a poem, but I think that was just sort of a starting place for Schubert." I wasn't really showing off. I was just so nervous.

This might be the best day of my life, but it was also pretty damned scary. I'm generally a confident person, but this? This was way out of my range of experience. And you can always tell when I'm nervous because my right leg bounces like crazy. Like now. My hands were shaking too.

And I was blathering.

To be really honest, I didn't believe for a second that I belonged here—in this place, in this car, in this suit—and I was scared to death that, before the evening was over, someone would figure that out. If I let my guard down, if I stopped flashing this smile, if I stopped being dazzling for even a second, someone would see right through me and know.

But hey, I'm Fletch, I reminded myself. I'll be fine, right? I'm always fine.

I just needed to keep that smile going, needed to keep the dazzle working, needed to keep up the act that I was born to all this.

In the meantime, if I talked enough, maybe my hands would stop shaking.

"For Schubert, I think it was mostly a kind of metaphor," I finished.

Darwin just blinked at me. "You do astonish me sometimes, Toots, simply astonish me."

"You thought I was just another pretty face."

"Not for a second, Fletch, not for a second. Okay, well, maybe for a second."

Yep, *that's* my name. Fletch. Fletcher Andrews. And I certainly do have a very pretty face, or I would never have found my way into that limo.

The car pulled forward again, and we were finally there.

Wow, the place was really lit up. The driver hopped out, ran around, and opened the door.

"That's your cue, Toots."

"What?"

"You're on!"

"Me first?"

"Go-go-go." Darwin goosed me out of the car.

So I climbed across the car, got out, and stepped aside so that Darwin could be seen coming out of this huge black limo next to the tall, blond trophy pet—which would be me.

"Know what time it is?" said Darwin as he got out and scanned the Plaza with a huge grin. "It's showtime!"

The plaza was really bright. And really loud.

There were people behind barricades who didn't care crap about opera but who were just there to see people like us. And for those slobs who actually *liked* opera but didn't have these stupidly expensive tickets, there was a gigantic screen in front of the opera house, stacks of speakers like a rock concert, and hundreds of folding chairs. At least it was a nice September night, if you're going to sit outside on a folding chair for four frigging hours, the poor bastards. As for me, for the first time in my life, I was on the inside looking out, so forgive me if I gloated just a little.

We walked across the plaza past the big fountain, me just slightly behind Darwin, and people took our picture. I thought there might be local TV there, but there were television crews from Italy, Germany, Japan even! There was a big clump of professional photographers set up with a gigantic board in the background saying Metropolitan Opera a thousand times in case people didn't know where they were, and we stopped there for a bit. Lots of pictures of Darwin, pictures of me and Darwin, a couple pictures of just me even. Somebody actually asked me who did my suit.

The photographers suddenly abandoned me. Ferris Bueller and what's-her-name—the *Sex in the City* woman—were coming up the carpet behind us. Damn—Ferris got fat. He was sooooo cute back in the day.

"Good Lord," said Darwin. "Just look what she's wearing. Who *did* that to her? A travesty. Merciful heaven, it just gets worse the closer she gets. And tomorrow, her picture in that walking nightmare will be everywhere-just-everywhere."

"You don't like it?"

"I could eat a bolt of taffeta and shit a better—darling!" And he pulled away from me to go gush over Mrs. Ferris. "That dress is stunning-stunning-stunning! I—I don't know *what* to say!" At least he didn't lie. Hugs, cheeks nearly but not really kissed. It was too early in the evening to mess up anybody's makeup—hers *or* Darwin's. Photographers went gonzo taking pictures of the lovefest.

From the middle of this clutch, Darwin stretched out a left hand to Ferris, who seemed a bit confused. I tried not to laugh. I mean what was he supposed to do, kneel and kiss the ring? And if so, which one?

Ferris settled on a wave, and then he waved to me a little, like maybe he thought he should know me. I smiled and nodded.

Maybe he *should* know me—I ushered his last Broadway show, so you'd *think* I'd be able to remember his name! That was *my* brush with show business until that point—I'd been a Broadway usher before Darwin whisked me up.

We went inside. The lobby was surprisingly loud, three thousand rich people all talking at once. Darwin schmoozed while I stood around behind him and tried to be decorative and tried not to show how unbelievably awkward I felt. Gradually people moved into the theatre, and we took our seats. The lights went down (they actually pulled the chandeliers way up to the ceiling, which I thought was incredibly cool), applause-applause for the conductor, and the music began.

The opera. Okay, real quick. It was *Otello*, from a play by Shakespeare, but the opera is by Verdi. Even though it's Shakespeare, they sang in Italian, which makes *no* sense, but they had these cool little screens on the back of the seat in front of you that ran subtitles.

It's about this guy, Otello, his wife Desdemona, and his best friend Iago. Spoiler alert: Everybody dies in the end, and I mean everybody.

The audience? Apeshit.

It wasn't as boring as you might think.

You won't be totally surprised when I tell you Darwin thought the costumes were awfuljustawful.

But I want to skip ahead because, little did I know, the big event of the evening was waiting for me at the party afterward.

Darwin seemed to know everybody, and anybody he didn't know, he *wanted* to know, so he was busy. Me, not so much. I stood around trying to look confident, trying to look like I belonged there, and trying to pretend that standing by myself in a crowded lobby surrounded by rich and famous people all yammering to each other while no one was yammering to me was exactly where I wanted to be.

Doogie Howser and his boyfriend crossed the lobby in front of me. Man-oh-man, they're so hot together. Wouldn't mind ditching Darwin and talking my way into *their* limo.

Anyway, there I was, six foot two, alone, and unmoving in a sea of expensive clothes, babbling faces, and jewelry. I felt like the frigging Statue of Liberty. Only prettier.

And then the miracle happened. I saw somebody I knew. Besides Doogie, I mean.

Coming back from the bar with two glasses of champagne was Tommy Radford. I hadn't talked to Tommy in a long time, but I always liked him and I was really glad to see him there.

"Hey, handsome," I said, coming up from behind.

He spun.

"Well. If it isn't the whore of Babylon."

"Wow, nice, Tommy. Real nice," I said.

"Thanks," he said, leaned up, and kissed me on the cheek. "You know I'm never going to forgive you."

"I know."

"I'm honor-bound as his best friend to hate you for all time. But da-yam"—that's a really gay *damn*, stretched to two syllables—"you look fabulous!"

"I know, right?"

"Of course you always did. But let me see. Here." He handed me one of the champagne glasses. "That's not for you." He pulled my jacket open to check the label.

"Sweet. Bespoke. Our little Fletchy is moving up in the world. No need to ask you what *you've* been up to."

"Don't be a bitch. It's really good to see you, Tommy."

"Yeah, yeah."

"Do you know any of these people?"

"Not a soul except for...guess whom."

"He's here?"

"Of course he is. How do you think *I* got here? He had to go tinkle, so I went to the bar. It's like a jungle over there. I backed up and stepped on Alexander Skarsgård's foot, and it was all I could do not to faint."

"How's he been?"

"Alex? Kinda cranky but still *sooo* hot!"

"You know who I mean, you twerp."

"Oh, him? Since you smashed his life to bits, you mean? He's fine, and while we're on the subject, you should go before he gets back."

"Go?"

"Do you *really* need to see him? And—way more important—does he need to see you? What's the point, Fletch? I always say when an ex calls, hang up!"

Ouch. I don't know what I really expected, and I guess I should have expected exactly *this.*

"You're right. It was good to see you, but yeah, I'll—"

And then I heard Roger's voice behind me.

"Gwyneth Paltrow spilled a glass of white wine down my leg, and then she was a complete jerk about it. You'd think it was *my*—"

He looked up from mopping himself with a paper cocktail napkin that was just leaving little white flecks of stuff on his navy-blue suit, and he saw me.

"Hey, Dweeb," I said gently as I could. I know that sounds sort of nasty—it wasn't. It was exactly the opposite. "This is for you," I said and gave him the glass of champagne.

I tried to hide my shivering.

"Fletch. Wow. This is weird."

"Yep, prit-tee much."

Roger's face is always a bit flushed, but it went almost pale now. Was he thrilled to see me again? Or outraged? Horrified, more likely.

"What brings you—I mean, kind of the last—why?"

"A date. His idea."

"Ah. Of course. You're with somebody."

"Hey, Fletch, you remember Katrina?" said Tommy, jumping to the rescue or I swear we would still be standing there, miserable, me staring at Roger and Roger staring at the carpet. "Katrina got the shingles, poor thing, and Roger got her tickets."

Roger. A little shorter than me, he looked up at me now from under this adorable clump of brown curls that always flopped over his forehead. He blushed through the scatter of freckles that ran across his nose and cheekbones.

I didn't really believe in love or relationships and stuff, but if I'd ever had a boyfriend, Roger had been it. No. I definitely had had a boyfriend, and it had been Roger. We had even lived together for like a year and a half. But there in the lobby of the Metropolitan Opera House—don't ask me why—it was like—I don't know what it was like. I mean he looked exactly the same, but somehow now, the cluster of freckles was the cutest bunch of freckles in the universe. Those big brown cow eyes were—I literally had to struggle to breathe. I'm not really the mushy type, but it kinda broke my heart, seeing him standing there. There should have been something I could say, but I had no idea what it was.

He looked so shy. Okay, he always looked shy. And he seemed embarrassed. And hurt.

"Hey, how about that Verdi, huh?" said Tommy. "I mean, they sure don't write tunes like *that* anymore!" Roger gave a little half-laugh. I couldn't stop staring at him.

"Did Gwyneth Paltrow really spill wine on you?" said Tommy, still valiantly trying. "That's frigging awesome! Although honestly, it just looks like you peed yourself."

"You look—wonderful," I said.

Roger pushed back the curls from his forehead and looked at me for a second.

"*There*-you-are-there-you-are-there-you-are!" My date was calling. You'd think I'd been hiding instead of standing here in the middle of the lobby holding my torch. "I've been looking all over for you, Toots."

There it was—Toots. In front of everybody.

"Darwin, these are some friends of mine," I said as Darwin put his arm around me. Darwin wanted to show me off. Okay, what the hell. I wanted to brag about him too. Look who brought *me* to the party!

"Tommy Radford, Roger Prescott, this is Darwin Stewart Harrison."

"Fletchy's little friends! Charming-charming-charming," said Darwin, extending a limp hand.

"Ohmygod, Darwin Stewart Harrison, the brilliant costume designer?" Tommy, of course.

"If there's another one, I'll sue."

"What a *thrill* to meet you!"

Darwin liked nothing more than a little fawning, and Tommy fawned with the best of them, pumping Darwin's hand.

"I've admired your work since—forever!"

Tommy handed me his champagne glass, and in no time he had his arm around Darwin to take a selfie. Darwin flashed his huge fake smile in time for the picture. Obviously Tommy was impressed.

I mean, c'mon—people wanted to take selfies with my date! How cool was that?

I turned back to Roger. Was *he* impressed? With my six-time Tony-winning date?

Roger looked at Darwin. Then he looked at me. Back to Darwin. And then—and then he just sort of looked away.

That was it.

That was all he had to do. And I suddenly saw the entire evening differently. I saw what Roger saw—Darwin, the preening old queen, sad and desperate, paying for the beautiful date he could paw and pretend. And when Roger looked at me, he saw that I was just today's eye candy, an expensive accessory like a watch. The boy du jour.

I was a joke these people would snicker about tomorrow morning. *And did you see who Darwin brought? Where does he* find *these guys?*

It was my worst fear come true. Someone had seen right through me—and of all people, it had been Roger, the guy who suddenly meant more to me than all the world.

My head buzzed.

Roger said something to Tommy, and Tommy said something. And they went. Darwin said something, and then he said something else that sounded annoyed. I think maybe I said something.

And I bolted.

I pushed through the crowd and out through the glass doors at the front of the opera house, and I walked away from there as fast as I could, past the guys piling the folding chairs onto carts, past the fountain, and past the waiting limos.

I can't tell you where or in what direction or even how long I walked. Somewhere along the way I must have turned around because when I realized where I was, I was right back in front of that damned opera house, sitting on the black marble edge of the fountain. The water was turned off now. There were some guys taking down the lights and the speakers and loading stuff onto a truck. A security guy was eyeing me.

It was a very different place now. The party was definitely over.

Only a few hours earlier I had been having the best day of my entire life. And now, I didn't know if this was really the *worst* day of my life—that's a tough one to call, so many to choose from, you know?—but it was right up there. And all because of one look from an ex-boyfriend, if that's even what he was.

I was twenty-five years old, and I'd come so far, or so I'd thought. You can't know this, and I don't want people to know from looking at me, but I didn't exactly grow up playing tennis at the club. Along the way, I'd done every crappy job you can think of and probably some you don't want to think of.

I'd had a ton of sex, way more than I should have probably, but it was always with hot guys, guys I *wanted* to sleep with. When Darwin came along and he was interested, I thought, *hey, maybe I been selling myself short—maybe I should be aiming a little higher.* But had I ever really *wanted* to have sex with Darwin? No. Not once. And I'd done it anyway. Did I ever find him attractive? Never. He's funny, he's bright, he's obviously crazy talented, and he knows everybody, he knows everything, he could be a hoot to be around. He was also a nag, a perfectionist, and an insecure insomniac, workaholic, paranoid hypochondriac. Truth be told—I didn't like him much.

I'd never taken money from him for sex. I'd taken plenty of other things, however, and some of those other things I'd even disposed of. For money. And if a guy gives you taxi fare, and then you take the subway…

Let's be honest—if you go on a date and can show a profit at the end of the evening, there's a word for that. And that's what Roger saw when he looked at me.

This was what had gone through my head while I walked.

I don't drink at all, not ever. Bad for the looks, and my looks were all I had in the world.

But I'm sure people thought I was drunk when they saw the guy in the fancy tux hurling into a trash basket in that little park across from Lincoln Center.

All because Roger had looked at me, so…how? It wasn't a disapproving look, he wasn't disgusted, he wasn't scolding. It wasn't contempt. He seemed just kind of sad. Pity? No. Disappointment. Whatever else he thought of me, he had expected more, he had thought I was better than this.

So had I.

I had disappointed Roger once before, and it was a terrible, miserable feeling. It had been two years since I'd seen him, and those big, sad, deep brown eyes could still rip me up.

This is what I thought about as I sat there on that fountain, watching the moon disappear behind that fucking opera house.

And I didn't have the tiniest glimmer of a clue of the roller coaster I had just climbed onto.

Chapter 2
How It Ended

ROGER

I hadn't thought about Fletch in forever.

Okay, that's a pointless lie. Who am I kidding, I still thought about Fletch all the time. Maybe not in that first-thing-in-the-morning-every-goddamned-day way anymore, but he was still sort of lurking, and little things could remind me. Lots of little things.

But now all I could think of was the *last* time I'd seen him—before seeing him at the opera, I mean. Not a happy memory.

The last time I saw Fletch…

We'd been living together for about a year and a half. And mostly it had been fantastic. I was really happy. I had this incredibly hot guy, who wanted to hang around *me*! Who'd have believed it? Why me?

He was way out of my league, and yet, there he was: Always glad to see me when I came home, always there in bed at night, always there at breakfast. And I felt really good about myself, the way you can.

When somebody looks at you as though you're really attractive and wonderful, you start to believe it. And, of course, you *want* to believe it. Life was just plain fun with Fletch. We laughed a lot.

And the sex was amazing.

I had had some inklings along the way. A couple unexplained things or improbably explained things. I ignored them. I believed the explanations. Because I was an idiot. Because I *wanted to* believe them. And he couldn't be cheating on me, I thought, because he was so sincere when he was around. That's honestly what I had thought.

But then there was that last day.

I was sitting on the couch cross-legged when he got home. I heard the door open behind me, and I didn't turn. My dog Haggis went to greet him. Haggis, my Scottish terrier, loved Fletch like crazy.

Yeah, me too.

On the coffee table in front of me there was just a wine glass, a nearly empty bottle of wine, and a small white plastic jar, labeled in large black letters, all caps:

LUBE

No mistaking that. Right to the point, no mincing words. It was a little pocket-sized jar of lubricant, so convenient for sex on the go.

With somebody not me.

He saw it, of course. I'm sure he recognized it. He came around the couch, and I could see the little cogs of his brain working, looking for another one of those improbable explanations that I just might be naïve enough to swallow. But it's not easy to explain away a jar marked LUBE.

"I wasn't going through your pockets," I said. "It fell out when I was pulling stuff out to give to the laundry guy."

"I just got that—you know, for us—"

"It's half empty."

"Roger—I'm sorry—"

"Don't. I've suspected before. When you smell of some cologne I don't recognize, when you come home and jump in the shower after you've taken a little too long going to the grocery store or getting a haircut. I didn't want to face it but there it is."

"Roger—" He went to sit down in the chair opposite.

"No, don't sit down. Because you have to go, Fletch. I can't. I'm not like you. I can't do this."

"I never promised—"

"Don't give me your crap about promises."

"I can only tell you—it had nothing to do with you or how I feel about you. It's completely separate."

"The thing is, Fletch—you knew what this would do to me if I ever got a clue, if I ever opened my eyes and caught on. You knew it would do *this* to me. It would tear me up from the inside."

"I didn't—"

"You knew—or you wouldn't have lied about it. But you went ahead and did it anyway. You chose. You could think twice about hurting me horribly, or you could get—whatever—with whomever. And we can see which was more important to you."

"That's not how it was at all, Dweeb, not ever. Don't say it like—"

"I don't want to hear it. I never really knew, but I had hoped somehow—that this"—I made a vague gesture to myself and the apartment—"had meant something to you."

"It did! It *does* mean something to me, a lot!"

"While you were screwing around constantly."

"It wasn't constantly."

"What was it then? Once a month? Twice a week? What?"

"Please, Roger—"

"Yeah, you're right. God knows *I* don't want to talk about it. I just want you gone."

"Roger, it doesn't have to be the—"

"Oh yes it does, Fletch. It absolutely does. I've had all afternoon to chew on this, and the only conclusion that makes any sense involves you going and not coming back. So call Marco and tell him to make up the couch." Marco was an old friend of his, and Fletch had crashed there a few times before he moved in with me.

"I'm so—sorry."

"Come back and get your things when I'm not here."

Fletch went to the door.

And he went out.

I ran to the door and double locked it. I wanted him to hear the locks slamming behind him.

But I heard them too, and the sound was horrible. Final.

I turned, leaned my back against the door, and slid down to the floor. The dog was, of course, all over me. I grabbed him, hugged him, buried my face in his tough coat—and I bawled.

As if I hadn't already done that enough that day.

So if, two years later, I didn't seem all that overjoyed to bump into Fletch at the opera—now you know why.

Chapter 3
How It Started

FLETCH

"Hey, Fletch, look over there!" said Marco, pointing across the street. "Those guys gotta be goin' somewhere."

That's how Roger's and my story *actually* began. Almost four years ago now. Maybe I should have started with this, instead of at the opera, because if Marco hadn't spotted that group walking through Soho that Saturday night, the best thing that ever happened to me would never have happened. And the worst thing that ever happened to Roger.

Marco and I were out, bumbling around on those funky cobbled streets with only a few bucks between us. It had been one of those unexpectedly warm days in spring, a lot of people out and about with no coats for the first time. The kind of night when you *have* to go out, even if you're broke.

Marco and I made a pretty awesome team: Marco is gorgeous—Italian, tall, completely buff, with dark hair and eyes and the most amazing eyelashes. If you like Italian guys, Marco is your dream. By contrast, I'm a blond, blue-eyed boy, a little taller than Marco, super fit but not so beefy.

I'm *everybody's* dream.

We were both just twenty-one at the time. We'd been best friends and occasional sex buddies since our teens. Marco's family owns a fish market in Hell's Kitchen, where Marco also works. (And yeah, he smells a little of fish no matter how much he scrubs.)

So on this particular night—like many others—Marco and I had spent some time standing at the end of the bar looking picturesque and waiting to see what came up.

It can be fun, but the drawback to this mode of entertainment is that you don't necessarily attract the kind of people who attract you back.

So we headed out onto the street to see if we could find a party to crash, and lo and behold, there was a party on the march, right across the street—five well-dressed, professional-looking people, late twenties, all chattering away at once. As Marco had pointed out—they had to be going *somewhere.*

"Let's go," I said. We jaywalked across the street and fell in a few feet behind our new friends. Sure enough, at the next block, they went in a door and rang a buzzer. Marco and I stepped in behind them. They smiled politely, we smiled politely. They got buzzed in, we went in as well, and we all waited for the elevator together.

"Guess we're going to the same party," Marco said, flashing his grin. Marco was generally gorgeous, but his smile could be lethal. There were two women in the group, and you could see their immediate reactions to Marco. It was almost funny. The guys were obviously straight and there was nothing from them, but the two women seemed ready to have his babies, I swear. The elevator door slid open, and the five got in—but it was one of those ancient, tiny elevators, and it was already crowded.

"We can wait," Marco said.

"Don't be silly," said one of the girls and she grabbed his shirt. "There's plenty of room."

She pulled him in so they were scrunched together facing each other. I sort of backed in. It was like a rush-hour subway. There was a guy behind me—judging from the pudge against my back, he'd been skipping the gym for a while—and a pair of boobs squished themselves against my left arm. She smiled. I smiled.

Marco is decidedly more open-minded about these things than I am. I like guys. I've done the other, but I definitely have a preference. I don't think Marco cares either way. Any port in a storm, as they say.

We all smiled, polite, a little awkward. The elevator gave a lurch and we were moving.

"You guys aren't Goodkin Berdann," said the woman who'd pulled Marco in on top of her.

"No, ma'am," Marco said.

"Actually Bob suggested we should stop by," I said.

"Cool," said the guy behind me.

"Bob from Accounting?" asked the boobs to my left.

"That's the guy," said Marco.

It took forever to get to the third floor, which was apparently where we were going. Party noise increased as we rose, before the seven of us stumbled out of the elevator built for four. There was an open door just down the hall. The sound of chatter poured out the doorway, as did a smiling blond giantess. Late thirties, built like a Norse goddess. Like a Norse goddess with big hair.

The others now rushed to shake hands, kiss cheeks, greetings, greetings.

"The bar is toward the back, food on the right," said the goddess.

Marco and I came up politely behind.

"You must be Katrina," I said, turning on the smile.

"Yes, and you guys are…"

"Fletch."

"Marco."

"Friends of Bob's," said the paunch from the elevator.

"Bob's? Really?" Apparently she didn't think we were Bob's type—but she didn't seem to mind. "One blond, one brunette. A girl doesn't know *which* to choose."

"Why choose?" said Marco.

Katrina's eyebrows jumped a good three inches. And yeah, we'd done the three-way thing before, too.

"You boys just come on in!" she said, stretching out an arm to us. "The bar is toward the back and on the left—food on the right."

We slipped in through the crowd. Katrina stepped up to greet some new people, and Marco let his hand slide across her backside as we went by. She seemed surprised, but she certainly didn't seem to mind. Clever boy—we weren't getting thrown out of here any time soon.

I don't actually drink, so while Marco aimed for the bar, I veered off on my own. It was a chatty group, all talking shop as far as I could tell. I kept looking for a conversation I could slide into, but everywhere I turned they were babbling about motions and subpoenas. Oh sweet mother of us all, I thought, it's a bunch of frigging lawyers. Hardly the ideal party crowd.

There was a guy sitting alone on a radiator by the window, balding, mid-thirties, looking shy and awkward. Approachable, but not really what I had hoped for on a Saturday night. And then I noticed another guy off by himself, studying the bookshelf, looking, well, just as shy and awkward as the radiator sitter but with an important distinction—the bookworm was seriously cute.

He was maybe my age, maybe a bit older. Curly brown hair that fell across his forehead. Big brown eyes. He wasn't really my type—and yet somehow, man-oh-man, he was completely my type. Maybe it was the shyness that was so appealing. The bookshelf was obviously a hiding place, to avoid dealing with the other boys on the playground.

A waiter was setting out several glasses of champagne on the bar. I swung past, snagged two, and moved to the bookshelf.

"Hey," I said as I stood behind the wannabe wallflower. He was startled and he jumped a bit as if he'd been caught at something. "This is for you." I gave him one of the champagne glasses, and reached over his shoulder to set the second glass on the bookshelf behind him. "Fletch." I extended the right hand.

"Roger. Roger Prescott," he said, shifting the champagne glass and shaking my hand. "Trusts and Estates."

"Fletcher Andrews," I said. "Biscuits and gravy."

"I beg your pardon?"

"I don't know what you said either, so we're even."

"Oh."

I think I had scared him.

"Thanks for the…" he said, lifting the glass.

"No problem. Hey," I said, leaning against the bookshelf next to him. "I'm going tell you a secret, if you promise not to tell anyone ever."

"O-kayyyy," he said, clearly not okay.

"You see the guy nibbling on Katrina's ear?"

"Yeah."

"That's my friend Marco. He and I crashed this party—"

"No way."

"Way. And we don't know a soul here—although it looks like Marco is getting to know Katrina pretty well. So, I ask you, because I know you will know. Who *are* all these people?"

"Wow. Well, let's see." He turned to the room, and pushed the curls back from his forehead, which, of course, fell right back onto his forehead. Maybe the single most-adorable gesture of all time.

"It's nearly all lawyers, mostly from my firm. Katrina's firm, I mean. She's a partner. I just work there. Katrina's my boss. She's head of Trusts and Estates."

"Trusts—and estates?"

"My department. That's wills and trust funds and things. You know how you hear about a zillionaire who pays six dollars in income tax? We make that happen."

"Wow. Useful skill."

"So yeah, that's my department. I recognize most of the others, but I don't know a lot of them. I'm new, just a first-year, so…"

"First-year what?"

"Attorney," said the baby-faced attorney.

"Really."

"And you're not? An attorney, I mean."

"Not even close. You don't mind, do you?"

"No! No, not at all actually."

"So—shouldn't you be out there working the room or something? Schmooze your way to the top?"

I scooched myself just a little closer.

"You're probably right. I mean, of course you're right. I'm just not very good at it. The firm is really—competitive. And I'm just not." He glanced at me, saw I was just that much closer to him. His cheeks seemed to be permanently blushing, but now he really blushed—but he didn't move away either.

My trusty gaydar went *Ding! Ding! Ding!*

"So you write wills for, like, old, dying people?"

"Old, dying rich-rich people. Normal rich people? They can't afford us. And I only do the boring bits. I'm just a first-year."

"You said."

"Sorry." He was sipping the champagne to avoid looking at me.

"No, it's okay."

At this point Katrina came over with Marco draped on her arm like one of Calvin Klein's obsessions.

"So you know Roger too?" she asked.

"Oh absolutely," I said before Roger could answer. "Roger and I go way back, don't we?" The poor kid was in no way up to this improvisation. "Summer camp," I said, explaining to Katrina.

"I see," she said, totally not buying it. "Someone said you're a friend of Bob's?"

"Uh—yes." I'd forgotten all about Bob.

"He's over there, by the window." Bob, it turned out, was the balding radiator sitter. Bob from Accounting, it all made perfect sense.

"Oh! I didn't even see Bob," said Roger. "I should go say hello."

I laid my hand on his arm to keep him with me and left it there. The bicep through his shirtsleeve was warm, nice. Not massive or anything, just—I don't know—nice. And Bob could wait.

"You and Marco seem to have hit it off," I said. "And I'll tell you something. You can take it from me—he's fantastic in bed."

Katrina looked from Marco to me to Marco. Marco just raised his eyebrows and smiled.

"You boys aren't lawyers, are you?"

"No, ma'am," said Marco, leaning on her shoulder.

She patted him on the head.

"And you, Roger," she said, looking at him and then me, and smiling, shaking her head a little. "It's always the quiet ones."

She turned and led Marco away—who looked back at me over his shoulder and grinned. Roger gulped his champagne.

"Damn, Marco works fast," I said.

"So you guys know Bob?"

"I lied. I figured the odds were good somebody would be named Bob."

"Wow—you do this a lot."

"Sometimes."

"For what, just free food and booze?"

"I don't drink, but yeah, free food, sure. And some laughs. It's something to do. And maybe I've just been hoping all this time that I'd meet some adorable young attorney with lots of curly brown hair."

"What?" He wasn't used to getting hit on.

"Seriously. I think you're about the cutest thing since bunny rabbits, with the most gorgeous eyes I've ever seen."

"Oh." He went to drink some more champagne, but the glass was empty.

"Take this one," I said, and I handed him the glass I'd set on the bookshelf.

"You sure?"

I nodded.

"I brought it for you."

"Oh." He sipped. "Bob's really nice. He's in Accounting."

"I've heard that about Bob."

"He's a friend of mine."

"Hey, Roger, as long as I'm flirting with you and stuff, I feel I oughta ask you before I go any further—does anyone here belong to that hickey?"

"What?" I swear, his voice cracked like he was fourteen. "Oh this," he said, rubbing the hickey on the left side of his throat. "It's not a hickey. I play violin."

I thought about that for a second.

"I'm glad," I said. "Is there—a connection?"

"Oh. If you play violin, a lot of violin, I mean, you tend to get a mark there where you neck bends over the instrument. It doesn't go away. Look, you can see Katrina has the same hickey—mark, I mean. She plays too."

I looked across the room to Katrina. If she had it, it was somewhere under Marco.

"And Bob!" he added.

"He plays violin, too?"

"No, cello. So no hickey. Unless it's like—on his thigh somewhere."

We both looked over to balding Bob on the radiator.

"Don't go there," I said.

"Seriously." He turned back to me. The champagne was starting to relax him. "Anyway, we play together, the three of us, Katrina, Bob, and I. I mean there's also Janine. I don't think she's here. She plays viola. We play quartets."

"So much easier with four people."

"I'm being an idiot—sorry."

"No! Not at all, I swear. Tell me, what kind of quartets?" Like I knew anything about this, but I wanted to keep him going.

"We've been doing Schubert mostly, lately, but we've been working on a Beethoven quartet too."

"Which do you like best?"

"Between the two?" He was gaining courage as he went. "I really love Schubert. If I had to pick a single all-time favorite, it would definitely be Franz Schubert. But lately I've been thinking the late Beethoven quartets sound like they were written last week. I'm always hearing something new in there every time I open a score." He explained some more about these quartets, and there was something truly charming in the way he talked about this stuff, like he believed I could somehow relate to it or even had a clue what he was talking about. His eyes were completely sexy and sparkly when he was even a little excited, and he was apparently pretty stoked about his late Beethoven.

Were those freckles that ran across his nose and cheekbones? How was anyone supposed to pay much attention when he had freckles like that?

Then he got suddenly unsure, and that wonderful enthusiasm was gone in a second.

"Jeez, you must think I'm a total dweeb," he said, "talking chamber music to a guy at a party."

"Dweeb? No, that was not what I was thinking, not even close." Man-oh-man, would ya' look at those eyes. "Hey, can I ask you—are you like—in the closet? I don't want to out anybody at the office party or anything."

"No, why? I mean I guess I'm out at the firm, as much as anyone cares…"

"Not a big presence around the office yet?"

"You could say that."

"Come here, turn to me. That's it. Now lean your shoulder against the bookshelf like me—and look at me."

He did as he was told.

"There that's better. I really meant it about those eyes of yours."

"Stop," he said, trying to pull away.

But my hand caught his arm and he stayed. So did my hand.

"The reason I asked about the closet and all is that I'm about to kiss you."

"What?"

He tried to pull back again, but my hand was firm. I leaned to him, moved my hand up to his chin, and held it with just the fingertips of my right hand. I tilted my head and kissed his lips, very, very lightly at first, then with a little more contact, and then a full-on kiss.

Is there anything better than a first kiss? Always a little tentative and sensitive and electric. He tasted of guy. And champagne. All good things.

"And you know what?" I said, pulling back only a little. "Monday morning, everybody in your office is going to be talking about that cute guy Roger from whatever your department is—"

"Trusts and Estates—"

"Trusts and—that's not the easiest thing to say: Trusts and Estates—"

We said the last bit together, and man-oh-man when this kid smiled…

"They'll be talking about Katrina's party and that cute Roger guy from—Wills and Things—"

And he smiled some more for me.

"And the hot blond he was kissing."

Roger laughed, sputtering a little. I kissed him quickly on the cheek just because his laugh was so sweet.

"They won't."

"They will."

"Hey, Prescott," said a girl in a black dress and a string of pearls as she passed by.

"Hey, Monica," said Roger.

"How's it goin'?" She walked past, oh-so slowly, eyed me and then Roger, oh-so slowly, and then she kept going, still slowly.

Roger Prescott. And for half a second I was actually thinking that even his name was cute.

"See?" I said. "The gossip's starting already."

"Seems kind of high school, doesn't it?"

"If you say so. Now c'mon, you dweeb," I said with one last little kiss before he could panic. "Let's go talk to Bob." I put my arm around his waist and shepherded him over to the radiator sitter, grabbing a couple more glasses of champagne as we went. I was sure Bob would like some too.

Bob and Roger talked mostly about music and their quartet, but they made an effort to clue me in, which was really nice. And I loved watching

Roger's face, how animated he became talking about allegrettos and legatos and stuff. By the end of the evening I knew a *lot* more music words than I did at the beginning.

Eventually Roger said good night to Bob, and I did too. He waved good-bye to Katrina from across the room, and I did too. He eyed me a little uncertainly, but he didn't tell me to take a hike either.

"Where do you live?" I asked in the elevator.

"Chelsea. You?"

"Brooklyn."

Out on the sidewalk—probably because we'd just come out of Katrina's crowded, overheated apartment—the warm April day seemed to have turned into a frigging cold April night.

Neither of us had a jacket. Roger threw his arms around himself.

"Spring Street's not far," I said, meaning the subway stop. We started off at a really fast walk. As we turned on to Sixth Ave., still a few blocks from the station, it started to rain. Really cold rain.

We looked at each other.

"C'mon," I said. I took off at a run, and he followed. We pelted as fast as we could through the few people on the sidewalk with umbrellas, dodging cars as we dashed across side streets. I let him go down the subway steps in front of me, his feet just flew, and we came to a stop as soon as we were inside. We were breathing hard, and laughing—don't ask me why. Like two little boys.

"You okay?" I asked.

"Yeah," he panted. "You?"

"Me? I'm fine. I'm always fine."

We didn't talk much on the train, but he seemed a little more relaxed with me, after the run.

Did I mention this kid was totally not my type? The ones who usually pushed my buttons were the big manly guys, fit gym rats with muscles and stubble, guys totally comfortable with their sexiness. But this shy little violin-playing lawyer boy had found buttons in me I didn't know existed. I didn't understand it, and I couldn't get enough. As we sat on the train together, I wanted to put my arm around him, but I wasn't sure how he'd take that, so I just leaned against him a little. Nothing obvious, just sharing some body heat. He felt really nice there.

"You can change here for the D," he said at West Fourth Street. The D train goes to Brooklyn.

"I'll see you home," I said.

I should also tell you that I was pretty much a cut-to-the-chase kind of guy. Most guys, me included, want to get to the point of the matter and sooner rather than later. Generally, my idea of foreplay was seeing how fast I could tear open a condom.

But with this one, my mind wasn't racing ahead to the sixteen things I was going to do with him—which was how I'd usually be at this point. Instead, all I could think was how much I wanted to hold that sweet face in my hands and kiss him, kiss him all over. Crazy, huh?

It wasn't raining when we got to Twenty-Third Street, just cold, so we walked really quickly without any conversation. Two flights up, we were outside his apartment door, and he seemed more nervous than ever.

"You don't have to come in if you don't want," he said, a little out of breath."

Not quite the line I usually got at this point in the evening. He obviously didn't do this very much. From the other side of the door came an occasional bark.

"Are you allergic to dogs?" he said. "Because I have a dog." He was apparently trying to talk me into going away.

"I love dogs," I said.

"Oh."

"Look, I can go, if you want me to. But—I'd much rather come in."

"Really?"

"Really. And maybe, Dweeb," I said kissing him, "if you let me in, you could show me your Stradivarius." How had I come up with Stradivarius? Even I was impressed.

He turned and put the key in the door.

"I don't actually have a Strad, of course. Mine's from Mittenwald, a little town in—" He pushed the door open.

I gently guided Roger inside, and this little black dog started sniffing my ankles.

"But you don't really care who made my violin, do you?"

I kicked the door closed behind me while kissing him—a much-practiced move.

"Actually, Dweeb," I said and kissed him some more, "I wasn't talking about your violin."

And that, boys and girls, is how all the trouble began.

Chapter 4
Knock-Knock

ROGER

Maybe the oddest part of the whole story—we'd met at Katrina's party, and we'd seen each other exactly three times since. Each time he'd called, which had surprised the hell out of me. I mean I wouldn't even *think* about calling a guy who looked like Fletch, so why was a guy who looked like Fletch calling *me*?

But that's not the strange bit. The really weird part was when he *didn't* call—he'd just shown up.

I'd been practicing and was putting the violin away when the door buzzer buzzed. The buzzer always makes me jump out of my skin, and it doesn't help that Haggis also jumps out of *his* skin and barks like an idiot.

"That's enough, Haggis." He knew that command, and he settled down to growling and waited at the door.

I pushed the intercom button.

"Yes?" I said.

"Hey, Dweeb."

Fletch? He'd sort of adopted "dweeb" as his nickname for me. Part of me thought I should resent it, but I just couldn't. He always seemed so affectionate when he said it. I had a pet name. I'd never had a nickname before. Even if it was dweeb, it still seemed really sweet somehow.

Anyway, he called me dweeb, and I buzzed him in.

We'd seen each other a couple times, as I said, and, you know, things had happened, and he'd spent the night, but this was completely weird of him, just showing up. I really liked Fletch, and I had hoped I'd see him again, but I had no idea if he felt the same.

I mean, seriously, why would he?

I was a skinny little drip who liked classical music and he—well, for starters, *he* looked like Fletch. He was one of those sort of breathtaking people: blond, blue-eyed, yeah, but that doesn't tell the half of it. There was something about the shape of his eyes, almost almond, that made them extraordinary. The hair was longish in those days, with a little curl to it, not crazy curly like mine, just a little. His skin was very fair, tending toward pink, and flawless. Beautiful mouth, gorgeous smile, and the body—seriously, go to the Metropolitan Museum and look at the statues of naked Greek guys. *That* was Fletch.

He was sex in high tops.

So, as I said, I was the nerdy lawyer with the fiddle, and *he* was Fletch.

I was terrified of going to parties because what if I didn't know anybody when I got there? *He* deliberately crashed parties where he *knew* he wouldn't know anybody, because he also knew that whomever he met *would* like him. Unbelievable.

I opened the door and waited for him to come up the two flights. As he came around the bend in the stairs he was carrying a gym bag over his shoulder in addition to his usual shoulder bag. Curious. Then he smiled up to me through the railing—

Okay, let me explain something. I'm not really crazy about surprises. Truth is I'm not the most spontaneous person you'll ever meet? And I sort of had my evening all planned out, you know—pizza and an episode of *Masterpiece Theatre*. I know, pretty dorky, but still, it was what I'd *planned.* And I had *not* planned on somebody just turning up without calling. Even if it was an absurdly hot somebody.

But when he smiled at me through the railing like that, nothing else on earth mattered.

"Hey," I said, trying not to grin like the village idiot.

By now Haggis was dancing around Fletch, and he was fiercely wagging his tail. Haggis, I mean—which was in itself remarkable. He was not a terribly demonstrative dog. Fletch had never had a dog, he said, but he had somehow connected with Haggis from the get-go.

"I'm really sorry to barge in like this," he said, barging in. Okay, he didn't really, he gave me a peck on the cheek on the way by, which was nice—and then he plopped the gym bag in the middle of the floor. "Hey, Haggis," he said squatting down to the dog. Haggis immediately scooted away from him, which was just a game he played with everyone. "Doesn't he like me?" Fletch asked me.

"I think he likes you more than anybody—he just dances away from everybody like that."

"Ah. Playing hard to get," observed Fletch. "Haggis, you gotta teach me that one."

"That little dance is Scottish terrier for 'can't touch this.'"

"Dweeb, was that a pop music reference?!"

"Enjoy it. I get about one a decade. But to be honest, I stole that joke from my sister. So—what's up?"

"I—I have a huge favor to ask you. And no is a perfectly okay answer."

"Good, because I am *not* helping you with your laundry."

He laughed. I'd made a joke and he laughed!

"It's worse than that." He looked sheepish. "Can I kinda crash here for a few days?"

"Here?" Jeez, talk about surprises!

I looked around at my little one-bedroom apartment. It was a nice place—for one. The living room was a good size, big enough that I used it occasionally for quartet rehearsals. One side faced the street and had three big windows. On the opposite wall was a small galley kitchen separated from the rest of the room by a counter and bar stools, with cabinets above. The place was sparsely decorated—clean, modern-y furniture. A console piano against one wall. There was a series of framed artsy photos on the wall that my sister had taken of my violin for a photography class, some shelves of CDs. I kept the scads of music scores in the bedroom.

And now there was this guy. Well, he was certainly decorative, but...jeez. Did I like him *that* much?

"My landlady," he started. "It's a long stupid story, but I have this not entirely legal apartment, and my not entirely legal landlady is not entirely sane. So yesterday, she starts nagging me, and maybe I said something back, and then today when I get there, there's this gigantic padlock on the door, and she's standing in the stairs screaming—Hungarian, Czech, I never figured out *what* she is—but whatever she is, she'd clearly forgotten her Zoloft or something, and—"

"Hey, sit down. Just move the Haggis steps."

"These are so cute, by the way," he said, setting aside the little steps I have for Haggis to climb up on the couch. "I was gonna ask—he can't get up on his own?"

"His legs are only five inches long. He can't jump up that high, and if he jumps down, his nose hits the floor before his front feet do."

"Ohhhh!" he said full of sympathy.

"Would you like some—water or—something?"

"Yeah. I'm wrecked. Thanks."

"Where do you live?" I asked on my way to the fridge.

"Brooklyn."

"I knew that. Brooklyn. Very hip."

"Not this part of Brooklyn."

I handed him a bottle of water.

"Hey, I was just going to order some food. Have you eaten?"

"No, I've been a little…" He made a sort of stressed-out face.

"Yeah, obviously. Pizza okay?"

"Wow, I never let myself have pizza. You know—the body and all." He lifted his shirt to show me his abs. Wow.

"Should we—would you—" The glimpse of Fletch's tummy had pretty much short-circuited the language center in my brain. "Th-there's other—" Of course I'd seen him naked but still. I was never going to get jaded about seeing those muscles, the shallow little belly button. "Menus—" I forced myself to say. And jeez, that little bit of blond hair that—"Chinese?" I practically yelled it. "Sorry. I got—distracted."

"Don't sweat it." He grinned at me.

"You're enjoying this, aren't you," I said, going to find menus.

"I always enjoy it here."

"Good line."

"It's not!" He followed me toward the kitchen and leaned against the counter so he could see me under the cabinets. "I mean, yeah, it *was* a line, but seriously, it's true. Dead honest—this day has been straight from hell, but as soon as I saw you, I felt better."

I had no idea what to do with that. *Did he mean that?*

"So…Chinese? Sushi?"

"Absolutely not, now that you've tempted me with pizza."

"Okay." I cleared my throat and tried to concentrate. "So what do you like on it?"

"My favorite thing is anchovies, but *nobody* ever wants anchovies, so you choose."

"I love anchovies."

"See? You and me—it's fate," he said and stepped over to me, all mock romantic with one arm around my waist, and he bent me over backward in this huge black-and-white-movie dip. "It's no use fighting it," he said doing some kind of vague accent. "It is written in the stars."

"Green peppers?" I asked, still bent over backward in his arms.

"Perfect." He kissed me on the forehead, and it was really sweet. "God you feel good like this."

Which really embarrassed me. I wriggled out of his arms and stood up.

"Mushrooms or no?" I asked, pushing my hair back.

"Love 'em."

"Me too."

"See? Now if *Scooby Doo* is your favorite cartoon, I think we should go ahead and start a family."

"Drinks?"

"Water for me."

I called the pizza place.

"So you're sure it's okay?" he asked. "Me crashing here?"

"Um, yeah, I guess. I mean, jeez, we hardly know each other. You really have no place else to go?"

"I'm sorry to ask. But it's not like we're total strangers after all…"

"No."

"And we get along. Don't we?"

"I think so."

"I definitely think so! I borrowed some clothes from my friend Marco, and I'd have crashed with him, but they're in the middle of this huge reno—and Marco's already sleeping in the living room as it is." He looked at me with sad-little-orphan-boy eyes. Breathtakingly beautiful sad-little-orphan-boy eyes. "Oh come on, Roger, please-please-please?"

"Well, you can't sleep in Penn Station. But—you're thinking—what?" Fletch was so far out of my league it wasn't even funny. I didn't dare entertain the thought of anything—is *serious* even the word?—with him. I would never in a million years hit on a guy who looked like Fletch, and here he was—what? Crashing? We'd seen each other four times total—and it had been incredible. And he'd stayed the night, which surprised me. I mean, a guy like Fletch, you'd think he'd be the kind of guy who would make a quick excuse afterward and bolt, sort of in and out. That sounds bad, but you know what I mean. He'd be sort of come and go. Jeez, that's way worse.

What I'm trying to say is that he'd stayed the night *and* he'd hung around for breakfast, and he even talked to me, told me about his day, asked about mine. Not just grunted at his coffee mug. Not that I brought guys back here every other night or anything. I get most of this stuff from Tommy's dating horror stories.

But Fletch stayed the night and with him it really was great, the sleeping over, I mean. You know how it can be impossible to sleep with somebody else right there? But with him…I'd never slept so well. He was a terrific cuddler without getting all grippy. He held me, I held him, it was somehow relaxed and fine, and in the morning, I loved waking up with him there, all warm, his gorgeous arm around me. I never wanted him to leave.

So was that he was thinking? Or was he thinking more along the lines of—

"Couch?" I asked.

Now he looked as insecure as I was.

The couch was a nice size for an apartment, meaning it was small. Not long enough for you to be able to stretch out on.

"That would be great, if that's what you want."

"If that's what *I* want?"

"Well, honest, I really enjoyed the time we've spent together and all, but if you don't want—I totally understand. This thing folds out, right?"

"No. This is it."

"Really?"

"Really. And you're so tall, so…"

"So, in that case"—he leaned over and kissed me—"I think you're saying I can't possibly sleep on your couch. Is that it?"

"It wouldn't be right." He kissed me again.

"And I'd really much rather sleep with a beautiful guy." He kissed me again.

"Great," I said. "Do you know one?"

"Fortunately for me…" He kissed me again.

"Pizza's coming, don't forget." Still kissing.

"Damn. Of course. I'll behave," he said kissing me back.

"Promise?" And the kissing continued.

"I don't know, Dweeb. I'm not very good at promises." His hands started migrating south.

After a good half minute of tongue wrestling, I pushed him back.

"That buzzer's going to ring."

"Yeah. Pizza."

"Pizza."

He sat up and I sat up, and we tugged at our pants to arrange things. His pants problem was particularly conspicuous. One more thing about him that put him out of my class.

He reached over, grabbed the end pillow from the couch, and plopped it in his lap. He handed me the other one.

"There. Now I'll be good. Hey, I know," he said with a sudden idea. "Until the pizza guy comes—would you, maybe, play something for me? I've wanted to ask you before, but it's always been so late. Is it like a huge deal?"

"No. I mean, sure, of course I can play something." Cold sweat of sheer panic sprang to my temples. I got up and pulled my violin up out of its case—but its cozy brown color didn't calm me, the familiar weight in my hands didn't give me confidence. I was scared to death.

Here was this really cool guy sitting on my couch. And he wanted me to play violin for him? How frigging uncool was *that* going to be? What should I play? Gilbert and Sullivan? I plucked some strings to check the tuning and adjusted, feeling my throat closing up. But what could I play that *wouldn't* make me look like the incredibly boring dork that I was? My instrument didn't really lend itself to hip-hop. Not that I knew any hip-hop. I wiped some rosin on the bow—sticky stuff to help the bow grab the strings better. My hands were sweating. I wiped some rosin off. Anyway, it was something to do while I stalled.

This was it. This was the end. Nice while it lasted, but whatever interest this fabulous guy had had in me—it would be all over now.

"I'm sorry," I said finally, giving up about a sixteenth of an inch from tears. "I'm a little—and honestly?—I have no idea what to play." Jeez, I sounded pathetic.

"Hey!" He saw what a mess I was. "Hey, I didn't mean to flip you out, Dweeb." He had jumped up, and now he held me in his arms. "I'm sorry. Put it away, you don't have to play for me! I don't want to make you miserable!"

"It's so stupid," I said, violin and bow still in my hands. "I've been playing since I was a kid. I'm probably more comfortable with my violin than I am anywhere else. Definitely more comfortable."

"It's okay, you know. If you make a mistake or something, I don't care. I probably won't even know."

"It's not that I'm going to make a mistake. I play really well. And part of me wants to show off. Me and my little violin—it's me at my best. It's just..."

"What then?"

"You'll think I'm such a geek."

He pulled me tighter in his arms.

"I don't. I won't." He backed up a little to look at me. "Look—only if you want—you can play me something really simple, something not stressful. And if you don't want, that's okay too."

"Okay, I know. I told you—I know it's really nerdy—but we have this string quartet?"

"It's not nerdy. Katrina's in the quartet?"

"First violin."

"Does Katrina strike you as nerdy?"

"Well, no."

"So. Definitely not nerdy."

Good point.

I tuned.

"I'm putting together an arrangement for the quartet of some Gershwin songs?"

"Gershwin, the songwriter guy."

"Yeah. So I've pulled together some of his songs into a medley for the quartet, and this is from that. I arranged it so each of us gets featured, but, since I'm putting it together, second violin gets the best solo."

"Sly."

"Okay." I took a deep breath. "Okay." I took another deep breath. "Please don't hate this."

"I bet I won't."

"Okay."

He was startled by the first notes—people are always surprised by just how much sound a little violin makes. My chunk of the medley was the song "They Can't Take that Away from Me." The words, which I obviously wasn't going to sing, are about this guy's memories of a relationship and how, no matter what, nothing can take those memories away. The piece wasn't particularly difficult or anything, just a terrific tune, lots of opportunities to let the violin really sing, with a few variations and flourishes and a fancy coda to a long high note at the end. I'd written myself some sort of tricky bits, some flashy runs, some awkward double-stops that I liked that I didn't really expect him to be able to appreciate. Still, he seemed to listen. I didn't dare look at him. I held out the last long note and let it slowly fade on the E-string. I tried to "savor the note," as Mrs. Kleinmeyer, my first violin teacher, once told me to do, but I was way too scared to savor much of anything. And then I stopped.

"That was—amazing."

Was he making fun of me? I looked up, and he jumped up and threw his arms around me. I still had the violin and bow in my hands, and I was suddenly very aware of how much I had pitted out with worrying, but he held me tightly.

"My God, Dweeb, I had no idea. You really are good! That was the most beautiful thing I've ever heard." He grabbed my head and kissed me.

"You mean it?" I didn't believe him for a second.

He kissed me again, he kissed me *lots.*

"Absolutely. Is that how you pick up guys? Because that must work like a clock."

"No way."

"Way. Take my word for it, Dweeb. You play like that, you'll have like Chris Hemsworth and that hottie from *Game of Thrones* duking it out over you!"

"Both those guys are totally straight, I'm pretty sure."

"For you, they'll go gay."

"Shut up!"

Like I had ever picked up a guy in my life. Can you imagine me walking up to some even *not* sexy guy and striking up a conversation? The way Fletch had done with me at Katrina's? He could do that because he was ballsy, and stunning. Two things I definitely wasn't.

"I mean it. That was the sexiest thing I've ever seen anybody do! And I once went out with a sword swallower at Coney Island, so that's saying something."

"You are so full of it!"

"I would never joke about something as serious as dating a sword swallower."

"Jerk."

"He *was*! A total jerk, but you know, a sword swallower, you can put up with a lot. But he was nowhere near as dreamy as you."

He kissed me again.

"Let me—" I said, raising my hands with the violin and bow.

"Yeah."

He held me from behind with his head over my shoulder next to mine, while I put the violin in its case and relaxed the bow, and jeez Louise it was nice. So much better than *Masterpiece Theatre.*

And lest you think I'm completely shallow—it wasn't *just* his gorgeous eyes that melted me. Fletch was fun to be around. He was funny and so sweet. I really liked him, and I really liked being around him, even though he made me nervous. I laughed more around him. And when he left, I always felt the room was dimmer, quieter without him. Emptier. I hated when he left.

And he had gorgeous eyes.

"You don't think I'm a dweeb?"

"Of course I do." He kissed me and then held me tight against him. "But you're *my* dweeb."

He took my left hand in his and began to kiss each finger.

"Don't," I said. "My fingers are so ugly—the callouses."

"Your fingers are amazing," he said and kissed them again.

It was awkward for me, and embarrassing—and wonderful. No one had ever…

I suppose it was about then that I really started to fall in love with him. To have somebody just plain admire you for what you do, the way that he did that night? Who wouldn't fall in love with that? He was in awe. Of *me*. Can you imagine???

"Thank you," I said. "I was pretty nervous about playing."

"I don't know why, Dweeb."

"Because—I wanted to impress you."

"Man-oh-man, you're this intelligent, educated lawyer guy, who just happens to have huge brown eyes and the cutest freckles, and the best ass ever in in the long and rich history of human assdom, *and* on top of all that, you have this astonishing talent. And you worry you need to impress *me*?"

"Yeah. Pretty funny, huh. Oh, the irony."

"And I bet you probably went to law school at like Yale or something."

I made an index-finger cross and hissed.

"Harvard."

"Get out. How did *I* end up in your living room?"

"You invited yourself in, remember?"

"Oh yeah, that's right." He put his arms around me. "I better behave too, or you'll toss me out."

"Not very likely." I laughed. "Hey, you want a beer while we wait?"

"No thanks. I really don't drink."

"I knew that. Sorry. Any reason? Of course you can tell me to mind my own business."

"Hey, of course it's your business if we're living together."

The words suddenly hit me. *Living together.* Like boyfriends? That's kinda what it sounded like. Is that what he meant? Is that what this was? Did I just fall into a relationship? Were we a thing now? That was crazy.

What would any of my friends say, if I told them I was living with a guy I'd sort of dated a couple of times? They'd tell me I was going to come home to find my apartment emptied out. Or wake up in the middle of the night because the police were raiding the meth lab he'd set up in my bathtub. Or I'd just wake up dead.

And yet I mostly couldn't believe that I could be so—lucky—that a guy like this—but what if he's one of those nutjobs you read about who ties up his victims and tortures them for days before finally killing them off?

"Fletch," I said, catching myself. "Reality check. We—we hardly know each other." I sat down. He sat with me.

"We'll get to know each other. Ask me anything!"

"Jeez. Okay. You're Fletcher...Andrews?"

"Yes."

"Roger Prescott."

"I knew that. How do you do. Very nice to meet you." He shook my hand.

"Charmed. So." Thank God we at least knew each other's last names before we got this far. "Are you a serial killer?"

"No."

"Drug dealer?"

"No, and I don't do drugs either. Don't even smoke. Nothing."

"Did you ever tie anybody up and torture them for days?"

"Just the once, and that was only because he asked me to"—?!—"And if it makes you feel any better, I didn't enjoy it."

???!!!!

I could only stare at him. I mean, seriously, what was I supposed to say to that??? The room started to spin.

"Oh my God, it was a joke!" He pulled me into a hug. "I was kidding! Don't wig out!" he said, kissing me on the side of the head. "Sh."

"Don't scare me like that."

"I won't. I'm sorry. No, I never tortured anyone ever. Ask me another."

"Okay." I tried to shake myself out of it. "Back on track. So. Do you have—like—a job?"

"I do!"

Okay, four questions, three right answers. And one that I needed to forget.

"Good. Where?"

"I work for the Nederlanders." This meant nothing to me.

"You're a—houseboy?" I guessed.

"No! The Nederlander Organization, they own a bunch of Broadway theaters, and I'm an usher for them. These days I'm at the Gershwin Theatre—Gershwin, like your song, I think. They have a nice exhibit about him in the lobby. Anyway, that's where I am. *And*, roomie—added bonus here—if you ever want to hear something from *Wicked*, I know aaaaaaaaall the songs!" I had to laugh. "Most of my days are free, so I can help with the dog and anything else, Laundry or marketing or whatever. Cooking…"

"Oh wow. You can cook?"

"Nooooo, but I can learn! Come on. Think how much fun this is gonna be!" He snuggled up against me. "It'll be like a slumber party."

"A slumber party?"

"With condoms."

We looked at each other for a bit—me, trying to think through what the hell I was doing here; him, making those incredibly blue sad-little-orphan eyes again. I didn't stand a chance.

"I'll make you crazy. I practice all the time—"

"Awesome! Can't wait."

"And I'm sort of…fastidious."

"I'm sure, when I look that up, it'll be one of the things I most admire about you. Look, I really, really like you, Dweeb. I'm not just saying that because I need a place to stay. I keep calling you and stuff because—when I think, gee, what do I want to do today, I think about you, and I realize—I just wanna hang with Roger some more."

"And you always do what you want?"

"Yep, prit-tee much." There was that smile. "So here I am. And you know what? Right now I want to do this."

And he pulled me close and he kissed me, and he kept at it, and just as we were both getting pretty-well warmed up—the door buzzed. We both jumped a mile, and Haggis exploded into his usual chorus of Scottish outrage.

"You know, for a little dog," said Fletch, "that is a helluva big bark."

"You should see his teeth."

I buzzed the delivery guy in.

"Do you need…" said Fletch, reaching for his wallet.

"No, I got it," I said as I went to the door.

"Good, because I don't actually have…"

At least he was honest about it and funny.

We sat down to plates of anchovy pizza and bottled waters on the coffee table.

"So," I said as we started. "Tell me about your landlady."

Which he did. It basically came down to his living in an illegal apartment, meaning that since it didn't meet city building code requirements for a rental apartment, his landlady, a certain Mrs. F. Szanko, first name unknown, hadn't registered it with the city. He told me further that he, for reasons he didn't share, hadn't actually been paying his rent, or at least not all of it, for a while, and this greedy bitch-slash-slumlord-slash-scumbag Mrs. Szanko had finally resorted to the age-old stratagem of wronged landladies everywhere—she had locked him out. With all of his things locked inside, as hostage.

So.

The next morning I was in my office, majorly underslept after a strenuous night—*and* morning—with my new roommate—I wasn't complaining—and I was on the phone with the aforesaid Mrs. Szanko, explaining that I was Mr. Andrews's attorney.

I should explain that my firm took a dim view of their lawyers taking on clients independently, paid or otherwise. In fact, we were explicitly forbidden to do so. Had Mrs. Szanko decided to check up on me and had she called my firm, I could easily have found myself—and a filing box of my personal possessions—escorted out onto the Sixth Avenue sidewalk by a nice, burly security guard.

Knowing all that, I made the call anyway.

You should further understand that I was actually in the Trusts and Estates Department at my firm—far, far removed from real estate law. On top of that, New York tenant law is its own special area of expertise. People make careers out of it.

Conclusion: I was way out of my depth.

My only hope was that once Mrs. Szanko realized Fletch had brought in a lawyer, she'd be intimidated and back off.

That afternoon, I was in my Manhattan lawyer suit and expensive shoes, standing in a fairly miserable studio apartment in a seedy and seriously inconvenient part of Brooklyn. (I know, Brooklyn is cool, blah-blah-blah, but I really don't like going to Brooklyn.) And I was doing my damnedest to bluff this landlady into releasing Fletch's stuff.

I failed.

In contrast to me and my ignorance, Mrs. Szanko knew as much as she needed to about the relevant law, and she was not the least bit inclined to back off. This out-of-his-depth little lawyer ended the negotiations by writing a personal check for Fletch's back rent. All of it. Every dime.

I was the world's worst attorney.

Mrs. S., grumbling the entire time, removed the giant padlock—with the stipulation that Fletch get his things and go. Whatever he had said and/or done, he had burned his bridges with La Szanko. He was homeless. Unless my apartment was home. I was stuck with him.

I tried to scold myself. I should have felt like the chump of the year for shoveling out a bunch of money for a guy I hardly knew—but I found I just couldn't care about the money and all I felt was—sort of giddy.

I could have danced back to Manhattan. Instead, I sat in the back seat of a livery car, staring out the window at the East River, with the biggest, stupidest grin on my face that I couldn't get rid of.

It was the last thing I expected, but I was ecstatic thinking about what drawers I could clear out for Fletch's stuff.

Fletch was moving in.

When I got back to the apartment, I told Fletch that I'd gotten the lock taken off his door and that he could retrieve his things—he looked at me with those blue eyes like I was a superhero. You can imagine how many times *that* had happened in my life—exactly zero point zip. But to Fletch,

I was a great lawyer and a staunch defender of the rights of man, I was Clarence Darrow, Atticus Finch, Abraham Lincoln, and Captain America.

I know it's pitiful, but I never told him that all I'd done was paid his back rent. I just couldn't.

I had my blue-eyed reasons.

Chapter 5

The Morning after the Opera—The Hell's Kitchen Edition

FLETCH

"Fletch! You look totally wrecked, my man," said Marco at the door yawning. As I'd expected, I had gotten him up.

After I'd ducked out of the opera house, I'd walked for a while, gone back to Darwin's to have it out with him, and then I'd walked some more before I turned up at Marco's. I'd lost the bowtie somewhere along the way, the shirt collar was open, but I was still wearing the tux, now considerably worse for wear.

By contrast, Marco stood in the door in nothing but a pair of tighty-whities, scratching his junk.

"Thanks," I said, pushing my way in past him. "Sorry I woke you up."

"Nah, I have to get up anyway. 'Sup, bro?"

"Can I crash here for a bit, man? It won't be long."

"That rich guy toss you out?"

"No, I left."

"Dude! That was a sweet setup you had. Are you crazy?"

"Probably. I'm gonna make some coffee, okay?"

"It's set, just hit the 'on' button."

I had screwed everything else up, but I figured I could probably manage to hit the on button.

"Wow," said Marco, yawning again. "I bet that suit was really something before you slept in it."

"Haven't slept," I growled. Totally true. And by now I hated the damned suit.

"Whatever. I'm gonna shower, bro."

He went into the bathroom and left me with my thoughts, which was where I'd spent the night, alone with my miserable self. I pulled the jacket off and tossed it on a stool at his kitchen counter and pulled off those ridiculous patent leather shoes finally. The bubbling sound of the coffee maker was comforting at least, as was the smell. I needed something to do, so I rolled up my sleeves and started breaking some eggs to scramble.

Marco and I went way back, so it was only natural I'd land here.

For a while, as a teen, things had been kinda tough for me. I was actually homeless for a good bit, sleeping in shelters or train stations or wherever, eating out of the trash bin in front of McDonald's. I met Marco, and he smuggled me into his house—not easy in a big Italian family—and at least I had a place to shower and sleep where I wasn't going to get beat up. Even after his mom caught on a couple days later, they let me live here, eat here, they gave me a job in the fish shop.

Of course one thing led to another, two randy teenage boys, sharing a bedroom.

But the thing is—I had been desperate, really desperate. I honestly don't know what might have happened to me or where I'd have ended up. There's only one reason my life got any better, and that reason is Marco Campobasso.

I would always owe Marco.

He came back a few minutes later, dripping and toweling himself off.

"So tell me what happened," he said, as I shoveled some eggs onto plates.

"I went to the opera, bro, and it changed my life."

I pulled the ketchup bottle out of the fridge for him.

"Get serious," he said.

"You'll never guess who I bumped into at the Met."

"Enrico Caruso?"

"Roger."

"The hell you say. *Your* Roger? From way back? He didn't make a big scene or anything, did he?"

"No. No, he hardly said a thing."

"So?"

"He saw me, and he saw Darwin—and I felt like my amateur standing was suddenly in question."

"Bro?"

"You know that little dog that Paris Hilton carries around in her purse?"

"Yeah…"

"My career model."

"Fletch, what are you talking about?"

"I just couldn't anymore. The only difference between me and that dog is that I had to *earn* my puppy chow."

"Wow. So whaja do? Howja leave it with the designer?"

"He was still up when I got in—the guy never sleeps—and I told him I was done."

"He didn't cry, did he? God, I hate when they cry. Or did he just get all cunty?"

"Just a little. Not bad, considering."

When I'd told Darwin I couldn't go on with him any longer, he'd sighed.

"It's just-as-well-just-as-well, Fletchy," Darwin had said. "I'm not going take umbrage or have a hissy. The opera gala was the big thing I wanted you for, and—until you walked out and left me there, and I *should* be totally put out with you—*until* then, you were fabulous-fabulous-fabulous, and besides, I just can't be put out with anyone with eyes like those. And think of it—tomorrow, your gorgeous picture will be everywhere-just-everywhere."

It was all I could do not to groan at the thought. I was not *just* a boy toy, I would soon be a *famous* boy toy.

"Right there next to Sarah Jessica and that godawful dress."

"I hope you can return the tux?" I offered.

"Keep-it-keep-it-keep-it! It looked so good on you, it would be churlish of me to take it back. Besides, Toots," he said, smiling grandly, "you earned it."

When I thought about what I'd been doing to earn a four-thousand-dollar suit…

He leaned to me, kissed me on the cheek, and he whispered sweetly—while casually groping my ass—"I'll have your things packed and left with the doorman."

"So you gave up that marble bathroom?" asked Marco, pulling me out of my funk. "All onna conna one dirty look from Roger?"

"Prit-tee much."

"Tha's messed up, Bro."

"Prit-tee much."

"Of course you can crash here for a while, but…"

"I'll make a few calls. I know a girl who's going into the *Kinky Boots* tour who was looking for an apartment sitter."

"Well, make yourself at home, my man."

"Thanks," I said and flopped onto his bed.

"I have to go downstairs and gut some fish."

"Lucky fish." I started pulling the shirt studs out and yanked the shirt off. It had some little puke spots on it. Charming. "I'm going to try to sleep for a bit." I kicked the pants off and added them to the heap. "And then I have to see if I can pull some ushering slots. I have to start earning an honest living again."

"If you say so. Steal some clothes if you need to. And keys," he said, pulling a set from a hook by the fridge and he tossed them to me. "I don't have any plans for later, so, if you want, we can fool around some if that'll cheer you up."

"Not today, bro," I said. I pushed my head under the pillow.

"Suit yourself. You know where the porn is."

I groaned.

I never thought I'd say these words, but the last thing I wanted to look at was some guy's…

I heard the door close.

Alone, with my head under that pillow, I thought about the irony of it. Twenty-four hours before, I'd been on top of the world. My life was golden. Now it was garbage. All "onna conna" Roger.

So obviously the thing to do was to keep as far away from Roger Prescott as humanly possible, right? I'd gone two years without crossing paths with him—I could easily go another two, right?

And yet, pressed under that pillow, all I could think was—I need to see Roger.

For what? I asked myself. Explain things? *Yeah, I was doing it with the smelly, old rich guy, but don't think less of me, okay?*

I pulled the pillow tighter. Maybe I'd suffocate.

I should clarify—I'm not one of those sappy pansies who cries at the drop of a hat. Honestly, I didn't think I could cry. I never had—not even as a kid, not that I could remember—which was just as well because where I came from, crying could get you into some serious trouble.

But alone and under that pillow—for the first time in my life—I wished I could.

Chapter 6

The Morning after the Opera—
On the Avenue of the Americas

TOMMY

Roger and I were standing on line at the Starbucks across the street from work on Sixth Ave., the same as every other weekday morning.

Like so many things in New York, the morning ritual at Starbucks was, for me, a love/hate thing.

I hated it because the place was tiny and mad crowded, and everyone was so effing rude.

Rude is like a badge of honor in New York. It marks you as belonging here. If you're polite, you must be from out of town and therefore insignificant. If you're cheerful, you're less than insignificant and probably insane. If you're downright chipper, someone will likely push you in front of a bus.

Only if you're complaining will you get taken seriously here, I swear.

Of course, listen to me—complaining. I'm starting to fit right in.

But I also *loved* this little trip through what was otherwise Starbucks hell because of—drum roll, if you please—the barista boy! I was seriously crushing on the new kid behind the coffee counter. I didn't know anything about him, not his name, *nada.* As in *nada* damn thing. For all I knew, he was straight, but I didn't think so. What I *did* know was that he had wavy dark brown hair and bright blue eyes. And really, who needs to know more than that, I ask you? With some guys I swear you can just tell from the shape of his eyes that he's a raving maniac in bed. You know, narrow eyes that go kind of crescent-shaped and get that teasing sparkle thing going when they smile at you sideways? This one's eyes were odee wicked. He was delicious, and he was *mine*, goddamnit. Not very tall, but then I'm not very tall either. So clearly, we were made for each other.

"Hey look!" I said when I saw the menu. "They have those awesome pumpkin-spice things again! I *love* pumpkin."

"You know there's no actual pumpkin in there, just nutmeg," Roger said. "And it's probably artificial anyway."

Man, he was in a mood. New York was rubbing off on him. It's not as though we had stayed at the Met Gala until the wee smalls, because we hadn't.

"I totally don't care," was my devastating retort. Of course I had a pretty good idea what was bothering him.

"By the way," Roger said, "in case it comes up in front of Jeff—Katrina gave you the opera ticket, not me."

"You didn't even offer it to Jeffrey?"

"He'd have wanted to go! He'd have thought it was a chance to network. He doesn't get the music thing at all."

"Neither do I."

"You understand music lots more than Jeff. I told you, I took him to that little recital at the Frick, forty-five minutes long…"

"And you said he wrote e-mails on his phone the whole time?"

"And then got all huffy when somebody asked him to turn his damn phone off."

"Yeah."

"So I don't take Jeff to things anymore."

"Too bad about him, then."

The line had moved up so we were now in front of the glass case, at least as far as the pumpkin bread, pumpkin scones, and pumpkin cream cheese muffins.

"It's not really Jeff's fault. He just doesn't get it. And besides, it was more fun with you."

"It *was* fun, wasn't it. Until he-who-must-not-be-named showed up." I watched for his response. He looked down at his phone. I wasn't sure how he was taking seeing his ex, not to mention seeing his ex with somebody else. All I knew was that two minutes *after* seeing his ex, we were walking down Broadway to the Columbus Circle subway station at warp speed.

The line inched forward.

"He looked amazing in that white tux though, didn't you think?" Roger made a noise, but God only knows what it meant. "Of course Fletch would look hot in a burka, so we have to hate him."

"Why was he even there?" Roger said, annoyed.

We took another a step forward and were even with the marble loaf. Almost to the cashier.

"I'll get my own today." Normally Roger bought because he was an atty. making piles and piles of the cold hard, and I was a measly admin. asst., and didn't.

"O-kay," he said slowly with a quizzical look.

Fine, he could look quizzical all he wanted. I had this idea—all right, I'd stolen it from somebody's Facebook page—but it was genius, and I wanted to try it. I was just *sure* this trick would finally get my barista's attention.

All right, so I'm an optimist. My mother says I'm cockeyed, but I don't think she means it like it sounds.

"Skinny latte—grande," said Roger.

"Name?" asked the girl at the counter with waaaaaaaaay too much eye makeup.

"Roger."

He paid and moved to the side as best he could through the shoulder-to-shoulder horde of miserable people, all jonesing for caffeine. It was also hot and stuffy. Think black hole of Calcutta—with smartphones and attitudes.

"Grande pumpkin-spice extra-foam cappuccino, please," I said.

"Name?" asked Miss Maybelline.

Are you ready for it?

"My darling," I said.

"My darling?" She looked up at me. Each of her freakishly long fingernails had a little teeny-tiny jack-o-lantern on it.

"That's right. Just put 'my darling' on there." I waggled an index finger at the cardboard cup in her hand.

And she actually scribbled it on the cup—after making just an oh-so-subtle face and rolling her eyes up into the violet eye shadow. *I hope your face sticks that way someday, you great effing muppet*, I thought. I smiled at her sweetly and paid.

"Love your nails," I lied.

"Thanks," she said and gave me my change. I bet she could gut a bear with those things. I crabbed sideways through the bodies over to Roger.

"I guess he was there with Darwin Stewart Harrison," I said, answering his last question.

"What?"

"Why Fletch was at the opera gala. He was there with Darwin Stewart Harrison."

"Oh, yeah. That guy must be like fifty."

"He's also rich. And famous. And he uses Tony Awards for doorstops."

"And he's fat. And all those rings on those fat fingers?"

"You're not jealous."

"Of course not, not at this point. I'm just—it's just that—I never thought of Fletch doing that. I mean really, a sugar daddy?"

"Grande café latte skinny for—Roger," yelled the cutest barista in all of Manhattan.

Ohmygod, it was my turn. Would he say it? Would he laugh? Would he say how incredibly hot I looked today in this green silk sweater that really set off my eyes?

Probably not.

But just to hear him refer to me as "my darling," that would be worth it. And maybe it would distract Roger from his whole Fletch funk.

"Grande pumpkin-spice cappuccino for—for my darling," said my sloe-eyed beauty. From clear across the shop he was looking right at me. How'd he know it was me? He could maybe smile a little.

I pushed my way through the sea of shoulders.

"Thanks," I said. I reached for the cup, but he was still holding it, not letting go—which meant ohmygodohmygodohmygod our fingers touched. He looked at me blankly. Those eyes. *Pitterpat, pitterpat.* Be still, *mi corazón.*

"Nice try," he said. With that he let go of the cup and went right back to work.

Well, da-yam. What did *that* mean? Nice try, keep trying? Or nice try, douchebag? Did that mean he liked it, that he thought it was funny? Or was that like straight-boy talk for go fuck yourself?

I pushed my way over to the napkin thingy, where Roger waited.

"I guess I'm just disappointed is all," said Roger.

"I'm mostly confused. What am I supposed to do now?"

"What are you talking about?"

"My barista boy!"

"Oh, yeah, I heard, cappuccino for my darling. Smooth."

"I touched his fingers."

"That's progress, I guess."

"But the way he looked at me…"

"Good?"

"Not so much." I pushed the door open, and we were out on Sixth Avenue in the fresh air. All things being relative.

Roger and I worked at the same law firm, by the way, Goodkin Berdann & Dunkel LLP, and no, Roger didn't get me the job. Roger was an attorney but still way too puny to pull any strings, even for his besty. After *he* got the job, I applied as legal secretary, lied lied lied about my experience, and voila! I got the job on my own, totally bogus, merits. "So what were *you* talking about?" I asked.

"Three guesses."

"Ah. Something that rhymes with—Fletch."

"Bingo."

We threaded our way through the morning rush, the usual tourists *and* a construction barricade to get to our building.

"Can I tell you how much I hate this?" said Roger.

I assumed he was talking about the sidewalk congestion and construction, because that's what *I* was thinking, but he went on.

"I can't believe Fletch is back in my head again. I've wasted way too much time and energy thinking about somebody who's basically nothing more than pretty eyes and a penis."

We were inside, and we waved our keycards at the security gates.

"Yeah, but they're really pretty eyes." I said as we waited for the elevator.

"And don't even start me on the other thing."

"Ummmmmmmmmmm," I said, wagging a finger as we and thirty-two other charming New Yorkers squeezed into the elevator.

Ah, don't you just love this town? It's sooooo glamorous.

Chapter 7
On the Sidewalks of New York

FLETCH

So there I was, minding my own business, leaning against a building on Sixth, and if I just happened to be directly across the street from Roger's office building, it was a complete coincidence. And if I just happened to have been here yesterday at this same time, likewise.

At least yesterday, Wednesday, was a matinee day. I could tell myself that I was just in the neighborhood, that I had an excuse to be in Midtown, that the theatre wasn't far. Okay, it was two avenues over and six blocks up. It was still walkable, so I clung to my totally lame excuse.

I had been really lucky to pick up a schedule back at the Gershwin, and I was defying gravity all over again at *Wicked.* Seemed like old times.

Anyway, that was yesterday. No matinee on Thursday, so today I didn't even have *that* laughable pretense.

I was just there. Just 'cuz. Onna conna, as Marco would say.

It was lunchtime, and Roger would come outside sooner or later. And I could wait. I just wanted to see him again.

That's not a crime, is it?

Well, yeah, I suppose, after a while it probably is.

So why am I here? I kept asking myself. What did I want?

I wanted to see him again, but why? We'd had a thing, and I messed it up, and that was long ago. I'm not really the sentimental type, know what I mean?

Let me be really straight with you. My life hasn't been all sunshine and roses in the morning dew.

Confession:

I don't believe in love.

I've seen a lot of crap in my life, but I've never seen anything, outside of the movies, to convince me that love is real. I believe in sex, yeah, obviously. It's been a major hobby of mine. I look around, and I see sex all over the place, and people doing really stupid things because of it. Just look at the *Daily News* any day of the week. But I'm convinced—what people call love is just your gonads lying to you so that you'll give them what they want. And something else I've learned going through life with these pretty blue eyes wide open:

Gonads are fucking fickle.

The next time they get a bright idea, *bam*! Those little fuckers have got you convinced you're in love with some *other* jerk, and before you know it, you're making all kinds of promises that you've already made to somebody else—promises your gonads have no intention of keeping to this new person either—but you'll say *anything* to get those little bastards whatever it is they want.

So:

I don't believe in promises.

That's what I think. And:

Monogamy is an even bigger swindle than love.

Monogamy is easy if only one person is asking. But for me, since I was a teen, the world has been pretty much like a gigantic all-you-can-eat buffet, and I've been able to take my pick. Young, hot, buff. Actors, models, dancers (Broadway *and* ballet). A completely drop-dead gorgeous baseball player at the start of his Major League career who shall remain anonymous—no problem. When Disney on Ice comes through town, man-oh-man. Let me tell you, those boys have moves. And there's a *lot* of 'em!

And it's like that buffet is already paid for, there's no check at the end. At least not until Roger, and then—well, yeah, there was a terrible reckoning, and I guess—since I was standing around on Sixth Avenue with a cardboard cup of cold coffee in my hand—maybe I was still paying.

I had ruined something, something that should not have been ruined. And I'd hurt someone badly who truly deserved better.

That was my only experience with "Relationships" with a capital *arrrrrrr*. It had been a total disaster.

Conclusion:

I don't believe in relationships either.

In spite of not believing in promises, I promised myself to stay clear of relationships no matter what.

And yet.

And yet there I was, loitering, lurking, like a TV detective.

What was wrong with me?

Twenty feet away, at the corner, waiting for the light to change, the strawberry blond in the blue suit—sweet. The lanky bike messenger in spandex with the obligatory Brooklyn scruff—total sex, with amazing hazel eyes, and he was clearly digging me. For cryin' out loud, the UPS guy in the little shorts was completely built and a frigging ten on anybody's scale. And instead of looking at them, I was staring at the front of an office building, hoping to get a glimpse of somebody who was *not* a model, *not* buff, *not* something off the cover of *GQ*, but who was just—Roger.

So the first question I had to ask myself was, Was this—whatever it was that I was doing here—just part of one of those little lies your gonads like to tell you to get you to stick your doober wherever they've decided you should be sticking your doober?

Or...

Was this maybe something else, something that I didn't actually believe in?

A deeply disturbing thought.

And there he was. Roger, coming out the revolving doors. And Tommy, of course. And there they went. Down the street.

They walked into the sunlight as they crossed Forty-Second. That mess of curls hanging over Roger's forehead shone a little in the sun. And then they slipped into the lunchtime crowd of Bryant Park.

I could have followed them, but—hey—I had to draw the line somewhere.

I wasted how much time—for *that*?

Further to my earlier line of questioning:

Was I just being a brat all of a sudden? I had had something, I had lost it, but now that it was clear I *couldn't* have it, I *had* to have it. I *needed* it. In fact, I'd go frigging *crazy* if I didn't get it.

Is that what this is? I wondered.

Because if *that's* what this is, then I should just go home and watch some porn or something. Or go find that bike messenger.

But somehow that second option didn't seem any more attractive than the first. For some reason, today, whether alone or not, it all seemed like just so much jerking off.

I tossed the cold Starbucks dregs in a trash can and headed for the D train.

Chapter 8
And God Bless Julia Child

ROGER

Seeing Fletch had brought up a lot of memories from the time we were together. And although it ended miserably, which spoiled everything, if I could look beyond that—and let's face it, I hardly ever could—but when I *could* look beyond that, I could see that it had been a fantastic period of my life. I knew it at the time. I'd never been happier, and I had thought it would go on like that forever.

Oops.

Our law-firm quartet rehearsed regularly and we tended to rotate the location. The first time that it was at my place after Fletch had moved in, I was a little embarrassed about it. About him. Not that *he* was embarrassing, because he was the opposite, but just the fact of him. I hadn't mentioned Fletch at work, and I didn't know how to explain this guy suddenly being in my apartment. The whole how-long-have-you-guys-known-each-other thing. Tommy had only recently found out, and that was by accident. But now it was time to out myself as—what? Somebody who had a boyfriend? That wasn't so bad. It was outing myself as this incredibly careful, orderly, circumspect person who had chucked all good sense out the window and done this really crazy, impetuous thing. *That* was embarrassing. Not that I regretted it, because I didn't. But still.

The four of us were marching up the two flights to my apartment—we're all fairly mobile except Katrina, who, instead of using a collapsible music stand like the rest of us, always brought her own heavy, not-so-collapsible music stand wherever she went. She was a big woman, and it didn't seem to slow her down much. Third story, not bad, but then I wasn't carrying a cello. Bob, the one with the cello strapped to his back, brought up the rear behind Katrina, keeping a safe distance from the music stand, because Katrina could be a little careless.

"My new flatmate is probably home," I sort of mentioned as we clomped up the stairs. How's that for casual?

"You have a new flatmate?" asked Katrina. Nothing gets past her. She was behind Janine, who was behind me, but I swear I could *hear* her ears perking up.

I opened the door.

Our chairs were already set up in a little semicircle, and my music stand was in front of the second chair.

Fletch. I hadn't asked him to do that. He just had.

"Hello?" That was me.

"Hey!" Fletch was in the kitchen—just separated from the living room by a countertop. He was wearing an apron with giant roses and flounces on it—an ironic gift from Tommy I obviously never used—and he had a little bit of flour or something on one cheek. "Hi," he said wiping his hands on the apron. All very Martha Stewart, but on him it was totally cute.

"Fletch?" said Katrina. She looked from one of us to the other, as Fletch gave me a squeeze and a kiss on the cheek.

Well, I guess *that* little kitten was out of the bag.

"Katrina," said Fletch, "it's great to see you again."

"Bob, you remember Fletch from Katrina's party," I said.

"Of course. Hey." He too seemed a little surprised and looked from me to Fletch to me. I guess I might have warned them.

"Janine," Janine said, shaking hands.

"Viola," said Fletch.

"I thought your name was Fletch. Kidding!" Music nerds. We never really learn how to make a joke.

"Don't tease me," said Fletch. "I'm nervous enough already. I don't really know what a viola is even."

"A viola?" asked Janine. "It's sort of like a violin—only better. Not so runty."

"Like a swollen violin," said Katrina.

"A violin with a head cold," I said.

"It's more like a violin," said Janine, "whose balls have dropped."

From meek, little Janine, that struck us music nerds as pretty damned funny, although it's probably not funny to anybody else.

"So," Katrina said, eyeing me and Fletch. Keep in mind that Katrina was not just first violin in the quartet—I'm second—she was actually my boss as well. Janine was a corporate attorney, and Bob did something in the Accounting Department. I wasn't really sure how much of my personal life I wanted to share with the entire law firm, but here was my personal life in a floral-print apron and grinning. With my thumb I brushed the flour from his cheek.

"So," Katrina said again. "You guys are old friends from summer camp?"

"Camp Onnaconna," said Fletch, nodding. "It was a very progressive camp." He gave me a squeeze as he said it. I blushed to my hairline.

"And an old friend of Bob's?"

"Me?" asked Bob, pulling out his cello.

Fletch waved to him.

"Don't bother," Katrina said. "Marco told me you guys crashed."

"The rat!" said Fletch.

"So you two boys met at my party. And now you're…"

"Of course!" said Janine. "You're the guy Roger was making out with at Katrina's party!"

"We weren't making—" I started. "Hey, you weren't even there!"

"I know, but it was all over the office the next day."

"Tolja." Fletch said, beaming.

"And you guys are—living together? Already?"

See? It was embarrassing.

"Well—yeah!" Fletch explained, not in the least embarrassed. "It was pretty fast, but you know, it's worked out really, really well so far, hasn't it, Dweeb?"

I heard some Brit on TV use this word once—*gobsmacked.*

It was all too much, and I was good and gobsmacked.

Fletch—the wild and beautiful boy who crashed parties and flirted with Katrina, who dated sword swallowers—was saying he was happily domesticated in *my* apartment? I was too gobsmacked to answer.

"Dweeb?" asked Janine.

"When we met, Roger was talking about music, and then said he felt like a dweeb for talking about classical music all night, and then, well…"

"We should start calling you that around the office," Katrina teased.

"Fletch," I said, fluffing a flounce of his apron, "what's with the…"

"Almost forgot! I've been cooking!" He turned around and pulled a towel from two platters.

"That's the fabulous smell," said Bob.

"I figured you'd be hungry."

He'd made hors d'oeuvres? They looked like little cream puffs.

"I didn't want to ask, but my mouth's been watering since we walked in the door." That was Janine.

"These are cheese-filled"—he pointed—"and these are crabmeat."

And they dug in.

"Where did you get the platters? I don't have platters."

"Kristy." Meant nothing to me. "The woman downstairs?" he explained. "With the French bulldogs."

Fletch knew the neighbors? I'd lived there *how* long? I didn't know the neighbors. He held up one of the hors d'oeuvres for me, and I bit it. Wow.

"Oh, Fletch! This is delicious," said Janine.

"Julia Child. That woman was a genius! And Marco gave me the crabmeat. He says hi, by the way."

"Still warm!" Bob said.

"Fletch, you should take up catering!" said Katrina.

"I can't cook!"

"Oh, contrary," said the accountant, being stupid.

"Maybe we should try to get started?" I was hoping to steer things back toward rehearsal, but it was completely futile. They had fallen on the little puffs like zombies at the brain buffet. There were *mmmms* all around. Janine *mmmm*'d in on a G-sharp with a rising attack and a short glissando down from there. Bob did the same, but being the cellist, an octave lower. Leave it to Katrina to *mmmm* a step higher than the others. Mozart couldn't have done it better.

Fletch put his arm around my waist, beaming.

"Try the crabmeat, Roger. They're really good," he said, feeding me another one.

And they were. They were really delicious. It was the end of the workday, we were all hungry, and these cheesy pastries with this warm creamy filling—they were out of this world.

I was stunned. By all of it. The hors d'oeuvres. The others. Julia Child and Fletch. Me. Me and Fletch. My reaction to me and Fletch. Office gossip about me and Fletch, for God's sake. It was all just nonstop smacking of gobs.

I had had no idea where things really stood with Fletch and me. I always felt Fletch was holding back a little. I knew how *I* felt. I was getting definitely way more wrapped up in Fletch than I'd ever been with anybody. Not because of the body and the looks but mostly because he was so *nice* to me. That sounds totally stupid, I know. But usually the really pretty ones were arrogant dicks, and Fletch? Fletch made *me* feel like *I* was the special one. He made *me* feel attractive, sexy even. Imagine.

And if I *hadn't* been goofy about him, those crabmeat things would have cinched it.

I didn't dare tell him I was falling for him because—you know—he was so out of my league. And I had no idea how he'd respond. Or *if* he'd respond. Or if he'd just laugh. Maybe he was really nice to *everybody*? I was never quite certain how much of his moving in with me was because he actually liked me and how much of it was because he just wanted to get in out of the rain.

But here he was making this deliberate show for my friends.

Make no mistake, he was announcing:" This is my boyfriend. We are a couple. This is our home. This is our kitchen.

I hadn't even realized how much I wanted such a thing—a boyfriend, *this* boyfriend particularly. I had been perfectly content, or at least I had thought I'd been, just me, my little Mittenwald violin, and Haggis. The quartet. I was never like Tommy, who was always looking. I had never really felt the *need* for a boyfriend, and now I had one, a staggeringly wonderful boyfriend, who was grinning at me as if somehow *he* was proud of *me*.

I smiled at him, and mouthed a silent thank-you. He shrugged a little, modestly, but he was obviously completely pleased with himself. All of a sudden, this crazy and impetuous decision, letting Fletch move in, seemed like the smartest thing I'd ever done.

"You two look so good together," Janine said, licking melted Gruyère from her thumb. "I'm really happy for you."

"And you met at *my* party. I think that's so sweet."

Katrina, sentimental? In the office she always seemed so tough. Even with the quartet. With Katrina on first violin, it was sort of like Diana Ross and the Supremes. Katrina and her backup girls. She brooked no difference of opinion about anything—her tempos, her phrasing, everything.

"So what all are you all working on?" asked Fletch as we crowded around the kitchen sink before we moved back to the living room to get our instruments.

"Franz Schubert," I said.

"It's always Schubert," said Bob.

"Not always," said Katrina.

"We like Schubert," explained Janine.

"I like raspberry Schubert." Bob. He was both an accountant *and* a musician. Double-nerd—his was a hopeless case.

"What's it called?" Fletch asked.

"This one actually has a name," said Janine.

"It's called 'Death and the Maiden.'" Bob read the title out like a lurid headline out of the *New York Post*. By now, bows were tightened, instruments were out.

"Cool," said Fletch. "Should be a horror movie."

"The title is from a poem," Katrina explained.

"But it doesn't really have a lot to do with the poem, I don't think." Janine again.

"I don't know," said Bob. "There's a lot of death music in there."

"You think?"

"Death-*ish*."

"Not so much maiden," said Katrina.

"I think it was kind of a jumping-off point for Schubert," I said. "A metaphor."

By this time we were all in our seats, tuning, tuning. Fletch took his cue.

"Okay," he said. "I'll be quiet now. You guys, be—tremendous."

We all smiled. There was another round of thanks for the pastries. Fletch called the dog, and they withdrew to the bedroom.

Okay, here's a secret for you, in case you were wondering (and I'm sure you weren't). There's no conductor in a quartet, so how do we all come in together? The answer is everybody sort of tunes in to the body language and breathing of everybody else and, especially, to the first violin. After a while, the connection feels almost psychic. A quartet becomes like a living creature all its own, and if one part is sick or out of sorts, we all feel it. Later on, when things went south with Fletch, I was maybe less than stellar for a while, and they hated me for it.

I mean, there we were, working on Beethoven's opus 133, the "Great Fugue," one of the last things he wrote and considered by lots of people to be possibly the greatest sixteen minutes of music ever composed. *And* it's a total bitch to play. So they were all scraping away, striving to give expression to this titanic vision that Beethoven had managed to put down on paper, despite his complete deafness and at the very end of his life, in his desperate need to articulate his view of his place in the vast, incomprehensible chaos of the universe—and right smack in the middle of this herculean work sat the second violin, aka, the Great Wall of Bummer.

I couldn't care about Beethoven; I didn't care about his place in the frigging universe. I only knew I wasn't supposed to be alone—and I was utterly alone. Not really the right mind-set for an intimate collaboration.

After a couple weeks, I bowed out and they went back to playing trios, which is what they were doing before I came along. Eventually Katrina had had enough of my sulking, and she dragged me back by the forelock.

Okay, she actually just scheduled a rehearsal at my place, and they were suddenly all just *there*. She threw a spanking new set of parts to Schubert's "Rosamunde" quartet on the stands, which she had obviously just bought for the purpose because she knew I had really wanted to play it, and without another word about it—we were a quartet again.

Thinking back, I suppose it was my salvation.

So. Body language and breathing and coming in together for the first attack. Katrina always brought us in with a sharp inhale before the first note.

No doubt that's more than you wanted to know.

On this particular day, I was obviously pretty keen. All I wanted in the world was for Fletch to like me, and he had done all *this* because he wanted *me* to like *him!*

"Shall we?" said Katrina.

We nodded. She was still for a second, then she took a deep breath—and four bows hit the strings at precisely the same instant.

Daaaaaaaaaaaaaaaaaaaaaah—
Dadada dum.

I had a really gifted string quartet made up of really good friends; I had the greatest boyfriend imaginable sitting in the next room with my dog, listening to us play my favorite composer; I had a tummy full of crab puffs.

I was feeling pretty damned good about myself and my own particular place in the vast, incomprehensible, and truly marvelous chaos of the universe. The fingers of my left hand seemed to work on their own. They were always magically in exactly the right place at exactly the right instant. I can tell you, I'm a pretty good violinist, but that afternoon?

That afternoon I was—tremendous!

We *all* were.

Chapter 9
Some People Might Call It Stalking

FLETCH

It was a few days after the opera, and there I was, minding my own business—and if I just happened to be hanging around the streets that just happened to be in Roger's neighborhood, it was a total coincidence. I swear. Yeah, I know, it was getting beyond creepy, and I had vowed to stop. Soon.

Chelsea Park is just a couple blocks from Roger's apartment, and I'd decided to take a break from staring at Roger's windows—yep, it had come to that—and I was enjoying the sun in the park on a very warm day in late September.

The first thing I saw was the dog—Haggis. I haven't talked about Haggis much, but he's important. He's a Scottish terrier, this little black thing with ridiculously short legs and a tough coat—it's not soft at all—with two black eyes that you can see glinting under looming eyebrows. Roger keeps him really well groomed, so he's this totally sharp little dog. Gets a lot of attention on the street.

So there I was, minding my own business, hanging around in Roger's neighborhood, and there was a well-groomed Scottish terrier. They're not very common, so to see one in Roger's neighborhood—well, it *had* to be Haggis, right?

But it wasn't Roger on the leash. Dog walker? Nice-looking guy, tall, blond, sunglasses. Then I realized that I knew this guy from somewhere. Then I realized from where. I knew him from ushering, and no, I don't remember every single person I hand a program to. Just some.

"Haggis?" I said when I was about fifteen feet away.

It was definitely Haggis. He flung himself at the end of the leash, ears back, and it was like his whole body was wagging. I squatted down and let him jump all over me and lick my face and spin in circles.

Two years later and he still remembered me. And he didn't hate me, which made for a nice change.

"I'm sorry," said the blond, a little perplexed. Not me, the other blond, the one on the other end of the leash. "He's never like this with strangers."

"That's because I'm not a stranger. Am I, Pupper-nickel? Nooooo. We're old buds."

"Oh."

"So who are you, and why do you have Roger's dog?"

"I'm—I'm Roger's boyfriend."

Whoa. Hadn't considered that possibility. A boyfriend. I'd just assumed—what? I guess I'd just assumed—self-centered, arrogant asshole that I am—that poor, lonely Roger would be waiting for me, pining for me, and *not* moving on to somebody else. And yet here was the somebody else. I'd have to rethink.

But if this guy's the boyfriend, I thought, why was Roger going to the opera with Tommy? Where was this dipwad when the fat lady was singing her fat little heart out?

I stood to look at him more carefully—and I made a discovery. Okay. There's pining, and there's pining. The guy is tall, blond, has blue eyes…

"Of course you're the boyfriend!" If you were going to cast somebody to play *me* in the movie, this would be the guy.

"Hey," said the Fletch type, a little embarrassed. "We—we've met before?"

"I think so," I said, enjoying his discomfort.

"Nobody else needs to know about that, do they?"

I squatted back down to the dog.

"I don't know," I said to the dog. "I've never been very good with promises."

Then I saw Roger walking toward us. You know how Haggis reacted when he saw me? That's exactly how I felt seeing Roger coming across the park in the sunlight. I felt my heart flip over in my chest. I just wish I'd had the guts to run across the park and make an idiot of myself the way that Scottie did.

Roger was completely focused on the two soft-serve ice cream cones he was carrying. In a striped t-shirt, jeans, and Adidas, he was—you know—just another guy out a on a warm afternoon, and at the same time he was—breathtaking.

"They only had vanill—"

Even behind his sunglasses, I could see the moment he recognized who was scratching his dog.

"Fuck me."

"Which one of us are you talking to?" I asked. "Because Haggis here's been neutered, so that leaves only..."

"Fletch," said Roger. "What are you..."

I stood up to look at him and pulled off my sunglasses to see him better.

Poor guy. I had bushwhacked him twice in just a few days, and if there's one thing I know about Roger—he doesn't like surprises.

"Hey, Dweeb. You have no idea how good it is to see you."

"Um—thanks. You've met Jeff?"

Poor Mini-Me was standing there, looking sort of bushwhacked himself.

"You could say that," I said. "Hey Jeff." We shook hands. "I'm Fletch."

"Jeffrey Bornic," he said.

I've spelled it right, but that last *c* is pronounced like a *ch*, so it rhymes with—well, nothing, really.

"Wait," said Jeffrey Bornic. "*You're*—Fletch? *That* Fletch?"

He looked to Roger.

"I don't know, Roger, am I *that* Fletch?" I was enjoying this.

"You are definitely *that* Fletch."

"Well, then, I suppose I am. So, Jeff—"

"Jeffrey actually. Nobody calls me Jeff."

"Roger just did."

"Besides Roger, I mean. Roger calls me Jeff."

"I'll bet he calls you Fletch sometimes, too," I said.

"I don't either!" Roger snapped. Bull's-eye. "What are you doing here, Fletch?"

"I was just in the neighborhood, and I saw a Scottish terrier that reminded me of Haggis, because it turns out he actually *is* Haggis. And then I wanted to know what ratbag loser had stolen Haggis, and the ratbag loser turned out to be Jeff—rey—and now here we are."

"Okay, it was nice bumping into you again but—"

"Like at the opera the other night." I turned to I-can't-believe-it's-not-Fletch. "Did Roger tell you we'd seen each other at the opera a few days ago?"

"No, he didn't in point of fact."

"No?" I knew it. "What a pity you couldn't be there, Jeff. Really glorious music—in point of fact. Roger's boyfriend, I'm sure you must be crazy about classical music."

"Actually—"

"It wasn't all that much fun, Jeff," said Roger. "Starlets flinging glasses of wine left and right—"

"That Verdi," I said. "They sure don't write tunes like *that* anymore. You should eat that ice cream, Dweeb, before you end up wearing it."

He looked down at his hands, dripping with melting soft-serve.

"Here," he said, shoving a cone at Jeff almost angrily.

"Um, thanks."

Roger tried to lick carefully around the ice cream—he was always fastidious. He ran his tongue slowly around the base of the ice cream, first in one direction, and then in the other. He nibbled some of the white cream off his index finger with his lips. He had absolutely no idea. Completely oblivious. He could have sold tickets—it was like the hottest sex show in town. He noticed me—and then Jeff—staring, and he looked at us, smiling, embarrassed.

"What?" he said, not getting it.

There was some ice cream on his bottom lip still—which he realized and his tongue slipped out and licked it away.

"I should go," I said, clearing my throat. I dropped back down to Haggis and used the silly voice. "It was soooooo good to see you tooooooooo," I said, rubbing my face on top of the dog's wiry head. I stood. "Nice to meet you, Jeff."

"Yeah, you too."

I had extended my hand—but Jeff was awash in dripping vanilla. I smiled and pulled my hand back. A little wave would have to do. I turned to Roger.

"It's really good to see you, Dweeb. We should get together some time, and catch up. I'd really like that."

He pushed back the curls from his forehead, while he was thinking how he was going to tell me that he *wouldn't* really like getting together to catch up—but before he could say anything, I leaned in and kissed him on the cheek. He didn't see it coming. Me either, to be honest. It was totally spontaneous, but damn! I was so glad I did it.

Especially with Jeff behind me, watching, dripping.

"Buh-bye!" I waved and walked away.

It was all I could do to keep myself from skipping like a six-year-old.

Chapter 10
Grooming Lessons

ROGER

Sunday. I practiced all morning, and now the only plan I had for the rest of the afternoon was for me, the dog, and the grooming table. Too bad about Haggis. The wire coat takes a *lot* of brushing out. Even with a ton of conditioner, it pulls. Sorry, buddy.

A No-Jeff day. That sounds terrible, that I should say something like that, like it's a good thing, but I occasionally need some time.

Jeff is at a different firm and a couple years more senior than I. He's also in litigation, which is a very different world. His workload can be really awful.

One of the great advantages to being in Trusts and Estates is that there are very few real crises. Your clients are either healthy and not expecting to die—I mean, who does?—and you have all the time in the world to do whatever; or they're dead—and in that case you have even *more* time. It's only when somebody's on his deathbed that things get hairy, and for that only Katrina will do.

Not so in litigation. They have deadlines—real ones—all the time. Complaints to file, briefs, motions, affidavits, discovery, God knows what all. Most of Jeff's practice is in advertising claims law. That's where somebody's ad on TV says their antacid works twice as fast or that their detergent will get your whites whiter, and Jeff's client feels that in actuality, *their* product produces the whitest whites—Jeff (and his firm) to the rescue. The other side will produce a study showing that *their* whites are whiter, and Jeff will argue that the study is flawed and that his client has their *own* study proving conclusively that *their* product will get your whites way whiter, blah-blah-blah. And all of this adds up to a mountain of billable hours.

If you're thinking this is a gigantic waste of time and money when there are starving children in wherever, you're not alone. But I don't say that to Jeff. He didn't choose it; it just sort of worked out that way. And you can scoff all you want, but Jeff just bought the apartment below his and is turning it into a gigantic duplex.

Honestly, I don't know how he does what he does. If *I'd* gotten stuck in advertising claims, I wouldn't have lasted a week. Of course, it wasn't as though we in Trusts and Estates were exactly working on the side of the angels, helping the affluent stay that way.

Anyway, it isn't an antacid ad that's the cause of my No-Jeff day. No. Today is Sunday, and on Sunday God created that most sacred of things, the holy of holies—professional football. I won't see Jeff on a Sunday until after the Jumbo Bowl or whatever it is they play in February.

Jeff doesn't get music; I don't get sports. So we're even.

Haggis, you get these terrible mats in your little armpits. Hold still while I snip this out.

I mostly went into Trusts and Estates because people told me to.

The clients are all über-rich, and it sort of helps if you come from that kind of background. And yeah, I come from that kind of background. My dad's family hasn't got all that much, but my mother's family is ridiculous. Are you impressed I went to Harvard? My great-great-grandfather endowed a building; they *had* to let me in.

Hold still. I don't want to nip you.

And, of course, the family could always use a crackerjack trust attorney.

At the office, the assumption has been that I should be good at this because I know how to talk to people who went to the same kinds of schools I went to, who know the same people, who know my grandparents, blah-blah-blah. And—although it's never been said out loud—I know the firm is also thinking about the people who would *like* to know people like my family.

I'm bait.

I'm supposed to be hustling some new über-rich clients for them, which in theory makes some sense, but in reality, I'm too shy to hustle *anybody,* a fact my law firm and Katrina are slowly beginning to grasp. If I were only good at the hustling, nobody would mind that I stink as a lawyer—but alas.

Trusts and Estates. The only thing I'm missing is the pearls. There are a lot of women in T&E, and I swear, they all wear pearls, genuine or otherwise. It's like a uniform, the mark of gentility. Genuine or otherwise. Tommy thinks I should get some pearls too, like the other girls in the department. As he points out—pearls go with everything.

So today it's the dog and I. Which is good. It calms me. Tomorrow I'm having my monthly lunch with my father—an event that always stresses me out a little. I don't know why. I truly like my dad. But still…

My father is also an attorney, senior partner at his firm. That's part of the reason he makes me nervous. He's such a good lawyer, and I—well, not so much.

In my defense, I'd like to point out—this whole lawyer thing? It wasn't my idea.

But the dog is terrific. I depend on him more than I like to admit. He's not really big on displays of affection, and neither am I. It's enough for me to have him in the same room. If I'm watching TV or reading or whatever, he'll climb up the little Haggis stairs to sit next to me.

He centers me.

Like my violin—he seems perfectly suited to me.

After the Fletch fiasco, I cannot imagine what I would have done without him around. Haggis was companion, teddy bear, furry hot-water bottle, and tissue box.

We've been through a lot together.

But today, lots of brushing, now a little trim, and then I just have to wash the conditioner out. I groom him myself because I took him to a groomer once and my beautiful Scottish terrier came home looking like a schnauzer. So, instead of changing his name to Hansel, I Amazoned some clippers and taught myself. And I enjoy it. If you stay on top of it, it's no big deal.

It used to stress me out. I would let it go for weeks—big mistake. And then I would stare at this dog, this mass of matted fur, a great black shrub. He would look more like a Scottish cow than a Scottish terrier, and I couldn't imagine how I was supposed to cut something out of that mess that would end up looking like the Monopoly dog. And, of course, if you make a mistake, you get to take your lopsided dog around the neighborhood for the next six months while your mistake grows out. So I would stress, and I would stare at him for like half an hour, paralyzed, overwhelmed. I didn't know where to begin.

And then eventually, I would. Begin, I mean. I'd start cutting somewhere, sometimes one end, sometimes the other, sometimes in the middle. Once I'd started, it was just a matter of evening things up.

It took me a while to stop stressing out, but then I realized:

> It doesn't really matter where you begin, so long as you do.

Profound, isn't it? I should get it printed on a t-shirt. It seems to me I should be able to apply this lesson to other aspects of my life.

No idea how.

Okay, Haggis. Bath time.

Chapter 11
Help Wanted: Dog Walker

FLETCH

It was crazy, I knew, but I could no more stop myself than the lemming who's standing on the edge of the cliff saying, "Hey, guys, are you sure about this?" No, there was no choice, I had to jump. I had set things in motion, and I had to follow through. And—as bad as this idea was—it was better than standing across the street staring at Roger's windows.

Besides—the neighbors were starting to notice. The six-foot-two blond was not exactly inconspicuous. Sooner or later somebody was going to call a cop.

So. A few days after seeing Roger in Chelsea Park, I was standing on the stoop in front of his building, with my usual shoulder bag and a big bunch of gerberas from a little Korean market. I was pretty damned sure that this was not *just* a bad idea but a truly *disastrous* one. My sweaty hand reached out for his buzzer just the same. This little lemming took a deep breath, yelled, "Geronimo!" and pressed the door button. I could hear the distant eruption of terrier fury from above. I smiled.

Roger's voice came out of the little speaker by the door. "Yes?"

"Hey. It's me."

"Fletch?" He was understandably surprised. The barking had stopped.

"Yep."

There was no buzz. After a few seconds:

"What do you want?"

"Just buzz me in, Dweeb."

"Stop calling me that," said the tinny little voice.

The door buzzed, I pushed my way in and bounded up the two flights. Deep breath. I knocked.

After a second the door opened. There he was. There was Jeff, too. That was okay. I was prepared for that. Jeff was sitting on the couch, watching one of those singing competition things on TV. Poor Roger.

"For you," I said and stretched out my hand with the flowers.

Haggis was spinning around in circles in front of me.

"Flowers?" he said, taking them. Roger I mean, not Haggis.

"Hey, Barka-Lounger," I said, squatting to Haggis, who was beside himself.

"Hey, Fletch," said Jeff, standing to greet me, and he mercifully muted the girl wailing that song from *Dreamgirls.*

"'Sup, Jeff." I stood up.

"Why?" Dweeb asked.

"Why what?"

"Why flowers?"

"Because I never gave you flowers when I should have. It doesn't make up for anything, but I saw them at a little green market, and it seemed like the thing to do."

"Well—thanks," he said, as he went over to the kitchen counter to put the flowers in water.

"I've got something for you too, Jeff." This was shameless, much worse than the flowers even. It was another spontaneous idea on the way over, and once it was in my head, well, you know how it is. I reached into my shoulder bag and pulled out a Yankees baseball cap. "There was a guy on the street selling these. Here, try it on."

Jeff was more perplexed than ever. He turned that hat over in his hand, a little suspiciously, but then he shrugged.

"Go Yankees."

"Go Yankees," I echoed.

And he tugged the cap on—backward, of course, because, you know, Jeff "In-Point-of-Fact" Bornic, he's so gangsta. And vanity being what it is, he immediately checked his reflection in the mirror by the door.

"I liked them so much," I said, "I got one for me, too." I pulled a second, identical cap out of the bag and tugged it on—also backward. I stood next to Jeff and turned to Roger. "How do we look?" I bent my knees a little bit so I was the same height as Jeff. "Eh? What do you think?" I pointed from Jeff to me and back and turned to our reflection, smiling affably at the two matching blondes in the mirror. "Brothers?"

"So not funny, Fletch," Roger said.

"I'm just sayin'. So tell me, Jeff, like, who's your dad?"

Jeff snatched the baseball cap from his head and pressed it against my chest until I took it.

"What? Don't like that one? Wanna trade?"

Nobody quite seemed to be able to rise to the humor of the moment, but *I* couldn't stop grinning.

"Let me just say," said Jeff, "A, because you and I are both tall and blond doesn't mean anything; B, from what I understand, you and I are nothing at all alike; so, C, your little joke is more annoying than funny; and D——I'm going to go, Roger," he said over my shoulder, giving up.

I guess he didn't have a D. after all. "I'll see you…"

"I'll text," said the voice of the gerberas.

"Does he always number his paragraphs like that?"

Jeff was getting his jacket from the hooks by the door and picked up his briefcase.

"Lawyer-speak," said Roger.

"You don't talk like that."

"I'm not a very good lawyer."

"He's a fine lawyer," said Jeff.

"So you don't live here, Jeff?"

"No," said Roger.

Interesting.

"Don't forget we have the Legal Historical Society benefit on Saturday," said the Bornic creature.

"Ugh. Is that *this* weekend?"

"I knew you'd forget."

"Do I really have to, Jeff?"

"So important to network, baby. We've talked about this."

"Baby?" I mouthed silently to Roger, disbelieving. He answered me with one of his don't-start-anything looks. And then, Jeff did this awful thing, this truly repulsive, contemptible thing.

Jacket on, briefcase in hand, he turned back to Roger in the kitchen and kissed him a quick good-bye. On the lips.

I could see it coming. I should have turned away, if only to be polite, but something made me watch. Like I needed to see it or I wouldn't really believe it. But there it was, this boring little nothing was kissing Roger, *my* Roger, right in front of me. Roger's hands moved automatically up to the jag-off's waist.

I saw a pirate movie once where this guy got killed with a red-hot poker being shoved right through his chest. And this was

Just—

Like—

That.

It was quick, Jeff didn't make a big thing out of it, it was hardly a kiss even. But you know what? It was exactly *because* it was so off-hand and casual that it was so—what?—repugnant. Because it said "*I* get to do this *all the time*."

And in that moment, man-oh-man, how I hated this little pseudo-me.

And what the fuck was up with that? Jealousy??? Where was this coming from?

This was *completely* new to me. Honestly, in my whole life, I don't think I'd ever been jealous—until that moment. I'd always thought that that was because I was a bigger person than petty jealousy, but obviously that was a lie. Apparently I was plenty petty, because I was suddenly, miserably, desperately jealous. Maybe it was just because I'd never had anything worth being jealous of—until now.

But, of course, I didn't *have* anything. I sure as hell didn't have Roger—this constipated twerp did.

At least Roger seemed a little surprised by the gesture and embarrassed about it, like he didn't want that to have happened in front of me or something.

"So," I asked all cheery, like none of this was a big deal, "how long you two kids been together?" This was something that had been bugging me, and I wanted to get it clear.

"I'm not sure—what is it, baby? Not quite a year?" said Jeff.

Baby? Really?

It bugged me when Darwin called me Toots, but this was so much worse. Hearing Roger called 'baby' by this slug totally skeeved me.

"It was just before the holidays, remember?" said Roger.

"Must have been so nice for you both."

"Anyway," said Jeff. "Gotta go. Fletch, are you leaving as well?"

"Actually, I kinda have a couple things to talk to Roger about, but you go on ahead, Jeff."

"Jeffrey."

"—rey," I amended myself.

"It's okay, Jeff," Roger said.

Jeff was clearly not happy about leaving me here, but he went.

Silence for a few seconds. Roger set the well-arranged gerberas in their vase on the coffee table.

"I'm glad you didn't feel the need to keep your boyfriend around for protection from me."

"What do you want, Fletch? Why are you here?"

"I just want to be friends. After I saw you the other day, I couldn't think of any reason why we shouldn't be friends. Look around. You've moved on with your life, the past is past. And you can never have too many friends, can you?"

"Fletch, I don't know. I know it's the grown-up thing to do and all, but I'm not sure I'm all *that* grown up."

"You can't still be mad at me. After all—although I'm incredibly sorry for what happened, Roger, and for what I did—please believe that—but if you think about it, if what happened between us *hadn't* happened, you'd never have gotten this wonderful happy ending with Jeff."

My eyes were wide, my face glowing with innocence. Not a hint of snark.

Even so, I knew he could read me like a Schubert quartet. He knew exactly what I was doing. He couldn't argue with me because then he'd have to admit that what he had with Jeff was maybe something less than paradise—and I was getting a good idea that the whole Jeff–Roger thing wasn't even in a far-flung suburb of paradise.

"So, can we be friends? Please? Please-please-please?" Puppy-dog eyes.

Roger made a scrunchy face, and I knew I had won.

"Fine. We're friends. What do you want to do, go to a movie?" Such attitude.

"No, I just thought we ought to be able to see each other without being uncomfortable or embarrassed. You look so miserable when I see you."

"I'm not miserable."

"Good, I'm glad. That's because we're friends. And you know, if you ever need anything, or, I don't know, need someone to sit with Haggis or whatever, you can always call me."

He paused.

I let him think about it, while I gave him my best smile, with the dimples.

Of course I understood his dilemma. Did he really want to bring an ex-boyfriend back into his life? An ex-boyfriend who had treated him so badly?

He had Jeff to consider. What would the current boyfriend have to say about bringing me back into his life and into their world? I wasn't sure I was going to win this round. If the dimples didn't do it, I might have to fall back on my last resort, my secret weapon, and I wasn't even sure that that would work.

I'll tell you this on the condition that you promise to reveal to no one just how much of an A-1 louse I can be. *But*—if you yawn and stretch oh so casually, your t-shirt will ride up and reveal a peek at your awesome abs, if you happen to have awesome abs, which I do and which Roger hadn't seen in two long, lonely, ab-less years. Did I mention some people consider me hot? I knew Roger certainly did, especially my abs. The yawn was a despicable move, a pathetic maneuver by a desperate boy at his wit's end, and I was totally ashamed of myself for even considering displaying my happy trail just to manipulate the Dweeb.

"Well the funniest thing is," Roger said, just as my arms were moving up into the stretch, "I really *do* need a dog walker tomorrow. I don't know why, but my dog walker totally flaked out on me, and I'm kinda screwed. Could you? I mean, I know it's short notice, but—"

"No problem!" I said, putting my arms down, happily spared the indignity of exposing my navel.

Now, I'm sure you're thinking, this thing with the dog walker—What a coincidence! Right? But actually—and talk about desperate—here's the part I didn't tell you.

I had staked out Roger's apartment, for no real reason. I swear I had no plan whatsoever, I had no idea what I was getting out of staring at Roger's windows. I was just standing across the street staring at Roger's windows because why not?

Well, yeah, there are obvious reasons for why not, but none of them seemed to outweigh my need to stare at Roger's windows.

Then I saw the Haggis coming out with this hipster girl. Aha! I said to myself. *This* must be the dog walker. And without a single moment's thought about what I was doing, I approached her, I chatted, I made with the dimples, and I asked her if it would be a really big inconvenience for her if she *didn't* walk Haggis anymore. The dimples got me exactly nothing—maybe I should have tried the yawn?—but she finally agreed, once I promised to pay her what Roger had been paying her.

Per week.

Plus fifty dollars.

Also per week.

To *not* walk the dog.

It was a crazy, spontaneous, and, yes, a desperate and underhanded and truly pitiful thing to do.

I didn't plan it, and I can only claim temporary insanity as my defense.

In case you're thinking Broadway ushers are like Broadway stars or stagehands and get paid truckloads of money, let me tell you: We don't. We're at the bottom of the food chain. This added expense in my modest little life was going to be a huge bite.

"Can I depend on you?" Roger asked. "I mean—aren't you sort of—busy—being a..."

"An usher? No, I don't think so."

"Oh, you're ushering again. I didn't know. Honestly, after seeing you at the opera with…I thought, you know, maybe you were…"

"A personal escort?"

"Well, I wasn't sure—"

"My kept-boy days are over, thank you. I've turned in my union card and everything."

"You got to keep the white dinner suit, I hope."

"I threw it away."

"What!"

"By the end of the night, I hated the thing."

"You hated it? It looked great!"

"Long story. I'll explain sometime. Anyway, I thought about eBaying it, and then I figured it would be too much hassle, so I tossed it on a dumpster."

"No way."

"Way. Somewhere out there is one seriously sharp homeless person."

"You're insane."

"Totally. The really stupid part is I forgot that the shirt studs and cufflinks were in the jacket pocket. *Those* were worth some money. But it was all—what?—ill-gotten gains."

"Ah. Like blood money."

"Same principle, although the bodily fluid in question was actually—"

"O-kaaaaaaaaaaay! So. Now you're a dog walker. I'll pay you what I was giving the girl who was doing it."

"Don't even think about it. I should pay you for letting me hang out with Haggis."

"He does love you."

"Do you?" I said in my goofy doggy voice, squatting down to the dog. "Do you wub me, Haggis?" He squirmed. Haggis, not Roger, although probably Roger too.

"You're sure? Easy enough to write you a check."

"Definitely sure." Perhaps "temporary" insanity wasn't quite accurate.

He handed me a set of keys, no doubt the same set that that moneygrubbing hipster had just given back.

"Are *you* sure?" I asked. "Jeff and all…"

"I need a dog walker. *Jeff's* not going to walk my dog. He'll get over it." This could not have gone any better, could it? "Tomorrow is going to be a crazy day—*and* I have the quartet rehearsal here tomorrow after work on top of everything else."

"No worries. The dog and I will be fine. How's it going with the quartet?"

"We're doing one of those recitals on Sunday for an old folks' home."

"Cool. The geezers probably remember when Schubert was in the top ten."

"Not quite. You remember, for them we mostly play popular stuff. I've arranged a new medley of sixties' show tunes."

"They'll eat it up. I would love to hear it."

"You haven't lived until you've heard the highlights from *Hello Dolly!* played by a string quartet."

Man-oh-man, I loved listening to him talk.

"Hey," I said finally.

"Hey."

We looked at each other for a bit—and held the look about half a second too long. Long enough that he was suddenly awkward and unsure again and I was too.

"I should go. I'm sure you have stuff to do." I bent down to the dog. "I'll see you tomorrow, Haggles," I said and stood. "I'll leave Jeff's hat here for him then?"

"Asshole."

"I know, right?" I grinned and pulled *my* cap back on, not backward this time, and I tugged it way down over my ears and eyebrows so I looked deliberately dorky.

"Go," he said, opening the door but smiling at my dorkiness.

As I went past him, I leaned in for a quick kiss on the cheek again—but got a firm "Don't!"

Oh well. It was worth a shot.

Chapter 12

The Weirdest Déjà Vu

ROGER

What a day. Work was awful. Katrina had totally chewed me out (deservedly) over a dumb mistake I'd made—then, being a good boss, she'd immediately forgotten about it. I, being a neurotic employee, had obsessed about it for the rest of the day. And now, here I was leading the quartet—with Jeff tagging along (why? why? why???)—up the stairs to my apartment.

Don't misunderstand. The quartet was the best thing about the job. I picked Goodkin Berdann over the other firms because Katrina had told me at the interview that she was pulling a quartet together. I truly loved the quartet.

Mostly.

Nearly always. But sometimes...and today of all days Jeff decided he wanted to network with my friends, and that definitely had me on edge.

We trudged up the stairs, our own little parade, with Jeff in the rear carrying Katrina's music stand.

And the door wasn't locked. What the hell?

Had the dog walker gone without locking the door? The dog walker who was now Fletch, I reminded myself. That made no sense. Whatever else Fletch was, he wasn't irresponsible. Well, okay, I mean, he was *utterly* irresponsible but not *that* kind of irresponsible.

Anyway. As I opened the door, the dog came tearing around the corner from the kitchen to bark. He skidded to a stop when he saw it was me, but then he barked a few more times, just on principle, I guess.

The semicircle of folding chairs was already set up, and my music stand stood in front of the second chair.

"That's enough, Haggis" came from the kitchen. The dog was immediately quiet and went about sniffing everyone's shoes for a couple seconds before tearing back into the kitchen to—Fletch. Of course.

Even more incredible—judging from the smell—Fletch had been baking. In *my* kitchen.

Had he completely lost his mind???!!

"Fletch?" said Katrina and she looked at me, her eyebrows floating somewhere above her face.

"Fletch?!" said Jeff. "Did you—" he started to ask me.

"Hey, Fletch," said Bob.

Bob and Janine looked a little uncomfortably at Jeff, at Fletch, at each other, at me, and they were obviously wondering what kind of ménage-à-something they had stumbled into.

"So. Golly gee, Roger," said Katrina, thoroughly enjoying the situation. "What's new?"

"Fletch is helping out walking Haggis for me—I think?"

"*He's* the new dog walker?" Jeff asked.

"I was going to tell you—"

"Great to see you guys," Fletch said, stepping out and tossing a kitchen towel onto the counter behind him. "Hey, Katrina, how are you feeling? I heard about your shingles. I'm not really sure what they are—"

"You don't want to know either," Katrina said as they kissed each other on the cheek.

"I hope you're feeling better."

"I'm a miracle of drugs. Feeling much better. Thanks."

"Hey, Bob, Janine."

Greetings all around while Jeff looked at me for an explanation, which I didn't have.

"It's a pity you missed the opera, Katrina." Fletch was on a roll. "But it was so nice of you to give the tickets to Roger."

"He didn't take *you* to the opera, did he?"

"No!" I said.

"No, I bumped into Roger there, and look! Now I'm the dog walker."

"Go figure," said Katrina.

"Roger took Tommy to the opera," Fletch explained. And then he turned to me, all fake innocence—as if this had only just now occurred to him. "Hey, why didn't you take—"

"You remember, Katrina," I said, trying to keep this from skidding any further out of control. "You gave the second ticket to Tommy, remember?"

"Oh yes, of course I did," said Katrina, taking my hint. I gave Fletch a look, which he naturally ignored. He knew he'd found a sore spot. "And then you ran into Fletch," Katrina went on, "at the opera gala of all places. How funny is that?"

"After Roger told me you guys had a rehearsal today," Fletch jumped in, "I thought it would be great to see you all for a bit before I run to work. So I made my famous cheese puffs."

"Oh boy!" said Bob. "We haven't had rehearsal snacks since—ow!"

I'm not sure what happened, but Janine was right next to him.

"They smell amazing, Fletch," said Katrina.

"The pink ones are salmon."

"I hate salmon," Jeff said.

"I'm sorry, Jeff. I didn't know. The first time I made these, I made a crab filling, and I didn't realize until later that Janine didn't eat shellfish, and I felt terrible."

"Oh, Fletch," said Janine, "that's sweet, but the cheese ones were really delicious, I remember. And this salmon!"

"The salmon is courtesy of my friend Marco. By the way, Dweeb, did you know your dog is crazy about salmon?"

"Why do I get the feeling I've seen this movie before?" Bob asked Janine.

"Must seem like old times," said Jeff sarcastically.

"The salmon is fabulous, Fletch," Katrina crooned.

"I know, right?"

I didn't know which was weirder: That my ex-boyfriend had let himself into my apartment to use my kitchen to make hors d'oeuvres for my friends? Or that my dog walker had?

My head was spinning. Way back when, Fletch cooking for the quartet had become a regular event. But now?

"Fletch," I said, stepping into the kitchen. "Can I…"

He followed me. The kitchen was only separated from the living room by a counter and the upper cabinets, but I couldn't really drag him into the bedroom, could I? We would have to whisper.

"Do you have any inkling how wildly inappropriate this is?"

"Is it creepy? That's sort of why I baked, to make it not so creepy. Still creepy?"

"Duh!"

"I'll just finish loading the dishwasher and go. Oh—just so you know—you're out of eggs."

I had always admired Fletch for being so ballsy. I envied him even. If only I had one quarter of his moxie. But this—*this* was amazing. This was too much. This was jaw-dropping.

"These were just getting in the way out there," Jeff said, suddenly behind me.

He was carrying the vase of Fletch's gerberas. He pulled the flowers out, opened the cabinet under the sink, and stuffed them into the garbage—on top of the eggshells. Fletch shook his head and laughed a little. Even I had to roll my eyes.

"Everything okay, baby?" Jeff asked.

Brilliant. Jeff had decided now was the time to play the possessive boyfriend. He started to slip an arm around me, but I shook it off.

"Everything's fine, Jeff. I was about to explain things to Fletch. Just go back and—"

"Salmon puff?" Fletch held the little pastry out to Jeff between two fingers.

"I hate—"

"Totally forgot," said Fletch. "Sorry!" He bit the little pastry in half and then stood there smiling at Jeff, chewing, smiling. "Mmmm." Does *everyone mmm* on G-sharp?

"Please, Jeff, just..." I turned Jeff around and pushed him back toward the living room, and he went reluctantly.

"So you really like this music?" Bob asked from the living room.

"Not really," said Jeff.

"Actually, I meant Fletch. Actually."

Fletch stepped around me and leaned his elbows on the counter to bend under the upper cabinets to answer—and his shirt pulled up in back, uncovering a good couple inches of skin. There was this little bit of blond fuzz there that sort of glistened, right there above his boxers, almost golden in the light from the—

Oh-jeez, what was I staring at??!!

I looked away quickly and could feel myself blush.

"You should see my phone," Fletch was saying. "It's still full of stuff I stole from Roger—there's a ton of quartets in there."

"I don't believe you," said Katrina.

"Would Fletch lie?" Jeff chimed in.

What were they talking about? I'd missed some of this conversation.

"It was hard for me at first," Fletch was saying. "The instruments mostly all sound alike—no offense—it's not like an orchestra, all those different sounds. And for lots of it you're all playing at the same time."

"That's true—in orchestral music there's more sharing, trading off," said Janine.

"And more rests," said Bob.

"Don't encourage him," said Jeff said, laughing a little, but no one joined in.

"But once you sort of work your way inside the voices, then you hear all the intricacies and the interplay, the different lines, and the way the notes lie against each other—I don't know how to say it."

"Harmonies," I said quietly. It actually touched me how much he'd picked up about music.

"That's it. Harmonies."

I mean, he was totally stupid, of course—but he wasn't.

"That's very well put, Fletch," said Katrina.

He was actually *listening.*

"Did you ever play anything, Fletch?" That was Bob.

"Once," he said and looked at me, smiling. "Roger let me play his violin one time."

"Really?" Janine said. "I always thought Roger was like me, he never let anybody touch his instrument."

"It was just the once. You remember, Dweeb?" Fletched looked at me, all wide-eyed innocence.

Let me point something out for you, in case you missed it: Nothing Fletch does is ever, ever innocent.

"I remember," I said.

Of course I remembered, and I could feel the heat in my cheeks. Fletch grinned. That bastard, he knew exactly what he was doing.

We'd been living together for a few weeks, when one day after practicing, it occurred to me—I don't know why—

"Hey," I asked, "do you want to try?" I'd never offered that to anyone. My little German violin was precious to me. I had never even offered to let my father hold it—my father, whom I had dragged around through months of violin shopping—or my grandfather, who controlled the trust that paid for the thing.

But Fletch was far from just anyone. If I was ever going to trust somebody, I thought, it was going to be Fletch. (Oh, the irony.) I held out the violin and bow to him.

"That's a terrible idea, Dweeb. I'm sure it's really valuable, and I'm such an ox. What if I drop it or something?"

"Well, promise not to drop it."

"You know I don't do promises."

I didn't want him to be afraid, and somehow it was important to share this with him, even if only in a tiny way.

"Come over here." He stood and came to me warily. "Don't worry. I'm not going to hurt you, but let's try this. Here, you take the bow, in your right hand." He did. I moved around behind him. "You're so damned tall." I reached over and pulled out *Tort Law & Alternatives—finally* a use for that damned book—put it on the floor behind him, and stood on it. "There. I'll hold the violin in my left—lift your chin." He did, and I laid the violin's shoulder rest on his shoulder. "See? Now bring your jaw down onto the chin thing." He did. "There. See how it fits?" To do this, I was right up behind him. "Now bring the bow up, there, and set the bow down on the third string with your hand right up close to the strings so you can draw the bow down. Closer to the bridge." He moved the bow, but in the wrong direction. "Sorry. Move it away from my hand." I waved a couple fingers on the violin neck. "Little more. Perfect. You're really tense. Try to relax a bit, take a deep breath."

He did.

"There. Now—slowly pull the bow across the string."

"You sure?"

"I'm sure."

He pulled the bow down—and bow and violin did what bow and violin do. They sang.

All pretty matter-of-fact, no big deal, nothing magical about it, just bow on string. It's what I do about a million times every day, and he'd heard me do it about a trazillion times. But if you've never done it, if you've never heard the sound come out of the instrument when *you* play it, and if you're not a totally jaded fart and you can really hear things with fresh ears—it's a very big deal. It's a frigging miracle.

I looked sideways at Fletch's face, and I could tell that he had heard what I had heard.

He had heard the miracle.

It wasn't the prettiest note ever produced by man, but it didn't sound bad either. It sounded like a violin. It sounded like an A.

"Do it again, and keep going. That's it, pull your hand all the way down until you've run out of bow—and reverse." And he pushed the bow back up, still on the open A-string. My right hand, I realized, was around his waist on his tummy. "Keep going. With the left hand we can change the pitch." I moved my left hand through the positions to play an A scale up through an octave, all legato because he was doing the bowing.

"That's incredible," said Fletch. He had stopped bowing.

"Do it again." He laid the bow back in place, and pulled again. "This is a glissando, going up." I slid my hand toward his face, and the pitch slid up. “And down.” I slid the hand back. He looked at me like I could walk on water and I’d brought him along for a stroll.

“Here, you want to try something? We’ll do that again. Bring your hand up for the down stroke.” He laid the bow back on the A-string in the same place. “I think this’ll work. Go.” He drew the bow slowly down, and with my left hand—don’t ask me why I picked this off the top of my head, I just wanted something that I thought he’d recognize—I played the bridge to “Over the Rainbow,” this pretty eighth-note line, while he kept bowing. And then on through to the end of the song.

There’s a little coda at the end.

“Move to the next string,” I said. He laid the bow across the E-string and bowed, and I took the coda up an octave. At the very end—where the bluebirds are flying and she asks, “Why oh why can’t I?”—I took a big fat ritard, and I wanted him to hold that last high note.

“That’s it…don’t stop….keep going…just like that.” Together we let that last, sweet note sing out. “Stop,” I whispered, holding him a little tighter.

We stood there, still pressed against each other, our faces very close. Somewhere in here, his left hand had reached around and gripped the back of my thigh, as if he needed something to hold on to. We looked at each other now, as best we could, with his face so close to mine.

“Do you have any idea how sexy you are?” he asked quietly. I didn’t, but I was perfectly content to let him explain it to me. “That was the hottest, most erotic thing I’ve ever done in my entire life,” he said, and he turned around to me. Arms around each other, him with a bow in one hand, me with the fiddle still dangling in my left behind him, we were pressed against each other, and it was pretty obvious just how erotic he had found violin playing to be. Me too, apparently.

“Sexy? Seriously?”

“Absolutely. Sharing that with you—the sound, you know, how it sort of hits your chest and your face, and it’s right there under your ear and the violin vibrating against your body, and with you behind me, and watching your fingers on the neck of the thing. Hot. Damn.”

“It *was* fun, wasn’t it?”

“I’m telling you—I once spent a weekend with identical twins, and this was hotter than that.”

“Now I know you’re making fun of me.”

“I would never joke about something as serious as identical twins.”

May I tell you how earth-shaking it is to discover that somebody likes you, genuinely likes you, thinks you’re sexy, wants to spend time with you because you are exactly who you are? It wasn’t for some pose I’d copied from somebody, not for the shirt I bought in the hope that it might fool somebody into thinking I was attractive. Not because I had successfully hidden the fact that my entire adolescence was spent locked in practice rooms and it had left me with zero social skills.

Here was somebody who wanted me *because* I was so inept. He didn't like me *in spite of* my unbelievable awkwardness. He liked me *because* of it, *because* I had no social skills and *because* I had never learned how to flirt or pick up guys or make a joke.

I've mentioned enough how Fletch was this Adonis—and he was—but after that night, that was *so* irrelevant. I was hopelessly, blissfully, bark-at-the-moon crazy in love with him because he was the most beautiful guy I had ever met—and that had absolutely nothing to do with gorgeous eyes or a handsome smile.

"Hey, are you all right?" Fletch asked very softly.

Lost in the memory, I slowly realized it was a quartet rehearsel. The others were talking, but I had no idea about what. I was still in the kitchen and Fletch seemed to be standing really close, between me and the gap under the cabinets.

"Dweeb? All of a sudden you looked so—"

"I'm—okay," I said. It was somewhere on the underside of triple *pianissimo*. As in "not quite audible."

"Hey! I'm sorry," he said, still whispering. He reached up, and—with the cuff of his sweatshirt—he brushed something off my cheek. "Don't, Dweeb. Really, I didn't mean to—"

I was suddenly livid, and I guessed I was livid with Fletch. Anyway, he was right there.

"Leave me alone," I said in a broken whisper and pulled myself away from him roughly, wiping my eyes.

What was he doing here anyway? What was he thinking? What was *I* thinking??? Hiding in the kitchen with Fletch, whispering, and now he was wiping my face with his sleeve?! With everybody in the next room! Even Jeff, for God's sake! And—and—and he used all my eggs!!! Not that I needed the eggs, but it was the *principle* of the thing, damn it.

"Didn't you, Roger?" That was Janine, asking me something. But what? I moved to lean around Fletch.

"Actually—" I tried to say to the others, hoping to get the rehearsal started, but there was still this thing in my throat, and my voice sounded like a bassoon with a cracked reed.

"I learned a lot about playing from Roger," said Fletch, turning back to the living room conversation. Jeez Louise, was he—covering for me?

"I mean, I know it won't impress you guys, but I know all about arco and pizzicato, and the difference between a glissando and portmanteau, tremolo and martele."

"Nice vocabulary, Fletch," Jeff sniped from the couch.

Mercifully, everyone seemed to have decided to ignore him.

I went past Fletch to join the others, who all had their instruments out by now. *Concentrate, Prescott,* I thought. *Stop trying to figure things out. Just get the violin out and play.*

"Actually it *is* impressive, Fletch," Katrina said.

I tightened my bow. Deep breaths.

"Where'd you go to college, Fletch?"

Wait—what was Jeff asking? Such a dick.

"New York Public Library," Fletch said before I could find my voice.

"Good answer," said Janine quietly.

"What about you, Jeff?" Now it was Fletch who was challenging.

"Dartmouth. *Summa cum laude.*"

Katrina gave me a look that said, "Seriously?" And really, seriously?

"Summa what?" said Fletch.

"Summa cum laude." Of course Jeff's Latin pronunciation was perfect. Fletch's—anything but, especially "cum" which he pronounced more like…yeah, that.

The musicians were all suddenly busy with their instruments, waiting for this to be over.

"Cool. Know what I've learned about college boys, Jeff?"

"What? Do tell."

"Summa cum laude—than others."

Wait, what did Fletch just say? He didn't! I glanced around. And my well-trained and experienced chamber music colleagues exploded with laughter—in perfect unison. So yeah, I guess he *had* said what I thought he'd said. Katrina especially seemed to think this was about the funniest thing she'd ever heard. Of course *I* had to laugh too. Fletch went back to loading the dishwasher.

And Jeff?

Jeff just turned red. Then redder. I didn't even know he could do that.

"Funny, Fletch, really funny," he said. "But I should go." He stood up. "You too, Fletch."

Wait a second, was Jeff throwing Fletch out of my apartment? First the flowers, and now? I seriously needed to start paying more attention.

"You're so right, Jeff, I have to get to the theatre. I'll walk you out. It was great seeing you all."

Jeff went to the door and held it open for Fletch as if he wanted to make sure Fletch was leaving. Fletch wiped down the countertop; hung a dishtowel on the refrigerator handle the way he always used to do; said his farewells, kissing Katrina and then Janine on their respective cheeks—and all while Jeff stood by the open door. Jeff finally grabbed Fletch's jacket from the hook and threw it at him.

"Something on your mind, Jeff?" Fletch said, smiling, catching the jacket.

"We can talk about it outside." He indicated the door with one of those jerks of the head I thought only straight boys knew how to do. Everyone was watching them. My suitors.

Seriously? Were they going to go outside now and beat the tar out of each other? Over me?

They went out, and Jeff banged the door closed behind them. No one in the room spoke. We listened to feet going down the stairs, until we heard the front door pulled open.

"Roger, Roger," Katrina said finally, shaking her head. "It's always the quiet ones."

The other two positively erupted—again—into sputtering and snorting laughter.

"I'm so glad you're enjoying this," I said. "Can we get started now? We *do* have a recital on Sunday."

"Absolutely," Katrina said, although the viola and cello clearly would need a minute. "Okay, let's start with Roger's medley, shall we?"

I opened the music to the first page and stared at the notes I'd written for myself. Jeez Louise, how was I supposed to do this? Like I was going to be able to concentrate after all that. As if. I was still half expecting to hear something outside. What?—shouts?—a brawl?—pistol shots?

But the show must blah-blah-blah.

Everyone settled; scores were opened; bows were raised.

I think I mentioned earlier how when one member of a quartet is sort of off, it tends to throw everyone off. Today was going to be my day.

Katrina took a deep breath and

Well—

Hell—

O-o-o-o-o——Dolly!

Chapter 13

An Epiphany—on Forty-Third Street

FLETCH

In my junky high-tops, I rabbited down the two flights, while Jeffie thudded along right behind me in his Italian whatevers. Okay, I thought. Jeff wants to chat. No problem. Keep it short, and it will improve your chances of getting through this without hitting him.

I wasn't normally a violent person, but you know, for Jeff, exceptions could be made.

"Hey, Fletch," he said. "I feel like I should say something here, just to make sure we're on the same page."

"Make it quick, okay, handsome?" He was still on the last step while I was on the sidewalk—kinda pathetic, I thought. "Why don't you come down here and we can get to know each other better." I backed away from the stoop, arms stretched out to the side, inviting him to follow me. An asshole gesture, I admit. I'm blaming Jeff.

"Well played up there, by the way: 'Laude than others.'"

"Thanks."

"I don't imagine you know—it means 'with highest honor.' If you knew how much work went into getting that, you wouldn't think it was so funny."

"I don't know, Jeff. It was still pretty funny."

"You want to tell me what it is you think you'll accomplish here, Fletch? Hanging around like this?"

"Accomplish?"

"Yeah," he said. He was all kinds of frat-boy cocky, head tilted back, chest out. And man-oh-man, let me tell you something—I *hate* frat boys. "I mean what's your game plan, dude?"

"I don't think I have one, Jeff."

"Pretty sure you do. You're hoping to make an end run, score a few cheap points—like you did up there—weasel your way around me and back into Roger's life. Bit of a Hail Mary, but I always admire a little grit and determination—"

"Wow. Sports metaphors."

"—but you will *never* get Roger back."

"Get Roger back?!" What was he talking about?! "I'm not trying to get Roger back!"

Was I?

"No?"

No, of course not! I thought.

"No! Of course not!" I said.

"Then why are you hanging around here all of a sudden?"

Beats the hell out of me, I thought. Really, why *was* I hanging around all the time?

"I was just catching up with some old friends, Jeff." Improvisation.

"Seriously, dude? Because I'm not buying it."

I was starting to wonder about it myself.

"I just *like* hanging out with Roger." That much was true. "Don't you, Jeff? Rey."

"I'll tell you what I think your plan is, shall I?"

"Oh yes please!" I said all sarcastic. "Do shall!" He ignored my attitude.

"A, you're just going to hang out as much as possible because B, you figure you're so good-looking, you don't have to do a whole lot else."

"Why, thank you, Jeff, that's so nice of you to say."

"C, you'll be attentive and do him little favors, and you'll be all loveable and charming with his friends—and you're a pretty charming guy, Fletch, I admit it—"

"Jeff, tell the truth, are you getting sweet on me?"

"—and D, you'll manipulate things so you'll get your little moments, your little whispered conversations with Roger, like you did in the kitchen up there."

"Hey—Roger asked *me* into the kitchen. If there were whispers, well then…"

"And E, one thing will lead to another—"

"Wait—is this really *my* plan? I mean, it doesn't sound bad, but—"

"Look, dude, I know you had a really cozy deal with Roger back in the day. I can't blame you for wanting it all back, i.e., his credit cards, his fat paycheck, the nice apartment—"

"Wait-wait-wait—you're thinking I'm after Roger…for his money???"

"You're trying to tell me you're not?"

"That's really what you think?!" And you know, I had thought I had to take this guy seriously. He'd had me worried there, he might have been on to something, but forget that! "Let me try to explain this, Jeff, in language you can understand. A, I'm not chasing after anybody."

"Then why are you still here?"

"Two, if I *was* chasing after somebody, it sure as hell wouldn't be because of his money!"

"You expect me to believe the money doesn't interest you at all?"

"Pretty incredible, I know—Where was I, you threw me off. I'm not used to talking in bullet points. D! Now I'm starting to be suspicious of *your* motives here, you little flatworm, because you apparently can't see that that smart, amazingly talented guy up there has so much more to offer than a frigging bank account!"

"Fine, okay. Look. I'll cut you some slack here. I'll even admit that you might not be *just* the pretty-boy prostitute—"

"Actually, I never—you know, never mind. I'm not even going to try."

"I'm willing to admit that you might even *like* Roger a little. So if you *do* like the guy, do you think you're making him happy, hanging around like this? You're not. You're making him miserable. Roger's moved on, and you have to let him have the life he's *meant* to have."

"What's *that* supposed to mean?"

"You know exactly what I mean. You've met his family."

"No, never did."

"Really! Huh." He looked even smugger, hearing that. Man-oh-man, I could really get to hate this guy. "See, Roger's from this old blueblood family, and he's a lawyer at a big, fat New York firm. Roger needs someone like *me* next to him, helping him in his career. Not some male escort embarrassment."

"You know, Jeff, I don't even care what you say about me, but I can't tell you how much I'm starting to hate hearing Roger's name in your mouth."

"Look, I have this fantastic career, and with my guidance, Roger can have the same. Roger and I are going to be this fabulous power couple—the kind that everybody envies—and no little call-boy is going to keep that from happening."

"Dude, you really need to stop talking."

I may have mentioned that my childhood and adolescence weren't exactly all sunny meadows and marigolds, and to be honest, I had learned to fight from people meaner than you can imagine. If Jeff wanted to have a go—and holy guacamole, he was begging for it—I could promise only one thing: It would be quick.

"Roger's not your boyfriend anymore," Jeff Bornic blathered on. "He's *mine* now. Roger belongs to *me*."

I was livid. Crazed.

"I'm gonna go." I turned and started walking away from him.

"Don't you walk away from me, you little—"

I heard his feet on the sidewalk, trotting after me, and he grabbed my arm.

There are reflexes you just never unlearn. My right hand was around Jeff's wrist like a rattlesnake strike. Man-oh-man, did I want to follow through. So easy. Lay him out right there. But Jeff's head was going to hit the sidewalk when he went down, and you just never know how that's going to go, and I had my reasons for not wanting to do anything that might possibly end with a squad car, flashing blue lights and me in the back seat.

Been there, done that.

So I held his hand where it was for a couple seconds, tight enough that it had to hurt, and then I pushed it away.

"Don't ever."

I turned around and walked away while he was still too stunned to say anything stupid that would make me change my mind. I actually jaywalked right out in front of a car—she wasn't going very fast, but she laid on the horn anyway. I didn't even turn my head. I just needed to get away from there fast. I stomped off onto the avenue, and started uptown toward Fiftieth Street. I was walking so fast it's a miracle no one was hurt.

I was so damned mad. I was shaking all over. My eyeballs ached I was so pissed.

Who did this guy think he was?!

"He belongs to me now"??? My teeth were grinding.

First, if Roger needed defending, he'd do it himself. He clearly had no problem telling me to go to hell—he'd done it before.

I was stopped, waiting for the fucking light at Twenty-Third Street to change. *I fucking hate Twenty-Third Street*, I thought. *Has to be the fucking ugliest—*

Walk light. I pushed my way past people in front of me who didn't move fast enough and strode off.

But the thing that *really* set me off—damn it—was that Roger was nobody's property, and he was so much more than a paycheck. If I was going to chase after Roger, it wouldn't be because of his great-aunt's trust fund or what-the-fuck-ever.

Of course, I thought to myself, my totally losing it like I did, and then storming off—wasn't exactly a terrific move strategically. I'm sure Jeff thought he won this round.

That's because he did, you dolt. You let him get to you.

Fuck.

And why? Why was I getting so sweated up about it anyway?

If Jeff felt the need to get all macho and flex his testicles with me, it just meant that he saw me as a threat. Good. Let him feel threatened.

And why should I care? None of this had anything to do with me. I wasn't trying to break anybody up.

Didn't have to, anyway. They didn't have a chance. They were a terrible couple. I ask you, how long could Roger put up with *America's Got Talent*? I know how Roger hears music, and a girl belting out some inane power ballad at the top of her lungs—and slightly flat—had to give him hives. Not to mention Jeff's master plan of steering Roger's career, turning Dweeb into Jeff Jr. Can you imagine???

I just wanted Roger to be happy. Jeff was never going to make Roger happy. That was clear. Power couple. For cryin' out loud.

I wanted Dweeb to see that this Chia Pet wasn't good enough for him.

He could do so much better.

And no, I wasn't thinking of me. I wasn't suggesting for a *nanosecond* that *I* would be better. Because I had been terrible for Roger. I had never understood why Roger took me in in the first place: the Harvard lawyer and the gutter kid. And I had proved myself to be the worst thing *ever* for Roger, as I'm sure he'd cheerfully tell you. I was so *unbelievably* not good enough for Roger.

I was stopped again at Thirty-Third Street.

But I had to ask myself—was part of me, some tiny, stupid part me, thinking about me and Dweeb? *Was* I chasing after him? Is that what all this stalking and bribing of dog walkers was about?

I didn't wait for the light and just dodged across.

If not, then why *was* I hanging around, being all cute and adorable and nice? Hmm???

I *like* Roger, I thought. I always have, ever since we met at Katrina's that night. So if I wanted to hang around—there didn't have to be some great big *reason* behind it, did there?

But was there? A reason, I mean?

So let's suppose one day Roger turned, looked me in the eye, and said, "Hey, Fletch, I want you back." Would that be what I wanted?

My pace had slackened.

Was that what I wanted—back together with Roger? Like before?

No!

Of course not!

I mean—I don't know.

Maybe.

But no. Not like before. I couldn't do that to Roger again. It would have to be different.

How different?

Don't be an idiot. You know exactly how it would have to be different. Was I ready for that? Was there suddenly a part of my miserable, undereducated, oversexed, juvenile-delinquent brain that was actually entertaining monogamy as a possibility?

Here's the thing. I really like sex. I really like guys. I really like sex with guys. I love guys' bodies. I love guys' wieners. Was I ready to say that I'd seen the last wiener I was ever going to see, except for mine and his? Could I live with that? I was only twenty-five, for cryin' out loud. Too young to retire, don't you think?

On the other hand, let's be real—I'd probably seen more wieners than most guys do in a long lifetime. I'd certainly seen my share anyway. I mean Disney on Ice alone…

And after a while, after you've racked up a body count like I had, they tend to blur together anyway.

And then there was Roger.

Was I really thinking that? That, if it was possible—and, of course, it wasn't possible and this was all pointless—but if it *was* possible, that I might spend tomorrow and the next day and the next with Roger? No one else but Roger, day in, day out? Like before, but without the distractions? Listen to Roger's arpeggios every damned day, day after day? Nothing but classical music out the wazoo from now 'til Doomsday? Take care of Roger when he gets one of his awful colds? Let him take care of me? Get old with him? Watch *him* get old? For years, decades? For *forever*???

For forever—until somebody *dies*????

Because that's what we're talking about here, and seriously, why would anybody agree to that? It's crazy! Terrifying!

And it also sounded—you know—like it might be…

I needed to think this through very carefully.

Because if I *wasn't* ready for forever and ever, 'til death do us, etc., I should bail right now. I should walk back to Chelsea, kiss Roger on the cheek, look him in the eye, and tell him to have a nice life—and vanish.

Never see him again. Never think of him again.

How could I do that, when all I seemed to be able to do these days was hang around Roger, look at Roger, or stare at the ceiling and think about the next time I might see Roger again.

But! I had lived without Roger for two years, no problem. Why couldn't I do that now? What had changed?

Good question, Einstein.

The answer was lurking right there, just out of the corner of my eye, and frankly it scared holy hell out of me.

I had come to a full stop in the middle of the sidewalk on Eighth Avenue at Forty-Third Street. People pushed their way around me like they were the stream and I was the rock.

This was the last bit of the old cheesy Times Square. I was standing in front of one of the few sex shops that were left. There used to be a million of these places. I stood there and stared at a blue neon sign in the shape of a naked babe. Booths still only twenty-five cents, said the sign. Ladies welcome.

Why do I mention all this?

Because it was a really strange place for a life-changing moment, and I was pretty sure that's what this was. It was like something biblical: The skies opened up, and I could see with a new and brilliant clarity.

I had stopped breathing anyway.

At first I was gripped with a kind of panic, a paralyzing fear. And then the fear just slid off and fell away like an old raincoat, *whoosh*, and I felt—what?—relieved? No. Fantastic! Ecstatic, even. Transformed.

Because I knew the answer to my questions. I knew what had changed.

Was I really ready to spend the rest of my life with someone, and *just* that someone, and no more fooling around, not ever, never? The answer came singing to me through the noise of Manhattan traffic like a high, clear note from a violin.

"Yep," I said. No one shoving their way around me even noticed. You have to do way more than talk to yourself to get anybody's attention on a Midtown sidewalk an hour before twenty-nine Broadway shows go up.

"Yep. I am."

If that person was Roger, then that was my answer.

Chapter 14
Cancun Should Be Lovely This Time of Year

ROGER

I was practicing, working through some old etudes I hadn't touched in a couple years, when Fletch let himself in. He had said he'd drop off some dog food today. I played through to the end of the page before I looked up.

"Hey."

He didn't answer at first, and I saw he was looking at some stuff Jeff had left on the coffee table.

"It's none of my business, but what's all this?"

"Jeff was here—we're planning a vacation. January."

"Cancun?"

"It'll be nice to get away from the winter weather."

"Ah. All that tropical sunshine?"

"Yeah, something like that."

"Roger, you hate the sun."

"It's a vacation."

"And you hate lying around doing nothing. What are you going to do in a resort?" he asked waving a webpage printout.

"Jeff's going to teach me to play golf."

"Now I *know* you're yanking me."

"Sadly, no. But Jeff really wants to go. His boss went there last year—"

"Why don't you go to Europe, hear some music, see some art? Didn't you tell me every little town over there has its own opera house and a concert hall and a little orchestra?"

"Yeah, but I can't haul Jeff off to Europe to go to concerts on his vacation. The music is meaningless to him. He'd just sit there, Facebooking on his phone the whole time."

"He doesn't."

"Anyway, I can't drag him off and make him miserable."

"So he can drag *you* off and make *you* miserable?"

"It'll be nice."

"You get sick if you sit in the sun!"

"Yeah, I know."

"Does he?"

"Here's the thing, Fletch: He's my boyfriend, and we're going to spend some time together. It's a commitment, and sometimes you make compromises. But I wouldn't expect *you* to understand that."

"I understand this much. A compromise is when you want to go to Austria, he wants to go to Mexico, and you go to Spain."

"It's just for a week or—"

"But if you want Austria and he wants Mexico, and you go to Mexico—that's not a compromise. That's caving."

Fletch was right, of course, which was just unbe-*liev*-ably irritating—and what was it to *him* anyway?

"Spelunking," I said.

"What?"

"It's a fancy word for caving." Music major, remember?

"Ha ha, Dweeb. Totally lame."

"I know. Look, not that it's any of your business, but Jeff really wants to go, and I don't care that much. And there's nothing wrong with Mexico."

"But why?"

"Why?" I was putting the violin and bow back in the case, but I could feel myself tensing up, grinding my teeth. "You want to know why?" I spun around to him. "I'll tell you why! Because he's dependable! That's why!"

"I didn't ask, 'Why Jeff?' I meant—"

"Unlike some people I could mention!"

"And why is this about *me* now?"

"Of course it's about you! Everything's about you!" For some reason I had a steady crescendo going here. "You're so astonishingly, breathtakingly vain, you think the only possible reason I could be with Jeff is because he reminds me of *you*!"

"Isn't that why you picked him?"

"No! Your hubris is positively mind-boggling!"

"I don't even know what that means, Dweeb."

"I'm sure you'll look it up!"

"I will! Sorry, I didn't go to Ivy League schools like you two—"

"I don't care—"

"When did you become such a snob?"

"I'm not a snob!"

"You and what's-his-name are a better couple than I thought!"

"We are not either!"

"*A-ha*!"

"Damn you!"

"Tell the truth, Dweeb. The only reason you picked that gutless wonder is because he looks like me!"

"No! I picked that—Jeff! I picked *Jeff* because he's *not* like you! In fact he's the *opposite* of you! He's dependable—"

"So you said—"

"He's educated, he's smart—"

I was bulldozing right over the top of him.

"And Ivy League, you pathetic snob."

I was going to *make* him understand finally.

"He's methodical, he's—"

"I'll tell you what he isn't. Funny. Or fun. Caring, spontaneous—"

"I knew you were going to say that, and spontaneity is so over—"

"—and at least *I* never called you baby! Why do you let him? Make him stop, Dweeb, it's creepy."

"You call me dweeb! Like that's any better!"

"Totally not the same thing, Dweeb—"

"And stop calling me—"

"—and you know it!"

"What I *know* is—there's nothing wrong with baby, and there's nothing wrong with Mexico, and it's none of your business anyway, and your little costume designer called you Toots!"

"When *he* calls you baby, it's *so* much worse—"

"Does that make any sense to—"

"Yes!"

He snatched up the bag of dog food and headed into the kitchen. "But I wouldn't expect *you* to understand—"

"Great!" I followed him. "Then let me help *you* understand something." I had added an accelerando to the cresc. "Jeff is smart! He was top of his class at Princeton Law, he has a terrific future, he has tons of friends, he has incredible connections, he's going to make partner, probably next year. He looks out for me, he—"

"No he doesn't."

"He takes care of me!"

"He takes you to Cancun, Dweeb."

"And he's really—reliable!"

He leaned back against the refrigerator, arms crossed. So goddamned full of himself.

"Really?" He smirked. "I bet he's dependable, too."

"He is! And *he—he—he—*" Okay, by now I was way out there triple forte, but Fletch's attitude—so damned cocky, so sure he'd won the argument—really pissed me off. I was sure I looked like a tomato, like a stuttering tomato, but I would have done *anything* to take that mocking smile off his face. "At least *he* doesn't cheat on me!"

Fletch didn't seem to know how to answer. He pushed himself off the refrigerator, his arms fell to his sides, and all of his arrogance had vanished. He looked like he'd been slapped.

He turned and leaned on the kitchen counter, staring at the marble. I could see his jaw muscles clenching.

All of a sudden I was scared.

I wasn't scared of Fletch. I was scared I had somehow gone too far. People who don't normally express anger are usually really bad at it when they try.

Case in point.

I waited for him to look up at me or *something*, but he didn't. I had definitely crossed a line.

"I put the dog food in the cabinet," he said quietly to the countertop.

"Fletch—" I wanted to try to apologize—but for what? I hadn't said anything that wasn't true, had I? But still.

Fletch was scooching past me sideways in the narrow galley, holding his hands up, making a big thing out of not touching me.

"Fletch, wait—"

He didn't even close the door behind him. Converse sneakers boomed in the stairwell, two steps at a time at least.

What the hell.

Chapter 15

The Greeks Had a Word for It

FLETCH

You have picked up by now that I have been more than a little bit of a tramp. I slept around a lot before I met Roger, I slept around a lot after Roger kicked me out. Unfortunately I also slept around some while I was *with* Roger, which now strikes me as astoundingly stupid, but it seemed like a really good idea at the time.

So I certainly am not going to bore you with the details of every little sexual adventure, even if I could remember them all, but there's one that's important.

Once upon a time…

I was at work. Ushering. The Longacre Theatre. It was a short run, a production of a Greek tragedy called *Medea* that's about a million years old. It's about this woman with a dickhead husband and two adorable little children, and the husband dumps her for some bimbo—which just goes to show that nothing's changed in the intervening millennia—and the dickhead then expects full custody of the little darlings. Instead of calling a good lawyer like a sensible girl, Medea takes matters into her own hands. She kills off the bride-to-be, and then, since the hubby wants custody of the two adorable little children, she butchers them and then flings the two adorable little corpses at his feet. I swear the classics are just dressed-up slasher movies—lots of screaming, lots of blood and dead bodies all over the place.

I may have got the plot a little muddled, but I think it's clear—this was *Medea*, not *Mamma Mia*!

But even without a single ABBA song, *Medea* was sold out for the run because it was this famous English actress—if you've ever seen a Harry Potter movie, you'd recognize her.

So that's where I was, handing out programs and helping people find row K, because apparently nobody knows the alphabet, and it was my job.

And there was this guy. Nearly as tall as me, seriously nice-looking, dark blond, and he was totally checking me out. I walked him down to his row. I smiled, and I flirted.

"Enjoy the show," I said.

"Thanks."

"But not too much."

"Excuse me?"

"Don't have too much fun. It's a tragedy." A weak joke, and he laughed weakly.

"Thanks, I'll keep that in mind."

"I'll see you at intermission," I said and held eye contact a second too long to go unnoticed. I left him to think about *that* during the seemingly unending and completely miserable first half. In verse.

There was an empty seat next to him, and it stayed empty. I'm telling you the guy was ripe.

At intermission, I found him on his way to the stairs down to the restrooms.

"How do you like the show?" I asked.

"It's great!" he said.

"It's dreary as fuck."

He burst out laughing.

"Yeah, it is sort of."

"I noticed you're alone?"

"My date—has the flu."

"Lucky guy."

"The show's not *that* bad."

"It gets so much worse—*but*," I added, "if you're interested…" I was three-quarters set to go already, and now I stood close enough to him in the crowd at the back of the theater that his hip could feel exactly how set to go I was, "we could probably find something more amusing to do."

The chimes were going for the second half, and people were moving back in through the various doors.

"Seriously?"

"Does this feel like I'm kidding?" I pressed his hand where it wanted to be.

"Wow." His eyebrows rose in happy surprise.

"While everyone's heading back in, go downstairs to the men's."

I did my job for another minute or two, watched the houselights go down, and I slipped down the stairs to the lounge and into the john. He was standing at the sink, looking *very* nervous.

"Come on," I said, pushed him into the farthest stall, and I reached around behind my back to latch the door. And no, in case you're wondering, this was not the first time I'd done this. (*Now* you know how I met Darwin.) "This will be lots more entertaining."

I unzipped my fly and pushed my pants down.

"Wait—what about the play?"

"Don't worry," I said, ripping open a condom with my teeth. "I'll tell you how it ends."

The smart ones among you will have guessed that that lucky guy getting banged under the Longacre Theatre was none other than our old friend Jeff Bornic. (Remember when I bumped into Jeff walking Haggis in Chelsea Park, and I remembered I knew this guy from somewhere?)

Time to do some quick calculations.

Roger said they'd been together since just before the holidays. Let's say, November or so of last year—*ten* months ago. And Harry Potter's aunt brought her Medea over here just in time to be eligible for a Tony Award (she didn't get one), toward the end of April. So our sordid little second-act number was maybe—at most—hmm—*five* months ago.

Yep, I had—without knowing it—done Roger's boyfriend in a toilet stall while Roger was home, sick and miserable, and Harry Potter's Aunt Petunia was overhead, slaughtering little children and acting up a storm in a great work of the classical drama.

So.

Kids.

Imagine how I felt, hearing Roger defend this smug, self-righteous, hypocritical little prick because, unlike me, *he* at least was faithful.

Chapter 16

The Old Folks at Home

ROGER

Okay, it wasn't really a recital, just an afternoon entertainment for some old people in a senior citizen residence on the Upper East Side. Forty-five minutes, light music. We play for them a couple times a year, among other senior centers, and we've learned that if you play longer than that at these places, or give them anything serious, they will fall asleep. Some do, even so. Or the really batty ones will just start to yell about it.

So. Light music. We have an arrangement of "On the Beautiful Blue Danube" by Johann Strauss Jr., and we do a Latin number that's very camp and a lot of fun called "Tico Tico." That sort of thing. I had worked up this medley of show tunes they would know, and I had my Gershwin medley that I'd arranged a couple years ago.

Punch and cookies after. It's a party.

In any case, all of this music works for these occasions. We save the other stuff—Schubert, Beethoven, et al.—for other events.

Three of us were there, already setting up and settling in, when Katrina came barging through the double doors at the back of the room like a terrorist attack, lugging her violin case, a jumbo tote bag, and her famous music stand. As noted earlier, she's a big girl, and it doesn't seem to faze her.

Her coat was positively flapping behind her.

"My God," Bob said, "she looks like Cruella de Vil on an off day."

By which time she was on top of us, slightly out of breath, beaming, and started pulling off her coat.

"Wow, Katrina—is that Chanel?" asked Janine.

Katrina stopped, looking over her shoulder to Janine.

"Possibly." She smiled slyly.

"You should have warned us, Katrina," Bob said.

Under the coat, she wore a sleek black cocktail dress. And pearls, of course.

"What?"

The three of us were dressed considerably more casually—it was a warm day in October and sunny. Bob and I wore neckties, but I hadn't even worn a jacket.

"If you'd said something we'd have dressed up," said Janine.

"What, this? Don't sweat it—you guys are fine. But I have to get to a cocktail party *straight* after—Roger, I know you won't mind if you take my things with you. You can bring them to the office tomorrow."

Well, of course I minded. Lugging two violins, okay, no big deal, but hauling that stupid music stand back to Chelsea on the subway, not to mention carrying the goddamned thing through Midtown in Monday morning's rush hour? How incredibly rude of her to assume I'd do it, just to accommodate her social schedule. What an inconsiderate cow.

"No problem, Katrina," I said, smiling. Yeah well—the cow was my boss.

Mrs. Greenbaum, our contact at the residence, checked in with us, and then she opened the double doors at the back of the room. Immediately a group of about a dozen seniors came in, some more quickly than others. As it got to be time, I'd say we had about thirty or so geezers and geezerettes—mostly geezerettes. I didn't know if the men didn't like music, were deaf, or were just already dead.

Mrs. Greenbaum checked with us again. We were ready. The doors at the back were closed, and she was about to step out and introduce us when the double doors opened again, and—what the hell?

It was an old lady in a wheelchair being pushed in.

By Fletch. Of course.

Fletch was chatting away, flirting, and the old broad was giggling like a girl. I'm sure she'd have blushed if she'd had any circulation left. They seemed totally oblivious to everyone else, as he parked her chair at the end of the second row.

"Glad you could join us, Ethel," said Mrs. Greenbaum.

Ethel smiled, nodded, and raised a pale, blue-veined hand in gracious acknowledgment. You'd think she was Marie of Romania.

After he'd crouched down to her, said something that made her smile, patted her arm—and carefully set her brake, lest she roll off on her own—

"Thank you, Fletch," Ethel croaked with a voice that apparently hadn't spoken since the Crimean War.

—Fletch stepped to the back row and sat by the door.

He never used to come to these things. Of course I never used to invite him to these things. But then again, I didn't invite him to this one either. So why was he here? I wondered. Maybe he just wanted me to know he wasn't still mad about our fight the day before—the whole Cancun thing—whatever it was I had said/done.

He looked at me and gave a little finger wave. He looked so goofy that I had to smile a little, and I shook my head in dismay.

Whatever yesterday had been, we were good. I felt a lot better. I'm not sure why I cared, but apparently I did. Maybe I just didn't want to be an ass, not even to Fletch. Anyway, I was surprised how happy I was that he was there.

Mrs. Greenbaum welcomed us, and the old ladies clapped. It's amazing how they do it—you can see their hands moving, but there's no sound. You have to lean forward and concentrate to hear anything. Fletch clapped loudly in the back.

Instruments up, bows up, Katrina took a deep breath, and we were off.

It went well. The old ladies seemed to be lapping it up. The sixties' show-tunes medley turned into a hum-along, which was great. Somewhere during the "Blue Danube" I looked out over the top of the music stand—a couple of them were actually swaying to the waltz. And I saw Fletch, looking up at me, smiling. With this really stupid grin. Like he was proud of me?

And then he did it. Something terrible. He winked at me.

And I screwed up.

I don't even know what I did because by the time I looked back at the score, I'd totally lost my place. I stopped while the others sailed on down the beautiful Danube, so blue without me. I found my place and started playing. Out of the corner of my eye I caught the dirty look Katrina flashed me over her violin. I knew the others weren't too happy with me either. Damn Fletch, I thought. I glanced up for just a second to see if he'd noticed how badly I'd messed up, and I guess he must have. There he was in the back, head down, bent over, his shoulders bouncing in silent laughter. He looked up, all twinkling blue eyes, his lips pressed together, still trying not to laugh out loud. It was his turn for the dismayed headshake.

So what did I do?

I screwed up.

Completely lost my place. Again. Of course.

I flipped the page forward, no, flip back, no, flip forward. I'd gone too far, but I waited there for the others to catch up and joined in as they got there.

And I vowed—never, ever, ever to look at Fletch Andrews. Ever.

I need to focus, I thought.

I played very carefully, very mechanically, sweating the whole time, and when we got to the end of that damned river, I never wanted to hear about the blue frigging Danube again.

From there on, the concert went along okay. I had learned my lesson. Fletch was a landmine. Like I didn't know that already? *Stop thinking about Fletch!* I scolded myself. *Focus!*

The last piece on the program was my Gershwin medley. I'd crafted it as a shared piece. In addition to ensemble playing, each member of the quartet had a section where he was featured. It started with Katrina playing the clarinet solo from the opening of *Rhapsody in Blue*, while the rest of us played this super-reduction. After a chunk of *Rhapsody*, Janine took the lead with "Fascinating Rhythm." I'd given myself "They Can't Take that Away from Me."

Now, you may remember that which I had forgotten—that that was the song I had played for Fletch that first night he moved in, so long ago, back when it was all nervous uncertainty and getting to know each other and so much wanting and hoping, and I was so scared he wouldn't like me, and he had thought that the song was so beautiful, and how he'd kissed me after, and how wonderful it had been, how wonderful *he* had been.

That's probably what you're thinking, but *I* didn't think of it until I was playing it, and then there it was, this big, fat memory had plopped itself down in the middle of my head. In the middle of my solo.

Would Fletch remember it? I wondered. Of course he would. Was he thinking about that night right now, the way *I* was? Probably. And how would *he* feel about hearing it again?

I have to focus, I told myself.

But what was this strange feeling? I suddenly had this tightening in my chest, and I felt an enormous wave of a terrible sadness sweep over me. Was this—what? Nostalgia?

I needed to focus.

Why are my eyes burning?

Unlike the damned Danube, I'd played this piece a thousand times, and I could play it in my sleep. Muscle memory. Which was a good thing, because I couldn't see the notes any more.

I have to focus, damn it.

So I closed my eyes and played. And all this strange sadness in me, this devastating sense of having forever lost something enormously precious flowed down my right arm into the bow, and it sat in the vibrato in my left hand, and I played Gershwin's tune as I had never played it before.

The bow arm pulled the despair out in long strokes and then drove back up through the notes, pushing this aching void, this unbearable, fierce longing out into the world. The others played a supporting accompaniment, and then the melody passed back and forth between them, while I played this variation above them. My left hand moved of its own, improvising ornamentations I'd never played, the saddest I'd ever heard. I let the violin sing. No, it was more like some part of *me* was singing through that little wooden box next to my head. I realized that this was what all the practicing was for, this was what technique was for. So that when the time came, the technique wouldn't get in the way. I could forget about hand positions and double-stops, and I could just let this music open up in a way that it had never done before.

The end of the solo was a run of 16th note triplets with a ritard, to a long G way, way up there, and I held that last, long, very high note of the song, the ring finger of my left hand on the E-string not far from my face. I savored that note, as Mrs. Kleinmeyer had taught me so long ago, before I let it

gently,
gently,
gently
die.

But remember, this was a medley—another thing I had forgotten. And the medley wasn't over.

The last tune in the piece was "Strike Up the Band," a bouncing march that featured Bob on the cello. It started way down on the C-string in the bottom of the cello range, Bob would play the first line—*ba-da-bum-bum-bum*—and then we played this sort of flourish, and then Bob again, then flourish, and so on. By the time it got to the bridge, we were all playing, and it developed to a big flashy finish with lots of tremolos.

I'd written the damned arrangement, so I shouldn't have been so surprised when Bob came in, but I was, and the last thing I felt like doing at that moment in my life was striking up the frigging band. I had to wipe my cheeks with the sleeve of my bow arm, and by the time we got to the second flourish, I was able to come in only a little late. *What key is this thing in anyway?*

Not that one.

Jeez.

Focus.

In spite of me, we rallied and got to the big slam-bang ending. Well, anyway, as slam-bang as you can get with a string quartet.

The old ladies clapped enthusiastically. They must have really liked it because thirty old broads managed somehow to produce a sound like a couple of pigeons flying away.

I realized after a second that I didn't hear Fletch.

I looked out. He was still there, but not clapping. He sat quite still, his hands covering the bottom half of his face, just his bright blue eyes showed above the fingertips. I had no idea what that meant or what he was thinking. Maybe he was moved. Maybe he was laughing at me again.

Maybe he was horrified.

Mrs. Greenbaum thanked us, some old ladies came up and nattered, and then Katrina was talking to me.

"I don't know what happened to you with the Strauss, Rog, but you certainly redeemed yourself."

"I hope I wasn't too awful."

"To play a wrong note is insignificant, but to play without passion—"

"Inexcusable, yeah, yeah. You know Beethoven never actually said that."

"I had that poster on my wall for four years at Northwestern. Of course he said it. Anyway, he *would* have if he'd heard you today."

"He was deaf."

"Stop being an ass. That was really something today, and you know it." Then she seemed to think of something else. "And Fletch got to hear it. How nice is that?"

"Yeah, I didn't—you know—ask him or anything."

"He came anyway. Go figure. Anyway, good job today. I don't know where that came from, but seriously, Roger, I will never forget what I heard this afternoon."

Wow.

"Thanks."

"You are an *extraordinary* talent."

From Katrina—double wow.

Then she reminded me that she still expected this extraordinary talent to schlepp her stuff for her. And then Cruella swooped out the door in a whoosh of possibly Chanel.

One of the old ladies brought me a small plate of cookies, which I didn't touch.

I tried to concentrate on the immediate. Relax the bow, pack things away, get Katrina's scores in her tote bag, get *my* scores in mine.

What *happened* to me today?

Jeez, I need to focus.

Janine and Bob congratulated me on the Gershwin; I wasn't really listening. It only occurred to me later that I didn't know if I'd actually responded or just stared at them like a fish. When I finally looked up, there was Fletch, standing in front of me, waiting. How long had he been standing there? He was wearing a hoody, the kind with one big pocket in the front, white. A light behind him caught the golden curls like a halo. He was—just—dazzling. I could forget that sometimes.

He had Katrina's violin case slung over one shoulder, her tote in one hand and that damned music stand next to him. He opened a bottle of water and passed it to me. I didn't realize how much I needed it until it was in my hand and I gulped greedily.

"Subway?" was all he said. He took an Oreo from the plate, popped the whole thing in his mouth, and started chewing.

"Uh—yeah," I said after a second.

I collected my things. He snagged the rest of the cookies, and we walked outside.

And damn!

"It's freezing!" I said. It had been mild and sunny earlier, and I hadn't worn a jacket. Now the cold, damp air slapped me in the face. I was going to freeze my little butt off.

Fletch didn't say a word, he just set everything down, pulled the hoody off over his head and handed it to me.

"What are you doing? You'll need that."

"Put it on, Dweeb. You're still sweaty from playing. Feel your shirt! You'll catch pneumonia."

"What about you?"

"I'll be fine. I'm always fine." He took my violin from me and pressed the sweatshirt in my hand. "Put it on."

I did.

As I pulled the sweatshirt over my head, *pow*, I was hit with yet one more thing that I had not seen coming. The scent of Fletch. No, "scent" suggests something subtle, and this was anything but. With my head deep in the soft sweatshirt, still warm from him, it was just there. Male, earthy, animal, him. Something I'd forgotten but of course hadn't forgotten, a scent that was still immediately familiar, cozy even. And sexy. And very, very confusing. Two years later, and this smell brought a thousand memories racing at me, lots of them not exactly G-rated, and each one waving its hand and demanding attention. I finally pulled the hoody down and poked my head out. The sweatshirt that had been all snug and sexy on Fletch was, of course, laughably too big on me, and yet it was somehow amazingly—comfortable. No—comforting. It was like being held by him.

Jeez, listen to me, I thought. *I must be realllly tired.*

For the fiftieth time that day, I reminded myself. *Focus.*

He gave me my violin back, we picked up our things, and we walked.

I hate the Upper East Side. Jeff lives up here, and it's always a pain. You can never find a taxi, the subway cars are small and overcrowded, and they never go where *I* want to go—which is back to the West Side as quickly as possible. Inevitably I end up having to change trains to get anywhere.

For now we just had a longish walk, to the closest subway stop. Neither of us spoke. I half expected Fletch to put his arm around me, but he didn't, of course. What would I have done if he had? Bitten his head off, I suppose.

Walking together, wordlessly, but somehow in synch, in harmony. It was a lot like before. Maybe even closer somehow. It was like playing duets. When you just have the other person in the corner of your eye, you occasionally exchange glances, but you're somehow always together and you don't know how? That's what it reminded me of, a kind of silent duet.

What's wrong with me, I thought. *"Silent duet???" Jeez. Get a grip, Prescott.*

We waited for the train, the train came. Of course there were no seats, and poor Fletch with that dumb-ass music stand.

"Hey," said Fletch, "can I have my cookies back?" I had no idea what he was talking about. He gestured with his head and added, "In the pocket."

I stuck one hand in the big pocket in front of the sweatshirt—there was a bundle in a paper napkin. I gave him the little package, which he opened. Two cookies, one of which was peanut butter, which he held out to me, and I took it.

"Thanks."

He had something chocolate.

Of course he had something chocolate. He really liked chocolate. And I really liked peanut butter. We knew these things. History. I watched him chewing for a couple seconds, and he smiled a little as we lurched in the aisle of the train car.

We got off at Fifty-First Street, made a longish transfer, including an escalator that must be four frigging stories tall, and then we got on the E train, but this time we found an empty seat together.

It was what? Maybe five in the afternoon? And I felt completely drained. I found myself with my eyes closed, half leaning against Fletch's shoulder. So warm. When I realized what I was doing, I immediately sat up straight.

"Sorry," I said, a little embarrassed.

A little later, I was leaning again, nodding off.

I sat up. *I have to focus*, I thought. Today's mantra.

Another stop, and my eyes were closed and I was up against that warm shoulder again.

Screw the mantra.

Chapter 17
Pizza Night

FLETCH

I didn't want to wake him. He felt so warm and wonderful on my shoulder. I thought, who cares, let him sleep and we'll take this train to the end. As far as I was concerned, Far Rockaway wasn't far enough.

But that's the A train, this was the E, and it only goes as far as the World Trade Center. The poor Dweeb was obviously exhausted and probably as hungry as I was, so I nudged him gently as we got to Twenty-Third Street.

We had hardly said a word all afternoon, and it was somehow fantastic. You can't fight if you don't talk.

As we walked from the subway to the apartment, I thought it was a good thing I was carrying all of Katrina's crap. It kept me from trying to put my arm around him.

Instead, I had a violin slung over my shoulder, the world's biggest knitting bag full of a ton more music than they had played today, and a clunky music stand.

Why doesn't she use a collapsible stand like the others? I've always meant to ask Roger.

We got to the door of his building.

"Thanks, it was really nice of you to help me carry all this stuff."

"It would have been churlish to walk away and leave you with it."

"Churlish?" he said.

"Is that the wrong word? Didn't I use it right?"

"No. It's fine. It's perfect. Anyway, thanks."

"You can pay me back. Buy me dinner—I'm starving."

"Dinner?"

"You order pizza while I walk the Scottish terror." A familiar routine from back in the day.

"Deal." We went inside and set stuff down. We each bent over to pet the dog, who as always scooted away from us. I took the leash down from the hook, and Roger picked up the phone. He didn't need to ask what to get on the pizza any more than he needed to look up the phone number. Like violin fingerings, Roger had once explained to me. Muscle memory.

"Hey," said Roger when we came back inside. He was still wearing my hoody. "I forgot to say it—thanks for coming today. It was quite a surprise."

"Where else would I be?"

"*Lots* of places besides an old folks' home listening to a string quartet. You didn't used to come to these things."

"That's because I was a dick."

"And you're not a dick anymore?" he said, skeptical.

"Well, yeah, but I'm a much nicer dick now. And besides, I had nothing else to do." A lie—I'd given up a matinee to be there.

"And about yesterday—"

"Hey, Dweeb, don't." The last thing I wanted to talk about was a rehash of our conversation from the day before over his stupendous relationship with what's-his-face. "I had no business sticking my nose in. I'm sorry."

"No, I'm sorry. You know I'm not very good at—anger—and I'm sure I was way out of proportion—"

"Hey!" I said.

"What?"

"You don't have to apologize. Believe me. You don't need to apologize to me ever."

"Oh."

We stood looking at each other for a second. Oh man, I didn't mean for this to get weird, but I'd just made it weird. I needed to get us back. I went and flopped onto Roger's couch.

"I wasn't sure they'd even let me in—the old ladies, I mean."

"No problem?" he said, sitting in his usual chair.

"Somebody said, 'Can I help you,' and I said, 'I'm with the band.'"

"You didn't."

"I always wanted to say that. And she just pointed me toward the door. And then there was Ethel in her wheelchair, who wasn't going in because she hates music, she said, but I talked her into it, and we rolled on in together. She loved it, by the way."

"You talked her into it?"

"I told her that she *had* to go in because my boyfriend was playing, and he was brilliantly talented—and so good-looking."

"You lied."

"Only the very first bit."

"Anyway, thanks," said Roger.

It amazed me he could still blush like that over a compliment.

"And I could hardly explain that you'd *been* my boyfriend and how great it had all been and how crazy we were about each other, but then I screwed it up and I was really-really sorry—"

"Okay! You talked her into it."

"And the rest was true. You *are* brilliantly talented."

"Thanks."

"And so good-looking—" I teased.

"Stop!"

"Hey." I went for a new subject. "Did I see Bob and Janine get into a cab together?" I asked.

"I didn't notice."

"Is there something going on between those two? Are they a thing finally?"

"Beats me. Not that I know of," he admitted. "Finally?"

"Bob's been in love with her as long as I've known you guys."

"He has?"

"We should ask Katrina," I said—the *we* just slipped out. "She'll know."

"You're right. She'll know."

A silence followed. The silence between us on the train had been an easy, comfortable one, but this was a little strained.

"Hey," I said. "That waltz was really beautiful. I'm sorry I made you mess up."

"No you're not. You loved it."

"Maybe a little."

"Jerk."

"The whole program was really nice, Dweeb. And then—you know—there was that song."

"Yeah."

He knew which one I meant.

"I told Ethel you were brilliant, but I didn't know you were *that* brilliant."

"Thanks," he said quietly.

"Honest, it was really beautiful. Moving. I'd never heard you play like that."

"Me either!" He almost laughed a little. "I was pretty surprised, too! Even as I was playing, I knew I'd tapped into something. Wish I could figure out how to do that *all* the time."

"And, of course, you know, it made me think of that first night."

"Yeah. Me, too."

"It's a good thing I don't cry," I said.

"Get out," he said, and he hit me with the little couch pillow.

"I'm serious!" I said.

I had to wonder. Had he played like that—for me? Or because of me? At least a little bit? I know that sounds like more of my usual egotism, my mind-boggling hubris, but really—it couldn't be a coincidence that he played like *that* on *that* particular song, could it?

"Something I've always wondered about—but hearing you today—I mean—you don't seem to like being a lawyer much…"

"So why don't I pack it in and go fiddle for a living?"

"Yeah. Something like that."

"Weddings, christenings, bar mitzvahs?"

"You know what I mean."

"I know—I'll combine the two careers. I can write your prenup, play at your wedding, and then handle your divorce. Bundle, and save big."

"Dweeb."

"There's lots of reasons, and the first is that I don't think I'm really good enough."

"I can't believe you think that."

"Another reason is—I'm scared. I *might* make a living at it, but what if I end up playing *Phantom of the Opera* eight times a week?"

"Still…"

"And then there's the traveling. Face it, professional musicians travel. Can you really see me living out of a suitcase? In hotels? No Scottish terrier?"

"Someone—you know—somebody could look after the dog while you're—"

"Teaching." He pushed back the curls from his forehead. "I've thought about teaching. I taught some when I was an undergrad, and I really liked it. I could imagine doing that and being happy." His face was suddenly soft, all the lines vanished.

"I bet you'd be really good at it, Dweeb."

"And then playing on the side wherever. Chamber music—or who knows? Maybe even *Phantom*. But I absolutely draw the line at *Les Miserables*."

"So?"

"So—what do I have against *Les Miz*?"

"So why don't you?"

"Well, there's my family, my father, my *grand*father. There are expectations."

"But still, if you're really unhappy …"

"And, of course, there's a lot more money in helping rich people stay rich than in giving the kiddies fiddle lessons."

"We've never really talked about money, but, Roger, seriously?"

"Let's *not* talk about money."

"You brought it up." Of course I'd picked up—mostly from Tommy—that there was a lot of money in Roger's family, and a lot of pressure. "I'll just say this—how *les miserables* do you want to make yourself over something that doesn't matter? But of course if you stick with the law, Jeff has big plans for your career."

"Yeah, I know."

"Congrats, Dweeb. You're going to be New York's next big power couple. I'll look for you on page six."

"He didn't really say that about 'power couple,' did he?"

"You know I couldn't make that up."

He sighed.

"I'll go get plates." He got up. I got up to follow.

"Hey!" I took the hint and changed the subject. "I looked up *haggis* on the Internet. Did you know it's a real word?"

"Really?" He poked his head down under the cabinets to look at me.

"It is, it actually means something. It's a food! It's this disgusting dish. They take the stomach of a sheep, and they stuff it with oatmeal and other stuff you don't want to know about, and they cook it and eat it, and that's a haggis!"

"And you found that out, did you?"

"Don't believe me?"

"Is it by any chance a specialty in—oh, maybe—Scotland?" He let me think about that for a second. "Because—what a coinkydink!—he's a Scottish terrier." He came out with plates and set them on the coffee table.

"You knew that all along, didn't you. I'm an idiot."

"Oh no, not you." He was at that moment going back into the kitchen for something else, meaning he had to pass between me and the end of the couch.

"Why you—are you making fun of me?" I asked, and as he passed me I gave him just enough of a shove that he had to fall backward over the arm of the sofa. As he went over, he tried to catch himself by grabbing my arm, which was enough to pull me off balance—okay, I *let* him pull me off balance—and I fell over onto the couch as well, on top of him.

"Are you making fun me?!!" I asked again laughing, maybe tickling him a little. "Is the snotty Harvard boy making fun of the poor street kid?"

We were both laughing and tickling, and I was reminded just how amazingly beautiful and deep those velvet-brown eyes were and just how close I was to that beauty. He was still grinning and ready to defend himself against the next onslaught of tickling. I could feel his breath against my cheek, I could smell his skin.

And aside from the beauty of his eyes and all that, I was suddenly aware of two other things:

One was in my jeans.

The other was in Roger's khakis.

Talk about your muscle memory.

Roger was just a beat or two behind me, but I saw the moment when he realized, and in that heartbeat his eyes flipped from smiling to horrified.

"Get up! Get up! Get up!" he sputtered, pushing me off him with both hands, and I jumped to my feet.

"I'm sorry, I didn't mean—"

"I can't—"

"It's okay! I wasn't—"

"I'm not like you!" he snapped at me.

"Well what's *that* supposed to mean? You seemed every bit as keen as I was!"

"I wasn't going to *do* anything!"

"Neither was I!"

"As if!"

"Hey. Roger," I tried quieter, calmer. "Today was really nice. I really enjoyed being with you, hearing you play. Please don't wreck it."

"Too late."

"Please?"

"You need to go."

"Look, the pizza will be here, we can just eat. I promise, no touching."

"I know how good you are with promises."

"But I'm starving!"

"Tough noogie!"

"Roger, I'm sorry that happened, but it was no big deal."

"That's how it is with you. It's no big deal. It's never a big deal. It's not important. You're so frigging irresponsible!"

"Irresponsible? I will gladly take responsibility for exactly *half* of what just happened. How's that! Your turn!"

"Great, it's all just a game to you, a big joke. I'm serious!"

"So am I!"

"You go through life with your fly open, and you think it's okay! Well, it's not okay! I can't do that. I'm not like you, and I don't want to be like you!"

"Fine! I never wanted you to be like me or anybody else! I—I like you the way you are!"

In my frustration I had almost blurted out a different verb. Maybe I should have, but I was too chicken. Maybe if I had, it would have sped this along.

Or maybe if I had, he'd have thrown me out for good instead of just temporarily. Doesn't matter because, like I said, I was too chicken, and in that moment, I was more than a little peeved.

"Please—just go!"

"Fine!" Man-oh-man. It's funny, considering what a great guy he was and how clearly out of my mind I was about him—he could still really piss me off sometimes. "Fine! I'm sorry! I am so frigging sorry!" I yelled and threw my hands in the air as I went to the door. "You know, for somebody who prides himself on how logical and reasonable he is—you can be *so* stupidly *un*reasonable sometimes."

As long as everyone was yelling, Haggis decided to weigh in with a couple barks of his own. "You tell him!" I said to the dog. I pulled open the door and turned back to him. "So fine! I'm leaving! Forget I ever touched you!"

And *bam!* Then *thump-thump-thump* down the two flights.

Out on the street, I tried to calm down. Deep breaths. I had no idea what just happened.

No, that wasn't true. I knew. We had wandered across a border neither of us had intended to cross. And it scared him.

I took another deep breath. Holy moly, it was cold.

And the Dweeb had my hoody.

Chapter 18
3:32 a.m.

ROGER

"Forget I ever touched you," he said.

As.

Fucking.

If.

Chapter 19
For the Guy Who Has…

TOMMY

"It's weird having you around again," I said as we stopped at a corner.

"Admit it, Tommy. You missed me," Fletch said, and he gave me the hugest squeeze while we crossed the street. "Admit it, admit it."

"Okay! Okay! Cried-myself-to-sleep-every-night, now get off me, ya big palooka!" He did. *"Thank* you!" I shook my jacket straight again. "Now. What exactly are we looking for?"

"You know!"

We were bumbling through Soho with all those cute little shops, and they were all decked out for Halloween. Totally kitsch and I adored it. You don't even want to be *around* me between Thanksgiving and Christmas—I am my own Hallmark movie. But there I go, digressing again.

"I know we're birthday shopping for you-know-whom," I said, "but for what specifically?"

"I don't know—I want to find something that suits him, that he'll like, but that he wouldn't buy himself."

"That Jeff wouldn't think of."

"Yeah, well, that too. And thanks, by the way. For coming along and helping."

"Don't thank me yet. I'll probably be useless," I said.

"You know him better than anybody."

"You know him pretty well yourself."

"I suppose. But seriously I want to get him something that's—you know—perfect."

"Big chance to impress, eh?"

"Something like that."

"So you want to find something that will make him realize that you're actually this fantastic and deeply sensitive person, not just that cheating bastard who shattered his precious little heart into a million pieces."

I had to stop and turn around because Fletch was about twenty feet behind me and looking like Lot's wife right after she remembered she'd left the kettle on. From the expression on his face, you'd think I'd kicked his puppy or something.

"What?" I said.

"You know, if I didn't have that coming, you little twink, I'd stuff you down a manhole somewhere."

"I might point out that stuffing things into manholes is how you got into all this—"

"Okay! Okay!"

"Besides. You *do* have it coming, and by rights I shouldn't even be speaking to you. It's my best-friendly duty to be at least a little bitchy to you now and then, don't you think? But I figure, if Roger can put up with you…well c'mon. Let's go shopping." I led him across the street.

"You're a real human being, Tommy."

"I know. Of course if you blow it this year," I chirped cheerily, "you can always try again next year." And you wouldn't be*lieve* the dirty look he gave me. "All-right-already! We'll see what we can do!"

We kept walking.

"That sweater is the cutest thing," I suggested and went to the window we were passing to inspect it more closely. It was totes sharp. Black. Was that cashmere maybe? With the coolest asymmetrical collar.

"Roger would never wear that. Would he?"

"Roger?! Not in this life. But it would look fab on me, doncha think?"

"Tommy!" he said, scolding.

"Hey, I have a birthday coming up too, you know."

"In February, isn't it?"

"Right. Around. The corner."

"Tommy—concentrate."

"Okay, okay." I tore myself away from the window, making a mental note of the store. Da-yam, that place is always *so* expensive, but that sweater was *mine*, goddamnit. There were some nice shoes in there too. I heaved a mighty sigh, like the tragic hero that I was, before I scampered to catch up to Fletch.

"The thing with Roger is," I said, tugging Fletch's arm to slow him down—you can*not* shop properly at that pace. "He can obviously buy himself whatever he wants."

"Unlike you and me."

"Very unlike you and me. But, on the other hand, he doesn't buy himself diddley."

"Unlike you."

"Unlike me."

"Is he still convinced the law firm is going to let him go?"

"I think he goes to work every day half expecting to get canned."

"You know what's going on—is that really gonna happen?"

"Strictly between you and me and not a hint of it to Roger-Dodger—yeah, probably. From what I can tell, it's what they do with baby lawyers. They're testing out who's partner material and who isn't. They try 'em out, squeeze a few years' hard labor out of 'em, and then they start culling the herd. And every year there's another group of eager little first-years that comes in right behind the last one."

"That's messed up."

"Meanwhile, yon Jeff over at his firm is going to make partner in a couple years."

"Which is messed-upper."

"So. Whereas Jeff has all his shirts custom made for him, with his initials cunningly embroidered on the cuff so everyone will *know* his shirts are custom…"

"Roger still gets his shirts online at shy-gayboys-dot-com."

"Exactly." We walked a little longer.

"How is he?" Fletch asked out of nowhere.

"Who?"

He gave me a look.

"What do you mean? You see him all the time."

"He seems sad, or is it just around me?"

"He's been a real mess."

"Because of me?"

"Oh hells yes."

"Thanks. Now I feel so much better."

"That's not my problem, kiddo."

We stopped in front of a window.

"Actually, he's better since you resurfaced—do *not* read too much into that," I said, but I could tell he was starting to buck up. I wasn't at all sure that was a good thing. "It's just an observation, not an endorsement. But he was worse before."

Apparently that gave him something to chew on because he didn't say a word for the next two blocks, when something else caught my eye.

"Wouldja take a look at that," I said quietly. There, looking in the window of the next shop was an amazing work of art, a glorious natural wonder, this guy who had obviously just stepped off an Abercrombie shopping bag. The cheekbones alone made me momentarily light-headed. Then there was the jaw, those lips, and that chest! And my God did those pants fit nice. I wanted to applaud.

"What?" Fletch said. "Something else I can get you for your birthday?"

"If you did, Fletch, I would be for*ever* grateful."

He went over to the window and stood there looking at the mannequins inside. I was about to say something, but hey, I can be discreet, and besides, it might be fun to watch the Fletcher in action. I stepped away to go check out some headlines at the newsstand on the corner. From there I could still see really well, but I couldn't hear.

Fletch stood there, right next to Mr. A&F, and he didn't even turn his head. *Damn,* I thought, *how cool can you be.* This was what it was like, cruising in the big leagues. I obviously had a lot to learn. I waited for Fletch to make his move. Any second now. I bet you could *smell* the hotness from there.

Shopping-Bag Boy, in contrast to Fletch, had most definitely noticed the change in his surroundings, and he had lost *all* interest in winter fashions.

The guy said something. Fletch turned to him, smiled, and said something back. Okay, I thought. This should be good.

Cheekbones moved a little closer, with eyebrows raised. Fletch said something and the guy said something and put his hand on Fletch's arm. I figured that that was about the end of my outing with Fletch. And Fletch said something, and the model said something, and then Fletch came over to me, no doubt to tell me to get lost.

"I didn't see anything for Roger, did you?" he said instead, and he started walking again.

He was just walking away? He was going to leave all that unmitigated man-hotness standing on the sidewalk, untouched and looking stupid?

Well, call me Ishmael.

I jogged to catch up with Fletch.

"What was it you wanted me to look at?" he asked.

"You didn't notice the totally gorj runway model you were talking to?"

"What? Him? You idiot, I thought you were talking about the jacket or something."

"I can't even. So what did he want?" I said. He gave me another of those looks. Okay, stupid question.

"He said he wanted to buy me a cup of coffee"—and here he dropped his voice to a stage whisper—"but just between you and me, I think he had something *else* in mind."

"And you shut him down???"

"I've kinda sorta lost my appetite for it these days."

"Well. Da-yam," I said. I was nonplussed. Seriously, if *Fletch's* libido could shrivel up, we were *all* in terrible danger.

"Fletch, that was the most beautiful guy I've ever seen, present company excluded, and you turned him down?"

"He was pretty good-looking, but, honestly? You see hotter guys at the opera."

Wow. I was pretty sure he wasn't talking about Alexander Skarsgård. My turn to have something to chew on.

We walked for a bit longer, seeing nothing in the shop windows that called out "Roger-Roger-Roger."

"Tommy," he said out of the blue, "I want this more than I ever wanted anything."

"You're not talking about something from…" I gestured vaguely at the Banana Republic window we were standing in front of.

"No!" he said.

"Good, because that would be gross. You're talking about my best friend?"

"Yep."

"Soooooooo, you wanna know what I think your chances are, right?"

"Yeah, something like that."

"I don't know. I honestly don't know."

"I almost thought something was going to happen last Sunday." He started walking again, and I started walking again.

"Really?" I couldn't believe Roger would let anything happen.

"We got a little too close, and Roger sort of panicked."

"He's not like you, Fletch."

"Funny you should say that."

"*Roger* has a conscience. He's not going to cheat on Jeff."

"Jeff."

"But you know as well as I do, Jeffrey's not your real problem here. I think Jeff was a Band-Aid."

"And now, what? The wound has healed?"

"Scabbed over maybe."

"Ooh, real pretty."

"I try," I said. "You know me, always struggling to find *le mot juste*. But hey, listen. You better be serious about this, because if you hurt him again, I will personally hunt you down and—"

"I swear, Tommy. The last thing I want to do is hurt him again."

"Okay," I said. "You've been warned."

"So what *is* the real obstacle, do you think, if it's not Jeff?"

"That would be you, bucko."

"Me?"

"I don't know if he'll ever forgive you." Fletch sighed and he looked like he was the saddest Pierrot doll from my little sister's sad Pierrot doll collection. "You know," I said, "you're pretty cute when you're serious."

We never did find anything for poor Roger. Fletch still had a few days to come up with something.

We parted at the subway entrance, going different directions. I stopped at the top of the stairs and looked at Fletch for a second.

"Do you remember I said I'd never forgive you for hurting him the way you did?"

"Yeah."

"There's one way you can redeem yourself."

"Really? What do I have to do?"

I considered for a couple seconds what exactly I wanted to say and if I should be sticking my nose in here or not. Finally I answered him.

"Make it right," I said, and I turned and went down the steps into the subway—like Orpheus, I liked to think.

Chapter 20

No, Really, You Shouldn't Have!

ROGER

I was practicing when the doorbell buzzed, and Haggis launched into his usual imitation of a blood-crazed berserker. Between the buzzer and the dog, it shattered me. Every. Single. Time.

I figured it was Jeff coming to surprise me. It was my birthday, so it was possible, and I buzzed him in without thinking. Then I remembered—Jeff had his own keys. Must be a mistake. I went back to practicing until there was a knock on the door, and *another* round of barking mayhem, and now was I getting irritated.

Jeff wouldn't buzz and he certainly wouldn't knock. I went to the door, ready to yell at the Jehovah's Witness I expected to see there. Okay, like I would ever yell at a stranger at my door. Nor had a Jehovah's Witness ever actually come calling. Did Jeff send me flowers or something? Some salesperson probably.

"Haggis, I hear it. That's enough." He settled into a low growl as I pulled the door open.

No flowers. And for some reason, this salesperson had a little boy with her—a little boy clinging to a tiny violin case.

"Mr. Prescott?" the woman said.

"Yes?" I said with some worry.

"We're here for our lesson." Definitely not a sales person, definitely not a J. W.

"Excuse me?"

"We're supposed to explain—there was an ad for a free violin lesson, and we spoke to the man, and here we are, exactly on time, like he said. Hello, nice doggy," she said to Haggis, who was doing his usual in-depth ankle inspection.

"Haggis, stop. I'm sorry, but I didn't place any ad, and I don't teach." At this point my cell started ringing in my pocket. Jeez Louise. Never rains but it hails. All I wanted to do was practice! I was still holding the violin and bow in my left hand.

"Oooh, that's lovely," the kid's mother said about my ringtone, which was me playing a bit from *Scheherezade*.

"Thank you," I said, as I stepped inside to lay the violin on the piano. They followed me in, while I was fishing the phone out of my pocket. "I'm sorry for the confusion, but I don't know where you—" I was trying to explain over the violin solo.

"You should take that," she said of the call I was about to ignore.

"I beg your pardon?"

"He said to tell you to take the call. That'll be Fletcher."

"Fletcher." I glanced at my phone. She was right. Of course it was Fletch. "Just a second."

I swiped the screen on the phone.

"Have you met Trevor?" said Fletch before I could give voice to my compounding annoyance, or even say hello. And to piss me off still further, he sounded totally chirpy about something.

"Trevor?" I said. The woman nodded smiling and pushed the little boy forward half a step.

"He's adorable, isn't he?" Fletch said.

"Fletch, what *is* all this?"

"It's Trevor! He's your first student! You said you thought you might really like teaching, so…"

"So you hooked me up? With an eight-year-old?"

"Nine!" the woman said, pulling her child back toward her.

"Is this a joke?" I turned to the woman. "Is this a joke?"

"I hope not." She pulled the kid tighter.

"Fletch, you should have said something—why didn't you ask? I'd have told you, if nothing else, that today is not really—I don't imagine you remember, but it's my birthday."

"Of course I remember! And—ta-da! Trevor!"

"What?"

"I know you hate surprises, but still, look at him! I even bought the cutest, dinky violin, a 'liddle-fiddle.' Happy birthday, Roger."

"You're kidding."

"Definitely not. Now go play. Have some fun."

And the son of a bitch hung up on me.

A student? I stared at the phone. It was ridiculous! I had the day all planned out but now this, this Trevor thing. God, I hate surprises. Fletch knows that. And here was this four-foot-nothing surprise, whose little high-tops—exactly like Fletch's but in the teeny-tiny version—seemed to be a source of great fascination for the dog.

"Haggis," I said. He ignored me.

And this little surprise was standing in my living room!

You know, if Fletch wanted to give me a *real* surprise, he should leave me alone and not screw up my schedule. Now *that* would be a surprise, *and* something I'd actually like! But no, wherever Fletch finds order, he has to mess it up. He *is* entropy. The Prince of Chaos. He loves to make trouble for people, especially for me, and I'm sure he thinks it's really funny. I bet he's laughing himself sick right now, knowing that he's ruining my day—my birthday!

This was so like him.

No, it wasn't either. It was actually a new low, involving total strangers in his stunts. Doesn't seem to bother him in the least that he's embarrassing this woman, not to mention what he's doing to this poor little kid just so he can have a laugh and wreak his havoc in my life. Such a selfish, irresponsible, thoughtless jerk. I should really tell him—this whole let's-be-buddies thing isn't working out.

I looked down at my birthday present. Great. Just what I always wanted. A mop of hair.

Now what am I supposed to do?! The kid is here, in my apartment! How am I supposed to get rid of him now? I'm supposed to teach him? I don't give *lessons*.

Here. Have a student. Take two, they're small.

Fletch gave me a student for my birthday?

Yeah. He gave me a student.

He did.

It's ridiculous. People don't—

He gave me a—

I looked back at this skinny little kid staring at the floor, clutching a violin case the way another kid would hang on to a teddy bear. My first student. Maybe. Oh my God. Fletch gave me a little boy who wants to play violin.

Really?

It suddenly occurred to me that this was maybe the nicest thing anyone had ever done for me in my entire life.

My eyes were burning.

"Everything okay?" the woman asked.

"Yes." I cleared my throat. "Everything's—I'm sorry for the confusion." I tried to regroup and not be rude. "And I'm sorry about the dog." I grabbed Haggis by the collar and pulled him away from Trevor's little sneaker. "Haggis, go lie down somewhere." He went to the couch, climbed up his little steps, and watched from there.

"Don't worry. Fletch said it would go exactly like this, including the funny little dog. So you'll give us a lesson free? Like he said?"

"You're really here for violin lessons, Mrs…"

"*Ms.* Johnson, but call me Betty. Yes!"

"Roger," I said, shaking her hand. "Okay." Needless to say, I wasn't really prepared for a student. "Has he had any lessons so far?"

"No. There were some visiting musicians at his school, and I guess Trevor got to play a violin for a bit, but that's all. And then he was so excited about it when he got home, and he doesn't really get excited. He won't let it drop, either."

"Okay then." I leaned down to Trevor, hands on my knees. "Hi, Trevor. My name is Mr. Prescott, and it looks like I'm going to be your first violin teacher. That okay with you?"

He nodded.

"You really want to learn violin?"

He nodded a little more forcefully this time. He was obviously shy, and I could obviously relate.

"Okay then." I straightened up. "Do you have anything else to say before we get started?"

To my surprise, he nodded again.

"And?"

He didn't raise his eyes from the floor, and he spoke in the tiniest voice, no more than a cracked whisper.

"Happy birthday," he said.

"Thank you," I said over the lump in my throat. "Okay, Trevor, why don't you open your case, and let's see whatcha got."

Chapter 21
And Many Happy Returns

FLETCH

Option A: Everything went according to plan, Trevor had had his lesson, and Roger had maybe found something he really liked to do. All because of me. I would be covered in glory and could do no wrong, right? And if I, completely by accident, just happened to call smack-dab in the middle of dinner (I got Tommy to find out what time their dinner reservation was), Roger would still take my call because *I* was the golden boy.

So I figured, with a reservation for 7:30, fancy-schmancy eat-slow restaurant, if I called at, say, 8:45, they'd be nearly finished, but not quite. Make it 8:43, just to be safe.

I can be a total bastard sometimes. This was one of those times. And Jeff had it coming.

Option B: Good old I'm-not-very-spontaneous Roger *didn't* actually rise to the occasion, and he kicked little Trevor down two flights of stairs—in which case, I was toast.

Deep breath.

I had my phone in my hand, watching the time. 8:42:50. 8:42:55. Three. Two. One. I pressed the phone thing next to Roger's cell number.

"Hey!" he said, picking up. He sounded really happy. He did *not* sound like somebody who had heartlessly tossed a little boy out on his little keister.

Option A had won out.

Booyah!!!

The first thing I did was doodle-oo-do-do-doo—through a very fast "Happy Birthday" song.

"Thanks!" he said.

"So?"

"I wanted to shoot you, you know that, don't you. You know how I hate surprises."

"Yeah, yeah, yeah. So how'd it go?"

"Trevor's great, and adorable, like you said. He was scratching out 'Twinkle, Twinkle, Little Star' by the end, and I didn't know who was going to faint first, Trevor or his mother. Probably me."

"Was it fun?"

"It was a blast."

"Awesome. You think you'll take them on? Regular lessons?"

"Absolutely. Although that violin you bought him is complete crap. Can you return it?"

"I'm counting on it. I need the sixty-seven bucks back!"

"That is so wrong!" I could hear the grin on his face. "*So* wrong on *so* many levels."

"True, but my heart's in the right place."

"Your heart was never the problem. It was another part of your anatomy that was tough to keep track of."

"Roger!" I said, shocked. He'd obviously had some birthday champagne.

"But, seriously, I want to return the violin pronto and find Trevor something he really can play. What are you doing tomorrow?"

"Don't you have to work?"

"I can figure it out. I'll text you, okay?"

"Cool."

"And Fletch, thank you. That was an incredible birthday surprise, and I can't remember when I've had so much fun."

"I'm glad."

"I mean it, the best birthday present ever."

"Say that again."

"Shut up," Roger said.

"You shut up."

"No you shut up." I don't know what made it so delicious—that Roger was flirting with me like a fifteen-year-old with a crush? Or that Roger was flirting with me like a fifteen-year-old with a crush while Jeff was sitting on the other side of a romantic table for two? I wondered what poor old Jeff had given him for his birthday.

"Hey, Roger, it just occurred to me," I asked, suddenly sounding all concerned and stuff. "Are you and Jeff at dinner?"

"Yeah, but he's gone somewhere. There he is. You got our coats? What about dessert? Hey! What's up with you? Sorry, Fletch, I have to go."

"Happy birthday, Dweeb."

"Thanks. Bye. Why are you all of a sudden—"

That last was obviously addressed to Jeff, just as Roger hit the disconnect.

I sat in my little house-sitting apartment in Brooklyn, also known as the Top of the World, because that's how awesome I felt.

I knew it had been small and petty of me to make that obnoxious call in the middle of dinner, and I wouldn't have done it if ol' Jeffie hadn't been quite such a monumental dickhead the last time I'd seen him. But he *had* been, so I did it.

Poor Roger. No dessert, no birthday cake, no singing waiters with sparklers.

And one more thing I was pretty sure of:

No birthday nookie tonight!

A big-ass smiley face goes here.

Chapter 22
Diagon Alley

ROGER

It had taken some doing to get the little violin out of Trevor's little hands at the end of his first lesson, but I had managed it somehow, without tears, and with the promise of a much *better* violin for his next lesson.

Monday, I canceled a late-morning meeting and blew off my entire afternoon. I wanted to return the garbage violin right away, which meant a trip to Sam Ash, the store where Fletch had bought the thing. For a music store, it's really big. I'm sure, for the average thirteen-year-old with a garage band, it's a slice of paradise. For me, it's a waking nightmare.

They had some kind of light-rock background music in the front of the store and a different light-rock in the back of the store. I swear to God I'm not making it up. The string department, such as it was, sat on the cusp between the two, so we were lucky enough to be able to hear *both.* Add to this a woman, who could actually play a little—which made *no* sense to me—bravely trying a violin, *and* a woman behind us simultaneously testing a piano. Every cell in my body was howling, "Get me out of here!"

So, when this troglodyte clerk with more tattoos than brains started to give Fletch just the tiniest hassle over the refund, I had had it.

I explained that the violin was both untunable and unplayable, that they should be ashamed to offer such a terrible instrument for sale, and that even *calling* it a violin probably constituted fraud—*and* I cited a New York State statute about the cancellation of a retail contract, which was total BS. I mean there probably *is* such a law, but I was quoting subsections by number, making the whole thing up as I went. I don't know what got into me, and all for Fletch's sixty-seven dollars. But it worked. The manager couldn't ring up the refund fast enough.

"Wow," Fletch said as we went out past the wall of a thousand electric guitars. "Roger. You were amazing. I've never seen you so—forceful."

"A little soft rock, and I turn into a beast."

"Grrr! Kinda sexy."

"Shut up and get us a cab."

From there we were off to find a new "liddle fiddle" for Trevor. I knew a much better store than Sam Ash.

We went to the shop where I had bought my violin as a teenager—in an office building just north of Lincoln Center. I knew they'd have something appropriate for Trevor. I also knew it would cost considerably more than sixty-seven bucks—but what the hell. And you can always sell a good violin when the kid outgrows it. Or quits. Or switches to bass guitar.

We waited in the hallway—it looked like any office building—there was an accountant's office, a dentist, and one glass door at the end of the hall where we waited to be buzzed in. When the buzz came, we pushed open the door with a tinkling bell. It was a small shop, with dozens of instruments everywhere you looked, rows of them covering the walls and hanging from the ceiling.

Mr. Rosen came out to meet us. He, of course, wasn't likely to forget me, not after my father and I had bought a violin that cost as much as a car. A really nice car.

"Roger, so good to see you. Look what a man you've become! What can I do for you today?"

I explained the situation, and we discussed what the best size would be—I'd measured Trevor's arms—and he went on to set out some instruments for us to look at.

I didn't know if Fletch would be bored by this, but he didn't seem to mind. He was even a little awestruck by the whole thing.

When Mr. Rosen stepped away, he finally spoke, but in a whisper.

"We should have brought little Trevor with us, you know? Like in Harry Potter. Let the fiddle pick the wizard?"

"It does sort of look like the shop in the movie but without the dust." I weighed the first instrument Mr. Rosen had laid out on the counter for me, inspecting it all around and peeking inside. I plucked the strings with my thumb, tuning as I went. It was so different here from Sam Ash. No background music, just quiet. You could really hear.

"So how *do* you pick a violin? What are you looking for?"

"Right now, just a sense of the quality, the balance. And a little bit of the tone. I'll play them later. And I always look in the f-holes because I feel like I should, not because I really know what I'm looking for. I mean, I know there's supposed to be a sound post in there, but beyond that? But I figure if there's like a dead mouse in there or something, I should probably know that."

"Wait a minute. Are you telling me that's called an f-hole?"

"Well, yeah. I can't believe you haven't heard that, after all this time. For obvious reasons," I said holding up the violin by the neck and pointing to one of the two f-shaped holes, "it's called an f-hole." And then I heard what he heard. "How old are you, thirteen?"

"I'm just sayin'. Hey, nice f-hole, buddy."

"Grow up." I was working my way through the line of violins slowly.

"That guy at Sam Ash was such an f-hole."

"Stop."

Fletch let it rest. For about twenty seconds.

"Okay if I put my finger in your—"

"Hey-hey-hey!"

"Okay, okay. I'll behave. So how'd you choose your violin?"

"Well, I suppose the Harry Potter thing isn't that far off, now that I think about it. We'd decided I needed a better violin than what I'd been playing, and the shopping began. I looked at a lot of instruments over a period of about a year, I guess. The awful thing is the violin I have was one of the first Mr. Rosen showed me. It was really good, so much better than anything I'd ever played, but—don't laugh—I was only fifteen—I wanted something French or Italian. Something sexy, you know? And my heart was set on finding a violin with a dark red finish. In my head I knew I'd be brilliant with this beautiful dark red violin. You know, like in the movie?"

Fletch had clearly never seen the movie.

"Anyway," I went on, "I figured, we were going to spend all this money on the thing, so I should be able to get whatever I wanted, right? But Mr. Rosen had shown me this violin. On the one hand, it was fantastic. On the other hand, it wasn't red; it wasn't from Italy. It was from some town called Mittenwald? Not quite so sexy as Cremona. And it was too brown. Not dark brown, not golden brown, not honey, not amber. Brown. Shit brown. Diarrhea brown, when I wanted to be really vile about it. But when I played it—okay, sparks didn't shoot out or anything—it would have been helpful if they had—but it seemed somehow easy to play. It was easy to get the sound from it that I wanted. It projected beautifully, without being harsh sounding or cutting, although I could get an edgy sound from it when I wanted. That make any sense?"

I was working my way through the violins on the counter, although I had yet to pick up the bow Mr. Rosen had set out for me.

"And then?"

"Well. It was the wrong color. So I kept looking. Because I wanted that deep red lacquer, damn it. Of course I didn't *say* that to anybody because even *I* knew it was pretty stupid. And for the next few months, I looked at lots of different dealers all over, we visited shops in Boston, we took a trip to Philadelphia. We'd even talked about flying out to Los Angeles. I played a *lot* of really nice violins. I'd also come back here a couple more times, tried a couple more instruments, and each visit I spent a little more time with that humble brown violin from Mittenwald, mostly just to convince myself that I *didn't* want it, in spite of how nicely it played. To remind myself how very *brown* it was. But whenever I came in, Mr. Rosen was sure to set the Mittenwald out along with whatever else he was going to show me."

I picked up the bow from the counter.

"You were fifteen? You weren't alone on these shopping trips," Fletch said.

"No. My dad. My infinitely patient dad was taking me wherever I insisted we go next. My infinitely patient, high-powered nine-hundred-plus-an-hour litigator dad took the time out of his life to drive me and stand quietly in the background with his Blackberry."

"That's—really something."

"Yeah, it was. And I'm sure Mr. Rosen was probably sitting back there the whole time, wondering when I'd finally catch on and figure out there was a reason why I kept coming back to play the Mittenwald. He had heard what I had heard, how responsive it was. But I was an idiot, and I took a violin out on loan from a shop in Boston. I tried it out in my lessons and in the school orchestra. And I took it back. Then I borrowed another one and so on. And then I was back here, dicking around, deliberately avoiding playing the Mittenwald, and Mr. Rosen suggested I try it on loan for a month. What could it hurt? So I did, and then I asked him for another month, and finally one day in my room doing études, I realized—that plain, brown, German violin was it."

"The violin you have now?"

"Yep. This one is nice," I said about the third instrument I had been messing with.

Mr. Rosen came back with two more cases and slipped out again.

"Do you hate your little plain violin then?"

"Oh God, no! I love that fiddle! The thing was, after two months, it was time to give it back to Mr. Rosen, and—I didn't want to. That's how I knew. *And*—I have to add—when I told my father what I wanted to do, that after all this brouhaha, I had chosen a violin I'd tried in the first week of this yearlong search—do you know what my high-powered lawyer-dad said about all of his very expensive time I'd wasted? Not a word."

"Wow. Awesome guy, I guess."

"He is. I forget that sometimes. And back to your question, I definitely picked the right instrument for me."

"The violin chooses the wizard, Harry," Fletch said in a crackly voice. "It's not always clear why."

"Apparently. Because now—God's honest truth?—I wouldn't trade that little Mittenwald for a Strad."

"Seriously?"

"Seriously. I even love the very brownness of it."

"Mittenwald is in Germany? We should go there on a trip sometime."

"Yeah, we should! That's a great idea. It's in the Alps in Bavaria. I'm sure it's really pretty." But Fletch had forgotten himself, and so had I. I wasn't going anywhere with Fletch. "I mean, yeah, I should."

"Yeah, you should." He had heard the distinction. I played a little of the Bach Chaconne. "Or Cancun," he said a little louder. I played a little louder. "I'm sure the Yucatan is a *lot* like Bavaria," he said.

I hammered a couple of loud sforzandos at him in response. We looked at each other for a second.

"Don't be an f-hole," I said and I went back to noodling.

Each instrument had a little handwritten card with the maker and date—none of these was particularly old—and the price on the back. Fletch had just flipped one of the cards over.

"Whoa!" he said. "I had no clue it was going to be so expensive. I know this was my idea and all, but—"

"Don't worry. I'm buying the violin. It's totally okay."

"Are you sure you want to spend this much?"

"It's fine. It's not that much."

"I guess I shouldn't ask how much your plain brown Mittenwald cost then."

"No."

I picked up the bow and went back to the third one, a French violin from the 1970s. I tuned. Violin playing = endless tuning.

"Fletch, you don't have to stick around. This must be really dull."

"Are you kidding? The Dweeb in his element—I wouldn't miss it for anything."

He must be crazy.

After I'd played all seven violins on the counter, it came down to three, but I kept coming back to the French one.

"You sure you don't want the dark red one?" Fletch asked.

"I'm sure." The French was a very light blond color.

"I thought the chocolate brown one was the prettiest."

"No, this is the one."

I spent a little time picking a bow, a little more playing just to be sure, and Mr. Rosen and I settled on a price for the violin and case, the bow, a cake of rosin, a collapsible music stand, some beginner books Trevor could start with, and a couple books on violin pedagogy for me.

Mrs. Rosen wrote up the sales receipt. A small, round woman with curls that I remembered being red, but which were now gray, she smiled up at me as she passed me the charge slip to sign.

"For a little boy or a little girl?"

"A little boy," I said.

"Trevor," said Fletch.

"I'm sure he'll make you two very proud daddies." The woman positively beamed at us.

I sort of gasped, but Fletch—as always—was too fast for me.

"We certainly hope so," he said, beaming right back. "Don't we, honey?" He squeezed me with one arm and kissed me on the cheek, still grinning.

"Thank you for your help, Mrs. Rosen," I stammered.

"Thank *you*!"

Fletch picked up the large shopping bag, and held the door for me.

"Buh-bye!" he called to the Rosens, and we went down the hall to the elevator.

Neither of us said anything until the elevator doors were closing. We both looked straight out.

"Sometimes I just hate you, do you know that?" I said calmly.

"No you don't."

"I do. I really do."

We stepped back out onto Sixty-Seventh Street. There was a nasty, cold wind.

"C'mon, honey," said Fletch. "I'll buy you some hot chocolate."

Chapter 23
A Viking Raid

FLETCH

And do you think there was a pushcart around selling hot chocolate? No.

This is New York, you're supposed to be able to find anything, right? But we didn't, not until we were in front of that big, ugly, way-upscale shopping mall thing on Columbus Circle, where there was a truck in front that sold Belgian waffles and "dinges," whatever they are, and some seriously amazing hot chocolate. So we stood leaning against the marble façade next to a mannequin-filled window where we were out of the wind, and we watched the world go by. Okay, Roger was watching the world. You can guess who I was watching.

What a fantastic afternoon it had been. All this time with Roger, no fighting. Just being with him felt good. Maybe Roger was starting to think so too? And this Belgian cocoa was totally rocking my world. Roger even had a little bit of whipped cream on his nose—you tell me how this day could get any better.

I had also noticed that, under his coat, he was wearing my hoody. Way too big on him, it was over-the-top cute.

"Thanks for coming with me, Fletch. You must have been really bored."

"Not for a second."

"Really?"

"Really." A glimpse into Roger's world. I was fascinated. "I had fun, honest."

"Especially the two-daddies part."

"Yep, that was prit-tee special."

"Jerk."

The cream on his nose was finally too much for me.

"Hey, I was going to let you go around all day like that, but I can't."

"What?"

"You've got something…"

"Where?"

He wiped his mouth with the paper napkin.

"Your nose, Dweeb."

"My nose?!"

"Here, you want me—"

"No!" He pulled his head away from me, very Haggis-like.

"How's that?" he asked, looking at me over those freckles, his cheeks flushed even more than usual from the cold.

"Perfection."

It slipped out before I could stop myself. His eyes met mine for a second. He was surprised. I was totally surprised, too. My throat had closed up.

I looked at him, and I thought, *Just say it.* He was right there, so close. We were having a good time. *Tell him!*

I know you won't believe me, I wanted to say, *but I promise I won't hurt you. I swear—I swear on your beautiful, plain brown violin—that I will never ever hurt you again.*

We were standing a little too close, and the words were right there. *Say something!*

But while I hesitated, I was suddenly aware of a huge bulky shadow out of the corner of my eye. Somebody had stopped only a couple feet from us to stare. The sun was behind him, and I couldn't really see. Some homophobe security guard here to protect the public welfare? Or just some perv watching two boys having a moment? I didn't care.

"'Sup?" I said with the obligatory chin move, without really looking at the guy.

"Fletch?" the guy said.

I looked over—and up. Damn, he was big enough.

A huge Nordic type, a couple inches taller than me even, and lots beefier, pink face, some blond stubble that glinted a little. Wait, did I know him? A shock of reddish-blond hair hung out from under a navy-blue knit cap that went so nicely with his peacoat and blue eyes.

The bell dinged. Oh yeah. He had a Nordic name too, like Sven, but it wasn't Sven. Big guy with an amazing body that went on for days. Like a rolling landscape. A blast from the past—that needed to stay there.

"I thought it was you!" said the not-Sven.

"Hey-how've-ya-been," I brushed him off. I turned back to Roger. "Hey, you ready?"

"Oh-jeez," Roger said, glancing at the Swede, taking in the size of him. "Let me guess how you know *him*."

"Hey I'm sorry, Fletch," said Leif Ericson. "Are you two..."

"What? Us?" Roger said. "We're nothing. Absolutely nothing."

Man-oh-man. That did not sound good.

"Roger—"

"Fletch, dude, I looked all over for you—"

"Good, now go look for somebody else. Roger—"

"Hey, you boys go on ahead," Roger snarked. "Don't let *me* get in the way. You never did before, did you, Fletch?" He snatched up the shopping bag and started walking, tossing his cardboard cup in a trash bin as he passed.

God damn it!

Where was he even going? The closest subway entrance was behind us, but Dweeb was headed for the other side of six lanes of traffic.

"Roger, wait." Now *I* was annoyed. He kept walking across the huge intersection, for no reason other than he was apparently completely out of control. I followed, of course, but while Roger had the tail end of the traffic light with him, it changed as soon as I stepped off the curb.

"Wait, Fletch," yelled Mr. Stockholm, bumbling along behind me. "I don't have your number!"

"Good! Don't call me!"

"C'mon, don't be like that, baby."

Fuck. Because of traffic, we were marooned on the little island in the middle, and I turned to the big blond.

"Call me baby again, I'll put *you* in a corner."

I made a crazy dash across Broadway after Roger, who was already disappearing down the steps into the subway. Taxis were whizzing around Columbus Circle, honking as I ducked between them—and the frigging Viking was lumbering across the street behind me! How good in bed could I possibly be that somebody would risk their life to chase me across Broadway against traffic?

Okay, yeah, I was chasing *Roger*, but that was different, totally different.

"Roger!" I yelled.

"Fletch!" yelled the Norseman.

Once safely on the sidewalk, I yelled back at the giant.

"Listen, you lummox! Take a hint! Get lost!"

Poor Bjorn looked at me like I'd slapped him in the face with a dried cod, but I didn't have time to worry about his hurt feelings.

God damn, Roger could be quick when he was pissed, and his feet just flew down the steps, weaving through the crowd to the subway entrance, and then *whoosh*, his Metrocard slid through the thing and he was past the turnstile.

"Roger," I shouted, following him. "You can't be mad—"

Well apparently he could, because he'd already made his way around four gum-chewing high school girls clumped at the top of the stairs down to the trains, and he disappeared down those steps like a white rabbit on a bad day—while I was still stuck at the damned turnstile in please-swipe-again hell.

"Roger!" one of the gum-chewers yelled down the steps. "Your boyfriend's calling!" Huge squeals of laughter.

Fortheloveofgod, I swiped my Metrocard a fourth time, and I could finally push through. I skirted around the group of girls, giving them a dirty look as I went.

"Oooh, now I'm scared," one of the girls said, mocking me, which brought on more laughter.

"Shut up!" another said. "He's hot!" Now screams of laughter were following me as I trotted down to the platform.

It was getting on toward rush hour, and it took me a bit to find Roger. But there he was with the shopping bag, calmly looking down the track for the next train.

I stopped next to him and looked at him for a second. He didn't look at me, just kept looking past me down the tracks.

"Why are you angry?" I said evenly, if a little out of breath. I wanted to bring this back to the land of the reasonable.

"I'm not angry at all," he said perfectly calmly, still not giving me the slightest glance. "You don't owe me anything. That guy was seriously hot. You should totally go after him."

"Don't be like that, Dweeb."

"Stop calling me that. And I'm not mad. Why should I be mad? After all, he's just another one. I've been thinking we could have a club, you know? Him, me, *all* the guys? We could have our meetings in, say, I don't know, maybe—Madison Square Garden?"

"That guy is from like a year ago. Nobody was cheating on anybody!"

The train was pulling in. Roger watched the cars go past as the train slowed.

"Look, you don't owe me an explanation, and you don't have to hang around with me all day. Go, knock yourself out. No reason you shouldn't have some fun, and he looks like, oh, *lots* of fun. Call him."

"I'm not going to call him." The train doors opened and we stepped back to let some people get off. "I don't want to call him."

Roger stepped into the train and turned around as I started to follow him. He stopped me with one hand on my chest.

"What you *want*," he said, looking me dead in the eyes finally, "is the D train. This is the C." He snatched his hand back just as the doors closed, and I was left standing on the platform.

"This is so not fair!" I screamed at him through the door. Through the window I could see Roger stuffing his earbuds in as he turned away. The train pulled out, the cars slid slowly past, then faster, and then in a blur—and then the train was gone, nothing left behind but the backdraft. An empty potato chip bag whirled down the track after the train. A rat snuffled out and waddled along over the ties.

Lars.

The Viking's name was Lars.

Chapter24
Gym Boys

ROGER

I was in an English garden on a glorious summer day. The sun shone obliquely, the yellow light of a late afternoon in July. The lawn, the shrubs, the trees around me were all deep, deep green. Verdure, I thought. What a beautiful word, *verdure*. A dragonfly did his amazing dragonfly thing in the breeze, moving from the sunlight through the dappled shadows. I reached up, brushed some perspiration from my forehead, and—

—and that's when the earbud fell out of my left ear, and the magical summer garden—the one that I see whenever I listen to Ravel's String Quartet in F—vanished, without so much as a *poof!* I was reminded that I was actually at the gym, tired, hot and sweaty (the perspiration on my forehead had been real) and that I was furiously pedaling on an exercise bicycle going nowhere. As I reached for the earbud, I realized that it hadn't fallen out—it was dangling from Tommy's hand.

Aha! I thought, looking at Tommy. There's the poof!

"Talk to me," he yelled over the noise of the gym. "I'm bored." He was on the bicycle next to mine, of course, but sitting up straight, left hand on his hip, barely pedaling.

"You dick," I said to my dearest friend in all the world and retrieved my headphone.

Thursday evenings, we went to the gym. I suppose we went because it was the thing to do. We were twenty-something gay guys, and twenty-something gay guys in New York go to the gym. And all the gay guys who want to *pass* for twenty-something—which means pretty much every gay guy under forty. They *all* go to the gym—so we go to the gym.

Jeff, who'll be thirty next April, runs. Every morning. Blizzard, hurricane, he runs. We go to the gym. I went mostly to keep Tommy company. Tommy had his own reasons.

"Talk about what?" I asked, still pedaling.

"C'mon. Your life is way more interesting than mine these days. How's things with Jeff? How's things with the other one? How's things with Jeff *and* the other one?"

"Oh jeez. You remember Blossom Palaschak? From middle school?"

"The one we called June because she was busting out all over?"

"That's the one, and the boys used to get into fights in the lunchroom over her?"

"Yeah, why?"

"I'm Blossom Palaschak."

"Cool! You're getting boobages?" he said at the top of his lungs.

He lives for these moments, I swear. Fortunately, between the equipment noise and the headphones, no heads turned to check out my new rack.

"No, I'm not getting boobs, and it's not cool. Mutt and Jeff—they smile at each other, and then they don't. Then they swap dirty looks and snarl. I'm waiting for the fistfight in my living room."

"My, how thrilling! I adore violence."

I was beginning to hate this bicycle in a serious way.

"Is that why you've been sullen all week?" Tommy continued. "Jeff stress?"

"No."

"The other one then."

"Somehow it's always the other one."

"What'd he do now?"

"We went out on Monday to buy a violin for Trevor? And it was all fun, I was really enjoying it, and it wasn't creepy being with him, and then—and then we bumped into an old friend of his. One of his many, many old friends."

"Hell's belfry. Did the guy hit on him?"

"Yeah, kinda."

"And did Fletch…you know."

"No. He was actually really rude to him."

"Oh. So was this guy from when you two were…"

"He says not."

"Oh. Well. Rog, be fair. It's not Fletch's fault that you ran into the guy."

"I know that."

“I’m not sure I understand why you’re upset. I mean, okay, I’m sure it’s a *bit* weird, you know, when the three of you are standing there, and two of you have both ‘been to the fair,’ so to speak. Both sampled the goods and all. And I’m sure you were wondering if the two of *them* had done the same things the two of *you* had done and how did it compare—”

“And you don’t understand why I’m upset?!!!”

“Well, yeah, okay, I concede the point. But while I understand that it could be a teensy bit awks—it’s not like Fletch was deliberately trying to rub your nose in it.”

“No. He seemed pretty embarrassed about it.”

“And you can’t really be mad at him because he’s not a virgin…”

“Not a virgin? That’s a laugh. And considering how many of us there are, Fletch’s—whatevers. Fletcherettes.”

“Fletchlings.”

“Fletchlings? That’s funny. How long you been saving that one up?”

“Two years.” There were days when it wasn’t easy having Tommy Radford as your best friend.

“So, considering how many of us Fletchlings there are, it’s a wonder we don’t bump into each other more often. Face it, we are legion.”

“I know you don’t really equate yourself with all those one-nighters, do you?”

“No?”

“Fletch definitely doesn’t think of you like that.”

“I don’t know what he thinks. I’ve never seen any evidence that he does.”

“Oooh. You’re pissed.”

“I’m not pissed.”

“You look pissed.”

“I’m not pissed.”

Tommy thought about that for a second.

“You sound pissed.”

“I’m not pissed! Now shut up, before I push you down the StairMaster.” We pedaled some more, but I missed the Ravel. I’ve *got* to talk Katrina into playing that piece. But before I could get the earbuds back in my ear—

“We should get those inversion boots like Fletch had, remember?”

“I remember.”

All right then, I thought. *Enough of this goddamned bicycle.* I got off and put my face in a towel. Tommy did the same, mopping his imaginary sweat.

“We could have tummies like his,” Tommy said.

I moved over to the side to do some stretches and cool down.

Fletch had had this elaborate chin-up bar thing that he had put up in a doorway, and these contraptions he put around his ankles, anti-gravity boots, and he'd hang upside down, and do these like upsidedown sit-ups and twists and things. Hence his abs looked the way they did.

"Did you ever try it?"

"The boots? Once."

Fletch, of course, could hop up and flip upside down like an orangutan, no problem, but I couldn't possibly get up there on my own. He strapped me in the ankle things and pulled my shirt off.

"This'll just fall in your face," he explained.

He bent over sideways, put his arms around my waist, and flipped me so my feet were in the air, and he hung me up there, carefully; then he slowly let go and stepped back. I tried to do the crunches I'd so happily watched him do, but it was hopeless, and I felt sort of exposed, shirtless and skinny with my hands dangling toward the floor. I wrapped my arms around myself to hide a little, and at least my armpits weren't waving in the breeze anymore. But if I couldn't get up there by myself, I sure as hell couldn't get down.

"This isn't going to work, Fletch. Let me down."

"Are you crazy? You look so hot there."

"Don't make fun."

"I'm not! And now I've got you right where I want you." He came back, put his arms around me, and started humping his crotch against my face. "Oh, yeah, just like that, Dweeb, just like that." I had to laugh, with my face full of his shorts and what was underneath.

"Let me down, you jerk. All the blood's rushing to my head."

"Not all of it."

He started chewing on *my* shorts, and what was underneath, and what was underneath seemed pretty happy about the whole thing.

Eventually he grabbed me, unhooked me, and then there was nothing else for him to do but carry me into the bedroom and throw me down on the bed. And then, well…

"So you're not mad at Fletch about this guy in the street," Tommy said, interrupting my memory and pulling me back to reality—which was that I was standing in the middle of this noisy, hateful gym, covered in sweat, with half a stiffy in my shorts.

"No, I'm not mad," I said grabbing another towel. "I don't know. I guess I'm just disappointed. I mean, that's really my whole history with Fletch. Disappointment. I start to think he's better than he is, and then, when I'm reminded that he isn't, and wham-o."

"But he didn't do anything, not really, and if you think about it, he was the same guy at the end of the day, as he was when you picked out violins together."

"And he's the same guy he was two years ago when he was doing half of New York between the matinee and evening show."

"Ah. The sins of the Fletch."

I looked at my best friend.

"Seriously?" Because seriously.

"I'm not sure he's as bad as you think."

"He's a total whore."

"I don't think he is. We were out last week, and there was this guy hitting on Fletch, so damn hot, I swear, even *you'd* have done this guy right there on Broome Street, he was that gorgeous—and Fletch just left him standing on the sidewalk."

"When were you out with Fletch?" None of this made any sense to me.

"Birthday shopping for you."

"Oh. I didn't know." Why hadn't he said anything? I mean either of them?

"And didn't he end up doing this incredibly nice thing for your birthday?"

Wait. It was just dawning on me—Tommy was on Fletch's side? Since when?

"Yes, he did this incredibly nice thing for my birthday, and that's just it. If he could just be the same self-centered shithead all the time, it would be a lot easier. But he has these moments when he's really—I never know what to expect."

"As compared to Jeff."

"As compared to Jeff."

"With Jeff, you always know what to expect."

"Yeah!"

"Always always always."

"Is that such a bad thing?"

"Let me think—what was your extra-special romantic b-day prezzy from your boyfriend? Hm? An argyle sweater?"

"Hey, it's a really expensive argyle sweater."

"Will you ever wear it?"

"Maybe."

Tommy arched a skeptical eyebrow.

"When I'm fifty."

"My point precisely."

"Speaking of birthdays, I'm going to go before I get any older. I'm reading up a little on teaching."

I need to focus on that. On my student. My one measly nonpaying student—but I loved that I had one. I liked saying it. My student. I have to go, I have to prepare for a lesson.

Forget about Fletch, I said to myself. Think about Trevor.

"You can't go just yet. I need your help with some weights."

"Since when do you do weights?"

"Since that guy over on that bench started doing weights about fifteen minutes ago. Did you *see* those thighs? C'mon, you can spot me for just a couple minutes."

"Ask the thighs to spot you. I gotta go."

"C'mon, Roger. Be a sport."

I was already walking away, so he had to yell.

"C'mon! I'm not doing this for my health, you know!"

Chapter 25
Hanging Out with Fletch

TOMMY

Fletch's inversion boots. That reminded me of the first time I met Fletcher Andrews.

I knew that Roger was going to be stuck in the office late—even in T&E, it can happen. So it had occurred to me that I should hop over to Roger's and walk the Scotty.

When I got there, however, the door was unlocked. What the hells? I had my phone out, ready to dial 911 so they could at least hear my final screams while I was being viciously assaulted by the intruder, and, you know, maybe they could play the call on the Channel 2 news: beautiful, young, and tragically still unattached gay man violently cut down in a brutal attack, hear his final words at eleven, et cetera, et cetera.

I pushed the door open slightly. There was somebody in the kitchen, who stuck his head out over the counter to see who was there.

Gorgeous blond boy.

Hel-lo!

Hair tied back with a bandana like he was the cleaning lady. Not a lot of guys can really pull off the babushka look, but on him…

Who was he, and what was he doing here? Cooking apparently, judging from the sizzling and the smell.

Haggis poked his head around the corner and woofed once before he ran back into the kitchen with the blond. Who could blame him?

But the blond was still an intruder in Roger's apartment.

Brought up by my mother to be gracious, and ever conscious of the importance of good manners, I greeted the stranger.

"Who the fuck are you?" I said, with my thumb still poised to call in the Marines. He reached around, turned the burner off, and came out of the kitchen wiping his hands on a kitchen towel from a set I had given Roger two Christmases ago.

Holy cats, he just got better and better, the more of him you could see.

"Hi, I'm Fletch," he said extending his hand.

I backed away from him.

"Don't come any closer, I'm calling the—" Wait a sec. "Fletch? The hotness from Katrina's party?"

"Sounds like me, doesn't it? You're Tommy."

"Yeah, Tommy," I said, relaxing but still confused. My best friend had said zip to me about having an on-going *thing* with this guy.

"I was wondering when we'd meet," he said. "He's told me lots about you."

"I'm so glad because he's hardly said boo about you. And like seriously, I would remember if he'd mentioned giving somebody the keys to his apartment."

"Actually, it's worse than that. I sort of—live here—now."

"You don't either. Since when?"

"Three weeks? A little more."

"Get out."

"It's true. Look, he even let me put up my chin-up bar." He gestured toward the hallway door, where there was this thing that looked like a clothes rack with a couple bars. "So I think it's serious."

"Chin-up bar?"

"Not just chin-ups. I have these really cool inversion boots—to hang upside down, to do crunches. Great for your abs. I'll show you later." He went back into the kitchen. "You know anything about cooking?"

"No."

"Too bad. Me either. I'm making dinner. You'll stay?"

"I just came by to walk the dog. And you just said you can't cook."

"There was one of those guys on the street with a table full of used books, and he had Julia Child right there on the top for four bucks, and I figured—hey, it's a sign. And seriously, how hard can it be? It's chicken in a red wine thing, but I don't know how to pronounce it."

I glanced at the open cookbook.

"Coq au vin," I said. "And no cracks, please."

"Can you chop mushrooms?"

"Sure, why not," I said, pulling off my jacket.

"Quarter the caps. She's really specific. You might want to read the recipe."

"Got it." I checked to see what Julia had to say on the subject of mushrooms. "Wow, you weren't kidding about specific."

"The woman knows what she wants. Don't mess with Julia."

"So," I said, carefully slicing each mushroom stem on the bias, "why didn't Roger mention having a boyfriend? A live-in boyfriend?"

"I think he's a little embarrassed because it all happened so fast." Fletch was back to the stove where he was browning his chicken. "My fault, 'cause I got evicted. It just sort of—happened."

And somehow between us and Julia Child, we got chicken braising in red wine into the oven. The smell was enough to make you cry like a little girl.

Roger had told me that his party pickup was a vision of hot-nicity, but I hadn't really imagined Roger had snagged somebody *this* hot. In gym shorts and one of those loose, sleeveless t-shirts with arm openings that come practically down to the hip.

Roger, you sly dog.

If I had a guy like Fletch look at me twice, you'd have seen it on Twitter, Facebook, Instagram, Snapchat, and the Oberlin College Alumni Newsletter. In ALL EFFING CAPS.

While the casserole was in and we waited for Roger, Fletch showed me all about the chinup bar. And the antigravity boots. He strapped these weird dealies on his ankles, hopped up to the bar, swung his feet up and hooked the dealies on the upper bar. He fell back, and there he was, 190 pounds of grinning, amazeballs blond boy with his arms hanging down like a chimpanzee. If chimpanzees were hot. His knuckles were on the floor and everything. And then, while I sipped a glass of wine, Fletch showed me the exercises, like sit-ups, only hanging upside down, and what happens to your tummy when you do them.

I've seen Chartres; I've been to the Sistine Chapel; last year I went to India with my mom and we saw the Taj Mahal under a full moon—and like, seriously, they have *nothing* on Fletch Andrews hanging upside down, hands behind his head, doing crunches.

So yes, maybe I was quietly leching after my bff's new bf, but only in the most aesthetic way, the way you'd admire a painting or a racehorse. I would never touch Fletch. Some things are sacred. There are rules. Bros before—beaus. Or is it bros before hoses? Something like that.

But seriously, my best friend was sleeping with *this*??? Roger was coming home to *this* every day??? And the guy *cooks* too?!!! It is a testament to the strength of the bond between Roger and me that I didn't hate him forever and all time.

Eventually Roger came home. He was duly embarrassed and duly penitent about having kept Fletch a secret, and we all three sat down to the groaning board, aka the kitchen peninsula, because Roger had no dining room, and we had a fantastic meal of Julia's delicious coq, with parslied new potatoes and a salad, also Julia's ideas. It was brilliant.

And Fletch called Roger dweeb, which—when he said it—was just about the sweetest thing I'd ever heard.

I had to say that I was really impressed with old Rog. Not that he had landed such a blueberry stud muffin—although that, too—but that he'd done this totally reckless thing, that he'd tossed himself into a relationship like this. Having a guy move in after you've known him for like forty-five minutes was something *I* would do, not Roger—and something sensible Roger would try to talk me out of.

So I was thrilled for Roger. I was tickled fuchsia.

I, in my brief career, had had—at a guess and without counting—about a million boyfriends. Each of whom was special in his own unique—if not necessarily good—way, although I admit I may not be able to remember them all exactly.

Roger, by contrast, had had—well—not so many.

There was a guy sophomore year at Oberlin, this really pretty trumpet player from Austria named Dieter, who was a senior. (Dieter is pronounced like Peter with a D, not like a refugee from *America's Greatest Losers*.)

Roger and Dieter were a thing most of that year until Dieter graduated and toodled back to Kitzbühl or whatevs and was never seen again.

It wasn't until the *next* year, after Dieter had sung so-long-farewell, that Roger gradually learned who *else* had been sharing Dieter's little wiener schnitzel at the same time—which was apparently the entire horn section (male and female, including a guy *I* was dating at the time), two percussionists, a bassoonist who had hitherto slept only with girls, and a good chunk of the upper strings, including Roger's stand partner, Vivian. Who had hitherto slept only with girls.

Apparently Dieter's triple tonguing was *that* good.

Anyway, that was all about a hundred years ago, and since then, there had been nothing remotely serious in Roger's little world.

And now this.

But I noticed the strangest thing about Roger and Fletch together. They were shy with each other.

Sure, Fletch kissed Roger when he came in and all, like a couple. And he definitely made a thing out of being the boyfriend, lots of unnecessary touching, all very sweet. But they seemed somehow unsure of themselves.

Here's what I saw:

Fletch went into the kitchen to get plates, and Roger watched him, stared after him even. Not checking out his butt, like I would do, just watching. And it was so obvious to me that Roger was completely in love with this guy. I had never seen that look before.

And then when Fletch turned back, Roger looked away, as if he didn't want to get caught. And then I realized Fletch did the same thing. His eyes would follow Roger like he didn't want to miss a second of him. It was totally adorbs. And I thought, this is really going to work out because the gorgeous guy is clearly head over heels for our Roger. And then when Roger looked up, Fletch would be looking somewhere else.

The whole year and a half they were together, that never really changed. They got more relaxed with each other, sure, but never completely.

Later, after it all went to hell, I wondered if maybe it wasn't somehow all my fault.

I felt like if I had said something maybe, pulled each of them aside and said, "You know, he's crazy about you," maybe they'd have figured it out, and maybe all the crap that happened might not have happened. Who knows?

Looking back, I think they each felt the other was out of his reach. They had paradise, but they never trusted it.

Isn't life funny sometimes.

Chapter 26
It Was a Dark and Stormy Night

FLETCH

I was yanked awake by an enormous thunderclap. Sounded like it was right outside the window.

I was still curled up around a pillow, but with my eyes wide open. After a minute, I rolled onto my back, clutching the pillow to my chest, and I stared up at the darkened ceiling. Rain was pelting hard against the window.

Poor Haggis, I thought. I hadn't really thought of it in the last couple years, but now that Haggis was around again, or, more accurately, now that *I* was around Haggis again, I remembered: The little woofer was terrified of thunder.

The first time it happened, way back when, it wasn't the thunder that woke me up, it was the really loud barking right next to my ear. I nearly fell out of bed.

The dog never slept on the bed with us, until it thundered. Then he would climb up on the little steps Roger had for him, like the ones in the living room, and he'd sit on Roger's pillow and bark his head off. Mine too.

Roger rolled over and shhh'd him.

"That's enough, Haggis," he said.

The dog barked twice more, and then settled down to a low growl.

I rolled over and peered at Roger, his eyes sparkling in the darkness. On the pillow next to his head sat this black shadow, like a wire-haired gargoyle, still growling.

"Does he always do that?" I whispered.

"Yeah, sorry. Thunder really scares him," he whispered back.

I had said once it would be like a slumber party, and sometimes it really was. Even a barking dog in the middle of the night was sort of fun when you were whispering with Roger, like two little boys.

"It's okay, Scooby," I said. There was another rumble of thunder, and he started barking again.

"That's enough," Roger tried a little more firmly. "Wait 'til you see him on the Fourth of July."

Growling.

"Poor thing. Why do you think he barks?" I asked.

"I don't know. Scare it off maybe."

"Maybe he just wants to make sure we're awake so we know there's this really horrible monster outside."

"Could be. Could be he wants to protect us," said Dweeb.

I looked up at the dog. There was another low rumble, and the dog was shaking.

"Or maybe he wants us to protect him?" I said.

"Probably all of that. It's okay, pup," he said to the dog. "We're okay up here. Nothing can get at us."

"But don't try to get down on the floor," I said, "or the sharks'll get you."

"Alligators," whispered Roger. "I always imagined it was alligators under the bed or the couch or whatever who'd get your feet."

A distant rumble of thunder, and another bit of barking.

"Hey, Braveheart," I said. "Come here." And I reached up and pulled the dog so he was lying on his side between us, under my left arm, his back to me and his head on my right bicep. "There. You're completely safe, okay?"

There was no more growling.

"Wow, that's working," Roger said. More thunder. The dog was quiet. "His eyes are still open, but he's not barking." We lay there like that for a while. "It's funny," he said after a bit of quiet. "It's like a little family."

"Really?" I said. Seriously, how would *I* know what a family felt like?

"Really. Papa Bear and the other Papa Bear—"

"Sh," I said. "Don't wake the baby."

Chapter 27
It Was Still a Dark and Stormy Night

ROGER

The dog was sitting on the pillow next to my head, barking. It must be thundering. Sure enough, there it was. Rain was hitting the windows really hard, but it was the thunder that scared the dog.

"I swear I'm gonna open one of the living room windows and drop-kick that dog to Seventeenth Street," Jeff said from his side of the bed, still facing the other way.

"No you're not. Go back to sleep. Hey, Haggis, that's enough."

He stayed propped up on my pillow like a statue. Like a growling statue. Like a quivering, growling statue.

"Fletch used to do this thing," I explained, "where he'd put the dog under his arm somehow, and he'd go back to sleep. The dog, I mean. Well, Fletch too."

More thunder. More barking.

"Well, by all means," Jeff said, sitting up to glare at me, "let's call the Dog Whisperer and invite him over to keep the stupid mutt happy, shall we? Plenty of room for Fletch. Don't mind me. I'll just move over a little."

"Go to sleep."

"I'd hate to come between you and the Beastmaster."

The dog continued to growl.

"Shhhh." That was me. I'm not sure which one I was shushing.

There was another rumble of thunder, and Haggis barked again.

"Couldn't you at least teach that dog to use his inside voice or something?" Jeff snarled as he rolled back to the far side of the bed.

"That *is* his inside voice."

Just then there was this really terrifying clap of thunder. You could see the lightning flash at the same time. It couldn't have been far away.

The dog sprang up and started barking worse than ever, and even *I* jumped.

"For fuck sake!" Jeff took his pillow, grabbed a blanket from the foot of the bed, and started out to the living room. To sleep on the couch? Lots of luck to him.

"God, I hate that dog," he said, and he banged the bedroom door behind him.

I pulled the dog to me, the way Fletch used to, and snuggled up with him.

I stared at the closed bedroom door. I couldn't believe Jeff had said that.

Of course I had to wonder—how much was he annoyed with the dog, and how much with me? And how much was he annoyed with Fletch? How much was he annoyed with me *because* of Fletch?

Fletch—the great source, from whom all annoyance flows.

When the alarm went off, Haggis was still right there under my arm, the wire-haired hot water bottle. I scooched out from under him to hit the alarm on the phone, and to think about my day. Things to do: Deal with Jeff. Get ready for Trevor. Tommy's coming by later. Fletch was supposed to drop off dog food sometime.

I tiptoed out into the living room so I wouldn't wake the dog-o-phobe. I wasn't quite ready for Jeff if I could help it. But when I got to the living room, the couch was empty.

Sweet. The first item on today's to-do list, already scratched off.

There was a note next to the coffee machine.

Can't sleep.

Ha-ha.

Going to the office.

On a Saturday. Ha-ha some more.

Call me.

Yeah, sure, right. Before *that* was going to happen, Jeff needed to show up here holding a great big Nylabone—with a bow on it.

I grabbed the leash and turned to the dog.

"C'mon, Braveheart. Let's go piss on something."

Chapter 28
Detective Story—Part I

FLETCH

I could hear voices inside. I had a decision to make: I could knock, like a good boy. After all, this wasn't my apartment anymore. Or just use my key and let myself in. If it was just Roger and Tommy, nobody would really mind—which would be good. And if Jeff was there—well—he *would* mind, which would be even better.

I let myself in.

Sure enough, Jeff was watching TV. Was that golf? Seriously?

Roger and Tommy sat at the kitchen counter with some chips and salsa. Roger flipped through the latest copy of *Strings Illustrated*, or whatever violin magazine it was, while Tommy dicked around with his phone.

"Hey, kids," I said, hanging my jacket on the back of the empty stool. "Rog, if that's the swimsuit issue, can I have it when you're done?"

Wow, Dweeb, nice stinkface. I guess he was still sulking about our run-in with the Viking.

"Hey, Fletch," Tommy said as I helped myself to the chips. At least somebody was glad to see me. The Pupstar was too, and he was smooshing his face against my ankles. It's one of those weird Haggis things he does. I squatted down to the dog.

"Ah, Fletcher Andrews," Jeff said without turning away from the television. "Forgotten but not gone."

"Ha!" said Tommy. "I'm *so* stealing that."

"That's funny, Jeff," I said. "It really is."

"The name is Jeffrey."

What a piece o' work. My eye roll was only outdone by Tommy's, who could clearly have made a career in professional eye rolling if he'd wanted.

"Did you guys get the storm we had in Brooklyn last night?" I asked. "Wow, that was loud."

"It was pretty noisy in Queens, I'll tell you that much," said Tommy.

"I didn't hear it," Jeff said from the couch. "The dog was barking too loud."

"Awww, the poor thing!" I said about Haggis, not Jeff. Definitely not Jeff. Of course if Jeff slept somewhere else that would be fine with me. "I thought about you last night, Pupstar. I knew you would be hating it," and I squatted down to scratch the dog more seriously. "Diju keep Uncle Jeffie up all night with the barky-warky?" I cooed in loving baby talk. "Bad doggie." I kissed him between the ears and kept scratching under his collar. "Such a baaad iddow Haggis—"

"Fletch," Roger said, hoping to make me behave—

"So!" I interrupted him before he could get to the scolding part. "Tell me! How'd it go with Trevor and the new violin we picked out for him?"

"That's right! You guys had your second lesson today!" Tommy said. "I totally forgot to ask!"

I could see Roger thinking, deciding if he could still be pissed off at the guy who had given him his very first violin student.

He couldn't.

"He was great!" he answered finally. "He and his mother were both over the moon that I was loaning them this beautiful instrument. She couldn't believe I was letting Trevor take it home with him."

"Is it too big?" I asked. Roger had been a little concerned.

"No. He's a little stretched out, but his hand position is still okay, and he won't outgrow this violin right away."

"You think he'll stick with it?" said Tommy.

"Who knows? But he's really keen on it now, as is his mother, which is good. We'll see if it lasts."

"So you'll take Trevor on for real? As a long-term student?" I asked.

"Don't be an ass, Fletch. You knew I would."

"Yep." I couldn't help but grin. "Prit-tee much."

"I don't understand," said the voice from the couch, "why anyone would take on a student who can't pay."

"Trevor's lucky," I said, ignoring the jerk. "He has an inspiring teacher."

"Flatterer," Tommy mumbled. I thumped him on the arm.

"And if I may," said Jeff, still not taking his eyes from the television screen, "I'd like to interrupt this little meeting of the Mutual Admiration

Society to mention just how overwhelmingly *not* thrilled I am that my boyfriend's ex-boyfriend has keys to my boyfriend's apartment."

I had wanted to irritate Jeff, and bingo!

"Jeff," Roger said, trying to explain the obvious, "he's the dog walker. He has to get in when I'm not here."

"Okay, okay, *dog walker*." Jeff finally pulled his attention away from the all-important putt or whatever it was. "A, I would appreciate it if, on a going-forward basis, you could at least knock before you let yourself in."

"On a going-forward basis—is that more lawyer-speak?" Roger nodded. "Well then, Jeff*rey*, on a going-forward basis, I will try."

"And, B, why is the—dog walker—here on a Saturday when you *are* here?"

Oh man, my hackles were up, hearing this fuckface trying to bully Roger like that.

"I needed dog food," said Roger.

"*And*," I added, happily ending the conversation with Jeff, "I got some new treats for the Haggi-doodle."

"The Haggi-doodle?" Tommy said.

"Haggi-doodle, the Scottish poodle," Roger and I answered in unison.

"Or sometimes he's the Scottish noodle," I added.

By this point Jeff had turned back to the TV. Because you know how it is in the fast-paced, action-packed world of television golf, if you look away for even a second, God knows what you'll miss.

"Wait, there was another one," said Dweeb. "What was it?"

"You're forgetting the Scottish strudel."

"That's it. Just a few of the thousands of humiliating names Fletch has invented for my poor dog," Roger said, shaking his head. "You have robbed him of all dignity."

"At least, *I* never put a bow on his head."

"You did too!"

"That was—what?—two and a half years ago? And though I may have taken the fall for it, I didn't do it."

"You rat!" Tommy said, looking up from his phone.

"Honestly," I argued, "your dog showed up with a bow on his head, Tommy Radford was *right here* the *whole time*, and you blamed me. Does that make *any* sense?"

"When you put it like that…"

"Ow!" said Tommy, getting the overdue smack from Roger.

"*Anyway*," I said, and I tore open the bag of treats I'd brought, "I got these. There was a dog in the shop who was crazy for them."

"God, what is that?" Tommy said. "It looks like the world's biggest booger!"

"You're right, it does. And they're crunchy, too! Here ya go, Haggles."

He sniffed at it, took it, munched it, swallowed it, and then spun in a circle, jumped up, and bonked my leg with two front paws, demanding more.

"Wow," Roger said. "That's a keeper."

"What's in those things, canine cocaine?" asked Tommy.

"Are you ready for this? It's little chunks of freeze-dried cow lung."

"Ewww!" came the chorus from everybody, even Jeff—everybody except Haggis, who spun one more time.

"I don't want to hear another word about that dog's dignity," Tommy said.

"Anyway, Dweeb," I said, giving Haggis another piece and closing up the bag. "I'm really glad it's going well with Trevor."

"Seriously, Rog," said Tommy, "it's just a hoot to see you excited about something. I haven't seen you this happy since I don't know when."

"Shut up, Tommy," Jeff said, again without turning from the TV.

We turned in unison to look at the back of Jeff's head.

"I was just going," said Tommy. "Call me later?" He kissed Roger on the cheek, grabbed his coat from the hook by the door, came back, kissed *me* on the cheek, made a dismissive gesture in Jeff's direction, and he was gone.

"So, Jeff," I said after a bit—I mean, why pass up the chance to needle your nemesis? "Who's winning?" I'm not sure I was asking about the golf game.

In response Jeff zapped the TV off and got up to get his briefcase. Did I mention that's the kinda guy Jeff is? He's a briefcase guy. Not a backpack, not a shoulder bag. A briefcase. And golf on TV. He was what—*maybe* thirty? And the guy couldn't *wait* to be a middle-aged fart.

So, like I said, Jeff went for his briefcase, and I figured he was leaving, so I sat on the living room floor on the opposite side of the couch next to the dog. I pulled the squirming terrier half onto my lap, hoping to hear more about Trevor just as soon as what's-his-face was gone.

But what's-his-face didn't go. Instead, he sat *back* down on the couch and pulled out a file folder, which he laid carefully on the coffee table. What was he going to do, sell us life insurance or something?

"You know, Fletch, I had intended to do this with just Roger, but on second thought, since you're here and all, and—full disclosure—because you seriously piss me off."

"You have been nothing, if not transparent, Jeff."

"Thank you. So I've decided to give myself a treat and let you stick around."

"Jeff, what are you talking about?" asked Roger.

"A little surprise. And it concerns you anyway, Fletch."

"What could possibly concern me?" I asked the dog.

"Shhhh," Jeff said to me.

Shhhh??!!! WTF? I opened my mouth to tell him where he could put his shhhh, and he shhhh'ed me again before he went on. "Roger, I know your firm uses the same investigative agency as our firm for background checks and things."

"A private investigator?" said Roger, a little warily, as he sat in the chair instead of on the couch next to Jeff. "Not really a big part of T-and-E work."

"Well, it happens in other kinds of law, trust me, and since I had gotten to know one of the associates at the agency, and he sort of owed me a favor—"

"Was he cute at least?" I snarked.

"Fletch," said Roger, "not everyone networks the way *you* network."

"Oh my God, ask him! Just look at his face!" It was true, and Jeff's face gave him away completely. You could tell from a mile off that he and Junior Sherlock had done the deed.

"Jeff?"

"It was a long time ago, Roger."

"Good luck with *that*, Jeff. I tried that one just the other day, and I *still* got left on a subway platform—"

"The important thing *is*," he interrupted me loudly, trying to get his little train moving again, "I asked this detective guy to look into somebody for me. A certain—Andrews comma Fletcher."

Didn't see *that* coming.

What could he have dug up on me? I hadn't done anything I was ashamed of really. Okay, well maybe one or two things.

"You hired a detective? Jeff, why would you do that?" Roger asked.

"Totally for giggles," said Jeff. "I thought it would be fun."

"Since when do you do things for giggles?" Roger said.

"Well then, think of it as a scouting report. Or due diligence."

"Jeff, put that file—"

"Trust me, Roger. I got this."

"You know, I'm flattered, Jeff," I said, "but if you wanted to know something, you could have just asked."

"I learned some interesting things, too," he went on, ignoring me completely now.

"Really? What did you and Nancy Drew find out? Let me guess. I bet you clever boys put your heads together—among other things—and figured out my real name. Cool. It's Frank. Frank Szyfranski. I'd have told you, if you'd ever asked. I needed a name, and who really wants to go through life called Frank Szyfranski? What else? How about my birthday?"

"It's not June nineteenth?" said Roger.

"Kinda sorta, my ma was pretty vague about it, so I just picked one. Hey, here's one for ya. You know who my dad was? 'Cuz my ma told me she didn't know, and I was always inclined to believe her. Roger, if you want to know something, ask me. You don't need a detective, and you don't need to listen to this halfwit. Whatever you want to know, I swear to God to tell you the truth."

"Ohhhhh, I'm sure," Jeff said all sarcastic.

I had to ignore him or punch him, so I chose ignore.

What a mistake.

"Seriously, Roger, what do you want to know?" I tried to look up at him, over my shoulder, but I couldn't really see his expression. "That I was in foster care? That I lived on the street for a while? Is that in your file, Jeff? What?" My mind was racing. Jeff looked even smugger than usual, and it was throwing me into a panic. Oh fuck. "Juvie?" I looked from Jeff to Roger. "I never lied to you about any of this, Dweeb. It's nothing I like to talk about, but you never asked, so I…"

Why didn't Roger say something? If not to me, then why wasn't he telling this tool to go piss himself? *That* scared me more than this amoeba. Or was this just Roger's revenge—for all my crap? Maybe it was his turn to smile and watch me suffer?

"Hey, Jeff," I said. "I know something you might have in your folder there—you know where my ma is?" Talking about my past, I could hear my accent drifting back. "After I went into foster care, I never heard from her again." Damn, Roger, say something. "I don't know if I really want to look her up or anything, but I wouldn't mind knowin' where she's hangin' out these days."

"She's dead." Jeff flipped through his file folder. "In Philadelphia… four years ago. Vagrant. Of an overdose."

I was an idiot.

I stepped right into that punch, and it had landed.

Of course she was dead. The path she was on, it would have taken a miracle for her to survive this long. Even so, I didn't see it comin', and I had let this dickwad get one up on me. Roger's boyfriend.

And Roger was just sitting there. He was letting it happen.

The country-club boys. Of course they'd stick together, I realized suddenly. I could forget sometimes, but I was nothing, just like I'd always been. Who was going to be on my side? I was just the street rat—good for a fuck, and they'd both used me for that—but not somebody you took home to your parents.

That guy was Jeff. And that guy had won.

They had planned this together?

I had trusted Roger.

Another in a very, very long string of colossal mistakes. Roger obviously wanted to hurt me as badly as I had hurt him. Well, congrats, Dweeb. Bull's-eye.

I didn't know much for certain in that moment, but I was pretty damned sure that I couldn't talk.

I picked Haggis up from my lap gently and kissed him on the head, and then I set him to one side. I stood up. In two strides I was at the door, then in the hall, and my old beat-up chucks were flying down those two flights of stairs.

"Fletch!"

It was Roger above me.

Fuck Roger.

I pulled the street door open, and I was down the steps and walking east.

Blind.

Chapter 29
Detective Story—Part II

ROGER

Fletch sat on the floor, so pale. I'd never seen him like that. I should have said something but I didn't. It was all like watching some terrible accident happen, and I just sat there. I'd never seen anyone get the better of Fletch, ever, and I kept waiting for his response. I was sure he'd have an answer, something funny or devastating. Or he'd just haul off and belt Jeff in his smug face, which he so deserved.

But there was Fletch, looking like he'd been kicked in the stomach. Why didn't I say something?

He didn't move for a second. Then he set the dog to one side, and I started to reach out to him—but with those huge legs of his he was out the door before I could even think.

I ran to the apartment door—Fletch was already past the landing, but I could hear his feet thumping down the stairwell.

"Fletch!" I yelled. I heard the front door pull open, the noise of New York washed in, and then the door fell slowly closed behind him, and the street noise was gone again, muted.

I should have stopped this, I thought. I shouldn't have let this happen. Why was I such a wuss that I let this happen?

I turned around and went back inside.

"Jeffrey for the win!" That was my boyfriend, my utterly loathsome boyfriend, gloating on the couch. How had I ever…

"What did you say?" I said when I was finally able to answer him.

"It's a pity he bolted—I hadn't even gotten to my favorite part. But I guess it's a touchy subject for him."

"Jeez, did you really think it was going to be funny, telling Fletch his mother's dead?"

"Sorry. I guess I didn't take Fletch for the sensitive type, not with his background. But you know, I was really disappointed there was nothing about prostitution in the file."

"Why would you think there would be?!"

"C'mon, he was living on the streets, and he looked like that. Of course he was turning tricks."

"Well why don't you ask him, like he said—"

"People like that lie—"

"You don't know anything about him!"

"On the contrary"—he tapped his file—"I know a great deal."

"You know nothing important then."

"I know he had a meal ticket—you—and he moved on to this rich designer, and he's screwed that up, apparently. That much I learned from you. And now he's trying to get back in your pants."

"You're unbelievably wrong."

"You're right—he doesn't want in your pants, just your pockets."

I was pretty sure I knew what Fletch wanted, and it wasn't just sex, and it certainly had nothing to do with money.

"If that's what you think, Jeffrey, then you don't know a damned thing. Fletch has his faults—believe me!—but greed isn't one of them. You don't know him as well as I do."

I went into the kitchen just to get away from him.

"The whole point, baby, is you don't know him at all!" he said, following me. "Did you even know Fletch wasn't his real name?"

"Fletcher Andrews! His name's WASPier than mine! Of course it's not his real name. But that was how he introduced himself, and I never needed to know more than that."

"Did he tell you his mother was an alcoholic? And an addict, in and out of rehab?"

"That's so—I mean, it's terrible, but it's—irrelevant. There's nothing in that file that I need to know."

"How about that stint in juvie?"

"Juvie? Really?"

"Don't believe me? It's all in here." He tossed the file on the kitchen counter.

"It's not that I don't believe you. I'm not even really surprised. I just feel bad for him. In the end—I don't know—maybe it explains some things, but it doesn't matter."

"Of course it matters! He was in there for assault and battery! If that's not a game changer, what is???"

"Assault?" That made no sense to me. It just wasn't possible. Fletch? No.

"That wasn't easy to find out, either. Juvenile records are sealed, and the copy I got was heavily redacted, but from what I could make out, he put some guy in the *hospital. That's* the kind of criminal who has the keys to your apartment. *That's* the kind of lowlife you're so damned infatuated with!"

"I'm not infatuated! And besides, whatever happened, it was years ago. He's changed. He learns all the time. I *see* it. I mean think about it. Literally a kid from the street. Addict mother—foster care—juvie—think how far Fletch has come from that poor kid in your file!" And suddenly I realized something. "He's not even the same guy he was two years ago. He's changed, he's gentler, more considerate and—"

"Roger, stop being so damned naïve!" he yelled at me. "People like Fletch, they'll *do* anything, *say* anything. It's how they survive! And you know what else?—and you can trust me on this one, baby—people don't change!"

I looked at him for a couple seconds and took a deep breath.

"I certainly hope that's not true, Jeffrey," I said quietly. "If only for your sake."

"What's that supposed to mean?"

"It means you're a prick. And I hope someday you outgrow it."

"I'm the prick? You just don't get it, do you? I'm not the bad guy here. I'm the one looking out for you!"

"Don't you dare..."

At the thought he was now going to pretend that he had somehow done this awful thing for *me!* For *my* benefit—I don't think I had ever been so angry in my life. My whole body was shaking.

"You should be thanking me!" he said.

I had to take a second before I could speak, which I did calmly, staring at the lines in the granite countertop.

"You should go. I can't talk to you, and honestly, I can't stand the sight of you right now. Just go."

Jeffrey picked himself up, got his things, carefully left the folder on the kitchen counter where I could see it, and snapped his briefcase shut. I couldn't look at him. He stopped at the door to say something but went without saying it.

Haggis nudged my ankle.

Chapter 30
Riffraff in the Hallway

FLETCH

I stormed out of there and kept on walking, and I walked all the way back to my flat-sit—yep, all the way to frigging Bushwick. I guess walking fast and far was how I was handling stress. I certainly seemed to be doing it often enough. Stress and anger and frustration—and hurt. Because this one really, really hurt.

I stopped on the bridge to watch it get dark for I don't know how long. It was soooooooooooooo cold up there and incredibly windy—only then did I realize I'd left my jacket at Roger's—but it felt good, too.

I should cry or something, I thought. After all, my ma was dead. I didn't have a lot of cozy memories of her, but she was still my ma, you know? There was a time she took care of me, or tried to. Mostly I remembered taking care of her. Seven years old and worried my ma wasn't eating enough.

I looked back toward Manhattan through the bridge and watched the sun set on the other side of the city until it was nearly dark. The only tears in my eyes were from the wind.

Even as a little kid, I didn't cry. My ma commented on it. I think I freaked her out, like there was something wrong with me. Her little cherub-faced sociopath, I guess, but I had somehow missed the crying gene.

And here I was.

I've told you how I didn't believe in love. Trust is another really tough one for me. But I'll admit to this much: I had loved exactly two people in my life. One of them, I'd just found out, died on a street in Philadelphia. And the other one—one I'd actually trusted, which was something I couldn't really say about my ma—*that* one had sat by and watched me get sucker-punched by his fuckstick boyfriend, by this miserable, insignificant, contemptible jag-off.

I'd loved two people in my entire life, and I'd lost them both in that one afternoon. And even then, I didn't cry—couldn't.

By the time I got to the apartment building, I was done. I was emotionally empty, I was fucking freezing, I was exhausted and shivering, and I only knew I wanted to go to bed. If I woke up again, or if I didn't, it didn't really matter.

I stepped out of the elevator, turned left toward the apartment, and stopped. My door was at the far end of the hall—where there was a Scottish terrier curled up next to a guy with white earbuds sitting on the floor, head fallen forward on his chest, a big shock of brown curls hanging down over his forehead.

Man-oh-man, I thought. Good thing I don't cry.

Haggis picked up his head, and then jumped to his feet and tugged at the end of the leash, tail wagging furiously—which woke Roger up.

"Hey, Dweeb," I said, hoarse.

Looking up, he pulled the earphones out—I could hear the tinny version of a string quartet. What a dork. What an adorable dork.

"It's about time," he said.

I leaned my back against the doorframe and slid down to sit beside him—he scooched to the side a little, but we were still shoulder to shoulder, looking straight out, not at each other. I did notice he was wearing my sweatshirt. That *had* to mean something, right?

"What are you doing here?" I said after a while.

"You forgot your jacket." He handed it to me.

"Ah. Explains why I'm freezing. Thanks." He leaned against me a little more. Body heat. "You came all the way to Brooklyn for that?"

"And people say I'm not spontaneous."

We sat for a bit.

"What did you think about Jeff's—revelations?"

"I'm so mad at him I can't even talk about it."

"You're not—mad at me? Or disappointed—or something?"

"No! God no!"

"I should have told you."

"I might have asked, too, but I didn't. And it was fine."

"I'm glad you brought the dog."

"Me, too."

I reached across Roger and scratched the dog under his collar where he liked it, and Haggis tilted his head and leaned into my fingers. Man, I loved this dog.

"I wasn't sure I'd ever see you again, Pup-sicle."

"Why would you say that?" Roger said.

"I thought maybe you and Jeff—had planned that."

"No! How could you think I would ever—"

"You didn't say anything, you just let him go on, and I thought—"

"You're right. I'm sorry, I should have stopped him, but I thought you—And honestly, I never saw you so—Once you were gone, I tore into him."

"Yeah? I don't suppose you…"

"Broke up with him? Not yet."

"Too bad. But you're thinking about it."

"None of your business, nosey!" But he was smiling when he said it. "But if it helps, I seem to remember calling him a prick."

"Dweeb, you didn't!"

"I did. Feel better?"

"Much."

We settled back next to each other, and sat for a bit without saying anything, and I just enjoyed his warm shoulder against mine. And him.

"And I *know* why you brought the dog, Dweeb."

"He doesn't get out enough."

"Because you're afraid of Brooklyn."

"Shut up."

Long pause.

"I'm not supposed to call you Dweeb anymore. Sorry."

"You can call me Dweeb."

We sat there for a bit, and then he let his head fall over onto my shoulder. I leaned my head against his, and I felt those soft curls against my cheek again, after all this time. I closed my eyes.

If that wasn't enough, the dog put his head down next to Roger's leg and sighed.

All I could think was—*I never want to move again.*

Chapter 31
When the Gingham Dog Met the Calico Cat

ROGER

I was sitting on the floor with Fletch in a hallway, and I did not want to think. I was through with thinking. I was just comfortable; I was where I wanted to be somehow. And I *couldn't* think about that. Because if sitting on a floor in a hallway in Brooklyn, leaning against the strong, warm shoulder of my ex-boyfriend, was where I wanted to be, it was obviously rather telling, and what it was telling, I did *not* want to hear.

Besides, I was too tired to think. I was too tired to stand even. I was certainly too tired to go back to Manhattan. But what then? Overnight here? With Fletch? Seriously? And what about Jeff?

If I was really dumping Jeff, I should probably tell Jeff *before* I spend the night with somebody else. Because that's what nice boys do, isn't it? And was I really the kind of guy to hop from one bed to the next? Not that there had been much activity in bed with Jeff in the last weeks. And why was that? Oh-jeez.

I definitely needed to stop thinking, I decided.

Was I sure about Jeff?

Okay, I should work this through, I thought. Was there any reason to keep Jeffrey around? I couldn't think of any. I wasn't in love with him, and I doubted he was in love with me. We had different interests, different goals, blah-blah-blah. And he threatened to drop-kick my dog.

Yeah, definitely done with Jeff. That was decided.

That just left—the other one.

And? At one point I could have pushed the other one onto the subway tracks and whistled a cheery tune while I did it.

But now? No, I was past that. How far past—that was another question. Another question for another day. I couldn't think about that now. For now, I was content to nestle myself a little closer on the other one's shoulder.

I definitely needed to stop thinking.

I should learn from Fletch. He wasn't thinking. Somewhere along here he'd reached over and taken my hand, and I bet he hadn't thought about it. And I had let him—without thinking. See, it wasn't so bad. In fact, it was kinda nice.

If you thought about it, *not* thinking was clearly the only intelligent thing to do. Particularly when you were overtired, emotionally drained, and leaning against a nice warm body. A nice warm, well-muscled body. In an outer borough.

So there I was, sitting on the floor, too whatever to call myself a car and drag my tired little butt back to Chelsea. But seriously, what did I expect was going to happen if I stayed? Sleep with Fletch or just sleep with Fletch?

If I didn't want to go, what *did* I want?

I wanted to stay. Obviously.

I was terrified of staying. Just as obviously.

And I wanted to stop all this *thinking!*

I could just stay here, stay overnight, and it didn't have to be sexual, did it? This wasn't sexual, leaning against him like this, even holding hands. It was just nice. We could call Chinese. I bet they have Chinese in Brooklyn. We could watch an old movie and just curl up on each other like this. And no groping. All perfectly innocent, I swear. Mostly.

And how long would perfectly innocent last? Certainly not until morning. I knew Fletch better than that.

I shouldn't try to kid anybody—I knew *myself* better than that.

Is *that* why I brought the dog? So I could spend the night without feeling guilty? Without feeling guilty about the dog anyway?

Did I *want* to sleep with Fletch? Of course not!

Of course I did.

I mean of course I did, but I didn't.

I mean, *part* of me did, for sure. A part of my *psyche*, I mean—not *that* part of me. Although yeah, *that* part of me seemed to be definitely voting yea on the motion. *All in favor, please raise your...*

And a part of me was scared. Let's face it—a part of me was always scared.

And maybe I *should* be scared. This is Fletch we're talking about, I reminded myself. What did I just realize about Fletch? You start to think he's better than he is and *wham-o*. He will disappoint. So don't go in with a lot of hopes jingling around in your pocket.

Please place all expectations in the gray bins before proceeding.

I should be more like Fletch. I should just let it happen. Maybe that's what I wanted. Maybe I just wanted to stop thinking and to stop worrying and to stop being afraid.

Maybe I just wanted to feel something.

Of course, by this point, mostly what I felt were my left leg falling asleep and my bladder calling out for attention. When I started to stir, both Fletch and the dog picked their heads up, and the moment was over.

"I'm sorry," I said.

"We can't sit out here forever."

He stood stiffly and helped pull me up.

"I should warn you, though..." he said, turning the key in the door.

Oh God what new hell was this? What new revelation did Fletch have for me?

"What?" I knew it. I just knew it. Here it comes ...

"I'm not just flat sitting."

Wham-o!

"You're not alone."

"Wait 'til you meet him, Dweeb—he's really nice, and super cute. But I don't know what he's going to think about the little Pup-tart here." I had already turned to go, but Fletch grabbed me and held me there. Damn, I'd forgotten how strong he was.

"Tybalt?" Fletch called into the dark apartment.

Tybalt? Fletch's little live-in fuck-weasel was called Tybalt? Like the guy in *Romeo and Juliet*? What kind of precious, artsy-fartsy, pansy-ass poser calls himself Tybalt? What*ever*, I was under no circumstances going to meet Fletch's new sex toy who was apparently allergic to dogs. He was more than welcome to keep my ex, my cheap, slutty ex. I could feel the sting in my eyes, I was so mad. Damn him. And to think, two minutes before, I had actually been contemplating the possibility of—

By now he had both arms around me to keep me there and I was still trying to wrench myself loose—when a large orange tabby came bounding to the door. He braked abruptly when he saw Haggis. His hackles rose up huge.

"Easy, Tybalt," Fletch said over my shoulder. "Don't wig out on me here."

He finally let me pull free.

"That's your roommate?"

"Cat sitting," Fletch explained. "Meet Tybalt."

What a monumental ass. He had deliberately let me think... I punched him hard in the arm.

"What? What?" he asked, so innocently, grinning. Then he saw me push a tear off my cheek. "Oh, hey, Dweeb!" And he pulled me into a hug. "Don't—I'm sorry, Dweeb—"

I wiped my eyes on his shirt, and then I pushed him away.

"That's Tybalt?"

We turned our attention to the animals at our feet.

Haggis had never really been around cats. He saw them at the vet occasionally, where they had a couple cats that wandered loose, but I had no idea how he'd respond to an enormous tabby, all up close and personal.

Apparently I had even less of an idea how the cat would respond to his first contact with a Scottish terrier.

The cat slowly arched his back, a low growl came out of his chest, and he hissed once. And did my little dog turn into a bloody killer? Did he suddenly direct the famous Scottish terrier ferocity on the poor, defenseless pussycat? No. He wagged his tail a little nervously, which, in case you don't know, is dog-speak for "please don't bite me."

Lesson of the day (among soooo many others):

> Cats do not understand dog-speak.

In music there's this thing when you have a particularly nasty page turn, and you have like maybe a bar rest to flip the page and get your bow back on the strings—there'll be this little *v.s.* at the bottom of the page. The *v.s.* is for *volta subito*. (It can also be rendered as *volta stupido*, depending on the mood of your violin teacher at the time.) Italian for "jump fast."

I didn't.

The only one who did was the defenseless little pussycat, who *volta'd molto subito* onto the back of my Scotty. He landed, snarling and screaming. It was horrific, nightmarish. There was a ball of raging orange fur and black fur, with terrible guttural noises coming out of the cat and screams of pain from my fearsome terrier. I was frozen.

Whatever else you might say about Fletch, he's useful in a crisis. I don't think he's afraid of anything. He shoved both hands in to pull the two apart, and it was over in a few seconds. He turned around and carried the still-growling cat by the scruff of the neck, and he tossed the demon tabby—not so super cute after all, if you asked me—into the bedroom, and pulled the door shut.

"Fuck." It was not my day to be articulate. I crouched down to my dog to see how badly he was hurt.

"Is he okay?" Fletch asked.

"He seems—fine." I was as much surprised as I was relieved. After all of that, it seemed like *somebody* should be disemboweled or something. "I was mostly worried about—but no, he's still got two shiny black eyes, thank God. And otherwise—I don't see anything. I guess this awful coat is good for something after all."

"I'm glad."

There was still some orange cat hair floating around.

"How's the…" I asked.

"Tybalt? I'll check on him, but I didn't see any marks on him."

"Tybalt?"

"Shakespeare. Cat belongs to an actress, remember?"

I was still crouched down with the dog, when I saw the blood on the floor and looked around for the source.

"Oh my God, Fletch," I said.

The source was a steady drip coming from a huge wound on the back of Fletch's left hand. He had definitely gotten the worst end of the fight. His shirtsleeves were rolled up, and both forearms were scratched. The right one had a particularly nasty scratch that ran almost the length of the inside of his wrist to his elbow. But his left hand—that was no cat scratch.

Haggis had bitten him. But good.

"Oh, yeah," Fletch said, looking at his bloody hand. "Ouch."

I ran to the little kitchen and grabbed a dish towel and got it underneath his hand.

It's not likely that you've ever seen the inside of the mouth of a Scottish terrier. It's a truly scary thing. Cute little Scotties have the teeth of a much bigger dog, with enormous canines. A lapdog with the teeth of a German shepherd. I stood and carefully looked to see just how bad it was. I got as far as seeing that there was a large flap of flesh that was partly torn away from the back of his hand—and ohmysweetfuckingjesus, you could see something underneath. Was that tendon? Or bone? I fell back against the wall behind me.

"Hey!" said Fletch, catching me as best he could with his right arm. "You okay?"

"Yeah, yeah, I'm okay," I said, pulling myself together. "You aren't, though. God, Fletch, I'm-so-sorry-I'm-so-sorry-I'm-so-sorry."

"It's not your fault."

"It's *my* dog that bit you!"

"It's not his fault either! Who knew the cat would go all kamikaze batshit?"

"You need to see a doctor."

"Is your vet open late?"

"Ha. Ha." I asked the voice in my phone for the nearest emergency room. She gave me the answer.

"I'll be fine," he said. "I'm always fine."

"What? Is that gaping chunk of meat hanging off your hand going to heal on its own? I don't think so. And *I'm* not stitching that back together. Are we going to find a cab out here?" To me the outer boroughs were a completely foreign country. And not a nice foreign country like France, but a scary third-world, watch-your-wallet-and-don't-drink-the-water foreign country that there was no good reason to visit. Fletch was, of course, right. He knows I'm uncomfortable out here, and yes, I'd brought the Haggis along for just that reason. Combination security dog and security blanket. Pathetic, I know, but there it is.

I wasn't more comfortable now that it was night.

I had one of those Uber accounts that I never used, and I used it now. I ordered two cars, one to take Fletch to Wyckoff Heights Medical Center—in my entire life I had never even heard of Wyckoff Heights—and one to take me and Haggis home.

"Are you in a lot of pain?"

"It doesn't feel nice—but I'll survive."

"I'm-so-sorry-I'm-so-sorry."

"Stop saying that."

"Sorry." He scowled. I went to pee finally, thank God, while Fletch took a look at the cat, who was still surly but was apparently unhurt. I helped Fletch get his right arm into the jacket I'd brought, and I draped the rest of it over his left shoulder.

Fletch grabbed a library book from his shoulder bag.

"It's not a gunshot wound," he explained. "This could take some time."

We went down to the street to wait for our cars.

My car arrived first, but I made him wait until Fletch's car was also there. Fletch's driver took one look at Haggis and started to make noises. He wasn't going to have a dog in his car. I told him not to worry. *My* driver, Lord love him, *liked* dogs.

I loaded Fletch into the back seat of the terrier-free car—while I allowed my dog, unclean as he was, to piss contentedly on a rear tire.

"Okay," I said before I closed the car door, "I'm going to run Haggis home and turn right around and find you at the hospital."

"You don't have to do that. That's crazy."

"Of course I don't have to, but I'm going to anyway. Call me if you think of anything you need."

"Roger—" He wanted to argue some more.

"I'll see you as soon as I can." I closed the car door, and he drove off.

Haggis and I got in the other car.

As we were going over the bridge, I noticed that one of Haggis's ears had a bloody scratch on the inside. I flipped through his coat and found a couple other small spots that were already scabbing. Nothing serious.

Just poor Fletch.

Chapter 32
Paging Dr. Scruff

FLETCH

At the hospital, I checked in at a desk at the emergency entrance. I was told to wait and to fill out my entire medical history. Great. With my bloody left hand wrapped in a dish towel, while I tried to hold the clipboard on my lap with my left forearm, I could barely write my name, but sure, no problem. Fortunately my medical history was mostly limited to checking "no" in about a thousand little boxes. There's just no end to the diseases I've never had. Did they really need all this, or was this just to cheer you up? I was sitting there, gushing blood into a dishtowel with sunflowers on it, my left hand felt like somebody was whacking it with a rubber mallet with every heartbeat, but—Hey! At least I didn't have dengue fever!

And there was a section about family medical history. Parents, still living or not.

Father:

Ha. Don't know, don't care.

Mother:

Like a bucket of ice water.

In all the craziness—finding Roger waiting for me, an insane cat, my throbbing hand—the other events of the day had sort of faded. But there was the reminder on this stupid form.

Mother:

My poor Ma. She was so beautiful. I suppose every kid thinks his mother's beautiful, but mine really was. Soft blond curls, like an angel. And bright blue eyes. And so messed up.

I'd gone into foster care a couple times, but she'd always come back and gotten me. Until she didn't. You're a kid, so you keep thinking. Two years later, four years later, still a kid, you're still thinking. I left the whole foster-care system somewhat prematurely, and after that—well—let's just say after that I wasn't a kid anymore.

I looked down at the form.

Mother:

I suppose, later on, I could have gone looking for her when I was living out on the streets—but I didn't. I don't know. She hadn't come looking for me, so…

Mother:

Thanks to Jeff and his private dick, I could answer that one. How did anyone as sweet and wonderful as Roger *ever* get tied up with such a royal asshat as Jeff Bornic?

I was still grumbling about that as I filled out the rest of the form. Finally I got parked in an examining thing—a table for the patient and a tall chair on casters—separated from the rest of the large ward by curtains. I sat on the exam table like I was told, and worked my way out of my windbreaker—which was a lot harder than it sounds.

Obviously, just separated by curtains, you could hear everything going on everywhere, and a woman down at the far end was having a much worse day than mine, judging from the noises coming out of her.

A granite-faced nurse came in and unwrapped the towel from my hand. If she was the least bit impressed by the carnage, she didn't let on. She held my left hand—or what was left of it—over an aluminum bowl and picked up a plastic bottle with a long nozzle from the counter.

"Is this going to hurt?" I asked. I'm not a baby, but if that was alcohol Nurse Torquemada was about to pour over my hand, I'd just as soon get a little heads-up.

"It's just water, tough guy," she said. "Cowboy up."

Sweet bedside manner.

"I bet you say that to all the fellahs."

She ignored me.

I looked down at the wound. Yipes. With one bite, the dog had really done a job on my hand. Props, Haggis. And to think, I used to sleep in the same bed with that dog sometimes. Naked.

She squirted some water around the wound, and then cleaned the blood from the flap of hand-meat with a piece of gauze. Ow. Ow, ow, ow. Ow. She laid another piece of gauze over it. Then she wet a piece of cotton with something from a different bottle—I could smell the alcohol from four feet away, and I instinctively pulled my hand back as she came toward me.

"Hang on, Rambo," she said, taking my *right* arm. "I've got to disinfect this." She indicated the ten-inch-long scratch down my forearm that was still oozing a little blood. Then she added in the same emotionless tone, "And this, by the way, is going to hurt like a screaming bitch."

I gave her my steeliest James Bond smile until she was done, had put the alcohol away, and was gone. And then? Holy guaca-fucking-moly did that ever hurt! I sucked in some air between my gritted teeth. Even the throbbing in my left hand was momentarily eclipsed. I wanted to pinch my arm to hold off the pain, but of course, my left hand was frigging useless.

I contemplated the drop-ceiling tiles until it subsided, which it did in a couple minutes. There was a drunk on the other side of the curtain that cops had picked up off the sidewalk where she had passed out. A doctor was trying to talk to her, but he wasn't getting very far.

Made me think about my ma again.

After a while, a doctor came in.

On another day, in another life...even—what?—six weeks ago I'd have been seriously glad to see him. He was really young for a doctor, under thirty, tall, gym-rat body, short dark hair, huge brown eyes, thick lashes, really good-looking, and oh-man he hadn't shaved in a couple days. Completely my type.

"Hello," he said. "I'm Dr. Stone."

And you know what else? As soon as he opened his mouth, I could tell—I was his type, too.

But—it *wasn't* six weeks ago, and I had zero interest in a hot young doctor or anyone for that matter, except for guess who. Not to mention my throbbing left hand, which wasn't exactly putting me in the mood, if you know what I mean. Poor Dr. Scruff was going to have to learn to live with disappointment. I would need to fix this.

"You hurt your hand, Mr. Andrews?" he said, glancing at the clipboard.

"Oh-yeah. And call me Fletch—please." I was sitting on the examining table.

"Okay, Fletch. Let's see what we have." He pulled on a pair of latex gloves and stood really close, much closer than he needed, so that his thigh was against my knee. He took my hand and removed the gauze.

"Ah. Excellent."

"Thank you. Glad you like it."

"Sorry. It's just something I say. I learned it in med school because you don't want to look at a patient and say, 'Oh, fuck.'"

"And I guess my hand is pretty much oh-fuck-worthy."

"Most definitely oh-fuck-worthy." With a little clamp thing, he lifted up the flap of flesh. You can imagine how nice that felt. "'Oops' is the one you really want to avoid." He poked around a little further. "Your chart says dog bite. Is that correct?"

"Yep," I got out between clenched teeth.

"What dog—Cujo?" He dropped the clamp in a metal bowl with a clang. "Okay. There's no bone damage, but we're going to need to clean that, reconnect some tissues, and close it all up." He pulled off his latex gloves. "First things first. Dog bite. Do you know the dog that bit you?"

"Yes."

"The issue here is rabies. Is there any chance that the dog is sick?"

"No, I'm sure he's completely healthy and up-to-date with his shots or whatever—the owner is quite fastidious."

"You're absolutely sure. People still die from rabies, and from what I've read, it's a really nasty way to go."

"Absolutely sure," I said. And then I thought—now's as good a time as ever. "It's my boyfriend's dog." Not entirely true. Okay, not remotely true, just wishful thinking, but it would accomplish what I needed to accomplish without hurting anybody's feelings.

"Ah," he said.

"Ah," I said, agreeing.

Message sent. Message received. Lieutenant Uhura couldn't have done it better. His leg was no longer pressed against mine. Good. The last thing I needed was to have Dr. Sexy-Eyes here passing me his phone number just as Roger showed up to take me home.

"Okay." He started scribbling on the chart on the clipboard. "So. Let's do something about the pain."

"I hope you got something stronger than Tylenol."

"On a scale of one to ten, how bad would you say the pain is?"

"Twelve and a half."

"Okay. I think we can do a little better than Tylenol. The nurse will get you started, and I'll be back in a bit."

Nurse Beeyotch came in, as promised. I sat up straight to show her what a manly little fellow I could be. She didn't seem to notice.

She gave me a couple really gigantic pills with water.

"You doing anything later?" I asked between pills. Not the tiniest reaction. "Have you ever thought about roller derby?" was my next attempt. "Because I think we'd make a damn fine team."

And she went out through the curtain without a word. In the end, she wasn't really a talker, my nurse. I guess she'd given me all the chitchat she had.

After a while, I noticed something a little odd. The dimensions of the little curtain-cubicle thing seemed to change, depending on how you looked at them. And none of it was really square. All the angles were kind of wonky. I closed my eyes and shook my head, hoping things would stand still again.

I was still trying to focus on the ceiling tiles, one eye at a time, when Dr. Scruff came back.

"The pills may make you a little woozy," he said.

That explained a lot.

"Woozy?" I said. "Is that what you call it?" It had been a kinda freaky twenty minutes. Or an hour. Or whatever.

"Well, hopefully it doesn't hurt quite so badly now. How do you feel?"

"Like Salvador Dali."

"How many fingers am I holding up?"

"Two. Maybe three."

"Excellent."

"Is that like 'oops'? Or was that an 'oh fuck'?"

"Depends. Look at me." He had this little flashlight that he pointed into my eyes while he pulled my eyelids open, then he clicked off the flashlight. "That's an 'oops' then. No biggie." He put his little toy away. "You're just going to feel a little funny for a while."

"You have amazing eyes," I said when I could see again. I guess that was the feel-a-little-funny part talking. He was writing something on his clipboard.

"Thank you," he said without looking up.

"Roger's eyes are prettier."

"The boyfriend?" He had a tray with some syringes on it, and he started to fill one.

"Yep."

"Is he here with you?"

"Coming to pick me up."

"Good." He carefully wiped around the back of my hand with wet cotton.

"Is this where you tell me I'm going to feel a small prick?"

He shook his head, smiling.

"I think we've both heard that joke before, Fletch. You *will* feel the needle but only for a second or two at the most." And he made three injections around the wound. "I'll leave word at the desk about Roger. It's good there's someone to look after you," he said, snapping the last syringe into the hazmat thing.

"He's very good at looking after."

"Fastidious."

"Fastidious."

"You should probably lie back."

"Good idea." I started to lie down.

"This way," he said, "with your feet at that end so I can get to your hand. I'll be back in a bit when the shots have taken hold."

I think I nodded off somewhere along here.

Chapter 33
Under the Influence

ROGER

There's another reason I don't like the outer boroughs. They're so frigging far away. I know Brooklyn's just across the river, but it always seems to take forever to get anywhere.

I got home, smeared some antibiotic stuff on Haggis's ear, gave him a piece of freeze-dried cow lung, and got back in the waiting car. I was off to the unknown regions of Wyckoff Heights. After a small eternity, I was finally able to thank my driver profusely with an absurd tip—he liked dogs, after all—and I ran in through the emergency entrance.

I thought for sure I'd get a hassle trying to see a patient who was no relation, but they just pointed me in the right direction.

All the doctors looked like they were in their twenties. It was like going to the frigging Apple Store. Seemed to me a little adult supervision wouldn't hurt.

I heard moans and grunts coming from different curtained-off cubicles, and I walked past a snoring woman on a gurney, until I finally heard Fletch's voice coming from behind a screen.

"He has the most beautiful hands you've ever seen. Long and thin, and so pale, they look like porcelain, except for these funky callouses from the violin—"

I stuck my head around the curtain. What the hell was Fletch going on about?

"Dweeb!" He was sitting on a table, and he was thrilled to see me for some reason. In his exuberance, he had yanked his left hand away from the doctor, who was in the middle of doing something with it.

"Hey!" the doctor said. "You have to hold still." He caught the hand in the air—with the needle and thread still swinging from it. Oh-jeez. I had to close my eyes. "You must be the boyfriend."

My eyes popped open. Was he talking to me?

"Y-yeah." That explained how I got in here so easily. Clever Fletch. And maybe a sympathetic doctor. I wasn't totally certain, but after just a glance I guessed he batted on our side.

"Dweeb, meet Dr. Scruff." Fletch was being awfully boisterous.

The doctor turned around to me briefly and nodded, smiling.

"Roger Prescott." I nodded back. Wow, leave it to Fletch to get the hot doctor. Wait a minute. Dr. Scruff couldn't be his real name, could it?

"Dr. Stone," Dr. Scruff said, anticipating my confusion. "Joel." Jeez, he was like my age.

"Fletch doesn't seem quite…"

"Yeah. He's not quite. He's having a bit of a reaction to the pain meds. Unusual, but not unheard of. You've seen that YouTube video of the kid coming home from the dentist? This is that. He'll be fine with a little sleep."

"Okay." I was trying not to watch as the guy used these like pliers things to push the needle through the skin, and then he tied it off and snipped the threads. And then he prepped another stitch.

"I'll give you something different to take home with you," the doctor said as he drove another needle in.

"Thanks." I couldn't look, but I couldn't really look away either.

"Have you considered a muzzle?"

"For—Fletch?" No, but I obviously should have. And a really short leash.

"For the dog," he explained.

"Muzzle Haggis?!" said Fletch, outraged. There went the hand again.

"If it's one of these pit-bull things," the doctor said, retrieving the hand and dangling thread, "you should really—"

"No, he's a small terrier. Scottish."

"He's the best dog in the world," said Fletch. "He called Haggis 'Cujo,'" he whispered to me.

"The dog didn't go after Fletch," I explained. "He was attacked by a cat—the dog, I mean—there was a horrible fight, and Fletch broke it up. And he got bitten doing it."

"I see. You didn't tell me you were a hero, Fletch."

"You'd be surprised at the things he can neglect to mention," I said.

"Oh, Roger, really?" Fletch said, pouting. "After today?"

"You're right, you're right," I conceded. "Yes, Doctor, he was definitely a hero."

"You do that really well," said Fletch, calmly observing the needle go through the living flesh of his hand. How can he watch that?

"Thank you," said Dr. Joel. "There." He snipped off the thread, examined his handiwork, and snapped the latex gloves off. I stepped over to Fletch.

"How are you doing, Fletch?"

He looked at me with the goofiest expression.

"I've missed you, Dweeb," and he hopped off the table, arms open wide to hug me. But his legs weren't quite steady and he grabbed onto me. As if *I* were strong enough to hold him up, which I wasn't.

"Excel"—the doctor rolled his stool under Fletch's backside—"lent." After waiting a second to be sure Fletch was more or less stable on the stool, he pulled a pen from his breast pocket, clicked it, and began making notes in Fletch's chart.

Of course Fletch was more or less stable because he was clinging to me like a drunk on a lamppost, with his head pressed sideways against my chest.

"Missed you," he said again, squeezed me, took a deep breath, and sighed.

I hated that I was blushing and didn't really know *what* to do with Fletch just *there* and me with my arms in the air like an idiot.

"I brought the rabies tag with me, Doctor," I said. I was pretty weirded out by this new, messed-up Fletch. I let my left arm fall around his shoulders—there wasn't much else I could do with it—while I fished the metal tag from my pocket. "Here, in case you need it."

"Your voice is so sexy like this," Fletch said with his ear pressed against my chest. "Say something else."

"Careful with your hand, Fletch," I cautioned.

"Rumble, rumble," Fletch mumbled, still pressed against me. He flipped his head around to try with his other ear.

"The nurse will come and put a bandage on that as soon as she's free," said the doctor.

"She's crazy about me," Fletch lolled.

"I have no idea if we need the rabies tag or not, but I'll put the number in the chart just in case. The dog is completely healthy?"

"Absolutely."

"How does your hand feel now, Fletch?" the young doctor asked.

"It doesn't. I can't feel it at all."

"I'm afraid that won't last. Are you guys here in Brooklyn?"

"Chelsea," I said. Obviously I couldn't dump Fletch in his apartment alone like this. The doctor glanced at his watch.

"By the time you get him back to Manhattan, the pain may have started to kick in again. Give him a pill when he needs it. I've given him an anti-inflammatory, which should help with the swelling. It's already better than it was. And a tetanus shot, just in case. He'll want to sleep—let him."

"Thanks," I said.

"You'll be looking after him?"

"Uh, yeah." Would I? Yeah, I guess I would be.

"He said you were fastidious."

"He said that?" It was dumb, but I couldn't help thinking about that night when he first moved himself in, uninvited, and he didn't know what *fastidious* meant. He had actually looked it up—and then later in bed, when we were doing—whatever—he teased me about whether this or that was particularly fastidious. I had to smile, and then I realized my left hand was stroking Fletch's back a little.

I could immediately feel my face glowing like a space heater.

"He's obviously very fit," Dr. Scruff said, whose actual name I had forgotten. Stone. Name tag right there. "No exercise for at least a week, until that wound is good and closed, and then take it slow. Common sense."

"I'll make sure."

"And the same with sex. Common sense. Nothing strenuous for a few days."

"Hear that, Dweeb?" Fletch said while he slid around and pushed his face under my arm. "No. Rough. Sex."

I wanted to pinch him soooooooo hard.

"You dolt," I said.

He nuzzled his face a little deeper.

"I'm not mad at Haggis, you know that."

"I know."

"I love that dog." He was still talking under my arm.

"I know. I do too."

"And I love you, Roger." And my heart stopped. He squeezed me tighter. "Did you know that? I need you to know that. I'd do anything for you, anything, because I love you so much."

I was paralyzed. The doctor cleared his throat.

"I'll just get those meds for you, and we're done." And he stepped out.

Fletch had never said that, not ever. At one time, I'd have given the world to hear that from him, even in a drugged-up stupor.

Why hadn't he ever said it? Why hadn't *I*? Would it have changed anything, if he *had*? Of course I'd been too cowardly to say it. What if I'd told him? Would it have stopped him maybe? Was this really all my fault in the end? All this loneliness and this terrible emptiness? All because I was such a miserable coward and now he loves me? I knew it didn't quite make sense, but still. I closed my eyes, lest they start gushing, as I continued to tailspin.

I had been so scared he'd just laugh at me, but maybe—

"Ah," said the doctor.

I looked up and quickly wiped my eyes on my shirtsleeve. I hadn't heard him come back. We were both a little embarrassed.

"Excellent," he said.

Fletch pulled his face out to look up to me.

"That's a code word. Did you know that?" He smiled at me. "It means 'oops.'" His head fell back into place, and I felt how hard his arm muscles were as he pulled me tight to him.

The doctor smiled, sheepish.

"Congratulations, by the way."

"Congratulations?"

"He told me—you're getting married."

"Shhhhh," Fletch said to the doctor. "That's a secret. Don't tell Roger." And he did his ostrich thing under my arm again.

"I think that's wonderful," said the doctor. "Honestly, when he told me his boyfriend's dog had bitten him, I thought *that* can't be good. But obviously you two are fine. I envy you guys."

And he went out through the curtain.

Fletch snuggled a little deeper, as though he couldn't get close enough.

I wondered if maybe *my* head was spinning more than Fletch's. I'd forgotten—but when Fletch was around, there was just a hell of a lot of gobsmacking.

After the nurse had bandaged his hand up, I walked Fletch carefully out into the waiting room. I managed to dig his wallet from his back pocket and then plopped him more or less upright on a chair. I could only hope he'd stay that way while I went off to deal with checking him out of this place. He had to have an insurance card in his wallet somewhere, didn't he?

Okay, lots of guys carry a condom in their wallet. Because hey-you-never-know. If an opportunity comes along, you want to be ready. Doesn't mean the guy's a slut. It shows he's responsible, blah-blah-blah. Perfectly nice guys carry a condom in their wallet.

But what guy carries *three* condoms in his wallet? Because hey-you-never-know when you might stumble into an orgy??? What???

I swallowed my anger. *Really, what did Fletch's condom collection have to do with me?* I asked myself.

I dealt with the woman in the window, signed half a dozen forms, and handed over my credit card to pay everything the International Alliance of Theatrical Stage Employees wouldn't.

Once again, I got one arm in his jacket and draped the rest of it around his left shoulder. I called a car, and I somehow managed to get him and his library book into it, where he immediately——fell asleep.

It was still night as we made our way back toward Manhattan. My thoughts were a mess. *I* was a mess. What Fletch had said wouldn't go away, and it left me with an uneasy thought.

It had been my observation that things people blathered when they were otherwise completely wasted—whether it was Mel Gibson or my dear aunt Hannah—were not necessarily the things that the blatherer *intended* to say, but they generally *were* what the blatherer honestly felt.

Gibson really *is* a bigot.

Aunt Hannah—well that's a whole other story.

And Fletch. I turned to him.

Fuck me.

Head thrown back, mouth open, snoring lightly. Still gorgeous somehow. With three condoms in his pocket. Because hey-you-never-know when you're going to bump into *triplets*???

Just how oversexed could one twenty-five-year-old boy be???

I was able to wake him up enough to get him up to my apartment. It took us probably fifteen minutes to get from the car to his falling face-first on my bed. I wrestled his feet up, rolled him over onto his back, and scooched him up so he wasn't hanging off the end.

Shoes off, socks off. Jeez, even his feet were sort of sexy, if that's possible. I counted to ten.

This next part could get hard.

Difficult. Not hard.

Nobody's parts were going to get hard. I'm just like a nurse, I said to myself. I can do this without it being weird.

I counted to ten again. I tried humming "On the Beautiful Blue Danube."

I opened the button fly of his jeans and then—moving to the ankle-end of things—I started working his pants down by pulling on the calf of one pant leg, then the other, and then back. It was slow but working. What I didn't realize until I looked up was—his boxers were coming down with the blue jeans.

Hel-lo.

Long time, no see.

Fletch never did go in for manscaping, did he.

Okay, nurse or no nurse, this was mad wrong.

I turned my head as far as I could to the side, scrunched my eyes shut, tugged his boxers back up, got everything safely back inside, and then finished—carefully—working his jeans down and free of his feet.

Now he woke up. Or at least enough to notice that his hand hurt, so I sat him up, gave him the pain pill he was due for, and I talked him into taking his shirt off, with lots of help.

I'm just like a nurse, I said to myself. I don't notice things—like the tiny bit of golden chest hair that brushed against the backs of my fingers as I undid the buttons, or the galaxy of beautiful freckles scattered across his shoulders, or the lithe, easy muscles of his back that worked beneath his smooth pale skin as I pulled the shirt off his good arm.

Hardly noticed them at all.

With effort, I managed to get the remaining shirtsleeve off over his bandage. I laid him back down, propped his injured hand up on a pillow, and he started to snore quietly.

My hero.

And then I did something stupid, monumentally stupid. In a string of stupid things, I guess. I knew I shouldn't do it, but I looked down—his face was sort of turned toward me—and there was this clump of hair that had fallen over his face and his right eye. My horrific mistake? I reached down, and I pushed it back.

Remember—during the course of this very, very long evening, I had leaned on Fletch's shoulder and held his hand; I'd fumbled in the back pocket of his jeans while his ass was still in them; I'd practically carried him upstairs while he groped me the whole way; I'd even undressed him, which included, at one point, actually having to tuck his hoober-hobber back under the elastic of his boxer shorts.

All that had given me considerable stress and confusion, but it was nothing compared to the great smack in the gob that came from brushing that soft blond curl back from his temple, the shock that came from that one gesture, that one intimate, stupid, tender gesture.

I looked at his face, the closed eyes, the eyelashes—and a ridiculous noise came out of me, as if I'd hiccupped, while simultaneously trying to swallow the gigantic dumpling that was stuck in my throat. My eyes stung. I was hit with a violent, crushing wave of emotions. Clobbered. A wave of emotions like a tsunami. It was all there—affection, longing, desire—sure. And loneliness. And fear.

And oh-jeez anger. Lots and lots of anger.

All of them and all at once. I couldn't begin to deal with it. I turned away, went to the bedroom door, swallowed hard, flipped out the lights—and I pushed it back, all of it, everything, back. I looked at him for another second before I pulled the door shut behind me.

Fletch could have the bed.

This day had been about a week long, but no matter how exhausted I was—and I was so tired I could cry—I was never going to sleep.

As I sat on the couch and rubbed my face with both hands. Haggis climbed up his steps, made one full circle, and dropped in a puddle of Scottish terrier.

Must be nice to be you, Hags, I thought. *One quick turn and you're done.*

I, by contrast, was going to be doing to some serious tail chasing.

Had Fletch really said what he'd said? He was in a drugged-up stupor. He would never have said it otherwise. But dear old Aunt Hannah haunted me still. Whatever else, no matter how many rye Manhattans she'd tossed back—I knew that old crow meant every vicious word. So—did Fletch?

Jeff said he loved me once, just after Christmas last year. At the time, I sort of laughed it off and made a joke out of it. I didn't respond. It was too soon, I'd thought. And then as time went on, I thought that maybe—you know, after what had happened with Fletch—I couldn't. I figured that that part of me was permanently damaged. And done. I had had the great, passionate thing, and I had crashed and burned, and you don't do that twice. It was wrong to expect to find anything comparable to that with Jeff or *anybody*. And that was fine. I could live without the drama. No more youthful passion, no more *Sturm und Drang*, it was time to grow up and develop more mature—and, of necessity, less intense—attachments. Like Jeff.

But now? Maybe the problem wasn't me. I thought about Fletch's concern for me in Cancun, about how he had looked after me after the old folks' recital, or about that mischievous smile he got talking about f-holes, or about how it had felt leaning on his shoulder outside his apartment. Or brushing back a curl of soft blond hair.

Maybe I wasn't so broken after all.

Fletch had finally said he loved me.

But he won't remember it tomorrow, I argued with myself. So technically it didn't really count, did it?

Of course not.

Absolutely not.

Definitely not.

Did it?

I looked down at the dog next to me, the little wire-haired horror, his black eyes glinting up at me through his eyebrows.

"You realize this is all your fault."

* * *

When it was finally time to be up and about, I made myself a cup of coffee, showered, and then I tried to get dressed without waking Fletch. With my back to him, I dropped the towel from my waist, found a pair of underwear, and bent over to pull them on.

"Hello, hot stuff" came sleepily from the pile of bedding behind me.

"Hey!" I said. "Don't be a perv. I thought you were asleep."

"I was," he said, rolling over lazily, "and I was having this totally sexy dream. This adorable guy stepped out of the shower, and he dropped his towel and bent over—"

"Creep. How's your hand?"

"I can feel it."

"Need another pill?"

"Maybe not just yet."

"I'll make you coffee if you're up. Or go back to sleep. You can stay as long as you like."

"Thanks," he said, yawning. With his upper body free of the sheet, he stretched quite languorously, luxuriously, arms over his head, reaching, his torso twisting a little.

Fuck me.

Did he do that deliberately, do you think? For my benefit? I'd always wondered.

It wasn't until I saw him smiling that I realized I'd been staring—and he had caught me at it. I could feel myself turning scarlet. I spun around and pulled open a drawer, looking for a pair of sweatpants.

"Hey, does Jeff have his own key?"

"Yeah, why?"

"Because wouldn't it be totally awesome if he let himself in right about now?"

"Oh-jeez, that would be—" I was going to say awful, but then I realized, it would actually be pretty damned funny, the two of us in our underwear. "Yeah, that would be pretty awesome."

"He'd come in, all manly-like, and we'd both be clutching the sheet to our chests."

"'But, Jeff!'" I began.

"It's not what it looks like!" we said together, laughing.

"And it would be the first time I'd said that, when it was actually true!" said Fletch, which shouldn't have been funny but somehow was, and I had to sit on the edge of the bed, laughing, just thinking about Jeff's big red face.

"Owwwwwww," Fletch said, holding his hand which apparently hurt from laughing.

"It's almost too bad it's Sunday—which means a football game."

"Football?"

"It's absolutely sacred. He'll be at his friend Rebecca's watching some game. Or she'll be at his place. Better TV."

"He has one of those huge screens, I bet."

"Like a drive-in movie."

"Compensating for something?"

"Hey! In any case, I won't see Jeff today." Which was a relief for me because I wasn't really looking forward to the big talk I knew I had to have with Jeffrey, and I could use some time to think about my approach to it.

I tugged a pair of sweats on.

"Football? Man-oh-man, no wonder you two are together."

"What?"

"You have so much in common!"

"Shut up." I started rummaging through a drawer for socks.

"I bet he hates the violin, hates chamber music."

"Stop."

"Does he like the dog even? Because I notice Haggis completely ignores him."

"Haggis ignores everybody."

"Except me."

"Except you," I said. I threw a pair of white socks at his head anyway. Dick.

I pulled out another pair for myself and sat back down on the edge of the bed.

"Hey," he said quietly behind me.

"Yeah?"

"Thanks for taking care of me last night."

"You're welcome. Thanks for rescuing my dog."

"He's welcome."

Pause.

"Hey," he said again.

"Yeah?"

"I think I was kinda out of it last night."

"Um—yeah. You could say that."

"I'm sorry. You know I never lose control like that."

"I know. It was pretty funny. How much do you remember?"

"All of it, I think, especially you pulling my jeans off."

"You bastard! You were awake?"

"I woke up a little when I felt my boxers coming down."

"You jerk! Why didn't you say something? Why didn't you help me?"

"I was *hoping* you were going to try to take advantage of my condition—but noooooooo—you were the perfect gentleman."

"Sorry to disappoint. Ass."

"Actually, I was only sort of vaguely aware. In and out. Anyway. I'm sorry if I did or said anything at the hospital that was embarrassing."

"It's okay." I could feel the blush in my face. "I knew you didn't mean any of it."

We were quiet for a few seconds.

"Hey," he said.

"Yeah?"

"I never said I didn't mean it."

I looked at him over my shoulder.

"Go take a pill. I'm walking the dog."

"I gotta pee," he said and threw off the bedsheet.

"Oh-jeeeeeeeeeez," I said, looking away.

Okay, it happens to all guys early in the morning, but Fletch's had managed to pop out through the fly of his boxers. Fletch gave a goofy smile and shrugged.

"Excellent?"

Chapter 34
Paradise Regained—Temporarily

FLETCH

I knew where he kept his clothes, of course. I used to live here. I glanced through Roger's underwear drawer—not to be a creep but because I was hoping to find some fresh underwear maybe and something I could wear that didn't have dried blood clinging to it. The search for underwear, however, was a complete bust. Roger's skinny-guy bikinis were way too small. A boy could hurt himself. I had no choice but—commando.

I traded my boxers from the day before for a pair of gray sweatpants, and I flipped through his t-shirt drawer until I found a dark blue one—to set off my eyes. Both the shirt and the sweats were small and tight, with a gap between the two, and with no underwear—wow—the sweatpants did not keep a whole lot of secrets.

I picked up the socks Roger had thrown at me—there was no way I was getting those on one-handed. Maybe I could get Dweeb to help me?

I looked myself over in the mirror, adjusted a couple things, turned a little left and right, and checked out my ass over my shoulder. Just obscene.

Perfect.

In the kitchen Roger had one of those one-cup-at-a-time coffee machines—new since my day, and just the thing for the lonely guy, I guessed. I fixed us two cups, changed the dog water, and dumped some kibble in the dog bowl. I was rummaging around in the refrigerator looking for some eggs when I heard the boys come back in. Roger and Haggis, I mean. My boys.

The dog came tearing into the kitchen—it was breakfast time for him.

"Hey, Hags—remember me?" I said, waving my bandaged hand as he bolted past me on the way to the bowl. "I'm the one whose blood is still drying on your little black lips, you heartless man-eater." He was only interested in kibble.

Roger hung the leash up on a hook.

"Hey, I borrowed some clothes—hope you don't mind."

"No—" Roger stopped as he saw what I was wearing, and what I wasn't. "No, on you they look…"

"Yeah, don't they, though."

"Maybe you don't want to go *out* like that?"

"Promise." I watched the dog crunching his food. "I thought after they'd tasted human blood, they never went back."

"I think that's tigers, not terriers."

"Oh. I was thinking about fixing us breakfast."

"Don't—you'll pull a stitch or something. Hey, I know—" He opened the freezer and pulled out a box of toaster waffles. "Ta-da!" he sang, triumphant.

"You are clearly the most brilliant person who ever walked the face of the earth," I said.

"I try."

"And so damned cute." I let my good hand brush across his ass as he turned around.

"Hey!"

"Sorry. Accident."

"Just watch it. Don't start getting all boyfriendy."

I raised my hands in surrender and turned back to making breakfast.

"Toaster waffles. Julia Child—stand back. Pull up a stool, Dweeb, and I will work my one-handed magic."

I had seen maple syrup in the fridge, so I knew we were good. Roger pulled his tablet out, sat at the counter, and read the *Times* online while I made more coffee, pulled out plates and butter, and waited on the wonder-waffles. Spreading cold butter with one hand, however, turned out to be a lot trickier than it looked. Roger wanted to take over, but I insisted I would do it. In the end he held the waffles with his left hand while I put some butter on each with my right, all of which involved us being really close, lots of contact, and it was funny, so there was lots of laughing too. If Jeff had walked in at just that moment, it would have looked far more incriminating than when we were in the bedroom in our underwear, and this time it was *exactly* what it looked like. Two guys being totally boyfriendy.

Roger read to me what was interesting online, and he showed me funny stuff on Facebook, jokes that started with things like "This quarter note walks into a bar…." It was easy to feel we had magically turned the clock back and the last two dreadful years hadn't happened, nothing had ever come between us, and no one had ever been hurt. He even helped me put the socks on, occasionally looking up at me with those melted-dark-chocolate eyes.

It was a beautiful morning. October sunlight streamed in through the yellow leaves of the tree out front and onto the living room floor. Roger practiced while I flopped on the couch and pretended to read the book I'd taken to the emergency room, but mostly I just listened to Roger, watched Roger. We talked a bit about the dog, about Trevor, about ushering (it was Sunday, and I was scheduled for the matinee but had e-mailed in sick).

"Hey, Roger," I asked. He was studying a score on the kitchen counter while I continued to recuperate on the couch.

"Yeah?"

"You really enjoy teaching Trevor, don't you?"

"I do."

"People can earn a living teaching lessons, can't they?"

"Yeah, some do. It's not a lot of money. But teaching is an important part of music. Everybody teaches."

"Have you thought about it?"

"Course. And since Trevor, especially."

"You hate being a lawyer."

"I don't hate it. But I don't love it either. Katrina really likes it. My dad loves it. I'm never going to love it."

"So?"

"So why not teach? To teach in a school, I'd probably have to go back and pick up at least *some* education credits. Maybe even a master's, I don't know."

"Oh."

I went back to my book for a second, but I'd rather talk to Roger.

So we talked about music, or mostly Roger talked and I let him talk. When he lagged, I poked him with another question ("so explain to me about Beethoven"), but mostly he went on without any help. He talked about his new passion for everything by some French guy named Ravel and how the guy only wrote one quartet and Katrina hated it. About a critic at *The Times* who pissed him off regularly. He played me a live recording he had from the fifties where you could actually hear the conductor yelling at the orchestra and how amazing and passionate that was. How he'd rather hear a college quartet play with enthusiasm and mistakes than an older group (I won't mention any names) who play like robots.

I don't have the words to tell you how awesome it was to hear him talk like this. Happy about something. I was pretty sure he didn't share this stuff with Jeff. His eyes shone with excitement. I was sitting up now, chatting over the back of the couch with him. It was just as well that we had the back of the couch between us because the urge to pick him up and throw him on the bed was starting to talk seriously and I was starting to listen, and to hell with Dr. Scruff and his common sense.

It was at that point, we heard a key in the door. Jeff.

Man-oh-man-oh-man, did I hate that guy.

I flopped back on the couch, feet up, facing the door, totally disgusted.

Jeff let himself in.

"Hey baby—" He stopped when saw me on the couch. I grinned and gave the shithead a cute little finger wave with my good hand. "Fuckaduck. What's *he* doing here?"

"Me? I spent the night." I smiled at Jeff and adjusted one or two things in my sweatpants. Did I mention how obscene those things were?

"First of all, Jeffrey," Roger began icily, "I'm not even sure why I have to explain this, but I will invite whomever I want into my apartment, and I will give keys to whomever I want. Understood?"

"Okay, baby, I get it. I crossed a foul line. My bad. I'm sorry."

"And don't call me baby."

"I thought you—"

"No, I never did."

"Sorry."

"And don't even try to apologize to me until you apologize to Fletch."

"No need," I said, intervening. "Jeff and I know exactly where we stand with each other, don't we, Jeff? It's totally cool." I could afford to be generous, and I was already having too much fun watching them fight.

Jeff's days were clearly numbered. And it was a *really* low number.

"And another thing, Jeffrey," said Roger, "America's most-wanted criminal here earned his place on the couch. Show him your hand, Fletch."

I held up my bandaged hand and stuck my lower lip out like a five-year-old.

"Caught in someone's zipper?"

"Haggis bit me."

"Good dog!"

"A huge cat attacked Haggis—" Roger explained.

"And this cat is like straight from *The Island of Dr. Moreau."*

"Don't tell me you've read a book, Fletch."

"I have! Wanna see my library card?" I tucked my thumb in the waistband of the sweatpants.

He sneered and turned away.

Hypocrite.

"Both of you, chill."

"Chill?" I asked. Roger said, "Chill?"

"Fletch, don't even. And Jeffrey, yes he reads, and when was the last time you read something that wasn't a brief? Just so you know, Dr. Moreau's cat attacked my dog, and Fletch broke them up, but he got all scratched up by the cat, and Haggis bit him really badly. I didn't even count how many stitches are in there. And better his left hand than mine," Roger said, wiggling his long, elegant fingers.

"I risked my life for that hand," I said.

"Well, if you spent the night on that couch, I suppose you have my sympathies."

"Who said I slept on the couch?" You didn't think I was going to pass that up, did you? "Oh, but *you* have! Interesting!"

Jeff made a sudden move to the couch, and I was immediately on my feet. Only one good hand, but I so didn't care.

"Go ahead, Jeff. Please. You spineless, nutless—"

Jeff was shouting something similar, but I wasn't really listening.

"Okay, that's enough!" Roger yelled. "Have you guys totally lost your minds?! Fletch. Go get some clothes on. Time to go." Roger stood there for a second. Was he shaking?

"Hey, Dweeb," I said quietly and moved toward him, but he stopped me with one hand held up.

"Get dressed."

"Okay," I said. I wasn't going to push anything. "I should go anyway, check to see if that cat's okay. It will be really hard to explain later—'No, really, I'm sure he only had one ear when you left!'"

Roger smiled.

"It would serve him right, though."

Good. Roger needed to smile.

And he needed to think about me a little before he faced off with Jeffrey.

It was time for the ultimate weapon.

I yawned.

I stretched slowly in front of Roger. I let Jeff watch, too, I wasn't going to begrudge him. I reached both arms up and out to the sides and arched my back, in the certain knowledge that this tiny t-shirt would give a generous view of some abdominals, the belly button. And I turned around. The back side was as good as the front, with a little bit of butt cleavage.

Think about *that*, I thought, before you jump into an afternoon of makeup sex with Mr. Oh-So-Very-Wrong—who was now staring at my crotch. You wish, dick brain.

"Just give me a second to get dressed, boys," I said, excusing myself to the bedroom.

"For God's sake, you too, Jeff." I could hear them through the bedroom door I didn't bother to close as I peeled out of the sweatpants.

"Did you really sleep with him last night?" asked Jeff.

"No! He passed out from all the drugs he got in the emergency room. *I* got the couch—which, as you know, means I haven't slept at all, which is why you need to go."

"Roger, I think we should talk," said Jeff.

"Isn't there a football game or something?"

"This is more important. *You're* more important."

Roger sighed.

"You really want to do this right now?"

"I think we should."

There was a long silence.

"Fine," Roger said finally.

I considered trying to pull my boxers back on one-handed and decided the jeans were going to be hard enough, and they were. Trying to button the fly, however, defeated me. One-handed wasn't quite working, so I used my left hand as much as I could—which wasn't much before it started throbbing. I got three and bailed. My shirttail would have to keep me and the dark blond curls from getting arrested on the D train.

When I got back to the living room, Bornic was still standing, staring at the floor. Roger was flipping through a score. Neither looked at me.

"Dweeb, call me if you want?" Roger nodded. "And thanks again for taking care of me. See you 'roun', Jeff," I said all super friendly.

I grabbed my library book. I soooooooo wanted to kiss Roger good-bye and not just to be an asshole to Jeff. That would have just been a bonus.

But I restrained myself.

Chapter 35
Lunch with Father

ROGER

It happens on the last Monday of every month, although it tends to get lost during the holidays, so this, the October lunch, was probably the last one of the year.

I sort of dread these things, but I should be fair, and tell you that there's a lot I like about my dad. My mom too.

My mom figured out I was gay when I was about sixteen. No, that's not quite right. I'm not sure when she figured it out, but I was sixteen when she shared her conclusion with me. I just nodded in agreement.

Of course Tommy had already broken the ice.

Tommy and I had always been friends. Really, I can't remember a time before Tommy. His family lived nearby, and Tommy and I are actually second cousins on my father's side (Tommy's mother is a Prescott).

Tommy was always my best friend, and Tommy was always Tommy. He was always exactly as he is. He was a *fabulous* four-year-old. In third grade, he was talking about cute boys. He used to use his birthday money to buy Barbie clothes. For his G.I. Joe.

And it never occurred to him that I might *not* be interested in cute boys. He just assumed that I was as interested in boys as he was.

For the longest time I didn't know what to think. I mean, compared to Tommy, I was a goddamned lumberjack, so I was always a little confused. I was pretty sure I wasn't like the other boys, but I also knew I wasn't quite like Tommy either.

So yeah, I was interested in cute boys, but I was never *as* interested in boys as Tommy. But seriously, was anyone? Ever?

In the end, though, when my mother just sort of put it to me—sweetly and sensitively—as a statement of fact, with only the tiniest hint of a question mark in her voice, I had to admit—she and Tommy were right.

My dad didn't flip out. (Let's face it; lots of parents do. Tommy's dad, a doctor, didn't flip out; he was just quietly a total dick about it, until the dick finally ran off with his nurse. Whole other story.)

My dad, the lawyer, treated it like a case. When he learned his son was gay, he did what he always does with a new case.

Research.

I'm sure his secretary and probably a paralegal were pulling books and articles for him. I bet he dictated memos with detailed outlines and at least three levels of numbered subparagraphs, full of thoughtful analysis.

A family trait that I believe was passed down to us through the generations from our puritan ancestors: We might talk about someone or something, but we never actually talk directly *to* the person involved. That sort of thing isn't done.

I had inherited this trait, too, apparently, which explains why I'd never asked Fletch about his past. We don't pry.

My father couldn't talk with me about my being a gay teen because that would be intrusive and embarrassing; it would be rude. But he could go to a parents-of-gay-teens meeting. I swear to God. How do I know this? My mother told me.

That's how we communicate in my family: rumors.

My mother's reaction was completely different. I was in my room one morning—it was summer—practicing and moping, exactly like every other summer morning when I wasn't at Interlochen (orchestra camp, where I first discovered chamber music) or Kinhaven (chamber music camp, where I first discovered a couple of other things)—when my mom came in, made me put the violin down, and pulled me out to the car while I whinged, and we drove into the city.

First stop, Dr. Feldman, a dermatologist. Holy crap, there was actually something you could do about acne? Who knew!

It was going to be a day of revelations.

Second stop, Le Salon Lilo, a hideously chichi hair salon in pink, where Miles, the big oh-so-very-gay guy who did my mother's hair, plucked at the huge mass of curls on my head—it was a ridiculous shapeless blob, but I didn't have a clue what to do. He pulled it here, pushed it there, looked at me in the mirror, looked at my mother in the mirror, told her it was under control, and he shooed her out beyond the curtains.

The second miracle of the day—it was possible to shoo my mother. Miles was easily the most effeminate man I had ever seen, which, considering my best friend was Tommy Radford, was really saying something; but that day I realized—Miles was also the bravest.

And Miles cut my hair, leaving this big poodle thing of curls on my forehead, and that's how it's been pretty much ever since.

After the salon, Bloomingdales and then a handful of little shops all over. She bought me a boatload of new clothes, all picked out by her, and all much better than anything I'd ever have picked out myself. The woman has taste.

I remember being in a dressing room that day and seeing my reflection in the mirror. Cute hair, cute clothes.

Miracle number three—I could almost believe that maybe someday someone might want to go out with somebody who looked like me.

Imagine.

So. That was my parents' response to having a gay child. To my father, I was a case to be solved. To my mother, I was a home-improvement project.

I can't complain.

They coped as best as they could, and there was never a hint of judgment or disappointment from either of them. I have a sister and brother, so: There will be bloodline.

The sibs:

My sister Andrea. (Pronounced on-DRAY-uh. You probably knew that, but I have to be clear because she'll eviscerate you if you get it wrong.) She's a gorgeous girl torn between two roles—the spoiled rich princess and the stoner. She'll grow out of one someday, but I won't make any bets which.

My brother, Todd, is still in school, where he plays football. Harvard—of course. Not a school where you're likely to end up in the pros, but still, he plays college football, the games are on TV (cable, but still), and this is America after all. He is revered.

You can guess who's the center of attention at family gatherings. The violin phenom is so far overshadowed by the football player that it isn't even funny. That sounds like I resent it, but I so don't. It takes a *lot* of pressure off my sister and me. Nobody expects mere mortals like us to compete with a college football star—and we don't. We watch Todd bask in their attentions, and we exchange sly smiles. Then we go outside, make bitchy remarks, laugh, and I watch my sister get stoned.

If anybody, out of politeness, asks me about my law career—which is rare—or about my violin playing—even rarer—I say it's going well, thank you, and did you hear about Todd's latest whatever? Which is, of course, what they'd rather talk about anyway, because this is America, and then I excuse myself and go outside to make even bitchier comments and to watch my sister get even more stoned.

I wish I could like Toddy more and vice versa.

So my family coped with the eldest child being a pansy, but other aspects of my life were harder for them to swallow. I loved music, which they thought was all very nice, but enough's enough. My family has connections to Harvard that go back to its founding, which I believe is mentioned in the Old Testament, so it was blasphemous that I went to Oberlin College for four years. For music.

I loved Oberlin. The music nerds ruled, or so it seemed to us. If there was a college outside the music department, those of us *in* the music department hardly knew about it. Other students, non–music majors, were only—and just barely—a step above townies. (Tommy went with me, and as an English major, he was my connection to the outside world.)

My family tolerated my time at Oberlin, they indulged me for four years there, and they shoveled out all that money for tuition, for which I am truly grateful—and then it was time to get serious.

They made it very clear. I had lots of options. If I didn't want to go to Harvard Law School, that was perfectly all right. There was always Harvard Medical.

I grumbled, I kicked and I—spelunked.

And that's how I got where I got.

My dad may not understand being gay, but he's trying. What he can't begin to comprehend is not loving being a lawyer.

I ended up at Goodkin Berdann & Dunkel largely because of Katrina—and against my father's advice. GBD didn't, and doesn't, have the nicest reputation in town. Jeff's firm, Parker O'Neill, is proud of their firm culture of collegiality and would probably have been a better fit for me, a firm where people are actually nice to each other. Ironically that's where Jeff-the-barracuda ended up.

Goodkin Berdann, by contrast, is famous for developing the killer instincts of their lawyers. But Katrina had one look at my résumé, found out I'd been concert master at Oberlin while still a junior—which *was* pretty unusual—and I think she'd have promised just about anything to get me at Goodkin. Of course she was a great attraction for me, too. How bloodthirsty could a law firm be, I asked myself, that was actually going to field a string quartet?

So I landed at Goodkin Berdann & Dunkel. GBD. Even our e-mail addresses end @gbd.com. Say G-B-D to a musician, and what do we hear? A G-major chord. I thought it was a sign.

Oops.

But the quartet is really wonderful, and I wouldn't trade it, even if I had some trouble making my way at the firm.

I make jokes about not being very good at the whole lawyer thing, but it's true. I'm aware how much better everyone around me is. I see Katrina plow through a bewildering pile of documents that represents an estate, and she knows immediately what to do with it, what the dangers are, and how best to keep the government from getting their hands on all that hardly earned money. Of course she's got years of experience, and she's a senior attorney, and that's why she gets paid gazillions. But the thing I see is—she's like my dad. She loves this whole problem-solving thing. She loves the analysis.

Me, not so much. Truth is I just can't care.

I can't say that to my father, though.

"Good afternoon, Mr. Prescott," said Panjeet. Panjeet ran the dining room of the Harvard Club and had done so for years. He was getting a little grey now, but I always thought he was the most elegant man I had ever met.

Now, here at Ye Olde Harvard Club, we weren't just members; we were like royalty come to visit. We owned this place. There were members more senior than my maternal grandfather, but my grandfather had a dorm with his name on it.

My father, who also went to Harvard and who married into this august family, considers it an almost royal obligation to use the club as often as possible. So the Paternal Lunch is always here. And it's very close to my office.

I greeted my father with a handshake—we don't hug, we Prescott men—and we sat at the same table as always. We looked over the menu, and we ordered—the same thing as always.

Turtle soup, whatever fish was fresh that day, a cheese course to follow, and to drink: Perrier. We had offices to go back to.

You've heard of the puritan work ethic? My family invented it.

"So Roger, how are you?"

"Fine, sir."

"You look a little tense, if I may say so."

"I've had better weeks."

"Work stress?"

"No more than usual."

"Well, I'm sure you'll come through. Sometimes it's just a matter of putting in that extra hour at the end of the day. When you're getting ready to go, whether that's six o'clock or nine o'clock or eleven o'clock—just sit back down and knock in another hour. I've found that can take a lot of pressure off the next day."

"I'll keep that in mind, Dad."

"And who doesn't love another billable hour? I know your firm has a reputation for being sort of—"

"Cutthroat?"

"I might have said competitive, but yes. Try not to let it bother you. Just do what you do, and you'll do fine."

"I'll try, sir."

We ate the turtle soup. I know it sounds disgusting, but it's actually incredibly good.

"Anything else on your mind?" he asked when the bowls were cleared and the two plates of fish had been laid down in front of us.

"One or two little things," I said ruefully, "but nothing you really want to hear about."

"Try me," he said.

I looked up at him. Was that really my father across the table?

"Trouble with Jeff?"

I practically choked on my scrod.

"You could say that."

"He seemed nice enough when I met him. Sensible, good head on his shoulders, and I've heard good things about his future with his firm."

"You've checked up on him?" He just looked up at me for a second. Of course he had, How stupid of me.

"Well, I hate to disappoint you again—"

"You haven't disappointed me yet."

"—but I just dumped him."

"Well. I'm sure you had your reasons—and whether *I* liked him or not couldn't be of less importance. I hope you know that."

"Thanks," I said, a little embarrassed.

After I'd finally gotten Jeff out of the apartment, I'd gone straight to bed, exhausted.

If you ever find yourself deep in a messy emotional quandary, as I was, caught on the horns of a dilemma, and you're having trouble seeing your way out of a particularly difficult turmoil, I can tell you this much:

Wrapping yourself up in the sheets where your turmoil has just spent the night is not terribly helpful.

My father and I forked our fish.

"You remember my talking about Fletch? My—um—sort of ex? Couple years ago?"

"Ye-es," he said, sounding uncertain. Maybe my dad wasn't sure he remembered—I hadn't talked about Fletch that much—or maybe he just wasn't sure where this was going. I wasn't either. "Is he the one—you guys lived together for a while, didn't you?"

"Um, yeah. We did. Well, he's turned up recently." Was I crazy to confide in my father? Could he possibly understand? Everything was so clean and simple for him. He would never get himself in such a mess. Mayhem and my father had never been in the same room together. He was all about bringing order out of chaos. He could never understand why I would, or how I could, let such sloppiness happen in my life.

"So. I never met Fletch."

"No. He's not really the kind of—I guess I wasn't quite ready for that at the time."

"But now he's back. And you're thinking you might want to try again?"

"No!" Of course I was, who was I kidding? But not seriously. Yes, Sunday morning had been fantastic, being with Fletch could be wonderful and fun. The problem with Fletch was what he was doing when he *wasn't* with me. No. I wasn't seriously considering Fletch as a possibility.

"But Jeff had to go anyway? Nothing to do with the other guy?"

"Not how you'd think. When I first met Jeff, I thought he was everything I was looking for. Reliable, steady, professional."

"All good qualities."

"And everything Fletch isn't. But since Fletch resurfaced, I see everything the way Fletch sees it. Now I see Jeff through Fletch's eyes. Jeff's the same guy he was, but now all I can see is how dull he is, shallow, predictable. Not an original thought in his head."

"And overbearing," said my father.

I looked up at him again.

"Sir?"

"I *have* met the guy, you know."

"Well, yeah, he is kind of overbearing. And a bit of a bully."

"Everything that Fletch isn't."

"Exactly!"

"In Fletch's eyes."

"Well yeah, now *I* see Jeffrey like that too."

"It seems to me fairly significant that you care what Fletch thinks, don't you find?"

"I—I guess." Did I? Care what Fletch thought, I mean? Why hadn't this question occurred to me before, and what was the answer? And, more important, if the answer was what I thought the answer was, what did the answer mean?

And my father thinks I should be a lawyer???

Dad looked at me for a few seconds while my head spun, and then he did the most amazing thing.

He laid down his fork.

In the Harvard Club, that's the equivalent of a cry for help. If you jumped up and down on your chair and screamed fire, people would look away embarrassed and pretend not to have noticed. Set your fork down in the middle of the entrée, and waiters came running.

"Is there something, Mr. Prescott?" Panjeet said discreetly at his shoulder, fearing the worst.

"Everything's fine, Panjeet, but, when you have a moment, could you bring us two double whiskies. Ice?" he asked me.

I shook my head quickly, not because I'm really a big fan of warm booze in a glass, but because it seemed the thing to do, and frankly I was terrified of disappointing my father, not to mention Mr. Panjeet.

"The special?"

My father had a private stash of some ancient Scotch hidden away in a vault here.

"Yes, Panjeet," he said, handing over a small key, "the special whiskey."

I wasn't at all sure what was going on. This was completely new territory for me. I had never had such a conversation with my father, and I'd never had a drink with him either.

"I can't possibly give you advice," my father said. "I know these emotions can be complicated. Sometimes it's easy to know when you're in love with somebody and sometimes not. You think you're in love and then two weeks later you're thinking, 'My God she has huge teeth. I could never spend the rest of my life looking at those enormous teeth.'"

"Sir?"

"I believe the expression is—I am just saying." It's a hoot when he tries to get hip and slangy with his perfect Old Saybrook diction. Imagine Katharine Hepburn saying, "I don't mind telling you, B, this shit is actually quite marvelously dope. Yo."

I could only smile.

Mr. Panjeet was back with a tray, two glasses of the sacred stuff and a small cut-glass pitcher of water. I looked down at the glass in my hand.

"People will tell you things," my dad said, "like 'follow your heart.' It's completely asinine of course. If you knew what your heart really wanted, there would be no problem. It's when you *don't* know that gets you in so much trouble. And sometimes your heart wants two quite incompatible things at once, this one *and* that one. And it's not always easy to sort out if you're following your heart or your hormones."

I suspect my mouth was hanging open. If not, it should have been. If my grandmother had been dancing on the bar with a lampshade on her head, I wouldn't have been more astounded. My father was telling me that he understood and perhaps had even experienced emotional confusion? *My* father???

My father had hormones???

"In any case," he said and picked up his glass, "welcome to adulthood."

I picked up my glass—to which I'd added some water.

"My uncle George used to make a toast about moving from the infantry into the adultery. Or something like that." He took a swallow.

I sipped and tried hard not to choke on it. I had just been welcomed to adulthood. I didn't want to spit up ridiculously expensive hooch like a fifteen-year-old, even if it tasted like charred lawnmower clippings and it burnt like hell going down.

"It gets easier, the older you get," he said. After a few seconds he added, "I mean the Scotch. The rest of it is still hella confounding and utterly—what is it?—mad whack."

He looked pretty chuffed with himself too.

Chapter 36
Westward, Ho!

FLETCH

Sooner or later he'd call, right? He'd call when he was ready.

I kinda had the idea he was going to give Jeff the boot that day, the morning after the emergency room, but maybe he hadn't. Maybe he was giving the numb-nuts one more try. Roger needs to think about things. It was clearly inevitable, a total sooner-or-later thing, but Roger needed to be sure. And fair. That was just how he was. Or maybe he'd dumped the moron, and he just wanted a certain amount of time before he was ready to deal with me. I could understand that. He needed time, and I needed to be patient. Right?

But it had already been like a week and a half!!!

You see, the trouble was patience was never really my thing. I've always been more of a doer, you know what I mean? Act on impulse and think about it later, if ever. The opposite of Roger, which was why we were so good for each other, although I'm sure he would never admit that. The whole yin–yang thing. I challenged him to relax a bit, and I gave him a little more spontaneity. And he lent me a certain degree of circumspection. One of a billion words I'd learned from him.

But the yin–yang thing isn't always very comfortable, which is why he'd say I drive him buggy sometimes. And why this waiting while he thought about things was driving *me* buggy.

Patience.

In the meantime, with an evening off from my usual post in the mezzanine of the Gershwin Theatre, I thought I'd distract myself and kill some time with Marco. His family had carved out this fairly hip apartment for him from the old family house when his two older brothers moved out. It's always nice to hang with Marco, and it would help me avoid sitting around the apartment staring at the walls, talking to Tybalt and thinking about a cute violin player. And of course there I was, still thinking about the violin player.

We were sitting on Marco's bed, backs against the headboard, watching TV. Just like old times.

"So," he said after a bit. "You want to fool around?"

"What?" I said. "No." Yeah, that was like old times too—except for the no. That was new.

"C'mon," he said and put his hand on my thigh. "We haven't messed around in fuckin' forever."

"True, and we're not going to today either."

We watched TV. It was one of those stupid dance competition shows, and it mostly just reminded me of Jeff.

Maybe I should set myself a deadline. If I haven't heard from Roger by the end of the week or whatever. And then what? Call him? Say, "Roger, I have to see you"?

Then he'd ask why, and I'd have to explain, and explanations would kill the whole thing.

Forget about calling him.

"So tell me what happened to your hand," Marco said at the commercial.

"Long-ish story, but Roger came out to my apartment in Brooklyn."

"Seriously? That's a good sign."

"I thought so too. But I hadn't mentioned I was cat sitting, and he brought his dog with him."

"He brought his dog?"

"He doesn't like Brooklyn. Makes him nervous."

"You're kidding."

"No. As Tommy described it, 'he doesn't do boroughs.'"

"Ha! Tommy—I haven't thought about him in ages. So Roger brought his dog…"

"And the cat took umbrage."

"Umbrage?"

"Umbrage."

"Funny name for a dog."

"There was a big fight, and I had to break them up."

"A cat did that?"

"A cat did this," and I showed him the pretty scab that ran down the inside of my right forearm, "while I was carrying him out of the room—one good swipe with his hind foot. It was the dog who did this," and I held up the left hand in its bandage.

"So you got bit saving Roger's dog? Did he throw himself in your arms and say, 'My hero!'?"

"Next best thing. He took me to the emergency room, and then he took me back to his apartment because I was sort of out of my mind on the anesthetic."

"Really? I woulda kinda liked to have been there for that, son."

"You missed it, your one chance to see me fucked up."

"So you spent the night with Roger finally?"

"Nothing happened. He slept on the couch, I think. I was in la-la-land."

"But he let you stay."

"Yep."

"That's a good sign."

"I thought so too. And we spent a good part of Sunday together, which was really nice, and we didn't fight."

"Also good."

"I thought so too."

A commercial on TV.

I should give Roger another week. And then just show up at his apartment. And tell him everything.

Tell him what, exactly?

Tell him how I feel.

Wow. Just the *thought* of that gave me a cold sweat. People talk about panic attacks; maybe this was one. I even shuddered a little.

"So," Marco said, "you want to go out?"

"Not really."

"We could pick up some hot guy, bring him back, and screw his brains out?" he suggested hopefully.

"Tempting as that sounds, Marco, no."

We watched a little more TV.

"You used to be a lot more fun, bro."

"I know."

I should do it anyway, I thought. The thing with Roger, I mean, not the three-way with Marco. I should cowboy up, as Florence Night-sweats said. I should randomly pick a day, and then, if I haven't heard from him by then, I'll just hang out in his apartment until he comes home, and—what? Ambush him?

Marco was pointing at the TV.

"You'll like this guy, Fletch. So damned hot."

"I guess."

"I hope they win. Them or the other ones."

Dance, dance commercial.

"You really like this stuff?" I said of the TV show.

"Are you kidding me? Everybody loves this show. Why?"

"I know a nice-looking lawyer I could fix you up with," I suggested. "If he's not available now, he will be soon." It was the least I could do for Jeffrey. A couple nights of reality TV with Marco, and Jeff's little broken heart would feel lots better. A few other parts wouldn't feel so bad either.

Who were these stars supposed to be, anyway? I'd never heard of them.

"So how long you gonna keep this up?" Marco asked.

"Which?"

"Waiting for Mr. Rogers to drop trou."

"I don't know. I really don't know. And I don't know what I'll do if it comes to nothing."

"All onna conna some guy who's not interested. Move on, my man."

"Can't."

"I think it's making you crazy."

"I *know* it's making me crazy. And broke too. That hipster dog walker I bribed? It occurred to her that I must have my reasons for buying her off—and she insisted I cough up *another* fifty dollars a week, or she will suddenly make herself available to walk the dog again."

"Peace, love, and gouge thy neighbor."

"She's also threatened to explain exactly who paid her off *not* to walk the dog."

"I could ask my uncle Phil to talk to her. It would be no problem. You remember Uncle Phil?" It's a cliché, but Marco's family knows people, and I'm sure Uncle Phil could explain to the greedy little slacker that it was not a wise business practice to put the bite on a friend of the Campobassos.

"That's okay. And you're right, it can't go on for much longer."

We watched a samba.

"That looks like fun," I said of the dance.

Marco's hand migrated over to my thigh.

"Dude, I'm not some sixteen-year-old girl at the movies." I moved his hand.

"You sure act like one," he grumbled.

"Shut up and eat your popcorn."

Interview of sweating, panting dancers. The guy was way pretty. But not like Roger.

Wait a minute. Just wait a cotton-picking minute, whatever that means.

I looked at the samba boy again. Big mess of black hair, fiendish green eyes, cheeks flushed, dimples, big grin, delicious lips, shirt open, washboard abs, chest heaving, sweating—everything about this guy was unbelievably hot. And I was—bored? Marco was right, something was clearly wrong with me.

Ambush. I liked the ambush idea. I won't say anything. No words, I'll just pounce. As soon as Dweeb comes through the door, I'll grab his adorable face in both hands and I will kiss him like crazy from his hairline to his collarbone. And just when he wants me to keep going—– I'll split. He likes to think about things? I'll just leave him standing there, so he can think about things. His turn for a little circumspection.

"So," Marco said, interrupting my plan, "are you like never gonna have sex again for like the rest of your entire life or somethin'?"

"That's not exactly the plan, no, but I'm not going to have sex until I want it."

"Dude, you know you want it." He wiggled his eyebrows suggestively.

Puh-lease.

"What are you going to do? Rape me?"

He sat up and looked at me.

"Fletch! That would be like soooo hot! And if you want, you can rape me back! How's *that* for an offer?"

"That's messed up. You know that, don't you."

"Seriously, you're like the saddest story I ever heard. You're totally dick-whipped, and you're not even getting any dick."

"Pathetic, i'n it?"

"It's sweet that you're saving it for this guy, but the guy you're saving it for doesn't want it."

A little harsh but completely true. I should say something, to acknowledge his keen insight and mature, thoughtful observation.

"Shut up," I said.

Time for somebody else to samba, or maybe it was a cha-cha. Beats me. I should pay more attention.

Of course what happens if I pounce, and he fights like a demon and tells me to get the hell out of his life? Again? It was a possibility. Maybe I needed to circumspect this a little more.

"Hey," Marco said, trying again. "You know if it doesn't work out, and you know, you don't hook up with the Roger again, I've been thinking. I've been thinking about moving actually."

"You mean—leave this house? Are you nuts? Leave your ma's cooking?"

"I'm thinking about leaving the city."

It was my turn to sit up and take notice.

"I know it seems crazy and scary, but I've never been anywhere. I got some money, and you remember my cousin Joey—you met him—Little Joey's Joey? He's been out in L.A. for a year and he loves it. He's got a house with an extra bedroom and everything."

"L.A?"

"Think about it. We'll buy a used car—"

"I can't drive."

"Me either! It'll be a blast! We're young and footloose. Why not? You've never been anywhere either."

"Fire Island doesn't count?" I said, smiling.

"Fire island most definitely does not count." He smiled back. "C'mon, think about it. You and me in a brand-new city. Great weather. Lots of sun, lots of skin, lots of beautiful dudes, dude."

My knee-jerk reaction was "no way," but…I really had no idea what I would do if Roger decided to shut me out completely. New York just might be unbearable. I knew I couldn't go back to being the little concuboy that I was in August. And aside from Roger and Marco, there was nothing to keep me here.

California. Probably a better idea than jumping off the GW Bridge, which was another option.

"I'll think about it," I said.

"You mean it?" He was surprised.

"I mean—I'll think about it."

"Okay!"

"Thanks."

"What for?"

"For asking me."

"Shut up."

There was more dancing. You'd think a professional boxer would be able to move better than that, but there you go.

Monday. This was Thursday. I would give him until Monday, and if I haven't heard from Roger by then, I would do it. The pouncing, I mean. And screw the consequences.

"So, you just want to watch some porn and jerk off or what?"

"You know what?" I got up from the bed. "You're a gorgeous hunk of man, and I love you madly, but I'm gonna go." I kissed him on his beautiful, thick Italian hair on his beautiful, thick Italian head. "You obviously need to take care of something. Watch some porn; have some fun." I pulled my high-tops back on and started tying up the laces.

I wasn't angry, it wasn't his fault. Not that long ago I would have happily shoved my jeans down, and—showtime!

"You can stay and watch, if you want."

I just couldn't anymore.

"I'll call you."

Chapter 37
The End of the Story

ROGER

I'd come home a little early. When I got there, there was no Haggis. Unless he'd decided to let himself out and go party with the French bulldogs from downstairs, he must be out with Fletch.

Fletch. I hadn't seen him in two weeks. I guess I'd been avoiding him. Of course I'd been avoiding him. Carefully avoiding him. I hadn't called him after my go-round with Jeff, as I kind of said I would, and I hadn't called him since. We'd traded a couple texts about the dog, but that was it. I guess I didn't really know how to handle Fletch in a post-Jeff world.

What was I afraid of? I didn't know.

Now it seemed like it was time—which didn't mean I wasn't still scared, because I was. But even *I* can only put things off for so long, and truth to tell—I sort of missed him. Sort of missed him a lot. I found myself thinking of things to tell Fletch when I saw him, and then I deliberately didn't see him. Which, when I thought about it, didn't really make much sense. So here I was, intentionally home early enough to find Fletch.

I heard his key in the door, and he and the dog came in.

"Hey," I said.

He jumped about a foot.

"Whoa! Man-oh-man, you scared me!"

"That's funny. In the whole time I've known you, I don't know if I've ever seen you startled."

The dog wandered past me into the kitchen, giving me one ankle bump and two miniscule wags of his tail as he went by, and that was it. Love you too, Hags.

"It's just—" Fletch started to say. "I was going to—I mean I had this all planned out—differently."

"Had what all planned out?"

"Nothing. It's just—"

"Sorry. Didn't mean to rattle you."

"You know how you like to have things all laid out in advance and how you hate it when something—usually me—comes along and wrecks it?"

"Oh hell yes."

"Today—it's the other way around. That's all."

"You—want me to leave?" I offered.

"It's okay. I'll wing it. Remember me? The spontaneous one. So. Hey, Dweeb."

"Hey."

"I've kinda missed you."

"Thanks." I blushed, but I liked hearing that. I liked hearing it way more than I should. "Me too. I mean, I've kinda missed you too."

"So what are you doing home?" He glanced at his watch.

"Couldn't stand it another minute. It's okay, not even my secretary will notice. And honest? I wanted to talk to you."

"Good. I'd decided I was going to hang out here 'til you got home—I wanted to talk to you too."

"How's your hand?"

"Much better thanks! The stitches are gone, and you can see, the swelling's nearly gone too." He pressed it with his index finger.

"Will it scar badly?"

"Just enough to remind me."

"A souvenir of Dr. Scruffy."

"Or something. Oh damn it!" he said suddenly, interrupting himself. "Speaking of remembering, there was something I wanted to bring you. I can't believe I forgot, unless..." He rummaged a little frantically through his bag. "No, I left it on the little table right by the door—so I wouldn't forget it. Damn!"

"What is it?"

"A surprise."

"Fletch, you know how I—"

"Not a bad surprise, I promise. I'll have to bring it tomorrow, you'll see. Hey, did somebody steal some of your CDs? That shelf didn't used to be empty."

I looked around.

"I guess Jeff came by and picked up his stuff. No more Lady Gaga, I'm afraid. Or is it the other one?"

"Oh. So." He changed the dog's water. "What happened to Jeff?"

He was trying to sound casual.

"We had a little chat, and I told him that—on a going-forward basis—he should go fuck himself."

Fletch stood up from setting the water bowl down.

"Really."

"In point of fact. And before you think another thought, stop right there."

"What?"

"I know you, and I know what you're thinking, and in about three minutes one of us is going to have his pants around his ankles—but forget it."

"Okay! Okay!" He put his hands up in surrender and went to sit—but he had to tug at his pants to accommodate what was already going on down there.

"Unbelievable," I said, trying not to look at what he was adjusting. "Get a grip." Fletch's eyebrows leaped about two inches at this tiny hint of an innuendo. "Stop it." I sat on the couch, and he moved to sit next to me. "Over there." I pointed to the other end of the couch.

We each had a leg bent up on the couch so we could look at each other. I wasn't sure what I was doing here.

"You can't be totally surprised about it. Jeff, I mean."

"No—but what about you? You okay with that?"

"Yeah, I am. I seem to be totally okay with that. I suppose if I'm honest, I've been wanting to dump him for a while, but I kept thinking he should have to *do* something to deserve it. Giving him the heave-ho just because I'd decided I didn't much like him didn't seem fair somehow?"

"Only you."

"Yeah, I know. Lately he's been a total dick, and then that thing with the detective? So that sort of solved itself."

"So. No Cancun?"

"I know! To think I was *this* close to getting golf lessons."

"How did he take it?"

"Not well. I tried to keep things quiet and not have a huge knock-down-drag-'em-out, but in the end he pissed me off so much. I said some awful things."

"Good for you."

I hadn't been particularly eager to thrash things out with Jeff—but he had forced the issue, and I'd told him. *È finita. Das Ende.* And although he had been the one pushing to have the conversation, he couldn't quite take it in. It was obviously his first time as a dump*ee* instead of dump*er*.

"There's no way on earth you are breaking up with me; that's just not happening."

Seriously, that's what he said. Reason enough to dump somebody right there, wasn't it?

"Jeffrey—"

"I get it. You're pissed at me."

"I'm trying not to be, but you're not making it easy."

You've figured out by now that I don't do nasty very well, so I wanted to keep this as *un*-nasty as I could. I told him I thought we had different interests, different ambitions, blah-blah-blah, but poor Jeffrey's little frat-boy brain could only see this as a competition, and it was a competition that he had lost. Worse than that? He'd lost to Fletch. That was simply unacceptable.

"Never imagined you'd go for sex and a body over brains."

My patience was just about done, but I tried again.

"This isn't the big game, you against Fletch. This isn't a case, *Fletch v. Jeff*, Second Circuit, or whatever. It's just you and I. I'm not choosing Fletch over you. I'm choosing: Not. You. I'm sorry if that's harsh."

"Honestly, I never saw that illiterate piece of street trash as a serious rival."

"Okay, Jeffrey, now you're pissing me off."

"You used to call me Jeff."

"Yeah, and it was stupid. Sorry for that too."

"So you're passing on me in favor of your well-hung rent boy."

"I assume you're still talking about Fletch, and no, that's not what's happening. Fletch has nothing to do with it!"

"What a lie."

Was it? Maybe. Okay, probably. I don't know.

"So that's it, after everything that's happened between you and I."

Not sure why *that* was the thing that did it, but that did it.

"Between you and *me*, you pompous fuck!" So much for outward calm. "Everything *about* you is wrong! You hate dogs—"

"I don't hate dogs."

"You love practicing law, and you love schmoozing, and you want me to love schmoozing, and I *hate* schmoozing! You hate the violin, classical music, string quartets, and I bet, if you were really totally honest, you'd probably admit you don't even like *me*. If that weren't enough, you went to school for nineteen years and still don't understand how to use the accusative case! So. Here it is. I'll always treasure this time we shared, now for the love of all that's holy, take your goddamn Lady Gaga CDs and go!"

"Katy Perry!"

"Same! Thing!"

"I don't want to speak ill of the dead..." That was Fletch, pulling me back from the fight with Jeffrey that I *really* didn't need to relive.

"Yeah, me either. So what did you want to talk to me about?"

"Me? Um—no-no-no. You first."

"Okay. Well, you know how you said you'd tell me everything I wanted to know."

"I'm going to regret saying that, aren't I."

"Probably."

"So. What do you want to know?"

"I think it's time—tell me about Frank Szyfranski."

"Seriously?"

"Seriously."

"Where do I even start?"

"It doesn't really matter—just start."

And he did. He gave a deep sigh, and he told me.

Only child of a single mother. She was blond and blue-eyed, like him, and beautiful. And with a ton of problems. They lived in the projects; they lived in shelters; they lived with her boyfriends; they lived on the street.

"Occasionally she'd go into rehab, I guess, and I'd go into foster care, and then she'd come out, and we'd try again—and then, I think I was about nine, she just left me there. I lived in different places, mostly in Queens or Westchester County."

"Where'd the name come from?"

"Fletch? Where I was when I was ten, eleven, there were a few of us. The thing with foster kids is they come and go, it's not like a constant family. Everybody in the neighborhood knew we were foster kids, and they were either like "Oh you poor little dears" or they looked at you like they thought you were about to pull a knife. In *this* house, they must have had some doozies going through there, because people in the neighborhood totally shunned us. No kids could play with us. The woman across the street looked at me like I was this prepubescent serial killer. Most of my time there, it was me and two girls, one older, one not. What I really wanted to do was play baseball or shoot some hoops with the neighbor boys. Not happening—except for one guy. He was older, maybe fifteen when I was ten. And he was nice to us, always talked to us, and he would play basketball with me while the girls watched. They had huge crushes on him—maybe I did too, a little bit."

"Fletcher Andrews."

"Andrew Fletcher, but everyone called him Fletch. And then, for whatever reason, our foster parents decided they had had enough, were moving to Oregon, and they were out of the paid-parenting business. We were sent back. And then on to someplace else."

"Did you at least go together, the three of you?"

"Of course not."

I had this huge surge of sympathy for him. It's tough to hear about bad things happening to kids, but when it's somebody you care about, even as a friend…

"Tell me about Juvie," I said.

"Two thumbs-down, I don't recommend it. Even Cancun would be better."

"Just tell me. How'd you get there?"

He turned away a bit, pulled one foot up onto his knee, and hooked a finger in the lace of his high-tops.

"You didn't read the file?"

"Jeff said it was assault, which didn't make any sense to me. I knew there had to be more to it than that."

"Thanks."

"For what?"

"The benefit of the doubt."

"So. Assault?"

"I clocked our foster dad. With a girls' field hockey stick. Really, really hard."

"Cool," I said, trying to make it all a little less awful.

"It *was*, actually."

"What happened?"

"You mean why did I hit him? He was a douchebag."

"Fletch—"

"Look. I'm not ashamed that I went to juvie, and I'm not ashamed that I hit the guy. But it's still not a very nice story."

"Hey. It's me."

He took a deep breath.

"Okay. The douchebag's name was Brad. Brad and Susan were our lovely foster parents. I was there from, what?—thirteen?—until almost sixteen. There were three girls in the house and me. Big house in White Plains. No money. Foster parents never have money. I got a room to myself. Two girls shared, and the oldest, Theresa, had a room to herself."

"Lucky Theresa."

"Not so much. Every so often, Brad would drink a little. He wasn't a drunk; it wasn't an everyday or even an every-week thing. But every so often he'd have himself a couple or three after dinner, I think to give himself courage, and then he'd go to Theresa's room. *I* knew it. I could hear it. Susan had to know it. Everyone knew, and none of us did anything.

"And I hated myself. Every single time. I hated myself because I let it happen. I was such a fucking little coward. But you see, coming up through the system, you learn to keep your head down. There was no point in sticking your neck out and catching somebody else's crap, because you knew you were going to have your own busload of crap come raining down on you all too soon, whether you deserved it or not, so why take on somebody else's? And that's how I went on, with a pillow over my head that didn't really block out anything, and hating myself."

"Until you clobbered him."

"One night I heard him, but he wasn't in Theresa's room. He'd gone across the hall to the room with the two younger girls. And I couldn't do it anymore. I went over there, the girls were both crying, and he was pawing at Angelina and trying to shush her, and one of the girls' hockey sticks was leaning on the wall right by the door. Bam, from behind. As hard as I could."

"Oh my God."

"We stared at him lying there on the floor. Pool of blood getting bigger by the second. He wasn't dead, but we weren't sure of that right away. Susan came running in—*now* she was willing to come down the hall, the fucking cow. She started screaming, she called 911—ambulance was there, police were all over, Susan was pointing at me. And before you know it, I'm fifteen years old in the back seat of a police cruiser in a pair of boxers, a sleeveless undershirt, and handcuffs behind my back. In February. Welcome to the juvenile justice system of the State of New York."

"But if he was raping the girls…"

"The girls had come from the same background as me, and they probably had it worse, being girls. I mean Theresa—she wouldn't say a thing to help me, and why should she? Nobody, including me, had lifted a finger to help her all that time."

"But you'd stood up to him finally."

"Way too late."

"You were just a kid!"

"We were *all* just kids. So. The two younger girls, they would talk to the social worker, but neither of them would testify. And it wasn't like the paramedics saw Brad with his pants around his ankles and his pecker in his hand, because I had hit him before he'd gotten that far. No charges were filed against Brad and Susan. They said I had attacked without provocation. I could yell all I wanted. Brad and Susan were taken off the foster parents list, so there was that. Your tax dollars are no longer going to provide booty to a creep with a middle-aged wife and a taste for teenagers. But I popped a guy with a hockey stick. *Clang, clang!* Six months in the Westchester Juvenile Detention Facility in the town of—and you'll love this—Valhalla. As you would say—oh, the irony."

"Fletch, that's awful."

"So far beyond awful, you can't begin to comprehend. It could have been worse, though. Because of the circumstances—I had been a good kid until then, and nobody really believed the 'without provocation' part—it was only six months. I was also already a big boy. But it could still get—you know—pretty bad in there."

"And you got out?"

"And I got out."

"Sixteen?"

"Sixteen and still a ward of the state. Well, I didn't care *what* happened, but there was no way I was going back into the system. First fraction of a chance—a car door opened—and you never saw a kid run so fast."

"Where?"

"I hid in the city. I couldn't be Frank Szyfranski; he was a runaway. And I knew only one person in the world I had ever admired and wanted to be like."

"Andrew Fletcher. Fletcher Andrews."

"My personal tribute to the only decent person I'd met in my life."

"Let me guess. Did he say yep a lot?"

"Man-oh-man, he did. I'm just glad his name wasn't Horace or Gaylord or something. You'd have never let me move in, named Horace."

"Probably not. So how did you—survive?" I was afraid of the answer, but I had to know.

"I wasn't turning tricks if that's what you were hoping to hear."

"I think that's what I was hoping *not* to hear, but I certainly wouldn't think less of you if you had."

"I did all kinds of crap jobs but never that one. And you can imagine—pretty blond sixteen-year-old boy? I couldn't take a piss without having to turn some slimeball down."

"But you did."

"But I did. I scrubbed floors, I scrubbed toilets, I scrubbed the kitchen of a fried chicken restaurant—which was way worse than scrubbing toilets.

I shoplifted. I shoplifted *a lot.* I bussed tables, I waited tables. I tended bar in a really nasty dive behind Port Authority—they had fights in there at least twice a week. I was sixteen. After Marco took me in, I gutted fish for Marco's dad while Marco went to high school. And I did not drop my pants, at least not professionally."

We sat for a long time without saying anything. Finally I put my arms around him and hugged him. He hugged me back.

"I'm glad you told me," I whispered.

"I'm glad I did too. But—don't ask me about it again. Okay?"

I nodded.

We were still there, arms around each other, his head next to mine. It felt familiar, and good, something I'd missed. We were just there together. And then I felt Fletch's arm shift and pull me closer. I felt his head turn and his lips were pressed against my ear, and then my neck.

Okay, this is what you wanted, isn't it? I said to myself. *This is what's been working in your head since you saw him at the opera. You've wanted him; you've wanted to touch him, to be touched; you've wanted those beautiful arms around you again, and here he is. You've wanted exactly this, so don't pretend to be innocent or shocked.*

He pulled his head back, and his lips brushed against mine and then again, more firmly.

The feel of his face against mine, the scent of his hair, the familiar warmth that nothing had replaced. Jeffrey had been a terrible, pathetic mistake. He had never touched me like this, never affected me the way even a glance from Fletch could. And now this.

It was perfect.

But it wasn't. Something scared me. I felt him push his face against my neck—and my body was completely rigid. He kissed me, and then he moved his head down and nestled against my shoulder. Was it just old fears, old hurts that held me back? Because this was it. Everything. To have Fletch back, to have it all back. Like it was.

But like-it-was had nearly killed me.

"Stop," I said. He did. He just sort of froze there, without moving away, his face still nuzzled up against my neck and collar bone. "No, Fletch really. I can't." I pushed him gently back.

He pulled up his head and looked at me.

It was old fears and old hurts—and there was something else too. There was something that had been whispering at me the last couple weeks that I hadn't yet put into words. Until now.

"Fletch—what happened between you and Jeff?"

He blinked at me for a second.

"Besides mild dislike, which grew into a bitter contempt?"

This idea had occurred to me as a possibility before—even when they seemed to hate each other, there was something—I know it doesn't make any sense. But now I realized—Jeff had said something about Fletch, about his—Well, I'm not really the type to brag to my boyfriend about my ex-boyfriend's impressive equipment. To Tommy, sure, but not to Jeff. Of course I told myself that maybe it had just been that pair of my sweatpants that Fletch was almost wearing that day, when the impressive equipment was pretty much on display. But still.

"I have to know. Did you ever do anything with Jeff?"

Fletch clenched his mouth, and then he closed his eyes. Fuck. Fuck, fuck, fuck. What wouldn't I have given for a different answer.

"It was a while back; it wasn't since I saw you this fall or anything."

"Tell me."

"Oh God, Roger, what do you want, details? Comparisons? What?"

"How would you two even meet?"

"At work. It was a men's room, okay? Sleazy enough for you?"

"A theatre?! During a performance???!"

He didn't respond at all, just closed his eyes again. I think maybe he was praying. Maybe I was too.

"God damn it, Fletch."

"It's not like you and I were together. I wasn't cheating on you, you can't be mad at *me* about this!"

"I don't even know if I *am* mad. Maybe just mad at myself. I start to think…and then you remind me. I can't be mad at you—you're just who you are. You're just being Fletch. It's just that I wish sometime, just once, you weren't. I wish that that just once you'd have a story that didn't end with you reaching for your zipper. I wish that just once I'd think the worst of you—and I'd be wrong. But nope. You never disappoint."

"That's so not fair."

"You want to talk about fair??? You waltz into my life and smash it to bits—twice—and you want to talk about fair?"

"I didn't! Okay, yeah, I did, but that's not what happened this time!"

"In law, there's this concept of an attractive nuisance," I said slowly, quietly. "That's you. Like a swimming pool without a fence. You're this incredibly beautiful thing that looks safe—"

"Dweeb—"

"Don't," I said, pulling away from his hand, getting louder as I went. "You should have to wear a sign that says 'Stand Back Two Hundred Feet.'

You should have flashing yellow lights around you. People should have to execute a waiver so they know that, whatever happens, Fletcher Andrews takes no responsibility!"

"Please, Roger—"

"Don't try to explain."

"I can't explain. There's nothing to explain."

"Was he alone at the theatre?"

"An empty seat. Said his date had the flu."

The flu. I raised my hand feebly.

"Fever," I volunteered. "One hundred three."

Of course Fletch had figured out long before now that I was the empty seat.

"I couldn't know," he said weakly, staring at the floor.

I got up, and I went to the closet. I pulled out the hoody he had loaned me a few weeks ago. I'd been wearing it practically every day since.

Like a little girl with a crush. Why?

I'll tell you why.

Because I am the

World's.

Biggest.

Idiot!!!

"This belongs to you," I said and held it out to him.

He took it without looking to see what it was.

"I beg you, Roger. You must know by now—"

"Stop." I couldn't let him finish.

"Roger! I've been hanging around these last couple months because I can't do anything else. I can't live without seeing you, without being around you at least some of the time. Please, I need you, Roger."

Two years ago, that might have meant everything to me. Fletch was perfect. Since seeing him again, he'd been even more perfect, if that's possible. He was kinder, more considerate, gentler somehow. And as much as I didn't want to be, I was still in love with him. Probably more than ever. All I wanted in the world was to have Fletch back.

But here's a little reality check for you. He came to the old folks' home to hear us play, which was so sweet and wonderful, and yeah, it meant more to me than I let on, even to myself. But back in the day, when we were together, he never came to those things. It was okay, I didn't expect him to, it was no big deal, but—here's the kick in the teeth—and I certainly didn't know this at the time, but I can only imagine what he was doing while I was scraping the strings in front of a bunch of old ladies. Just take a wild guess.

So now he was being all charming and sweet and beautiful, and I was stupid in love with him even after all this, but what good was that? What good was *any* of that, if—if the moment your back is turned, he's reaching down to pull out his—

I couldn't even finish the sentence in my head, it hurt so much.

It took me a few seconds before I could speak.

"Leave the key," I said. "And Fletch—"

"Roger, I love you. That's gotta mean something."

"Don't come back, Fletch. Don't—come—back."

I couldn't watch him go. I heard the keys on the counter.

"Did you ever ask yourself, when I first crashed here, why I didn't go to Marco's?"

"You said you had nowhere else to go," I croaked without turning around.

"I lied. I wanted to be with *you*."

I heard the door open and I heard it close behind him.

Then silence. And I realized what I'd been afraid of:

This.

Chapter 38
I Hate Opera

FLETCH

I must have walked, but I was completely unaware of it. Where had I been? What had I done? No idea. Missing time. For all I knew, I'd been abducted by aliens. When I woke up or came to or whatever it was I did, it was hours later, I was sitting on the edge of the fountain in Lincoln Center—in front of that God. Damned. Opera house. And I thought:

You again.

The fountain splashed behind me, the water danced. November in New York, it was dark out, and cold. The plaza was empty. Huge. There were only a few straggling tourists wandering around snapping pictures. Assholes. Totally oblivious to the fact that the world had just come to an end.

Roger had given me the definitive answer. Go away, don't come back. I wasn't going to win this one after all. I had known it was a long shot, but for a while there…

I couldn't *not* try. After I saw him at *Otello*, I couldn't keep away, and there was no point along this path where I could have stepped out, given up, stopped myself.

I hadn't realized how much I'd missed him until I saw him here that night, only a few weeks ago—and then it was so clear how much was wrong with my life, and it all had to do with this emptiness where Roger had been. And I had hoped that maybe he…

I had something in my hand. It was the hooded sweatshirt I had loaned him. Even that hurt. Would it have killed him to keep the frigging sweatshirt??? Christ, he could be mean when he wanted to be.

So what now, Fletch?

Would I toss myself in front of the number 11 bus? No.

Would I survive? Yeah, probably.

Would I ever be the same? No. Obviously not.

I wasn't going to win this one, and I wasn't going to recover from this one either.

One thing I *did* know with certainty: *This* was hands down the worst day of my life.

But hey, I'm Fletch. I'll be fine, right? I'm always fine.

And you had to smile. Remember me? The moron who didn't believe in love? Well look at me now. Pretty funny, huh?

But I'm always fine, aren't I?

Sitting on the black marble rim of the fountain, I leaned back and looked up at the arches of the opera house windows, and I tilted my head back—so nothing would roll out of my blinking eyes.

I don't cry, I reminded myself. I couldn't.

I leaned over my lap and balled the hoody up against my face.

He'd been wearing it.

I was so not fine.

Bent over, with my face buried deep in the soft white fabric, I hoped that somehow, between the muffling sweatshirt and the splashing water behind me, no one would notice the wrenching sobs that ripped through my body.

Like meat hooks.

Like rifle shots.

Chapter 39

Your Slip Is Showing...and It's Pink

ROGER

"Hey, Alice," I said answering the phone. Alice was Katrina's secretary. She'd been at the firm since forever. The joke was that Alice could remember when that nice Abe Lincoln had been a summer associate. Alice looked like she'd been the model for those heads on Easter Island. That was Alice—a stone idol in a blond wig. My breezy, casual greeting to her on the phone was a complete front. When Alice's name came up on the phone, my blood ran cold. The woman scared the living bejeebers out of me.

"Brunhilde wants to see you," she growled. That would be Katrina. "Consider yourself summoned."

"On my way."

It wasn't as if I was doing anything anyway. I'd spent most of the last couple days staring out the window—wasn't quite sure how I was going to handle that on my time entries. Lawyers bill their time to clients, and if you *don't* bill any time, it tends to raise some eyebrows, to say the least. Honestly, I wasn't really sure why I was even coming in.

But I dutifully ran up the two flights to Katrina's floor, and I was just a bit out of breath when I stood at Alice's desk. She was, as always, reading a beat-up paperback. This one looked like it had already been read by the entire Bulgarian army. On the front cover was an impossibly handsome guy with a lot of black hair blowing in the wind, and he held in his beefy arms a girl in a period costume and a half-faint. Both parties were showing ample cleavage.

I never quite reconciled rock-faced Alice with the bodice-ripper paperbacks.

It had occurred to me that maybe she fantasized about being the bosomy babe getting ravished by the swarthy stud with the storm-tossed hair.

Then it occurred to me that maybe she fantasized about being the swarthy stud doing the ravishing.

And then it occurred to me that maybe it didn't really bear thinking about.

Alice didn't look up or speak, but she indicated with a jerk of her wig that I should go in. I tapped and peeked around the door.

"Hey?" I said.

"Hello, Roger. Come on in. Alice?" She raised her voice to reach the secretary. "Hold my calls please." She waited for an answer. None came. "Is she out there?" she asked me. I nodded. She rolled her eyes and called out again, "Thank you, Alice," and then said to me, "Close the door, would you?"

I did as I was told, but why? Did Katrina call me in to gossip?

"Hey, I've been meaning to ask you something," I began. "Is there something going on between Bob and Janine?"

"For about a year and a half, Roger."

"Oh."

"Why?"

"Fletch picked up on it, I guess. Obviously I hadn't."

"Hmmm," she said slyly. "Take a seat, Roger." I took one. "Roger, you've been here going on five years, and I've watched you grow, as a lawyer, and as a person."

Oh.

Ah.

Now I understood.

This was *that* conversation. I had to close the door so no one would hear me getting fired.

"Is this where you tell me..."

"That we don't see a long-term future for you here at the firm? Yes. Sadly."

"Um—okay. I'm—not really surprised."

"The usual speech I'm supposed to give you is: I'm sure you'll be able to take the skills you've learned here and develop your career with another firm or a financial institution that might suit you better."

"I've known for a while I didn't really fit in."

"Goodkin Berdann is pretty competitive, I know. And that's just not you. But consider maybe a boutique firm. You know you will have a glowing reference from me."

"Thanks."

"How are you doing otherwise, Roger? I'm asking as a friend—you seem a little stressed."

"It's been a pretty full week." A mild understatement.

"You've been lovely to work with. And the quartet has become a huge part of my life, largely because of you. So. In addition to the usual speech, as a *friend*, I feel I should suggest to you that you look on this as a real opportunity. I know that sounds like some lemons–lemonade Hallmark horseshit, but what I mean is—you're being given a chance to reassess. You don't have to jump into the next job you find. You can take your time here. And while you're taking your time and considering your options, maybe you should think about where your talents lie and what you're really good at."

"Because you think that that's probably not the law."

"Because you play a mean fiddle."

"And pretty soon you can catch me playing that mean fiddle in the Fourteenth Street Subway Station."

"Don't be dramatic. You know better than anyone how good you are."

"It's way too late to think about playing professionally."

"I don't know that that's true. What I *do* know is—you know more about music, and you hear music better, than anyone I've ever met. I've learned more about playing Beethoven from you than I did in four years as a music major at Northwestern. You complain that you're no good at analysis, and when it comes to Trust and Estates, yeah, well, you may be right. But I've seen you flip through a Shostakovich quartet that was completely opaque to me, and you knew exactly where to begin to find your way into the piece. You have students now, don't you?"

"Student. I have one beginner student who's on the Roger Prescott Scholarship."

"You could easily get paying students and more advanced students. Or you could teach in a high school or college situation."

"I don't think I have the academics for it."

"Well, I don't know anything about that, but this is the opportunity part I was talking about. New York has some of the best music schools in the country. I don't have to tell you. I know it's not the same kind of money as in a big law firm, but you've never struck me as somebody who needed a huge paycheck."

"You mean because of my family?"

"I mean because of you."

"It's something I've thought about. Teaching. Even Fletch was encouraging me."

"Good. Think about it. Talk it over with Jeff."

I made a face.

"Jeff's gone," I said. "We're done."

"Oh. I can't say I'm completely surprised. So then are you and Fletch finally?"

I made the face again.

"I threw Fletch out too."

"My. You *have* been busy. I'm sorry to drop this on you on top of all that."

"No, it's okay. I've expected it. In a way, it's a relief."

"You really threw Fletch out?"

"Yyyyy-eah."

"Wow. I somehow thought you two—and then when he turned up at the old folks' home to hear you play, and you played the way you did, I thought for sure—"

"Yeah well."

"Just didn't work out?"

"Guess not. Can we—"

"You know," she said, plowing over the top of me, "that first day when he was just *there* again, at our rehearsal—when was that? A month ago? There was a moment—and I'll never forget it—the two of you were in the kitchen, and I don't know what was going on in there, but I looked up just as he wiped a tear from your cheek with the cuff of his sweatshirt—and it hit me as the most beautiful, the tenderest..." She seemed to get lost for a moment and then came back, incredulous of my apparent stupidity. "You tossed him out?!"

"Yep. I sure did." And a little dose of Katrina in sappy mode wasn't making me feel any better about it.

"Because you know, I thought that day, if anybody ever did something like that for me..."

"Well, *anyway*. Let's talk about something cheerier. You were just about to give me the ax."

"That's right."

"And encouraging me to quit my day job because I stink at it."

She smiled.

"Not exactly, but yes."

"Now would you just explain it to my family?"

"I've watched you for four-and-a-half years, and I can tell you this much. You're a big boy, Roger."

"Thanks."

"I think it's fair to say that you tried it their way; you gave it a serious shot. And maybe now it's time to try your way."

"Hey, that's good. Write that down for me, would you?"

We both smiled.

"Play out your time here. No one has a problem with you staying through the summer, and then start school somewhere in the fall maybe. But whatever happens, you *have* to stay with the quartet."

"I'd like that."

"And here's something I should have done long ago. You should be playing first violin."

"But it's your quartet!"

"I knew from day one that you were a much better musician than I am, but I'm vain. And it *is* my quartet. But here's my proposal. From here on, you take over, and you play first on anything new."

"Seriously?"

"And you take over music selection."

"I'd like that. Wow. Thanks. You know what that means, though—"

"Ravel!" we said together.

"I knew it."

"Finally! And we need a better name than the Goodkin Berdann Quartet."

"Look at you. You've just been told to start job hunting. Usually I'm handing over a box of tissues at this point, and instead, you're sitting there grinning like the canary that ate the cat because you get to play first violin in an amateur quartet. I think if you look closely, you'll see that there is a tiny clue in there as to where your real interests are."

"You may be right."

"I'm always right. You're just figuring that out now? No wonder you couldn't cut it here."

"Wow. Nice, Katrina, real nice."

"And maybe think about this Fletch thing, okay?" Like I'd been doing anything else. "Now scram, before I sic Alice on you."

Chapter 40
One Skinny Latte and a Double Shot of Therapy, Please

TOMMY

The usual ritual, me and Roger standing on this incredibly long line in this incredibly small storefront for a goddamn cup of coffee. The overcrowded shop was even worse now that every man, woman, and child among us was wearing a great big ol' winter coat—in black, because it's New York. Roger and I pressed ourselves into the queue behind two chattering Latinas.

"I swear," I said, "if I have any more of that pumpkin crap, I'm going to turn into one."

I thought I was talking to Roger, but apparently not, because he completely ignored me, even to the point of failing to remind me that there was no actual pumpkin in the cappuccinos. Under the circs, one job and two boyfriends later, I suppose it was understandable that he'd be just the teensiest bit preoccupied.

"So, how are you holding up?" I asked him.

The deeply ironical part is that I could work for the next thirty years at the same law firm that was tossing Roger out onto the sidewalk. They paid the lawyers a lot better than staff and then treated them way worse.

Of course I had no intention of working there for thirty years. Sooner or later one of those hot young lawyer boys was going to chase me around the desk and I was going to let him catch me. And we'll get married, and I'll gladly stay home, watch soap operas, and make babies. Or die trying. Either that, or I'll sell my screenplay, as soon as I write it.

But Goodkin Berdann was going to be a miserable place without Roger.

Maybe I should shop around. Rumor was Parker O'Neill was dangling a giganto salary to work for some godawful partner. They're just on the next block, so I wouldn't even have to switch Starbuckses. *But*—and it was a big *but—but*—Parker O'Neill was Jeff's firm.

Wouldn't it just be a hoot and a half to go work for Jeffrey Bornic? Yeah, probably not.

Anyway, *until* some mad-handsome young esquire recognizes what's right under his gorgeous nose—I still had my morning pash, my little Monday-to-Friday heartbreak, my wicked-eyed barista. Not that it was going anywhere, because it wasn't, but he was sure nice to look at. Sigh. Let me do that again. Sigh.

But enough about me. Poor Roger was clearly in bad shape.

"I've had better weeks," Roger said, answering my question from not one, not two, but I think it was *four* digressions ago.

"You miss Jeff that much?" I knew better than that, but I figured it was a place to start.

"No. Isn't that awful? What does that say about me? It says I'm an awful person."

"Probably. But you were still smart to dump him."

"I suppose."

"So. What about the other one?" He looked at me. "He-who-must-not-be-named," I clarified, as if he needed clarification. Roger's turn to sigh. He did it much better than me anyway.

"Yeah. Him. It's always the other one."

"Are you moping?"

"No. Yes. Yes, I'm moping. I am in full-on moping mode. Stand back. I don't want to get any on you."

"So what happened? Honestly, I thought you guys were heading toward—"

"He fucked Jeff."

"My aunt Fanny," I said to express my disbelief.

The two girls in front of us, who had been prattling away nonstop, were suddenly mute.

"It's true," Rog said.

The girls turned their heads slightly to Roger, so they could hear a little better. I'm not really sure what it means to cock your ears, but I'm pretty sure—those ears were good and cocked.

Sounds mad wrong, though, doesn't it?

However, back to the subject at hand—I simply could not believe that Fletch, after all I'd seen and all I'd heard from him, would then jump on somebody else. And if he *had* jumped on somebody else, that somebody else would have been anybody on earth who was *not* Jeff Bornic.

"I don't believe it. It never happened. He hates Jeff, and vicey versy."

"Apparently, it wasn't always so."

"Oh. This was…a while ago?"

"I guess."

"Oh. And you know this because…"

"He told me."

"Oh. Jeff?"

"Fletch."

"Figures. So was this while you and Fletch…"

"No."

"While you and Jeff…"

He nodded.

"Also figures. So you're pissed off at Fletch because he shouldn't have told you? Or because he told you what Jeff *should* have told you but didn't?"

"That's not it."

The line snailed forward, our faithful listeners carefully keeping themselves in earshot at all times.

"Are you pissed off because Fletch slept with your boyfriend? Or because Jeff slept with your boyfriend?"

"I'm pissed off because nobody should have been sleeping with anybody!"

Roger was oblivious to the babes in front of us, who by now had given up any pretense of minding their own business. They were doing everything but taking shorthand.

"I'm mad because he's such a slut. And I don't want him to be. I want him to be—better than that somehow. He's—in so many ways, he's better than anyone I know. You know?" Roger's voice cracked. "He's—you'll laugh but—he's finer, somehow. So why does somebody need all that screwing around?"

"I don't know. Have you ever asked him?"

"I'm not going to ask him, 'Hey, Fletch, why are you a sex addict? What's behind this unhealthy need to be constantly desired? Why are you compelled to go around, letting total strangers slurp on your hoober-hobber?'"

Unfortunately, the two eavesdroppers in line ahead of us had just placed their orders and stepped aside—albeit not far—and we were now at the head of the line. In the meantime, my dear friend at the cash register, Miss Max Factor of some recent year, summoned her dignity and drew herself up to her full four foot eleven.

"If it's all the same to you," she said deadpan, "let's leave my hoober-hobber out of it."

At which point the Nosey Twins, quite understandably, burst into screams of laughter. It *was* pretty damned funny.

The cashier graciously drummed the register with her bear-gutting nails, each nail with a little teeny-tiny turkey on it.

"Uh—skinny latte—grande," said Roger. His face was roughly the color of a firetruck.

"Name?" Like she didn't know.

"Roger."

"Next?"

"Grande half-caf white chocolate mocha cappuccino, please," I said. "Extra foam."

"Name?"

"My Boyfriend." Our Lady of the Lavender Eye Shadow stared at me blankly. "C'mon," I said, and I waved my finger at the cardboard cup in her hand. "You know the drill. Just make with the Sharpie."

The same Sharpie you use for your eyeliner, apparently. I *must* try that sometime.

I knew by now that the Siege of Fort Barista was beyond hopeless, but I figured Roger could use the distraction of watching me make a fool of myself one more time. Over the last two months, I'd tried Sweetie-Pie, Snookums, and Honeybunch, so far without much success, although Old Blue Eyes had at least laughed at Snookums.

Roger and I moved to the side as best we could in the logjam of winter coats. It was like rolling over in a cave full of hibernating bears. One moves, *everybody* has to move.

"I don't think he is," I said.

"You don't think who is what?"

"Fletch. I get the distinct impression his hoober-hobber is pretty much a no-slurp zone these days."

"He screwed Jeff in a toilet."

"Appropriate somehow, and months ago. You should think about giving Fletch a chance."

"He had his chance."

"Another chance, then. Sometimes, Roger, you gotta take a risk."

"You know, I'm all in favor of that. But with Fletch, there is no risk. He's a known commodity. He's a given. He *will* screw around. It's not a question of if but when. He *will* hurt me."

"Ask him."

"Ask him what? If he'll break my heart again?"

"Yeah! The problem with you two all along has been that you're afraid to talk to each other. Because I swear, if he talked to *you* the way he talks to me *about* you, this whole mess would resolve itself."

"Why? What does he say about me?"

"Ask him!"

"No. I don't want to know."

"Ask him if he still wants to sleep around."

"I'm not going to ask him. I'm—I'm never going to see him again."

"Roger, you're like a whole lot smarter than I am and you always have been, and I have no business giving you advice—"

"But you're going to anyway."

"Oh hell yes. Your life is not—down the toilet, per se—"

"Gee! Thanks!"

"But let's just say it's 'in flux,'" I said, with air quotes. "And in the middle of this 'flux'"—more quotes here—"you're making some really, really big life choices, without maybe all the information."

"How much more information do I need to know? It was in the men's room in the basement of the Longacre Theatre during a performance of *Medea*."

If only I had my mocha cappuccino, I would have done a spit take.

"Aunt Petunia's *Medea*?"

"Aunt Petunia's *Medea*."

"Okay. Wow." It was going to take me more than a second to process this. "Hey, weren't *you* supposed to see *Medea*?"

"Exactly. And why are you sticking up for Fletch anyway?"

I thought about it for a second. Do I speak up or remain silent? Butt in or butt out? But seriously, he flat-out asked me. If that isn't an invitation to butt in, I don't know what is. I mean, technically, it's not even meddling any more, is it?

Besides, I'd already said too much, and like I always say—in for a penny, in for a pound cake.

"Because I'm pretty sure you're crazy in love with Fletcher Andrews. I was pretty sure you were crazy in love with him the first time I met him, and I'm also pretty sure you've been crazy in love with him ever since. I know what he did was terrible, terrible, terrible, but I thought it was a mistake to throw him out the way you did, and nobody suffered for that mistake more than you. But I didn't say anything at the time because I wanted to be supportive, and that was *my* mistake, but this time I think you're about to make *another* huge mistake, and so this time I'm saying something. I know you're scared, and you should be scared, and you should make him earn your trust and all that, and you should definitely *not* put up with a bunch of pointless promiscuity—but don't assume that he's necessarily still boinking all and sundry, just because he once was. Because what if he isn't? Think about that! Because I'm also pretty sure that that beautiful, amazing man really is crazy in love with you, and only you. You *have* to talk to him."

I'd gotten a little worked up, and I had to dab at my eyes with a brown environmentally friendly napkin.

"He is so right," said eavesdropping Bimbo #1 over my shoulder. "You should listen to this guy."

"I agree," said Bimbo #2. "You should definitely talk to Fletch, let him know how you feel and shit."

"Out of the mouths of babes" was all I could say.

Roger gaped with horror, like he was waiting for Edvard Munch to come along and do his portrait.

There he was, the scion of a proud and ancient Yankee family, backbone of New England society since the *Mayflower* crash-landed on that rock, the product of generations of Puritans, witch-burners, and blue-noses, and he was now faced with the realization that his love life was the topic of a group counseling session in a crowded Starbucks.

"Jeez-fucking—"

But before Roger could invoke the name of the unfortunate Louise—

"Grande latte, skinny, for Roger!" yelled the sexiest barista in the Western Hemisphere.

"Over here!" yelped Roger, snatching at his reprieve.

While he shouldered his way through the steaming crowd of black coats, I waited, and I pondered two questions about the immediate future.

Would Roger take my advice?

And would my beautiful barista call me his boyfriend right here in front of God and Starbuck and everybody? I could just see his face through the forest of heads. Devastating blue eyes, concentrating. He was finishing it; he was reading the cup; here it comes…

"Grande half-caf white chocolate mocha cappuccino for—oh for—White chocolate mocha cappuccino for—Tommy!"

Disappointment writ its name large across my face. I navigated the stormy sea of black, and wedged my way up to the counter.

"Hey!" I said. Now I was annoyed. "Look. Since you apparently know my name, you might occasionally say, 'Hey, Tommy, how's it going?' or 'Hey, Tommy, your hair looks really cute like that,' or 'Hey, Tommy, stop fucking hitting on me.'"

"Hey, Tommy, how's it going," he said. The eyes were starting to twinkle. "And your hair always looks really cute, and I didn't want you to stop. It was too much fun."

"Serious?"

"I look forward to it. But I'm not about to call you 'my boyfriend'—snookums."

"No?"

"Not yet anyway." It's possible you remember one of my first observations about this guy, how he could narrow his eyes down to little crescents and look at you kinda sideways in a way that promised a crazy demon in bed? He did that now.

I died. Right there, I died. I am still literally prostrate on the floor of Starbucks at Forty-Second and Sixth. Mourners may view the body during business hours. In lieu of flowers—

"I'm Javier, by the way," he said, interrupting my funeral arrangements. He's Latin, in case you haven't noticed, and that *J* is an *H.*

He turned my coffee cup, which was standing on the counter, and there, down the side of the cardboard cup, it said "Javi," and there was a string of numbers, ten digits, starting with nine one seven. His cell.

"Oh. My. God."

"It's what you wanted, isn't it?" The eyes sparkled even more than usual.

"Ohhhhhhhh-yeah."

"Call me. I'm free all week," said Javi, my Javi.

"The hell you are."

I sidled my way through the shoulders, shoulders, shoulders, back to the door where Roger was waiting outside.

"And?"

"Hold this a second—don't smear it!"

"What?"

"This!" I said, pointing, as I keyed the number into my phone.

"You got his number? Congrats."

"His name's Javi, which is obviously the cutest name in the whole wide world, and he gave me his number, and I'm supposed to call him, and we're getting married this weekend. Okay, the last bit is a slight exaggeration."

"Take your coffee back so I can high-five you."

I did, and we fived ever so highly. We made our way out onto the sidewalk.

"You go on ahead," Roger said. "I think I'm going to mope around in Bryant Park for a bit first."

"We're late already, Rog."

"What are they going to do, fire me?"

"Good point. And hey, Roger? Just don't mope for two years this time."

"I didn't mope for two years."

"You did, very nearly. And you know when you finally started staggering out of it? The night at the opera. What conclusions can you draw from *that*, besty?"

"That Verdi. They sure don't write tunes like *that* anymore."

The Snoop Sisters brushed past us on their way up Sixth Avenue. The one on the right looked over her shoulder, made the universal symbol for a telephone out of her hand, and yelled—

"Call that guy!"

Chapter 41
Just a Quick Good-Bye

ROGER

I'd been staring at the violin—in its case—for over a week now. Probably the longest I'd gone without picking up the Mittenwald since…oh, gee, let me think, since the last time I ripped Fletch out of my life.

I should be channeling all my misery into my playing, I thought. I should tap into my emotions the way I did at the old folks' home. I'd been trying to re-create that feeling ever since, with mixed success. Here was my perfect opportunity. I was miserable, I should play that. I should pull out the trusty old Mittenwald, throw open the windows, and let the neighbors know the full breadth and depth of my heartache.

O World, hear my pain!

But honestly? I'd rather not. I didn't have the energy, and really—what would be the point? And if I somehow *did* actually tap into this cold emptiness in my chest—it would probably kill me. Or the Mittenwald. Or both.

It was just as well. The violin would only interfere with my *new* hobby—looking out the window. You can see a traffic light from here. It changes colors. There, see, it was red; now it's green. In a little while it'll be yellow. Fascinating stuff.

I kept thinking it would get better, but it had only gotten worse. At first I'd gone to work, but that was useless. I started calling in sick on Wednesday. I'd blown off a quartet rehearsal by email. I'd even canceled a Trevor lesson, which made me feel *reallly* good and rotten.

In the days since, I'd only seen Tommy. He came by a couple days ago to throw shoes at me for a while, just trying to get my attention, but it didn't help. He'd been busy with Javier, who seemed to like him, and I'm glad. But…

Now it was Monday, and I *still* couldn't bring myself to go in.

At some point in this story I think I've said something about how I was over Fletch—that he occasionally crossed my mind, but not in that first-thing-in-the-morning-every-goddamned-day kind of way anymore. Well, he definitely was back in that position now, wasn't he. And if I were completely honest about it, he'd been there for a while. Certainly since the night at the emergency room. Before that. Since Trevor? Before that. The old folks' home? I mean whatever happened to me playing Gershwin that day, that had to have come from *some*where.

But I suppose, really, he hadn't left my thoughts since I saw him at the opera house.

So why didn't he text or something? I wondered. Maybe it was because I'd made it clear that I didn't want him to. Because I'd told him to go away and stay there. *What'll I do if he does*?

My phone sat permanently on the table in front of me, so it was easy to snatch up if someone *did call.* Or text. It was also handy to check every two minutes, just in case I had somehow missed a call or a text, which, of course, was impossible because the damned phone was sitting *right there.*

And what would I say if he *did* call?

> "I loves ya like crazy, ya big galoot"—?

Maybe. Yeah, maybe I *would* say that.

If that's what I would say, then I should call him and say it and stop being such a wuss. Or text him. Or I could put an ad in the personals, like they do in the movies:

> Please come home. All is forgiven.

But who reads the personals? Tommy and his backup girls said I should call him. And say what?

> "Yep." That's how Fletch answers his phone.
>
> "Hey, it's me."
> "'Sup?"
> "Just chillin'. 'Sup with you?"

Like as if. But seriously, what could I say to him?

> "Please come back. I'm sorry I ever threw you out"—?

Or how about—

"Please come back and you can screw around all you want—I promise not to notice this time"—?????????

Because that's what it came down to. Sure, Fletch said he loves me, and maybe he even meant it, and Tommy said that he thinks Fletch is just as nuts about me as I am about Fletch, which is all just swell. But does any of this mean that he isn't going to pull his boxers down for the next casual acquaintance or total stranger who looks even mildly interested? And let's face it—everybody's interested.

That's what Fletch does. That's how he is. Why would that change?

That was the killer.

The knowledge of that certainty was the paralyzing venom that had seeped through me and left me here in this fetid apartment, unable to do more than walk my dog a couple times a day and contemplate the profundities of that goddamned traffic light.

Compounding my overall depression was the incredibly annoying realization that I had *let* this happen. *Again.*

After the first cataclysm with Fletch, I'd sworn—I would never put myself in a position where someone could do that to me again. I would *never* let another guy have that kind of power over me. And here I was. Worst of all, it wasn't even another guy. It was the *same guy*!!! How stupid was that???!!!

Fool me once, blah-blah-blah. Fool me twice, just hit me with a speeding taxi, why doncha.

And what was I doing now as demonstrative proof that I'd finally learned my lesson? I was staring at my phone like a crazy person, because maybe, just maybe—

BUZZZZZZZ. Not the phone—the door buzzer.

I jumped about a mile, and fuck fuck fuck, I banged my shin on the coffee table. From the way Haggis was barking, you'd think the frigging Loch Ness Monster was humping his way up to the door.

Jeezus Lou-eezus, that hurt.

Wait—the door buzzer?

What if it's Fletch, I thought.

It's not. Of course it's not. It's-not-it's-not-it's-not. Don't start hoping because it's not, I scolded myself, *you know it's not, and it will kill you when it isn't. You want this way too much. It is not Fletch.*

But what if it *is*? I hopped one-legged to the intercom and pushed the button.

"Yes?"

My voice cracked. It occurred to me that I hadn't actually spoken to anyone in a couple days, not even to Haggis. I sounded like an oboe.

I stood in front of that intercom, a giant bubble of aching hope—just waiting to be obliterated when it turned out to be UPS.

"It's me."

OMYGOD it really was Fletch. It *is* Fletch. I slammed the buzzer with the heel of my hand. Ow.

The dog immediately stopped barking and started spinning. Jeez, Hags, you're worse than I am.

I ran to the mirror, I plucked at my hair, I straightened my t-shirt. I'd slept in this t-shirt. Twice. I tucked my nose inside the neck hole and sniffed. Oh-jeez. I ran to the bedroom, pulled off the shirt, grabbed a fresh one, and then went on to the bathroom, where I shoved a toothbrush and some toothpaste in my mouth for like five seconds before I spat and wiped my chin.

I looked in the mirror. It was completely hopeless. I looked like hell. I had bags, I hadn't slept, I hadn't eaten. I hadn't shaved, and I'm not one of those guys who look hot with stubble.

There was a soft *tap, tap* on the door.

Deep breath.

I flipped the deadbolt and pulled the door open.

"Hey," I croaked. I couldn't remember eating a great big hunk of bow rosin, but apparently I had because that seemed to be what was stuck in my throat. "Come in."

"I know I'm not supposed to be here but I needed to drop some stuff off for you and I was going to go to your office but you didn't answer your phone and the security guys wouldn't let me in. So I called Katrina to see if I could leave the stuff with her but no, she told me I had to come over and give it to you myself. So here I am."

"Katrina made you come over." Figures.

"Otherwise, I would never have come, I swear. Hey, you okay?"

"Yeah, me? I'm great, I just—yeah. I just needed some—you want some water? Or—something?"

"No thanks, Dwee—Sorry. I won't be long. I asked because—you called in sick and all. And you don't look so great."

"I look like dog barf."

"Prit-tee much."

"Thanks."

"So—are you sick?"

"No. Probably. I don't know."

Fletch hesitated. I could see the conflict in his face—*Concern v. Caution.* He was worried about me, but there were boundaries. Boundaries I had set. Fletch was scared of me. And I guess he should have been. In all of Fletch's rough, brutal life, with its poverty and abandonments, cruelty and unhappiness, probably no one had hurt him as much as I had. I was such a miserable human being, the lowest—

"I'll be quick," he said, catching me before my downward spiral brought me to suicidal. "Here. This is the surprise I forgot to bring last time."

He reached into his shoulder bag and pulled out a folder like you'd get at K-Mart for a sixth grader. There was a picture of Chewbacca on the front. He handed it to me. "Sorry about the folder, I know it's stupid. It was the Wookiee or a daisy. Anyway..."

I opened the Star Wars folder—did he notice my hand shaking? Inside were some brochures, class listings, schedules. From the New School. From Columbia. Music schools. I started to lay out the brochures on the kitchen counter. Manhattan School of Music, NYU. Graduate programs. What the—I looked to him for an explanation.

"You had talked about it—grad school, I mean—and I was in the neighborhood, so I went in and found their admissions office and asked, and you know, they gave me stuff."

"Fletch, these schools are all over the city."

"Okay, I was in a lot of different neighborhoods."

"Liar."

"Yep, pretty much."

I started straightening up the brochures and laid them carefully in a pile on top of Chewy.

"Fastidious," he said, smiling sadly.

"Yeah. Fastidious." I had to swallow really hard. "Sorry."

"Don't. It's cute." There was a long pause that stretched into unbearable. For him too, I guess, because the next thing he said was, "I should go."

"No!" The word shot out of me. I didn't want him to leave, not just yet. Okay, I knew that Fletch had to go. I had thrown him out last week, and I meant it. I was resigned to the fact that I was going to live the rest of my life Fletchless. Fine.

But there was no need to rush into it. I could start living without him... later. In a minute. In an hour maybe was plenty soon enough. He was obviously just as miserable as I was, so why couldn't we just sit here and be miserable together? I could always throw him out, you know, in a little bit. Or tomorrow, or...

"Don't go. Not just yet."

"No?"

"And thanks for the—stuff. I kinda need to rethink my life. The law thing doesn't seem to be quite panning out." I was feeling pretty light-headed, the longer I talked to him. Lack of sleep, low blood sugar, high anxiety—

"Did they…"

"They did! They did indeed. Katrina was super nice about it too, of course. And you know? She said the same thing. 'Go back to school, kid,'" I said, and I wagged a finger—nothing at all like Katrina. "So. First I throw Jeff out, and then I throw you out, and I go to work, and they throw *me* out. Here we are, all thrown out on our respective ears. Or asses. Depending. Pretty funny, don't you think? Oh, the ironing."

"Dweeb, are you really okay?"

Maybe I *was* sick. I seemed to be winding up toward delirium.

"When I suggested to Katrina that I could always busk in the subways, you know, me and the Mittenwald? She scoffed. Doesn't seem to think I have the stuff, but I'll show her. I got the goods. I can grovel; I can beg. I can play that awful song from *Cats* as well as the next guy. But hey, the good news is—she's going to let me play first violin in the quartet sometimes. Pretty cool, huh?"

Fletch had no idea what to do with me. I was more than a little lost myself.

"You need to sit down, Dweeb, and maybe take a breath."

"I think you're right. No reason we can't sit and talk to each other, is there? We're grown-ups, blah-blah-blah. We can handle this, right?"

"Absolutely, but first, shhhhhh." He shepherded me onto the couch. "Okay?"

"I'm okay."

"Want a glass of water, or something? Wine maybe?"

"That's probably not smart. I haven't eaten…since…no idea."

"Yeah. Me either," he said, bringing me the glass of water. "Or slept."

I sipped.

"Or slept. Want some?" I offered him the glass, and he sipped from it, too, and gave it back. He sat carefully at the other end of the couch.

"So—did you tell your dad yet?"

"Are you *crazy*? *IIIIIIIII'm* not telling him."

"Coward."

"Yep, prit-tee much," I said, doing my best Fletch imitation.

"I'll talk to him," Fletch said, and I had to laugh. Which at least broke the tension. "I'm sorry, Dweeb. Like you don't have enough going on."

We sat on the couch, opposite ends, each with a knee up so we could face each other. Just like the last time. I think we were each waiting for something, but it was something that was never going to happen. Because what we wanted to happen was impossible.

"So," I volunteered, "I need to rethink my life, sort of, and I don't really know where to begin. But there's something I learned from Haggis."

"What's that?"

"Sometimes when you don't know where to begin, it doesn't matter, as long as you do. Begin, I mean."

"Smart dog, Haggis."

"And good-looking, too." I looked down at the dog leaning against Fletch's ankle. "But so damned arrogant. Anyway, that's the lesson. I'm just not always sure how to apply it."

We sat for a few seconds without saying anything.

"Hey," he said suddenly, "I have something else for you. A Christmas present."

"It's only November."

"Yeah, but you know, considering—anyway." He retrieved his shoulder bag and handed me a small envelope. I looked inside: tickets. Carnegie Hall, four nights in February.

"What's this?"

"It's a competition for young chamber musicians. I remembered what you said about young players with passion, so…anyway. Merry Christmas."

"That's really—you know, for a shallow, egotistical asshole who's only interested in sex—first Trevor, now this. When did you get so…"

"It's a recent development. I hope you like the present."

"I do, very much."

"Better than an argyle sweater?"

"Hey, it was an expensive argyle sweater."

"That you'll never wear."

"That I'll never wear. Poor Jeff. Does Tommy tell you *everything*?"

"Only if I ask him. Hey, there's even a quartet on the program that's playing 'Death and the Maiden.'"

"Is that like 'our song'?"

"Maybe, kinda." He sang the first line with the dumb words he'd made up for it. "*Dweeeeeeb*!"

"*Where are my shoes*?" we sang together.

"That's so romantic," I said.

"I know, right?"

"No wonder we were doomed, if that was our song."

He waited a second before he answered.

"That's not why we were doomed."

"No. That's not why."

"I'm so sorry, Dweeb. You can't know. I'm really sorry to have lost you—but I'll never forgive myself for hurting you. Please believe that."

"It's just a metaphor," I said finally.

"Sorry?"

"You know, death, the maiden...."

"Somebody really smart explained that to me once."

"You might have kept the tickets. You could just go yourself."

"Without you it would be—I—anyway, I won't be here."

I looked up sharply.

"What?!"

"Marco and I, we're going to try Los Angeles for a while."

"Los Angeles? California?"

"I suppose there's probably another, but I only know of the one."

I was totally stunned by this. What was that—panic?

"But—why?"

"Change of scenery. Neither of us has ever been anywhere but here. And Marco wants to be a movie star. Or a gigolo—whichever pays better."

"And you?"

"I always wanted to be an astronaut, but heck, I can do that anywhere."

"Fletch."

"There's nothing for me here. I think maybe it's for the best."

Wow. Why did this shatter me so, to hear that he was leaving town? I mean I was the one who'd told him to get the hell out of my life. Why was I miserable at the thought that he was doing just that?

"Yeah. Maybe."

I hated this. I hated, hated, hated this.

"There's something I have to ask you," I said. "I know it's weird, but this wasn't my idea. Don't be mad at me—blame Tommy."

"Tommy?"

"Tommy said I should ask. In fact, it seems to be the consensus of the whole gang down at Starbucks that I should ask—and this is from some girls who look like they really know about these things."

"Dweeb, what are you talking about?"

"You see, the burning question on seemingly everyone's lips these days is—are you, Fletcher Andrews, still a tramp?"

"What?"

"Are you still being your usual slutty self? Or have you modified your past harlotty behavior?"

"Harlotty? Is that even a word?"

"You're avoiding the question. Are you still boinking all and sundry? That was the question Tommy told me to ask you."

"Thank Tommy for his interest and tell him no, I'm not."

"Based on what?"

"Well, I'm not completely sure about all, but I definitely haven't boinked sundry—I'd remember that. Come to think of it, there hasn't been any boinking of any kind in a while."

"Since…when? Lunch? Since…Wednesday? Since…"

"Since—*Otello*."

Wow.

"Really?"

"Really."

"Good answer."

"Thanks."

"For you, that's quite a dry spell. Must be some kind of record or something."

"I hadn't thought about it. Hmm, there wasn't a whole lot of action going on the first twelve years or so, but since then, yeah, I guess, pretty much a record."

Since he was twelve. *This* was the guy I had to go and fall in love with?

"So, you're telling me that you're really not tramping it up anymore?"

"Say amen, brother!" He held his quivering hands up over his head.

"Why not?"

"I went to the opera, and it changed my life."

"Yeah, yeah, yeah, I'm serious, Fletch."

He looked me in the eyes and took a deep breath.

"Well, if you're serious, I saw someone in the lobby of the Metropolitan Opera House who literally took my breath away, he was so amazingly handsome—it ruined me for anyone else."

"You are so full of—"

"Honest, I swear, Roger. I couldn't say it before because I was afraid I'd scare you away and you'd throw me out, but now—I saw you that night—you seemed so beautiful and so fragile and sad and hurt, and I knew it was because of me, and since that night all I have wanted was to make it up to you and hold you and protect you and to get it right this time—and since then—since then—since then I've just been hanging around you because I can't think of anything else to do with my life."

"It did feel like you were stalking me there, for a while."

"That's probably because I was. I skulked around outside your office, just to watch you go in and out. I followed you home a couple times. Stood across the street and stared up at your windows for like—days. And it gets so much worse. I bribed your dog walker to disappear."

"No way!"

"Way! And the bitch was bleeding me dry, too."

"You're joking."

"I would never joke about something as serious as bribing a dog walker."

"And now?"

"I don't know, Dweeb. I don't know anything anymore. Except that I love you so much."

"I thought you didn't believe in love."

"I didn't! And if I ever *had* believed in love, I certainly didn't think that *I* was capable of it. Like not crying when I was a kid. I always figured there was a part of me that was missing, or maybe I was just such a dick that I didn't fall in love, or maybe I was just too—you know—banged up by everything that I couldn't. But I was wrong. You showed me that. Because I am so in love with you, Roger, that absolutely nothing else matters."

"You've changed so much?"

"I was motivated." I had to smile. "If you gave me another chance," said Fletch, "I swear I'll prove it. Hey, you remember Dr. Scruff?"

"Of course."

"Totally hot, no?"

"Ye-ah." Kind of the last thing I wanted to talk about.

"I could have had him eating out of my hand, if I'd wanted."

"Out of your lap, more likely."

"Exactly. But instead—I told him all about you, my fabulous, gorgeous, talented boyfriend."

"I wasn't your boyfriend."

"That's not the point. I immediately shut him down. That ought to count for something."

"One time."

"First of many, but I gotta start somewhere, Dweeb. Look—you know, I don't believe in promises either, but I promise you, if you give me a chance—I will be the best boyfriend ever."

"You *were* the best boyfriend ever, except for one tiny detail."

"It's a detail I can live without." He paused for a second. "If you give me a chance, I swear to you, I swear on the entire town of Mittenwald—that I will never ever hurt you like that again. There will *never* be anyone but you. Ever."

That was what I wanted to hear, wasn't it? I mean, it was all perfect before, but for that one awful thing. So why wasn't I jumping at it?

Because I was scared.

Let's face it, Prescott—you're always scared.

"But you're going to California?"

"Unless you can think of a good reason why I shouldn't?"

I could get really, really hurt. That was me, continuing the argument with myself.

"Well, there's the concert tickets."

"There's that."

You're already hurt, genius. Take a look around. It doesn't get any worse than this!

I looked up at him for a second. Oh-jeez, those eyes.

"For God's sake, Dweeb—say something."

I tried to, but there was that damn hunk of rosin in my throat again.

"Don't." I managed to get out. "Just—stay. With me, I mean. Please-please-please? It could be like a slumber party."

"Really?"

"Really. And I always loved our slumber parties."

"You're serious."

"I don't know why it is—and I mean—why you, Fletch? Of all people, why you? But it is you, and I've tried to live without you. Twice. I'm just not very good at it."

He looked at me a while from his end of the couch.

"Damn, Dweeb. Took you long enough to figure that out."

We held each other very tightly after that, and for a long, long time, and we talked very quietly, and we each said about a thousand I-love-yous, and we each said we were sorry about a thousand times, and we made each other about a thousand promises.

And he gently kissed the tears from my cheeks.

They weren't all mine.

Chapter 42
Over the River and Through the Woods

FLETCH

Roger and Haggis stepped down off the commuter train out onto the platform ahead of me. I was slowed down, carrying the dog crate Haggis had had to use to get on the train. He'd come out as soon as we were moving and stood with his two front feet on my lap looking out the window the rest of the trip.

I'm generally not a nervous person, but when I am, you can always tell because my right leg bounces like crazy, which it had done pretty much since we left Grand Central. Because man-oh-man, I was scared to death. The dog didn't seem to mind the bouncing leg, and I was seriously glad he was there for moral support. Did I need it!

Out on the platform, Roger scanned the parking lot of the small suburban train station.

"There she is," he said and started walking. I stepped down and followed.

"Hey, Bro," said a thin, incredibly beautiful girl, blowing out smoke as she dropped her cigarette and stepped on it.

"Hey Andrea." They kissed each other on the cheek and turned toward her car. "This is Fletch."

"Hi," I said cheerfully. I didn't expect her to kiss *me* on the cheek, but I thought she might have *looked* in my direction. Nope.

What a mistake. This was all such a horrible mistake. I should never have let Roger talk me into this.

You've caught on by now that I wasn't exactly born speaking French and knowing which fork to use. I knew these people were going to spot me as a fraud before I even walked in the front door. I should get on the next train headed back to the city.

Roger followed Andrea to the car. I took a breath and followed Roger. Andrea opened the trunk with one of those remote control things on the keyring. I loaded the crate in and laid the hanging bag across it.

"Haggles and I can ride in back," Roger volunteered and clambered into the back seat of the two-door.

Wow. Real nice, boyfriend. Thanks *so* much. Make *me* ride up front with the scary sister.

I got in, and while I was fumbling with the seat belt, Andrea got in the driver's seat. She turned and stared at me. I looked back. Was she going to say something? Was she just *trying* to make me uncomfortable? It took every bit of self-control to keep my leg from bouncing again.

"Is there—something?" I said finally.

"Look straight out."

I turned front, but I kept a wary eye on her as best I could. She reached over—my first instinct was to pull a Haggis and duck away from her hand, but I gutted it out—and she pushed my chin a little higher.

"Andrea," Roger said from the back. "Play nice."

She pushed some hair back from my face. She looked over her shoulder at Roger.

"Respect!" She turned back, started the car engine, and headed out of the parking lot.

Apparently I had passed a test. No doubt unworthy in other ways, I was at least pretty enough. Today—I would take what I could get.

"Andrea, don't be a bitch."

As soon as the car was out on the street, Andrea pulled a half-smoked joint out of the ashtray, lit it, and took a longish drag. She held it out to me.

"No, thanks."

She exhaled.

"Christ, don't tell me you're as square as Roger."

"Oh God no. I'm much worse. I don't even drink."

"You may want to rethink that before the day is over."

I reached back between the bucket seats toward Roger, and he squeezed my hand.

"Hey," Roger said from the back, "did I tell you that I had a drink with Dad?"

"No, seriously?"

"Seriously, at the club. His special two-hundred-year-old scotch that was blessed by Saint Cuthbert or whatever that stuff is."

"Woot."

"It was all terribly grown up. Very man-to-man."

"And did he tell you about the birds and the bees?" she asked.

"Not yet. I think he's waiting for my voice to change. He did welcome me to the adultery."

"That old joke. So, Fletch. Did Roger give you the rundown on the family? All the rules and regs? Tell you where the quicksand is?"

"He told me some. If I can remember. Don't say anything bad about Harvard."

"Very good rule. I don't suppose you're Republican?"

"Ummm, not really."

"Avoid politics completely, although we're all totally hip on the *gay* thing because of old Rog being sort of light in the loafers, if you know what I mean."

"I've heard that rumor."

"Watch your back, that's all I can say. What else did he tell you?"

"The little brother—"

"Todd—"

"Todd—is a football player—"

"At Harvard," Roger prompted from the back seat.

"—at Harvard and is treated as a visiting deity."

"Good. What'd he say about me?"

"Bit of a pothead."

"Well, under the present circumstances, I don't suppose I'll argue."

"And that you're spoiled and can be unbelievably arrogant."

"You bastard!" she said, reaching back to slap Roger's knee and she managed to drop just two wheels off the road as she did it.

"Hey!" Roger objected—to the slap, not her driving.

"And what do *you* think?" she asked me. If she had even noticed the near miss with the mailbox that whizzed past my window, she didn't let on.

"He seems to be pretty much dead-on so far."

She glanced in the rearview mirror to look at Roger.

"He may actually survive this weekend."

"Should I be scared?" I asked.

"Oh God yes!" she answered.

She laughed and turned the car onto a paved driveway. We went past the front of the house, and she parked the car where she could. There were already at least ten cars in front of the biggest garage I'd ever seen.

"Holy moly," I said, looking up at the house.

"Don't be too impressed. If you are still around at Christmas, Roger will have to drag you to the *big* house where the grandparents live. Emphasis on *grand*." She did that thing with the key chain, and the trunk popped open. "That is, if you survive today."

As we retrieved our bags, Roger kissed me on the cheek.

"Happy Thanksgiving," he said.

"Yeah," I said. "Happy Thanksgiving." Of course I had a lot to be grateful for, obviously, or I wouldn't be standing here on this asphalt driveway with a hanging bag over my shoulder, with Roger, who was my boyfriend again. I had everything I had ever wanted. I should be all kinds of thankful.

But I mostly just felt scared. And suddenly seeing this house, those cars, and being faced with the fact that I was going to have to walk in there and try to pass myself off in front of those people—man, I had *never* been so scared.

"Are you ready?" Roger asked.

"Look, I think I forgot my toothbrush. You go on ahead, and I'm just going to walk back to the train station."

"It's eleven miles."

"Piece of cake."

Haggis, at the end of his leash, kicked his tiny hind leg up on a leafless shrub.

"Look at the dog," Roger said. "He's not scared."

"Easy for him! He was born out here. He's educated, mannered. He knows who his dad is!"

"If it's any comfort, they don't get along, Haggis and his dad. Happens in the best of families."

"I can't believe it. You're making fun of me."

"Only a little."

"Here." I pushed the hanging bag into his arms. If Roger could laugh at me, what would the rest of them do when they got a load of the trash that had somehow turned up in their dining room? "It's really not that far," I said, and I turned and started walking super fast.

"What the—" He ran after me and grabbed my arm. "Fletch, stop. Hey. Hey. I've never seen anything scare you. I didn't know—you *could* be scared."

"They'll see right through me, Dweeb. They'll take one look and know I don't belong here."

"If they see right through you, you know what they'll see? They'll see you. They'll see the fantastic guy that I see. They'll see exactly how much you *do* belong here, next to me, and that has absolutely nothing to do with what schools you went to."

"I didn't, remember?"

"Or didn't went to. Okay?"

"You're going to look across the table and wonder what you were thinking, bringing me here."

"I'll look across the table and wonder what I did to deserve to be so happy. Because I am."

"Just—don't make fun of me in there. Don't ditch me, okay?"

"Hey! What kind of an f-hole you take me for?"

I couldn't believe he could make me smile.

"I promise. I won't desert you," he said finally, with his face very close to mine.

All I could do was close my eyes and bow my head until our foreheads touched. I'm not really big on trust, but, you know, when somebody looks at you like that…

"I love you so much," I said.

"Oh God, you two!" Andrea yelled from the side door where she'd been waiting for us. "That is *so* gross."

Roger kissed me again and we followed the little brick walkway after Andrea, with Haggis out in front.

"But you know," I said as we walked, "no matter how hard I try, I will *never* be as cool as that dog."

"Me either. He's sort of a role model for me."

"Hey," Andrea said over her shoulder as we walked up to the door behind her, "did you warn Fletch about Aunt Hannah?"

"Damn! No," Roger said. "Remind me to tell you about Aunt Hannah."

Andrea pushed the door open and called into the house.

"I'm baa-aaack! And I found some pansy boys making out in the hydrangeas!"

You know how sometimes somebody will make a joke, and everybody laughs, and it releases all the tension and you feel better?

This wasn't one of those times.

I let Roger and Haggis go in first, wishing desperately I wasn't so damned tall, and I followed them into the kitchen—the smell of turkey and sage could make you faint. There was the sound of sports on television coming in from another room. A Hispanic woman was stirring something on the stove, and a woman with Roger's eyes was standing in the middle of the kitchen gripping her pearls as she turned to us.

"Oh, Andrea!" she said, exasperated as she pushed some brown curls back from her forehead with a gesture I'd seen a hundred thousand times before. "You're just horrid sometimes."

People started to come noisily into the kitchen through a couple different doors, and I could see some more were hanging in the hallway. The house was obviously full of people. The football player was easy to spot, as he leaned against the refrigerator, all casual arrogance. I was pretty sure I picked Roger's dad out of the lineup. The scary old broad with the highball—Aunt Hannah, had to be. They were all a little rowdy and jostling, but they were also all smiling and joking, and then they were all looking expectantly at us.

Andrea stood in the back, making faces.

"Mom, Dad, everyone." Dweeb looked back at me, grinning—like *he* was proud of *me*. He took my hand and pulled me up next to him. "There's somebody I'd like you to meet."

Man-oh-man.

It's a good thing I don't cry.

Maybe later.

Special Thanks

My first readers: Travis J. Sherrod, Neil Montiel, and Ophelia Julien (a fabulous author herself, whose books you should be reading).

Timothy Brown—who advised on all things musical, and whose literary criticisms were also spot-on.

Laura Frautschi, violinist—who offered technical advice on the stringy bits.

Sonya Lashua Fagan—who made some brilliant photographs of me and my writing partner at work.

And of course my writing partner, Watson, my own personal Haggis. Woof.

ABOUT THE AUTHOR

Chase Taylor Hackett was raised on a farm in the Midwest far from his current home in New York City. He has written most of his life, nearly all of it in musical theatre. His theatrical career peaked when a musical for which he'd written the book and lyrics opened on Broadway. Unfortunately, two weeks later it closed on Broadway.

One morning he woke up and found that he had a couple characters in his head, who, try as he might, refused to become a musical comedy. He wondered if he could possibly work them up into a novel, but, never having tried to write one before, he didn't have a clue where to begin.

And thus: *Where Do I Start?*

He lives in upper Manhattan with his partner Travis, and a Scottish terrier named Watson.

www.ingramcontent.com/pod-product-compliance
Lightning Source LLC
Chambersburg PA
CBHW020746250626
47155CB00003B/937

9781516104451